BACKSTORY

BACKSTORY

a novel

William Michael Ried

CKBooks Publishing

Publisher's Cataloging-in-Publication Data
Names: Ried, William Michael, author.
Title: Backstory : a novel / William Michael Ried.
Description: Belleville, WI : CKBooks Publishing, 2021.
Identifiers: ISBN 978-1-949085-37-2 (paperback) | ISBN 978-1-949085-38-9 (ebook)
Subjects: LCSH: College teachers--Fiction. | Secrets--Fiction. | Dublin (Ireland)--Fiction. | Hudson River Valley (N.Y. and N.J.)--Fiction. | Suspense fiction. | BISAC: FICTION / Thrillers / Suspense.
Classification: LCC PS3618.I39228 B33 2021 (print) | LCC PS3618.I39228 (ebook) | DDC 813/.6--dc23.

LCCN: 2021903502

Cover design by michaelstar*

The quote in Chapter 30 is the final stanza of Richard Marsh's poem *Over the Wall to the Trinity Ball*, ©1981 Richard Marsh, quoted with permission of the author.

The title page image is "New Campanile, Trinity College, Dublin," a wood engraving by W.E. Hodgkin, Welcome Collection Attribution 4.0 International (CC by 4.0)

CKBooks Publishing
P.O. Box 214
New Glarus, WI 53574
CKBookspublishing.com

Each man lives for himself, uses his freedom to achieve his personal goals, and feels with his whole being that right now he can or cannot do such-and-such an action; but as soon as he does it, this action, committed at a certain moment in time, becomes irreversible and makes itself the property of history.

War and Peace, by Leo Tolstoy (1869)

* * *

Whenever you get a new master you must directly give him a history (in which you need not adhere to the truth) of all your former ones, together with an account of the different ways in which they treated you.

Advice to the University of Dublin (P. Byrne, Dublin 1791)

* * *

The British tabloid articles on Ireland, as on other issues, have more in common with works of fiction—such as thrillers and romances—than with reporting actuality.

Ireland: The Propuganda War, by Liz Curtis
(Pluto Press Limited, London and Sydney 1984)

Exordium

2004

In one instant the quintessence of automobile design exploded into a burning mass, and it all came back to that night, when an ancient campus was washed by spring breezes.

In what felt like the shortest of years they had soaked up the spirit of Trinity College, the tranquility and mystery of the old buildings within high stone walls, the manicured lawns and rebel statues. Half a millennium of tradition and rebellion laid like a cloak over bustling youth.

In a week the American exchange students would go their separate ways home for summers, and senior years and the rest of their lives. But that was in the future. For one night more Dublin was theirs, the world stood still and wide open and history remained to be written. They had one more chance to clasp arms and bellow drinking songs.

Bud organized the party, as usual. He scored access to a snooker room in the Graduates Memorial Building and arranged for a keg. He assigned tasks to the other "McYanks," the six American students who lived on the same hallway in Botany Bay, attended the same Irish history seminar and often traveled in a pack. Tess and Molly nicked food from the dining hall. Ansel and Charlie got the word out and collected beer money. Dutch helped Bud move the keg and clear furniture.

They had barely cleared a dance floor when music started shaking centuries of dust from the ornate molding. This brought a trickle and then a wave of students. The beer flowed. A few bottles of whiskey appeared and quickly went to ground. The party soon overflowed into the surrounding hallways.

Dutch saw nearly everyone he had met at Trinity that year, from the crazy German pre-med student who always had weed to the annoyingly unsullied redhead saving herself for a boyfriend back in Galway. Dutch was no hoofer. A gimpy leg from a baseball injury and his broad shoulders made him a menace on the dance floor. But it was a night for release, so he whisked Molly and then Tess and then whomever else he could grab onto the floor and tried not to bump into anyone too hard.

He met two American tourists who had been invited by one of the Irish students. "Never seen a shag rug on a phone before," he shouted over the music to the taller one, pointing at the fuzzy pink phone case slipping from her pocket.

"Oh, thanks!" she shouted back. "I've lost it twice already." She had short auburn hair and a welcoming smile. Her friend went off to dance, and Dutch guided the tall woman to the keg, then out of the party room to where they could hear each other.

"Nothing like this at Santa Barbara," she said, gazing at the intricate staircase and running her hand over a carved wooden bench.

"UC Santa Barbara?"

"Yeah. The coast is gorgeous, but the buildings are nothing like this."

"Small world!" he exclaimed. She looked up.

"I went to baseball camp there one summer."

"That's amazing!" she laughed. "Yeah, I study there, and my folks run a diner right by campus: the Cosmo."

"I ate there! Best French toast in California…or so they said."

"That was probably my mother," she laughed.

"And hey, if you find this staircase impressive, you *have to* see the Debating Chamber."

She looked at him dubiously.

"Oh, it's safe; I promise. It's just down these stairs."

She gave him another close look and smiled. They descended half-way to the first floor, passing students crowding their way up. He led her onto the balcony overlooking a big hall with deep red walls and large windows. Pilasters rose two stories to the ceiling

"Wow!" she said.

"Shaw," Dutch said nonchalantly, nodding toward a bronze relief on the wall as if pointing out a classmate across the yard.

"George Bernard?" she asked.

"Well, no. Actually, it's George *Ferdinand* Shaw. I think he edited *The Irish Times*."

She smiled. He tried to think of another scholarly comment. Maybe it was time to suggest a tour of the statuary around New Square. But their cups were empty, and she was eager to check on her friend.

Back in the snooker room, Dutch sensed the California girl was looking past him. Following her gaze, he was not surprised she was watching Ansel and Tess. They were always the center of attention. But instead of their usual snogging as if no one was watching, they were arguing in the middle of the dancers. Suddenly, Tess stomped from the room. Ansel shrugged in several directions as if he were on stage and then looked over at Dutch.

"Trouble in paradise?" Dutch said sympathetically, although it was hard to feel too sorry for the king of the prom.

"Ah, women," Ansel said. "You can't live with 'em and you can't, you know...." He turned to Dutch's companion. "And this is?" he asked.

Dutch realized he had not asked her name.

"Reilly," she said, extending her hand to shake and nodding at Dutch in belated introduction.

"Yeah," Dutch said, recovering. "Reilly's from California, traveling around Ireland."

Neither of them heard what he said, and they soon disappeared onto the dance floor. He took his beer to where friends were singing along with the music. His father always said, "If you can't sing well, sing loud," and so he joined in emphatically and largely out of tune.

Later, Tess returned to the room and stood back by a wall, looking like she might take a shillelagh to someone's head. He made his way over. "You okay?"

"What?" she said, as if pulled from a trance. "Yeah, I'm fine. Come on, Dutch, let's dance."

She yanked him after her. As they swayed and spun, she tried not to be obvious but clearly was watching Ansel and Reilly, who held each other close. When Ansel kissed his partner, Dutch could feel Tess's shoulders tense.

At a break in the music, Tess charged across the floor. Face-to-face with Ansel she shouted, "You shit!"

Reilly looked startled. The crowd pushed back but everyone heard Tess growl, "Are you trying to humiliate me?"

"Slow down," Ansel replied, holding up his hands as if fending off an attack. "No need for drama. It's the end of the year!"

She took a wide swing at his head but he ducked. She stormed to the other end of the room.

Ansel could be arrogant but he and Tess seemed perfect together. He was darkly handsome, with the entitled air of someone whose family had a lot of money. She was a consensus beauty, thin and delicate with the face of a movie star. They had been a solid item from early in the year until that moment.

Ansel soon left with Reilly, but not before elaborate goodbyes all around. Dutch was relieved to see Molly take Tess in hand, and then Charlie finally arrived and helped out.

As the party wound down, Dutch helped Bud clean up and then they went outside into the cool night air. The campus was peaceful. They sat on the base of the Provost Salmon statue to polish off a bottle of whiskey.

"Well, that was quite a show," Bud said, handing over the bottle.

"An inauspicious end for the McYanks," Dutch replied.

"It all seemed good until that thing with Ansel and Tess. Who was that girl?"

"She's just passing through. I talked with her some, but all I got was she goes to school in California."

"Ansel can be a turd. How could he treat Tess like that?"

"I'll drink to that," Dutch said. He held up the bottle to see if there was any left and then drained it.

Dutch woke next morning to find Bud crashed on Charlie's bed. He wondered at this, but then remembered Ansel had kicked Bud out of their room so he could be with that girl. And Charlie? Last he remembered his roommate and Molly were comforting Tess. He rose gingerly and opened the shade to muted sunshine. There were police officers in the square.

"Oh, shit," he said to himself and then turned to his friend. "Hey Bud, the campus is swarming with Gardaí. This can't be about the party?"

He went outside to see what was happening. When he returned, Bud was peering through the window. "So what's up?" Bud said in a low rasp.

"It's not about the party," Dutch said somberly. "Last night Digory fell from the Arts Block. They say he's dead!"

Chapter 1

2016

Never let facts get in the way of history. That was Ansel Tone's mantra.

The April sun crept across the floor to his heavy glass desk. He turned in his chair to take in the view of silvery pools in the Hudson River. Spring slyly sprouted in the ribbon of park along the water. He could just pick out patches of bright purples and pinks peeking through the ground.

Spring was *his* time, rebirth, in a sense, his stock in trade. That thought drove him back to his laptop. He had started the outline, so the morning was productive enough. He could put off his agent, Leah, and the publisher, Harvey Bendel at John Wiley & Sons, for another few days. With something pithy in hand, Leah could ease Harvey's angst about Ansel's big advance. No sense selling cheap while the public was clamoring, and there was nothing like a pile of cash to prime the engine.

He glanced at several copies of *Time* magazine on the desk, the cover proclaiming him the "Golden Boy of Popular History." The photo was flattering, showing off his thick dark hair and chiseled chin, but next time he'd insist on the three-quarter profile his social media expert preferred. He was paying for her insight to the youth market and so should heed her instincts.

A rap song shouted from his pocket. He answered his phone.

"Ansel, finally," came over the line.

"Speak of the devil," he said to Leah's abrupt greeting.

"Don't mean to prod," said Leah, in a voice always too loud, "but it's what I do."

He waited, focusing on his fingernails. It was worth putting up with Leah's bluster because she knew her business and threw her sharp elbows on his behalf. When he said nothing, she continued. "How's the *Redux* outline coming?"

"So singularly you should buy me lunch before my class."

"I will, Ansel, because there's something we need to discuss."

"Oh, this sounds ominous," he kidded but wondered seriously what she had in mind.

Ansel was on track to be tenured at Columbia University in record time. It helped he had published his doctoral thesis on British revisionist history of Irish nationalism and spun the rewriting-the-past theme into two *Redux Revisionist History* best-sellers. His publisher planned a book franchise on any number of historical subjects under the *Redux* brand: how the victors write the history with only passing regard for the facts. It also helped his candidacy to appear humble with his department head, even though his classes were among the most popular at the university.

Along with an apartment on the Upper West Side and a good salary, his associate professorship assured him a captive, ever-young audience. He thrived on doling out a minimum of testable curriculum spiced with historical theatrics. The "professor" title also sold books.

His breakthrough titles were *Redux Hook-Up: A Revisionist History of the Sexual Revolution*, followed the next year by *Redux Stick It to the Man: A Revisionist History of the Radical Sixties*. In both books he took a cutting-edge view of how those in power crafted the raw material of actual events into their preferred story. Combined with Ansel's family wealth and seductive good looks, these best-sellers made him one of a rare breed of celebrity historian. He appeared on late night talk shows. He spoke to packed auditoriums. Undergraduates were said to swoon over his lectures.

The attention from admirers young and old and the bedroom doors opened by his celebrity status kept Ansel from sustaining any romantic relationship since his short-lived marriage in grad school. There just was not enough of him to go around—and freedom from entanglements suited his style.

* * *

Leah sipped her tea waiting for Ansel to show up at a quiet café west of Broadway. She carried a briefcase the size of an overnight bag to be prepared for anything. People thought they were polite when they called her "heavy-set," but she was resigned to being fat and knowing clothes would never hang right on her. Her nose was also large and her cheeks round but the intensity in her big hazel eyes behind horn-rimmed glasses usually got her what she wanted. She was tenacious in an industry that gorged on weakness, and Ansel was fortunate to have her batting for his side.

When he arrived she asked for an avocado salad, while he ordered a panini and a small-batch bourbon he spotted behind the bar. "Just one cube," he added and turned his attention to her.

She rolled her eyes at his drinking at this time of day, and the "one cube" shtick. But she refrained from commenting. There was business to do. "So when will we see the outline for the fake news book?"

"Well, you know, dear mistress of all things administrative, inspired creation cannot be rushed."

"Ansel," she said, exasperated, "we have to strike while you're hot."

He sipped, acting as if he hadn't heard her.

She shook both fists at him. "I'm serious. They love you now, but you have to stay current. The public will turn to the next thing in a heartbeat."

"Hey, what could be more current than the *Redux* history of fake news?"

"It's fortuitous the politics of the moment fits the *Redux* model, but you'll have competitors on this one, and you have to lead, not follow."

"Yes, I know, but let's skip the pathos. I'll spit out an outline, if you can just keep Harvey off my back. Meanwhile, this presidential campaign has the public wondering whether facts inform reality at all and so is priming my target audience."

"Politics aside," she said, "now we have to get serious." Her voice was unusually quiet, as if to avoid being overheard. This got his attention.

"We received a letter through the Redux site," she said ominously, "from a former student of yours...." She checked her notebook. "Karla Canterwail."

Ansel's smile dissolved.

"She claims you used her work in *Stick it to the Man*, a paper she did for your class."

"Bullshit!" he said, loud enough to attract attention from other diners.

"But you do remember her?"

"Sure. Good-looking short blonde; she wrote a paper on the Weather Underground for my History of the '60s class a few years ago. She was a good writer, but hard to say if I used any of it. This is history! It has to come from prior sources!"

"Yes, it's absurd but we can't ignore it. She doesn't seem to have told anyone else, so Harvey hasn't gotten wind, and I'm sure Columbia's in the dark. We can't have this kind of publicity. Not now. Not with the new book underway."

"Damn! How can I defend myself against a charge like that? It's not like her work was published. It was just a term paper! Probably no one saw it outside the class!"

"Well, it's more what can she prove, and how loud she'll be. I think we have to talk with her, or *I* should talk with her and see what she's got?"

"Why does this old shit have to come up?" he complained but

then added more calmly, "You're right. You'd better meet with her; find out what she has and what she wants. I assume we'll have to pay her?"

Leah sighed. She needed to have faith in her clients, but there was no telling what debacle Ansel was courting. "I'll set up a meeting."

"And let her know we won't be pushed around!"

"Yes, Ansel, but first let's see if we can make this go away quietly."

He drained his bourbon and looked to the bar as if he would order another but then shook his head and focused on his food.

She pushed her salad aside. He had a way of killing her appetite, but then he had a knack for writing what sold and was by far her most lucrative client. She just wished he didn't require so much mothering. "And another thing," she said reluctantly.

He stopped chewing. "Am I going to need another drink for this?"

"No, Ansel. And look, don't worry about the Canterwail thing; we'll work through it. No, it's about this 'social media guru' you found in a coffee shop. What's her name…Rebecca?"

"Just Becca," he said, clearly happy to change the subject. "I knew you'd love her—and isn't that name perfect?"

"'Love' is not the word I'd choose. And I don't understand why we couldn't use the normal recruiting process. We had a handful of impressive resumes." Leah had suggested getting a young person's advice on social media and posted a position online, but it was impossible to get him to look at resumes or schedule interviews. Then Ansel called out of the blue, so pleased he had hired the "perfect" assistant.

"She's cute," he gushed, "and smart and the politest person I've ever met. She *knows* that Instagram-Reddit-Twitter shit like she was born to it."

"And just happens to have a perfect twenty-year-old ass."

"I believe," he said, thoughtfully, "she is twenty-*four*. And while you and I may tweet or use LinkedIn, it's impossible to stay fluent in what platforms the young use."

"Just so you keep your thing in your pants and finish the outline," she scowled, feeling like she was scolding a child.

"Will do, chief. And speaking of noses to grindstones, I'm off; class at two."

"What's the course?"

"Propaganda in the Great War. I've taught it before but it's great fun, and I think I might get some gratis research for the book."

She wondered if he realized how incriminating that sounded after the Canterwail discussion. "Always working the angles," she said, shaking her head. "Just play by the rules, okay?"

He rose to leave, drawing a lascivious look from a woman at the next table. Leah watched through the window as he stepped up to a black SUV waiting curbside.

The waiter asked if she wanted anything else. "A client like Saul Bellow?" she said dreamily, but seeing his confusion she simply took the check.

* * *

"Afternoon, Henry," Ansel said to his driver, whose dreadlocks were pushed away from his face by a natty chauffeur's cap.

"You know you can ease up on the uniform," he added. The outfit was unnecessary, except when Ansel wanted to impress a date.

"Oh, but it assures me respect," Henry said, "most especially when driving for such a distinguished personage."

"You're a wonder, Henry."

"It is as well my honor to provide you with wonder."

Ansel laughed. Compliments gushed from Henry like water from a hydrant on a hot summer day. The trustees at Columbia might look askance at his dreadlocks, but Ansel's dates loved him, and the publishing types thought him chic. Also, the hair hid a large scar from a knife fight when he was a teenager. The car service dispatcher had sent Henry to drive Ansel one night and they hit it off talking about reggae and ganja. After that, Henry became Ansel's primary driver and reliable connection to drugs. Talking with him made Ansel feel connected with a rebellious world far from publishing and academia.

On the short run to the university, Ansel gazed at sunlight dancing on the Hudson River and mused. What was Karla's problem? He was sure he gave her an A on the paper and in the class. What more did she want, a fucking byline?

It brought him back, uncomfortably, to Dublin and his advisor Brandon Doogan. Brandon had set a firm date for Ansel to prove he had not plagiarized a book in his term paper. He insipidly called it Ansel's "*sprioc-ama,*" a Gaelic phrase for immutable deadline Ansel unfortunately had used in his paper's conclusion and Brandon now threw back in his face. But thinking about the run-in with Brandon hardly took Ansel's mind off Karla. He needed to compartmentalize, let Leah do her job and free his mind of worry. He focused instead on the opening that evening at an art gallery in SoHo. It would be the first one-man show for a graffiti artist turned darling of the art world. The paintings would probably be childlike but who cared? He'd be among the beautiful people, with Severine as his perfect date. He and Severine were *very* close, although most of the time geographically distant. She lived in Paris but was in town for a modeling gig. She texted she'd be ready at seven. He confirmed with a leering emoji.

As the SUV pulled up to the university, Ansel got Henry's attention. "I'll need you to drive me home after class, and then pick me up at my building at 6:45. And can you visit your friend in between?" Even in private, Ansel preferred to talk about drug purchases in code.

Henry smiled. "The usual?"

"Right," Ansel said, handing cash across the seat.

Henry pocketed the money and nodded.

Ansel was running late and walked across campus straight to the auditorium in the basement of Havermeyer Hall. He had asked Becca to come up with a multimedia piece for this class, which they could also use online. After two days she produced something to pin them back in their seats. She's on her toes, that one, he laughed, although with her long legs maybe it was best she stayed *off* her toes. His next "guru" would have to be a less intimidating height.

Outside the auditorium he paused to collect himself and then burst through the rear doors to a familiar buzz. An enthusiastic shout of "Professor T!" made him smile. He took the podium and noticed the admiring gaze of one stacked brunette seated on the aisle. How had he missed her before?

He quickly waved for quiet. "We have considered how propaganda has been used by democratic as well as totalitarian regimes, from ancient Athens through the medieval communes and the Renaissance to the Reformation, with at least as much fervor as the Bolsheviks in Russia. And now we focus on World War I, the first war in which propaganda was significant in informing the home front about events on the battlefield."

The room lights dimmed and the screen behind him lit up. Driving music accompanied images of ads and posters showing slogans printed over heroic images and photos of wartime atrocities. The music volume rose with the pace of the pictures, building into an audiovisual cacophony. Suddenly, the music stopped and the auditorium lights came up. Ansel said dramatically, "And some of these icons remain with us, even today." He looked over his shoulder at the static image of Uncle Sam on the screen, pointing at the viewer, and then turned toward the room, stretching out an arm to point to a far corner of the seats and moving his finger across the students as he intoned the poster's slogan in a low, rumbling voice "I...WANT...YOU." On the last word his finger rested on the brunette.

The students burst into applause. The dark-haired girl didn't clap but kept her eyes pinned on Ansel. He dropped his arm and smiled around the room. *Maybe I should call this class "History Histrionics,"* he laughed.

After class the usual brown-nosers surrounded him at the front of the room. He answered questions and then, glancing at the brunette, said, "I'm sorry but I have a meeting. *Please* come and see me during office hours."

He walked to the back of auditorium with one acne-faced young man still talking at him. In the empty last row, Becca was gathering her things. She looked up with a smile from under honey-blonde bangs and joined him to walk across campus.

"That went well!" he said.

"Really well! The poster thing had them eating out of your hand."

He stopped and looked at her, gesturing to go on.

"I guess I nodded off a little between psychological action and psychological warfare."

"Yes, well, my stodgy old department head insists I insert a bit of academics into what would otherwise be much more entertaining theater."

She smiled. "Well, I videoed the poster bit, like you said, with some shots of mesmerized students."

"Excellent! Ride along and show me in the car."

Becca was so refreshing: no crap about copyrights or faculty meetings. She obviously admired him and seemed willing to do *whatever* the job required—and those long legs *were* enticing. He had dropped carnal suggestions a few times over their months together, but she seemed oblivious.

* * *

Riding with Ansel in the SUV was fun, as was kidding around with Henry. In fact, Becca's whole job sometimes seemed like a fairy tale. Everyone knew Ansel, and with him she was treated like a celebrity. She couldn't help noticing his constant pursuit of women, but things were not like that between them. He kept it professional and she liked that, although he *was* awfully attractive. It was like having a movie star for a boss.

They stopped at his apartment to look over the website design and he offered a glass of wine in thanks for her help. Over a second glass, for the first time in their four months together he expressed interest in her studies and plans. She was flattered, and revealed more than she normally would to an employer about her hometown and her dream of doing professional photography. He was charming and engaged, so much more so than guys her age, who would buy her a beer and then ask her back to some crappy walkup just like hers. She wondered whether, if she worked hard enough, she could break into his circle of acquaintances. She might spend time with men like him, men of maturity and depth.

Laughing at a story about her dog, he touched her hand, gently and yet purposefully. She sensed things were about to change. When she accepted a third glass of wine, her head was spinning and, with no conscious decision on her part, they were kissing.

It was a turning point. In a way the thought of being with Ansel had been building in her subconscious these four months, ever since he appeared in that coffee shop and changed her life. But having a thing with Ansel had always felt like fantasy, so distant it was not worth examining. Now it felt too easy. An undertow was sweeping her out to sea. He laughed, apparently enjoying her bashfulness.

It was intoxicating to think someone famous and fascinating wanted her. And this was not just spur of the moment, not after they had worked together for months. She knew he respected her expertise and valued her advice. And she thought she cleaned up well the time she filled in as his date at his publisher's reception, and when they sat in the celebrity seats at a Knicks game. She knew she was just his default date but nonetheless was dazzled. She guessed she had had a crush on him all along.

Ansel showed her the view from his bedroom. Big windows faced the park and the river. She was nervous but he took hold of her and she relaxed in his arms. She was completely lost in the moment, the swirling sheets and muffled cries. He certainly knew his way around women. It had been months since she had slept with anyone; now it felt like she had been saving herself for this afternoon.

Afterward, he dozed and she lay looking at how the afternoon sun sparkled on the river, thinking what a lofty view this was of the world, so far from where she started. No one she grew up with in Wisconsin would believe this scene.

It was amazing how things had turned around in her life. One day she was unattached and unemployed and the next she was working for and romantically involved with a famous writer. She wondered what else might change. Would she attend elegant functions? Could she put on the sophisticated, bored expression so natural to his typical model dates? She hoped to meet his friends, who never came around the apartment. She also wondered about his family. He seemed distant from his father, but she could help fix that; she was good with older people.

She gave him a kiss on the cheek as he woke. "I've got to get going," she said. "My roommates are throwing a birthday party and I have to help set up."

He watched with an amused smile while she gathered clothes strewn around the room. As she pulled on her sweater, she added, "You could join us, if you have nothing on tonight."

He smiled but his phone rang and he took the call. "Severine," he said, sounding surprised. "*Oui, chérie.* You know I do." He waved for Becca to leave the room, and holding the phone to his chest said quietly, "And close the door, please."

In the living room she caught sight of herself in a full-length mirror, hair disheveled with a murderous expression she hardly recognized as her own. She tried to run a comb through her hair but it caught in a tangle and she threw it across the room. How could he treat her like that? They were barely out of bed!

She gave up on her hair and pulled on a stocking cap, grabbed her bag and left, shutting the door with a bang. Walking down the street to the subway, an image of her father popped into her head. Oh God, if he had seen this! What had she been thinking? How could she not see? She was not some actress from Ansel's world; she was just an assistant with a laptop, probably not even worth another notch on his belt.

* * *

As he dressed for the opening, Ansel heard his ring tone. The caller ID showing Jordan MacTone vanquished his smile. He grimaced and answered in a respectful voice. "Hello, Father. How are you?"

"Where are those tickets?"

He scrambled to remember his father had asked for tickets to a jazz concert sponsored by Ansel's publisher. "Right, yeah," he fumbled. "You know, I asked about tickets," which was a lie, "but there were none left."

He heard his father breathing heavily and was grateful not to be facing those seething eyes.

"I guess we waited too long," he added. "I'm sure I can get tickets for the August show."

"I'm not interested in *August*," Jordan said in a voice eerily quiet but cold like steel. "I asked you two weeks ago to arrange four tickets for *tomorrow*. Is that too much to ask from Wiley's best-selling author? Do you honestly mean to tell me you could *not* get this done?"

Ansel had forgotten the request and probably *could* get the tickets, even now, but he feared he had put his foot in it by saying none were available. He hated how his father made him feel like a misbehaved child and wished he could just hang up. But the ominous silence compelled him to say more. "Father, I've got to take a work call, but I'll ask again. Let me call you later."

"I'll be waiting."

Ansel wiped a bead of sweat from his forehead. How did that man have such control over him, and what the hell did he want, anyway? He had plenty of money to buy tickets. Why did he have to bother Ansel? This was just another in the countless ways to exert control and remind him he would be nothing without him. These stupid tickets were now one more thing he had to take care of. He'd be better off with no family.

He called Leah. Twenty minutes later she called back to say tickets would be messengered to Jordan. Ansel gulped down two fingers of bourbon before picking up the phone again. "No problem, Father," he said with forced cheerfulness. "The tickets will be at your house tomorrow morning."

"Not the house! I won't be *home* tomorrow. Send them to my office."

"Yes, sir, I'll take care of it."

This time Jordan hung up without another word. Ansel called Leah to straighten out the address. Then he sat on the balcony watching the river, thinking how much better everything would be if the old man would just fade away.

Finally, he headed out. Henry waited by the SUV, and in minutes they pulled up to Severine's hotel. Ansel stayed in the car to sample the cocaine Henry had delivered while the driver went to fetch his date. Ansel sat back, flexing under his suit. He felt powerful, dominant, a master of the universe. Then Severine appeared in a shimmery, form-fitting dress and Ansel forgot his father entirely.

Early the next morning Ansel called for Henry to drive Severine back to her hotel. The night had energized him and helped him compartmentalize the copyright dispute as "Leah Handling," so he could focus on his classes. He decided to assign his Propaganda class a final paper comparing the use of the term "fake news" with historical propaganda. Some of those kids were smart; there was no telling what they might contribute, if not specifically to his book, then to his general thinking. In the meanwhile, he deserved a nap on the balcony. He and Severine hadn't gotten much sleep.

He later often thought back to that moment, when he could have continued napping and not answered the phone. He could have gone out for a drive, his biggest problem being how to make sure he got tenure. But he did answer, and everything changed.

"Mr. Tone?" a woman asked.

"Yes, this is *Doctor* Tone." He suspected this was a solicitation and was about to hang up.

"Sorry. Well, Doctor Tone, there's been an accident."

"What accident?"

"A construction crane collapsed on Sixth Avenue. It killed the operator and injured four people on the street."

"I'm sorry to hear that but…"

"And your wife, Doctor Tone…"

"My wife?"

"Yes, doctor, your wife Florence was seriously injured. You should come to the hospital without delay."

Florence? Was this possible? He tried to think who could help. His father? Leah? But there was no one. He'd have to do this himself.

Florence was once his wife and the mother of his…. He panicked. His son True! Where was he?

Chapter 2

Charlie put his foot to the floor. The Jaguar jumped. A coin hanging from the mirror whipped up and clipped his cheek. He rubbed his face but saw no blood. Who cared, anyway? The Jag was flying.

Breakneck Road began to wind. This was the best part: stunning vistas and tight turns. There was no traffic, so he used the whole road, slicing corners and accelerating out of curves. He loved feeling in his core the force of the turns.

He rolled to a stop on the short gravel driveway that opened up in front of his detached garage. He revved the engine, as always, to hear the roar before shutting it down. Then he sat for a moment, savoring the exhilaration.

When he stepped from the car he was almost bowled over by a huge brown Newfoundland. "Odysseus, you old dog," he laughed, grabbing him behind the ears and tussling. The dog growled and slobbered on his arm. Charlie didn't care; it was worth the mess to have someone happy to see him come home.

His smile dissolved when he saw Tess's Volvo in the garage. She was never home in the middle of the day. He hoped she wasn't leaving on another trip.

Charlie and Odysseus squeezed together through the front door, not quite large enough for the task. He always thought the entrance understated for their sprawling "Mountain House," which commanded the ridge over a wide valley. The structure was built in the 1960s by a renowned architect with a penchant for unpretentious facades. Any renovation of the entryway would clash with the architect's vision, which of course must be respected above all things. Besides, any funds for home improvement would go first to fixing the terrace railing or updating the laundry room plumbing.

"Hey, Tess," he shouted down the hallway toward the master suite. "You here?"

"Out in a sec," came his wife's cool, confident voice.

In the open kitchen at the end of the great room, Charlie grabbed a mineral water from the refrigerator. Tess appeared, briefcase over the shoulder of a tailored blue suit. The skirt hugged her hips, and without being obvious showed off her legs. When his eyes rose to hers, he saw a frown.

"I've got to run down to Washington for a meeting in the morning. Back for dinner tomorrow."

"When did this come up?" he said, annoyed.

"Oh, Eddie's wife went into labor, so I have to cover. Shouldn't be a big deal."

Thunder rumbled in the distance. "You better check the weather," Charlie said. "A storm is moving up from the city."

"Damn. Well, if it doesn't clear, I'll catch the Acela."

Tess was always working. He only saw her at all because she worked on her train commute, filling out her twelve-hour workday. Her firm dangled the possibility of promotion to tie her to the job but it was far from certain a junior partnership would improve her quality of life. Charlie especially disliked her boss, Tom Carter, "super lawyer." Still, the money was good and was carrying them, given the dismal sales of Charlie's second novel.

He had published his first novel two years after graduating from Cornell, while he held a day job reporting on local politics for the *Ithaca New York News*. *Against the Odds* was an account of his bleak childhood in working-class Baltimore. His mother was a good woman, but years of marriage to a bitter alcoholic left her battered and hopeless. Her only joy came from Charlie and his sister, but she lacked the strength to protect them. When he was a teenager, Charlie tried to shield his mother and sister but that just provoked his father. His sister killed herself with pills. His mother faded into herself and died from collapsed hope.

It was wrenching to expose details of growing up, barely veiled as "fiction." He felt vulnerable and didn't want people to know it was based on his life and pity him. At the same time, he was afraid people might be horrified to know he mostly felt betrayed by his sister and his mother, when they died and abandoned him. But his sensitivity vanished when the novel hit it big and the publisher sent him on a lavish book tour. A wunderkind producer in Hollywood even picked up the movie option, just after Charlie and Tess were engaged. Charlie spent nearly the whole fee on his dream car. Tess thought the car extravagant, but it was clear she enjoyed the stares they got rolling through town.

She worked as a summer associate at Regis & Kessler, a white-shoe law firm in New York, and was offered a job after graduation. With his book topping the best-seller list for sixteen weeks and her salary, they were riding high. They jumped at the chance to buy a distinctive house in Cold Spring, a wooded town on the Hudson an hour and a half north of Manhattan, and "Mountain House" became their castle in the sky. The house was close enough to the train station to make commuting into the city barely doable, and yet it was nestled into its own private world. It backed onto a large terrace, bringing all the valley and sky indoors. Their guests raved about the architecture and the stunning view from all the rooms.

While the commercial success of *Against the Odds* stoked Charlie's ego, he aspired to establish "his place in the pantheon." He would not give in to pressure from his agent and publisher to write a sequel and turned instead to pure fiction. He spent months poring over literary theory: Forster and Kundera and Nabokov. He reconnected with his literature professor at Cornell and shared many glasses of scotch, debating the future of the novel form. He took to heart the words of

Hermann Broch, that the sole *raison d'etre* of a novel is to discover what only the novel *can* discover: an unknown segment of existence. He experimented for ways to push the novel in a new direction that would place him on par with Dostoevsky and Joyce.

The research and theorizing finally led to writing, and five years later he published *Apostate Agonistes*, a monumental treatment of the plight of one doomed village at the edge of the Cold War. He poured his soul into that book, striving for innovation in style and poetry in prose, while expressing important themes of loyalty and spiritual growth. He produced an important novel, while adhering to the ideal Aristotle found most admirably displayed by Homer: that the poet should speak as little as possible in his own person. This was a giant step for Charlie. No more time for fictionalized memoir. No more "small" books!

He waited for praise but the reviews were harsh, starting with *The New York Times*, continuing in *The Atlantic* and reaching overseas to *The Guardian*. The best anyone said came from *Publishers Weekly*, which noted the author of the best-selling *Against the Odds* here attempted to push the bounds of literature, though with results "tragic, like a slow-motion train wreck."

Charlie drank for days and threw books. After reading the review in *The New Yorker*, he kicked Odysseus, who yelped and tried to squeeze under a staircase. The idiot critics wanted stereotypes that appealed to the lowest common denominator! They utterly failed to perceive literary innovation!

He posted a rebuttal in the *Times* but the book-buying public ignored his defense, as it did his book. Lashing out at the reviewers also lost him friends in the industry, and his publisher cancelled a second printing and pulled the marketing budget. His agent, Joan Munchin, struggled to help him see that fans of his first book did not want to be *challenged* by the second book. She believed *Agonistes* offered precious rewards, but there was a limited market for "difficult" writing unless you were Thomas Pynchon or David Foster Wallace.

While Charlie worked on the second novel, Tess was moving

up the ranks at Regis. She was smart and hard-working and way more than presentable, precisely the kind of young lawyer the firm wanted to encourage. Her salary kept Mountain House from crumbling into the valley while Charlie stirred the pot of creation. This was only fair; he had carried her through the end of law school and ponied up the down-payment on the house. They were also able to go on the firm's medical insurance and take advantage of the other benefits. Charlie was certain his second novel would ensure their financial future and encouraged her to maximize contributions to all the retirement plans and insurance. Of course, one downside was she worked for that slave-driver Carter, which was massively inconvenient. He worked everyone crazy hours, and Mountain House got lonely with only the dog for company.

A horn in the driveway announced the car service. Tess grabbed her overnight bag, brushed Charlie's dirty blond hair from his face, kissed his cheek and turned for the door. "Oh," she said over her shoulder, "if you get a chance, there's dry cleaning to pick up."

She stepped into the car. He stood by the door to wave but she didn't look back. She never understood how it ate at him when people left. Why did she let the moment slip by, when a simple gesture would have made him feel connected? He wondered who she would be meeting in Washington and who would be taking her to dinner.

Late in the afternoon, Charlie was playing spider solitaire on his computer when the phone rang. "How's the reclusive novelist?" Joan said in her pep-talk voice.

"Ah, you know, just kicking around, wondering where my muse got to."

"Listen, Charles, I've been talking to Penguin. They're looking past *Agonistes* and want you to return to the formula that made you."

"Right, but I've already covered the tortured childhood thing."

"They don't want the *same* book, but they want you to go back to fictionalized memoir: first person, writing about something you know."

But speaking in my own voice as little as possible, Charlie heard Aristotle say as he shot a rubber band at the ceiling and caught it.

"Problem is coming up with a story. Maybe if I lived a more interesting life, you know, jumped a banana boat to the South Seas or joined the IRA. Hey, maybe I should skip the novel altogether and write a screenplay, some detective story set in early Hollywood. Think of the Oscar party!"

"Seriously, Charles, you signed a contract for three books, and you have credibility writing novels from life. The first one really touched people. You could tap into that audience with something real."

"I'll think about it, but I've got to go now. See you Tuesday for lunch?"

Joan sighed deeply. "They say you have one more chance, and they will not commit to near the same marketing, not until they see the finished product. And they want to see it *soon*! Penguin didn't call it an ultimatum but it sounds like one to me. Please bring good news Tuesday."

That evening Charlie microwaved stew and sat in front of the television to watch a movie. He kept returning to the idea of a screenplay. The one he co-wrote in college was terrible. Still, how hard could it be to write for the movies? It would give him an excuse to write directly for the masses, literary achievement be damned. Could they really make him write another novel just because he signed a contract?

All things considered, it would be safest to do what Joan and his publisher wanted and write a novel from his life. He tried to think of an anecdote to spin into a book, which might also be made into a movie. What Hollywood wanted was young love stories or young people on adventures; but his life, after the well-documented childhood, had been pretty dull.

Tess got home late the next night. Charlie was asleep when he felt her climb into bed. He fell back to sleep until his internal clock woke him at five a.m., an hour before she'd get up for work. He pressed gently against her. But she jerked abruptly, as if he had startled her, so he waited, envisioning making love once she was fully awake. When he woke again, he heard her in the shower.

After coffee and grapefruit, Charlie took Odysseus for a hike in the woods. He tried not to think about the morning, and turned his attention to the lack of novel-worthy material in his life since his escape from Baltimore. College was mostly a chance to work hard in school and live a student life without the trauma that filled his childhood, the nightmare just under the surface. He had hoped putting it down on paper would dispel the demons but instead it etched the details into his mind. If he could just focus on another story, maybe he could sleep without seeing his father's bloodshot eyes and feeling the strap across his back.

There was the year in Dublin, but where was the novel in drinking Guinness and emulating historic college pranks? And since graduation, well, the success of the first book distinguished him, but what was interesting in a book about a guy who wrote a book?

A squirrel darted by with Odysseus in pursuit, but the dog stopped on the driveway. He looked up at Charlie with a dumb smile as if to say he never intended to catch the varmint. Charlie laughed and petted his head.

"From a writer nicknamed Homer with a dog called Odysseus," he said out loud, "the world rightfully could expect more than paperbacks for beach reading." But he had to face the fact that the world would not let him live on his peaceful mountain with his beautiful wife and his big dog and just create art. He needed to dig deep into the muck where he found the first book, into something disturbing and real, something that would sell.

Chapter 3

Tess looked out the window when the car reached the switchback below Mountain House. This view across the valley always thrilled her; it was like throwing open a window from a speeding train.

The ride to the airport gave her an opportunity to think. Attending college at NYU had left her uncomfortably close to her parents in New Jersey. Her mother felt entitled to show up for surprise shopping visits, which Tess had to join if she wanted new clothes. And then she made Tess come to Montclair for events at the country club. Tess had few real friends left from high school, mostly hangers-on who seemed to think she was still interested. She wanted to leave that world behind, particularly her mother's prying. But any resistance on Tess's part always came back to who was paying for school and providing Tess the New York City life her mother thought should be hers.

So, with only a touch of Irish blood and no prior interest in Ireland, she saw the opportunity to escape for her junior year to Dublin. She signed up first and then got her father to persuade her mother.

The Trinity College campus was captivating, from its grand Front Gate to the lush green cricket pitch. She was enchanted by Examination Hall, with its chessboard floor that made you feel part of a grand game. She loved how snow blanketed College Park in winter and the magnolia trees bloomed in spring. Then there was Ansel, who was *so* good-looking and self-assured. She knew in an instant she *had* to have him and, for the first time since fifth grade, became the pursuer rather than the pursued. Early in Michaelmas Term they ended a pub night in his room and kicked out his roommate. From then on they were the couple everyone knew. She still carried images of looks they got walking across campus or through the city.

Ansel had a roving eye and competition from other girls came with the territory. But in late spring it got bad, particularly with one blonde from Australia, who kept pointing her big boobs at Ansel. And then there was that last nightmare of a party. That was a smack in the head. She was lucky Molly and Charlie were there for her.

That was probably the first time she looked seriously at Charlie and his pitiful mustache. He was so earnest and caring, which is what she needed right then. He kept Molly and her up half the night with stories in his terrible Irish brogue. But there was nothing more between Charlie and her in Dublin. She was not attracted to him then, not even a little.

They texted a few times senior year, when he was at Cornell and she finished at NYU. He came to the city once and they had drinks, but he didn't stay with her. Then she started law school in Ithaca, where he was working. It was nice having someone in town with a job and a car who could afford to take her out. He was attentive, and his apartment was much nicer than the dorm room she shared with a roommate. In a way she even liked how he didn't divert attention from her, the way Ansel could. He was also quite jealous, which was cute and so *unlike* Ansel that she found it endearing.

They saw a lot of each other that summer. She found a law clerk job in town and was relieved to have a chance to relax. They drove around the Finger Lakes and searched out wineries and odd attractions. They saw a concert outside Cooperstown and visited the Baseball Hall of Fame, where Charlie just had to see the Cal Ripken plaque. In between trips she was impressed by how hard he worked. He had such a strong sense of his destiny as a writer.

Her school workload eased up second year, and she continued

her law clerk job part time. In January he published his novel and was an instant star. He suddenly had money and was traveling all over. She was thrilled to join him at parties in Boston and New York City, finally headlining in an exclusive world. For her birthday, he bought her expensive sapphire earrings, her first real jewelry.

He quit his job at the paper to have time to promote the book and became a celebrity in Ithaca. Whereas earlier in the year he had to sneak into the university gym to play paddleball, suddenly he was a distinguished alumnus and guest lecturer with a key to the campus. People all around, especially young women, started paying attention and, Tess had to admit, that made her appreciate him all the more.

Then her father had a stroke and passed away. Once again, she looked around in crisis and there was Charlie. He cancelled a book tour to drive her to Montclair for the funeral. She needed every bit of his support to deal with her mother, who became unhinged. She told Tess what to wear to the funeral, how to act and how much she should eat and drink. Charlie bristled at this and her mother attacked him as well. After a loud argument, Charlie and Tess left without saying goodbye.

Two weeks back at school her mother wrote that estate finances made it impossible to continue paying Tess's tuition, so she'd have to find another way to fund her third year. Tess panicked, but once again Charlie calmed her down.

"You could easily take out a loan," he said. "You only have to cover one more year, and you'll make plenty at your job this summer."

She scrunched up her nose, grateful for the support. "Better still," he added, "you could marry me and we could start our own family, away from childhood memories."

He was not exactly the man of her dreams, but he worshiped her and would take care of her, which seemed more important. They married at the end of the summer. Charlie paid for everything. Tess's mother showed up only to criticize her dress, the ceremony and the groom.

The early days of marriage were fun and she really got along with Charlie. Then there were the bouts of artistic martyrdom, when living with "Gloomy Charlie" made her wonder if she even loved "Cheerful Charlie" or if her feeling was more gratitude for his help and excitement at sharing his celebrity.

She threw herself into searching for a house near New York City, thinking this would bring them together, and it worked for a while. After she graduated, they bought the perfect place. Mountain House was a little big and far from Midtown but it was distinctive, a building well known to architects. It was perfect except for some furniture past its due date. But then Charlie loved the well-worn chairs and sofas. He really was a real lay-around-and-watch-movies kind of guy.

Breakneck Road took some getting used to and was treacherous in the snow. But Charlie loved it. "It's the best part of the house," he once said, throwing his trophy car into gear. The winding road rose past the house to a peak. It was used so rarely, Charlie treated it like his private Le Mans track. She had to admit, though, she sometimes raced up the mountain in her Volvo.

It was hard to say when she and Charlie drifted apart, if they had ever really been together. In Dublin it was Ansel who took her breath away, so that might be why Charlie made no impression. But after graduation, when they fell in together in the same town, there was a lot to admire in him, holding down a day job and writing his book into the night.

Early in the marriage, he announced his second novel would be not just successful but "important." In the flush of his success with *Against the Odds*, this sounded more confident than pretentious, but as years passed with nothing to show, it came to seem like a way to justify self-centered behavior.

One typical Saturday morning she'd been inspired by a fresh breeze to air out the house. "What do you say to a little spring cleaning?" she asked over morning coffee.

He looked up from a clipboard. "Not today," he said and returned to his work.

"But it's such a glorious day, and this place is musty."

"Look," he barked, "I'm in rhythm. If you want to clean, go ahead and clean, but keep the noise down!"

That illustrated the "creative phase," when nothing could interfere with Charlie's work. He *must* have time to write. He must *not* be disturbed. At times she had to muffle all sounds and at others she could not escape the blaring bebop.

On a Sunday afternoon months later, she felt an urge unrelated to housekeeping. She tried on new perfume and a negligee and knocked on his door. When he answered, she said demurely, "I have finished all the housework, sir," turning to exhibit her figure to advantage, "and I wondered if there's anything else at all you might want of me."

"What," he said absently, barely looking up. Then he noticed her outfit and couldn't fail to see her intention. "Ah, very nice," he said. "But could we put it off until later? I'm in a critical chapter."

Yes, lovemaking was on *his* schedule, to feed *his* creative juices, just as invitations were turned down and mealtimes juggled on the altar of high art. In his fever of creation, he couldn't even pick up after himself, which made him like the child they never had.

Which was another fraught subject. She had made clear from the start she would not have children. She had no love for her parents and wanted to forget her childhood. Now that she was free to live the life she deserved, she would not be tethered to some snarling baby. She competed with men undistracted by diapers and day care. She liked being admired for her appearance as well as her work and could not see waddling into a deal meeting in a frumpy maternity outfit everyone pretended not to notice. And, even though Charlie wanted children, he was such a child himself that he would have been no help caring for them, except maybe between chapters.

Against the Odds made Charlie's childhood experience out to be as gruesome as hers, or even more so if you thought physical abuse worse than psychological torture. "Doesn't the reality of our own growing up make you see raising a family would be disastrous?" she pleaded.

"But kids!" he said, as if this made his point.

"It's insanity when you repeat the same thing and expect a different result," she said, exasperated.

"But we are *different* than our parents. We're better!"

"You're stuck in a sitcom life. But look around: no picket fence; no neighbors gossiping across backyards. We *are* different, and we're better off living the life we've earned. Anyway, you agreed, and it's too late to change your mind."

He pouted. She proposed a dog as a compromise, and he grudgingly agreed, although neither of them realized how much room and attention their cuddly Newfoundland puppy would take up in the end.

When the second novel bombed, Charlie went into a funk. It was all the reviewers' fault; they couldn't understand his genius. Their criticism of *Agonistes* bothered him more than the fact that no one exercised the film option on the first book. (She had heard rumors the option was lost in a poker game, but never shared that with her husband.) Over the last year, he drank too much and spent his time walking in the woods or detailing his car. With no book underway, for a while he became obsessed with making love, as if dusting off an old hobby. But she found it increasingly difficult to get excited by an unshaved partner who never changed out of sweatpants, and that inflamed his jealousy. It got to be a relief to go to the office, where people respected and admired her.

Her uninspired sex life could have left her open to temptation. If Tom Carter had been better-looking, who knows what might have happened on those overnight trips? And now she would spend another night in the same hotel as Tom. She thought it best not to mention that to Charlie. He'd make a scene, which would be totally unfair. Charlie's jealousy would be easier to bear if she had something to hide. Besides, Charlie and his agent were quite cozy. Maybe his guilt about Joan made him assume Tess was also looking elsewhere. She absently flipped through mental images of the partners at Regis, swiping left to reject each one.

Chapter 4

Ansel pulled on his shoes and started to call Henry but decided he shouldn't wait and asked the doorman to get him a cab.

As the taxi crept across town, memories flooded in. It was just after he had started his doctoral program at Columbia when he met Florence, a ballet dancer who grew up in Manhattan. At first he was attracted to her lithe body and enthusiasm in bed, but he gradually drifted into her ethereal world. Dance and music were all that tethered her to the ground. He lusted after her creative focus and was drawn to how little she cared about politics or finance. This was such a relief from his father and his study of historical data. He spent as much time as he could with her and the artists filling her life. When she moved in with him after two months, he hid this from his father, who surely would have forbidden it.

Two months later Florence was pregnant. Ansel told his father they were living together, but not about the pregnancy. Jordan demanded he end the relationship. Ansel wished his mother were alive; she would have taken his side. But thinking of her gave him the strength to push back against his father. He and Florence married at City Hall and settled into married life in their university apartment.

Florence continued to practice and hope for bigger roles but found it hard to push herself physically. This dimmed her prospects of making it out of the chorus. Yet, she would not consider giving up the baby and so was forced to look past her dreams. This took a toll on the unfettered joy that had attracted Ansel, and he turned reflexively toward his work. As months passed and her perspective focused more and more within, he found less enchantment with her artistic circle and new interest in his colleagues and his thesis. A shapely fellow student also caught his eye and encouraged him to begin writing about history for publication and also about collaborating with her in more personal ways.

Before the baby arrived Ansel and Florence agreed to divorce. There was no acrimony; they both realized they had never been well suited. She moved back with her mother, who would care for the baby while Florence qualified to teach. He agreed to see her through the birth and pay modest child support, but otherwise wanted a clean break, so they could pursue independent lives. He wanted no custody and no visitation rights.

She named the boy "True," as if she were a hippy living in a meadow, and added her surname. Each year in a Christmas card she thanked Ansel for the money and sent a photo of True. After the first couple of years, he just stuck the cards in a dresser drawer, unopened. He never told his father he had a grandson.

By the time Ansel secured his associate professor position on the history faculty and published his two *Redux* books, Florence's mother had passed away and left her the Chelsea co-op where she grew up. She was teaching dance and True, at ten years old, attended a Catholic middle school near their apartment. Ansel rarely thought about them, except when he noticed the nominal debit on his bank statement.

And then came the call on his balcony.

When he arrived at the hospital, Florence was stable but unconscious. The doctors said that was good, for now. Otherwise, there were some broken bones but apparently no internal injuries. They would keep her in intensive care and monitor the situation. Did she have a living will?

A living will? Was she going to die? How could this be? How could a freak accident pluck someone off the street like that? And how would *he* know if there was a will?

The nurse had found an insurance card in her wallet but kept asking questions he couldn't answer. What was her blood type? Was she on any medication? Finally realizing they were no longer married, the nurse asked, "Is there someone else we should call?"

"No," he said numbly. "No one I know of." No one but the boy. His mind turned again on True. He had to find his son!

"Then, as her next of kin, you will have to sign the release for her treatment."

"Me!" he blurted out. Why should *he* be making decisions affecting her treatment? They hardly knew each other anymore. Still, he had no choice and so he agreed to what the doctors recommended.

While he was signing the document, a call came to the nurse's station from Florence's neighbor, Helen, and a nurse handed Ansel the phone. Helen said her son was True's classmate, and they all lived in the same building. She brought True home after school Friday.

Ansel told her what he knew about Florence's condition and asked, "Can he stay with you?"

"Well, he's with us now. The boys, they think it's a sleepover. Of course he can stay, until you're able to come get him."

"Until I..." Ansel was startled to think this also was *his* responsibility.

"Yes you, Ansel, his *father*."

"Father" was a word that connoted no comfort. This was no role for him. How could this possibly work? He didn't even know the boy, had seen him only when he was first born. Where would he sleep? Who would watch him? There had to be someone else, but there *was* no one else.

Helen was firm, and they finally agreed True would stay with her until Sunday evening and then go home with Ansel.

* * *

Becca was in her apartment when Ansel called. She let it go straight to voicemail: "Becca, I know you're angry but something urgent has come up. Please call me tonight."

She played the recording for her roommate. "Wow," Roxy said, "he sounds genuinely concerned."

"Yeah, he *sounds* that way, but who knows what's real?"

"Look, you need the job."

Becca thought about it while she prepared dinner and then returned the call.

"You have a son?"

"Well, he was born after my divorce and always lived with his mother."

"But he's yours? When do you see him?"

"Look," he said, "this is not about being father of the year or making up for lost time. I just have to keep him with me for now. There's no other way until his mother's back on her feet. Can you help me keep an eye on him? I have no idea what to do with a kid."

The revelation about his estranged child fit her image of Ansel-the-Terrible. How could anyone lack an innate sense of how to be a father?

When she said nothing, he spoke again. "Look, I guess we cut things off abruptly the other day. But it was fun, right?"

It was a good thing they were not speaking in person; she would have broken that perfect Greek nose. But she calmed herself and looked at things objectively. He didn't care about her; she should just face that. She *had* to have more sense about men. They were basically all shits, and Ansel was no different, just better dressed. But that aside, she needed to find another job before she could move on, which was easier said than done. There was rent to pay, and she had grown accustomed to regular meals. Going back to restaurant work was not a pretty option. And something inside said that, stuck with Ansel as his father, this kid would need help. Also, Ansel needed *her* now, so he would have to respect her.

"I'll help get him settled," she heard herself say. "But I'm not going with you to pick him up. *You* are his father; you have to bring him home and let him know you'll keep him safe. Can you do that, Ansel?"

"Yeah. Yes, absolutely. But you'll come early tomorrow?"

"I'll be there. We'll sort this out."

She wondered how she ever became an abused employee slash babysitter. But somehow her roll in the sheets with Ansel had moved her forward emotionally, and maybe in terms of her job as well. Call it an education in what was really important. She knew right from wrong, which made her stronger than Ansel would ever be. She would help with the boy because he needed help and she needed the job.

In cut-off shorts and an oversized Boston College Football sweatshirt, she took her laptop out on the fire escape and stuck her feet through the metal railing. A brick wall fifteen feet away took up most of her view, but she could see a pear tree on the street if she leaned forward. She had photographed this tree in all seasons but this was the best time of year, when it was in flower. Still, the shots never fully communicated the comfort it gave her, the tiniest sliver of nature and home almost within reach. The spring breeze, anyway, felt delicious after the drizzly cold of the last few weeks. It was also liberating to be over her infatuation with her boss. He was her paycheck and a steppingstone to a career, nothing more. She should have had more sense than to believe he had feelings for her. Look at the way he treated his other women. Look at how he ignored his own flesh and blood!

She wondered, as she had so often before, how her life would be different if her mother had lived. She imagined an elegant woman, all kindness and understanding, taking her hand to show the way. Her father did his best, and he was the one person who loved her without reserve, but he was a man and struggled to understand her challenges, especially as a teenager trying to make sense of conflicting signals all around.

Then she had met Ansel and life swirled. She had arrived in the city fresh from college with a marketing degree and a determination to make her way. She still loved her hometown, where the pear trees, along with elms and oaks, filled the streets and anchored life to solid ground, but she refused to return there in defeat. Home now was a one-bedroom walk-up in Greenpoint shared with an ex-college roommate and another woman. She spent weeks following up job leads, but all the positions required experience, which was exactly what she needed. Ideally, she'd work with a photographer, get to know the business and make contacts, but to start she'd take anything related to marketing. Failing this she turned to waiting tables, which at least paid the rent, but it was hard on her feet and the hours were grueling.

On days off she travelled to parks and coffee shops all over Brooklyn and Manhattan, soaking up the ambience and taking photographs. She would splurge on a cup of coffee and sit for hours looking for jobs and keeping up with her social media accounts.

Submitting job applications one afternoon at the Hungarian Pastry Shop across from Saint John's Cathedral, she looked up to see a handsome, well-dressed man. "I'm thinking Vassar," he said. He was eminently sure of himself. She looked down shyly at expensive shoes.

"Boston College," she said, looking around at her absorbed neighbors, wondering if any of them thought this approach a little aggressive.

"Oh, not a *Red Sox* fan?" he smirked.

"The Brewers, actually," she said and realized she recognized his face. "Hey, aren't you that history guy?"

"Ah, my adoring public," he said and took the seat across from her. "And you majored in…?"

"Oh, not history, but I saw you on *The Tonight Show*. You were funny." And quite telegenic, she thought but didn't say.

"Well, 'funny' is something. But tell me, my intriguing Boston College Eagle, what do you do when you're not surfing the web in coffee shops?"

Before he finished his coffee, he had hired her to manage his online publicity and given her Leah's card to get things started. She wondered if that was all the job would entail or if she might get the chance to travel with him and gain entrée into his world. He was awfully good-looking, and famous. As it turned out, he really was interested in what she could do for his public image, both by working social media and occasionally standing in when he needed a date on his arm.

Then came their afternoon tryst, which confirmed what she should have known all along: he was a rat bastard like all the rest, or maybe worse than the rest. She should have known better. Going forward, she'd be smarter. He was too short for her anyway.

Ansel said the university wanted teachers to clear with the administration any video that might imply authorization by the university. So he told her to post the lecture video so the source couldn't be traced. She put it on a masked Instagram account and added hashtags to link it to his followers. She smiled. She was good at this stuff.

She held up her phone, raised her eyebrows to express reaching a cosmic revelation, and shot a selfie before the brick wall. She texted the shot to her father, asking him to share it with her dog Wolfgang. She captioned it: "Ingénue stumbles upon the secret of life."

Chapter 5

"Who are you?" True said suspiciously.

Helen had shown Ansel into her apartment and introduced the boy. He was four-and-a-half feet tall with bushy dark hair needing to be cut and a snarl on his face.

"I told you, True," Helen said. "This is your father."

Ansel nodded. "That's right, True, and your mom needs you to stay with me while she gets better."

"I don't even *know* you!" True shouted and turned away.

It took some time but Helen convinced True to go home with Ansel. He didn't fully trust Ansel but seemed to see he had no choice. On the taxi ride uptown, he watched out the window as if he were being kidnapped and was looking for a chance to jump from the car.

"When will Mom come home?" he whined before Ansel had a chance to close his apartment door.

"Uh," Ansel stumbled, "we don't know yet, but soon." Florence was still out of it, but the doctors remained confident.

"I want to see her!"

"The doctors say we can visit later in the week, when she's feeling better."

True's expression went from rage to pain, and then he cried quietly. Ansel looked around for help, but they were alone. What was he supposed to do? True was so small and frightened. Memories of his mother suggested Ansel should hold him, but his father's voice kept saying to let the boy cry himself out.

He finally sat beside his son and patted his shoulder. True jerked away and moved to the floor by his suitcase. "It'll be okay," Ansel said, wishing he sounded more convincing.

Ansel fixed up a bed for True on the sofa and left the boy sitting on the floor. True would not look up.

With his door ajar, Ansel got into bed and could hear True moving around. Drifting off, Ansel was awakened by sobbing. He dragged himself from bed to close his door.

Thankfully, Becca arrived early next morning. She brushed by Ansel and went directly to True, who lay on the sofa with his face buried in his phone. She sat on the floor facing the boy. "Hi, True," she said brightly. "I'm Becca. I work for your dad, and I think you and I should be friends, okay?"

"Um," True said, looking up. "Okay."

True was guarded but he kept watching her. She made breakfast, which he grudgingly ate, and then she sat him down in the living room.

"So, listen," she said, friendly but serious. "We promised your mom we would keep you safe until she's better, so there are a couple of things you have to remember. And this is really important. Okay?"

He avoided looking at her but he seemed to be listening. How was she able to get his attention like that?

"First," she said, "you see that cool balcony and the river and all? Well, it's a long way down, and it is *not okay* to play out there. None of us ever climb on the railing to look over or get up on the furniture at all. Right?"

She gently touched under his chin, and he looked at her. "Right?" she repeated softly but firmly.

"Right," he said in a small voice.

"That's great. And the other thing is you're in a strange neighborhood now. I know you're not a little kid anymore and can take care of yourself, but you don't know your way around here, and it's so easy to get lost or hit by a car or to find all sorts of trouble on the street, so you *can't* go out alone. Do you understand?"

She waited until he said, finally, "Yeah, okay."

"Awesome. So now let's fix things up for you. Your dad is used to living on his own and we need to make this a place for both of you."

She told Ansel the boy could *not* sleep on the sofa, so he handed over his credit card and she ordered a twin bed for his office. She emptied out the office closet for the boy's clothes, stacking Ansel's books and boxes in a corner. She asked True what kind of food he liked, and after no response called in an order while he listened closely. She dialed his school and made Ansel tell the principal True would be out for a day or two. She posted notices for a nanny to take him to school and stay with him when Ansel wasn't around.

Ansel looked on as if this was all happening to someone else. What would this do to his life? How could he work with a kid here? Was this going to take all his time?

Later, while Becca took True to Riverside Park to show him how to shoot nature photographs, Leah called to say she had arranged to meet Karla Wednesday evening. "You have to remain positive," she said, "and focus on the outline."

"I will, I promise, but there is a small complication."

"Oh, don't tell me the same old…"

"Oh, this is new. It's my son." He paused to let this sink in. "He's ten, and his mother had an accident. And, well, it sucks but he has to stay with me for a while."

Leah was silent for a moment. "Okay," she said decisively, "we can deal with this. Can Becca help until we line someone up?"

"Yeah, she's here already and knows what to do. They're in the park right now."

"Good. So, have her call me and I'll find a babysitter."

"Thanks, Leah. I think Becca already posted something, but you two can work that out. And I'll get you the outline as soon as I can."

Ansel tried to work but was interrupted by delivery of the bed and groceries. Then True and Becca returned, chased inside by a thunderstorm. She made True change into dry clothes and Ansel showed him his bed. True promptly claimed it as his personal space and sat on it looking at his phone.

"Is he all right?" Ansel asked Becca as she dried her hair with a towel.

"Well, let's see: his mother is hurt, he's separated from the only family he knows and he's stuck living with someone he just met. And yeah, he's only ten. So *no*, he's not *all right*. You've got to step up here, Ansel. This is your son, and he needs you right now."

Ansel had spent a lifetime repenting for what happened to his mother, and here was a new world of shame and obligation he didn't want and couldn't handle. Why was this heaped on him? Surely Ansel's father was never weighed down with caring for his son.

* * *

True heard Becca and Ansel talking in the living room. He believed Ansel was his father, but what did that mean? He was never around, like other dads. And who was Becca and why was she here? At least she was nicer than him. At least she thought about getting food he liked.

Ansel came in and sat on the bed. "So, True," he said, like he was talking to a little kid, "do you like school?"

"I guess."

"I bet you have a lot of friends there."

True didn't want to talk. He could see Ansel didn't care; he was just pretending.

At dinner Becca served pasta. It was not how his mom made it, and he didn't want to sit at the table with grown-ups. They just asked questions and didn't *tell* him anything. Was his mother really hurt? Why couldn't he see her? How long did he have to stay in this place?

Chapter 6

"John Sanderman on the line," Bud's assistant announced over the intercom.

"Johnny!" Bud bellowed.

"Hey, man. Just wanted to say thanks!"

"Oh, you know it, sport. Great weekend, right?"

"As always. You have to keep me in mind for the next trip."

"You know it, sport. So hey, give my regards to your lovely bride, and we'll catch up on the policy after you see how you like the fish."

He hung up and called out the doorway. "Lois, what've I got this afternoon?"

"Call with Helen Smith at three. Squash at five with Jerry Butler."

He pulled out his phone to check his notes. Trout fishing made a great weekend, but closing in on Jerry's business and cementing a friendship with John Sanderman paid the bills.

He opened the file on Helen Smith, widowed mother of three, dissatisfied with what she got from her husband's life insurance, looking for a more comprehensive policy for herself. He reviewed the names of her kids but was sure she also owned a cat. It was named something stupid like "Fluffy" or "Cuddles."

In the hour before his call, he went online. He checked social accounts and traded messages with friends and potential clients, or was it clients and potential friends? It was unfathomable why some agents made little use of the internet. It was instant research and networking gone nuclear, like working a room as big as a fat year-end bonus. Networking was the key.

Bud had graduated college with little distinction and was overjoyed to find a job, any job. That the position was with a well-known insurance company made it even sweeter. What he failed to realize until he had passed the required test and nearly completed his internship was the position paid *only* commissions, which also were split with his boss and his boss's boss. This provided a comfortable living for the higher-ups but left Bud no way to pay his rent and college loans while he built a business. His parents had retired and had no means to help, other than to offer sympathy and their guest room.

He thought about changing careers but had already invested so much time. And he was a natural salesman; it was sure to pay off. So, for years he worked all the time, selling insurance by day and tending bar at night. He quickly got over feeling uncomfortable about pushing policies on friends and family who might have more important uses for their money. Like his boss said, "You're not an insurance salesman to make friends." He had to sell to survive, which made everyone a contact. Anyway, it was not like he was pushing a scam; everyone was underinsured, and he could cover it all. He handled professional policies start to finish but could share the commission on insuring everything else from pets to vacations.

His thoughts returned to Helen Smith. He should ask her if she had a policy for the cat, if he could just remember the furball's name. Those vet bills could be murder.

Lois buzzed. "Jack Martin on the line."

Bud flinched. His new boss had resisted Bud's transfer from Boston and was leaning on him hard. "Morning, Jack," he said cautiously.

"Bud, how are things going?"

"Excellent. Prospects are lining up."

"Prospects are good, Bud, but there's a timeline on this."

"I know, Jack. Just put through an E&O policy, and a few other things are about to close."

"I hope so. I'm counting on you to make me look good."

And to fatten your wallet, Bud thought. "No worries, Jack. I'm on the case."

After he hung up, Bud took a deep breath. In one sense, life was good. No wife to slow him down but hook-ups often enough. After years of struggle, he finally had a steady income without moonlighting and every personal and professional reason for prime skiing and fishing. And in moving to New York, he had joined the insurance big leagues. True, he would have to start out living in Long Island City, but Queens was cool now, and anyway it was temporary; things would pick up with millions of new pigeons to pluck. But he had put himself on the line to fill the position Jack wanted for a client's nephew. He had to prove himself quickly.

There was no doubt he'd make it big. He'd been making deals his whole life. When he was nine, his father was livid that he sold his first bike—until he heard for how much.

Then came college. He once bought sixteen pounds of skunky home-grown weed from a farmer skulking around campus. It was scary moving it in and storing it in the dorm, but he unloaded it the next day for a quick profit. Then, there were the fur coats. One day the owner of a dry-cleaner offered him a raccoon coat someone had left behind years before. "What do you say I sell you this nice coat—real cheap?" the owner said. Bud just smiled. The coat looked like a prop from a Buster Keaton movie; it should have come with a ukulele. "No, really," the owner went on, "this coat must be a couple hundred dollars in the store. I give it to you for fifty." "Forty," Bud blurted out without thinking and the deal was made. He wore that coat for a few days and then sold it for eighty. And thus launched a year of canvassing dry cleaners for abandoned coats, buying cheap and selling slightly less cheap.

And now New York was his oyster. He would push every policy known to the insurance universe, and maybe invent some others, and earn his way to the top of the heap with minions splitting *their* commissions with *him*.

"Buttercup" popped into his head, and he added the name of Helen Smith's cat to his notes. He then flipped to Dutch Gilroy's profile on LinkedIn. Dutch was a good friend, big and square-jawed and solid as a fire hydrant. Since Trinity, they had exchanged Christmas cards and occasional online quips but had not gotten together.

Dutch worked in his father's business in New York. What was it, restaurant supplies? He typed Dutch's name into LinkedIn and laughed when the screen showed his name was Dilbert; he had forgotten that, although he remembered his "Plato" nickname from Trinity. Dutch was vice-president of Aljo Company, there since graduation, and the president's name was also "Gilroy." It was a private company that didn't report financials, but Bloomberg listed substantial accounts. Now that he was in New York, Bud would have to renew his friendship with Dutch, and the whole Trinity crowd.

He started a message, then toggled from LinkedIn to Facebook. Best to keep this non-professional; they were college buddies, after all, and had practically been roommates. In fact, he owed Dutch big time for one fateful night in Dublin. Bud had gotten into a jam in a pub, the sum of one drunk American plus three city toughs looking for trouble. The lads had Bud on the ground in an alley when Dutch blew in like a force of nature. His shout put the locals on their heels, and after he laid one out, they all vanished into the mist. Back at campus Molly and Tess fussed over him while Charlie wanted Dutch to go with him with cricket bats and teach the locals a lesson.

"No need," Bud said. "They're in bed by now having nightmares about Plato here."

He and Dutch never spoke about that episode, but they both remembered.

"Moved to town," he typed. "Seeking best pint of Guinness."

He was heating up a lasagna for dinner when Bud saw Dutch's response: "Swift on East 4th - any night after six."

Two nights later Bud found Dutch at the empty bar in the front of the pub called Swift. He looked solid as ever, dressed casually for a vice-president and quietly nursing a beer.

"So, a philosopher and a duck walk into a bar…" Bud said from behind.

Dutch spun around and got up to clasp Bud's hand. Bud pulled him in for a bear hug and stepped back to look him over. "Putting on a few, big guy," he said, patting his own stomach.

"Ah, you know how it is, too much sitting in an office."

"How *well* I know."

"And looking a little thin on top," Dutch said, brushing back his own thick hair.

"Ah, give me a break," Bud laughed. He caught the bartender's eye. "My good sir," he said, "two shots of your very finest Irish whiskey, if you please."

"Now are you sure you'll be wanting just that?" the bartender replied in a genuine brogue, reaching for a bottle of Midleton on the top shelf and placing it on the bar. "You're welcome to handle the bottle, but it's thirty dollars a shot."

Bud guffawed.

"It's what Daniel Craig drank when he was in," the bartender said with raised eyebrows.

"What the hell," Bud bellowed. "How often do I see a friend from the old country?" The price was steep but it would go on his entertainment tab.

Dutch held up his glass.

Bud nodded toward the head painted on the wall behind them. "Is himself who I'm thinking he is?" he said.

"And now who else *would* it be?"

"Then to our fellow Trinitarian!" Bud toasted.

"Jonathan Swift," Dutch said, and they downed their shots.

When he caught his breath, Bud said, "So how the hell are you, sport? I understand you've moved up to the C-suite."

"Yeah, the two rooms I share with my dad at the end of the floor. It's a living but not very glamorous."

"So Aljo's a family shop?"

"Yeah, Dad started the business thirty years ago when he inherited some money. We supply restaurants and food services, mostly the big equipment. The company has survived so far, but it's not easy dragging my father into this decade, which we have to do to compete."

"And the name?"

"'Al' for my mother Alice and 'Jo' for my dad."

Bud smiled. Dutch was just the kind of guy to be close to his parents.

"And what are you up to?" Dutch asked.

"Insurance game. Life, health, you name it. Calls for a lot of entertaining—golf, fishing trips—but I've learned to live with it." He grinned. "Learned the ropes up in Boston but couldn't stand the weather and the traffic."

"*We* have some traffic too."

"Yeah, but you've got the subway. Anyway, I got a chance to move to the big city where I can develop commercial sales."

Dutch eyed his friend and laughed. "Always pushing a scheme."

"Hey, I'm just a poor salesman trying to make my way in the world."

Dutch smiled. "So, are you in touch with anyone else?"

Bud didn't want the conversation to turn from Aljo's insurance needs but he had to avoid looking predatory. "You have to network," he said, "so I'm linked online with Ansel and Charlie, and he married Tess, right?"

"Right, strange as *that* seems. They bought a house in Cold Spring, up in Putnam County. I saw a magazine spread a few years ago; it's an amazing spot on the side of a mountain." Dutch looked into his beer glass, laughing quietly.

"What?" Bud said, a consequent smile forming.

"I was thinking of the 'Tonehenge' party we organized for your roommate's birthday."

"Oh, no!" Bud laughed. "I remember planning that but the details are lost in the Dublin fog."

"Which was inevitable."

"Of course. And when was excessive drinking *not* part of the plan?"

Dutch laughed again infectiously. "I can see Ansel with his blindfold after, what was it, our fourth pub?"

"Hey, we took it off so he could see his beer, and we never let him fall over in the street."

"Right—true comrades to the end—although we walked him in circles until he was too dizzy to know where he was."

"Well, we didn't go far in the end. And the unveiling…" Bud wrinkled his forehead. "I think I remember the unveiling. We photographed him by the Wolfe Tone statue, right, with all those granite columns?"

"Hence the name 'Tonehenge.'"

"And he was actually touched, I think."

"Well, Ansel shared the stage with only his famous ancestor, and he was pissed off his ass. Plus, it was photographed for posterity. Could the future historian imagine a finer moment in Irish history?"

Bud tried to piece together the memory. "So where did we end up that night?"

"I think Charlie went back to the dorm, but we crashed behind the bushes in Saint Stephen's Green. Ansel was in no condition to go anywhere and we were in no condition to carry him."

They smiled and sipped their beers. Then Dutch squinted. "You know, I think that's the only time I remember Ansel being serious. Or, that's not right; it was the only time he spoke seriously about himself."

"Yeah, that's when he told us about the ogre."

"Right, his father running roughshod over everyone. Even when Ansel was at boarding school the ex-football star was on his case, embarrassed that Ansel was more a squash and tennis guy."

"Did he ever mention his mother? It's a bit foggy in my brain."

"I think his mom passed away before he started college, but he didn't talk about her."

"Anyway, his father let him go to Ireland," Bud said.

"Yeah, because the ogre decided he should, as a nod to the Irish roots and a step in Daddy's plan for grad school. If Ansel hadn't taken the right courses, aced his big research paper and got the recommendation he needed, Ansel would have been afraid to go home."

After a swig of beer, Dutch said, "Well, he's done all right for himself. His books are all the rage."

"You read them?"

"Well, yeah. I mean, he *is* a friend. Somehow, even though we don't see each other, I think of you guys as the closest friends I ever had."

Bud held up his glass in silent toast and then said, "They're history books?"

"Sort of. He calls them 'revisionist history.'"

"What's that?"

"The people in power twist the facts to their benefit, like they say about wars: that the victors write the history."

"Does he write about wars?"

"No, but one of his books was about the Vietnam War protests. It talked about how commentators at the time said the 'Days of Rage' in Chicago were caused by hippies run amok, a generation later academics taught that they were really a courageous generation protesting an unjust war, and after 9/11 protesters were again portrayed as 'radical delinquents.' Same facts on the ground but told how those in power want it told."

Bud decided to get all the old friends out of the way so they could turn back to business. "So, what about Charlie?" he said, gesturing to the bartender for more beer. "He published a big book too, right?"

"Oh, yeah, *Against the Odds*. You can't have missed that. It was a bit depressing but over-the-top successful. I heard they were going to make it into a movie."

"And that was it? Nothing more?"

"Yeah, I guess that's where it unraveled. Never heard any more about a movie, and then a couple of years ago he published his magnum opus, *Something Agonistes*, and it bombed."

"Nobody bought it?"

"Worse than that, the townsfolk came out with pitchforks and torches. Critics called it 'sheer narcissism.' I read all eleven hundred pages, because it was Charlie, but…"

"Didn't do it for you?"

"Seemed like he wrote it for himself or posterity or something and dared the rest of us to figure it out. You remember how he used to quote Keats and Shelley and expect us to get the reference? For all I know, it's great literature but even the title is over my head."

"Well, I don't have much time for novels, and when I do read one, I want a thriller that keeps me on edge but doesn't tax my brain. I had enough 'great books' in school."

After two more beers, Dutch glanced at his watch.

"Got a date, Plato?" Bud laughed.

"No, not at all," Dutch said, seemingly embarrassed. "Just meetings in the morning."

"Oh, yeah, I was going to say the same." He wondered if Dutch was uncomfortable being asked about a date because he didn't get out much. He had never been much of a ladies' man. More important, however, was how to get back to talking insurance. Suddenly inspired, he said, "Hey, what do you say to a reunion? I could email Charlie, and maybe the 'Historian of the People' will spare us an evening."

"Great idea."

Bud watched Dutch down his beer. Maybe he could expand his network while repaying his debt to the big guy by pulling him out of his rut, bringing some life into his life. But the first priority was to sell Aljo a policy; everyone needs insurance.

Bud said he'd arrange everything. They parted on the sidewalk and melted into the passing crowd.

Chapter 7

The office phone snapped Dutch to attention. He'd been staring absently at a photograph of his Trinity College classmates on the wall. He loved that shot; their preposterous pose before the red brick of Rubrics. It transported him back to Dublin. That year was a precious memory, like a book he once read and hated to finish. There were always friends around, crazy parties and compelling conversations; even day-to-day he constantly experienced new things. He missed that time, those people.

Two years back he'd been shopping for an engagement ring when his girlfriend announced she was leaving Aljo for a job in Seattle. She gave no explanation, not even two weeks' notice on the business side.

Now he lived a straight-line commute from his apartment to the office to his parents' house. That day a store manager in Elmhurst was waiting on a refrigerator shipment, and the mix-up was sure to be traced to Aljo's version-challenged software. The lawyer was on the line about a facility they were buying; the sellers wanted more money to leave the fixtures behind. He thought about updating the company's website. He owed the accountant a call about a tax strategy that couldn't wait. In the midst of it all, his mother called five times. This didn't mean she had five different things to say or what she wanted to say was five times more important than anything. Most likely, she called to ask what to cook for supper Saturday and four more times because she forgot she already called.

He buzzed to see if his father knew why his mother was calling, but the president was gone for the day. Nothing new there.

He couldn't blame his father for being distracted, and it was best someone was home with his mom. Dutch could handle the business and for some time had, in fact, been running the company, but it was not clear anyone could deal with the situation at home. He wished his sister was more help, but she lived far away, and even in person it was hard to get anywhere with his mother.

He had to try, though, so he called the house.

"Sweet boy," his mother chirped, as if they had not spoken in ages. "It's so nice to hear from you."

"Hi, Mom. How are things?"

"Oh, just fine and dandy. You know, I've been meaning to invite you to supper."

"On Saturday, yes. I'd love to come."

"Oh, that will be so nice." She paused. "And there was something else; let me think."

"About what to cook?"

"Oh, that's right. It's such a treat to see you, I was thinking I'd make a pot roast. I know it's your favorite."

"Great, Mom. I'll pick up some bagels from that place you like and see you around noon."

"That'll be lovely, Dilly."

Dutch's assistant, Michael Devers, paused in the doorway until Dutch hung up and then came in with a letter for him to sign. Michael was an enormous help to Dutch and his father, anticipating their needs and serving as a go-between to the employees. All Michael's cheerfulness, however, did not soften the blow of the letter in his hand. It was a plea for a meeting with the owner of a large string of restaurants in Suffolk County who was taking his business to a competitor.

When Dutch passed the letter back, he held it tight until Michael looked him in the eye. "You're doing a great job," Dutch said, "Couldn't run this place without you."

"So, it must be time for a raise," Michael said, stifling a smile.

"Sure," Dutch laughed, "for you and me both…as soon as we turn the ship around. But first let's see how you do at getting me a turkey on rye—with a pickle this time."

"Right, Mr. Gilroy, pickle and turkey coming up."

For thirty years Aljo had been a successful company. Joe was able to send Dutch and his sister to private schools. They both got respectable grades, and Dutch excelled in sports, particularly baseball. Professional scouts came to some of his high school games and the Cleveland Indians offered him a spot in their farm system. But decent test scores and a phenomenal batting average also opened the door to Columbia.

Halfway through his sophomore season, he was starting for the Lions in right field when he tried to push a double into a triple and a torn ACL ended his career, and left him with a slight limp ever since. He had so long identified himself as an athlete that his accident left him rudderless. He lost touch with friends and interest in his studies and finally just wanted to get away. He thought about transferring outside New York but then learned of the junior-year-abroad program. This was a chance at a fresh start, away from sports, in a new place with new people.

The year in Dublin was a turning point; it revived him and returned him home eager to finish his degree and join his father's company. And a few years later he met Jennifer and everything was falling into place. But he must have been naïve or insensitive to her needs because she just left him stuck in place, with parents and a company to care for and no personal life. He found nothing to say to women he met online. It was simpler just to focus on the business.

But now Bud was in town. What a piece of work that guy was. Dutch wished he had half his energy. He'd be a welcome distraction, anyway, and it would be great to see the old crowd.

Saturday he drove out to Floral Park, over the county line in Nassau. The neighborhood around his parents' house hadn't changed in sixty years: small houses with front porches, tiny lawns and additions tacked on over the years. The mind-numbing traffic was also familiar.

He wished he didn't lose forty minutes to tie-ups each way, but at least he only had to make the trip once a week. If this was his daily commute, he'd have to shoot himself.

His father was trimming hedges when Dutch pulled up and walked over. "Dad," he said, with the informality bred of working together all week, "how's Mom today?"

His father shook his head. "Ah, she's in a tither, as usual. She's reminded me three times you'd be coming to dinner. You know how much it means to her when you come out."

"I was here *last* weekend."

"Oh, I know. But she loses track and she *always* wants to see you. Anyway, let's see how the feast is coming along."

Pot roast aroma spilled through the screen door. His first whiff of Mom's pot roast was always an epic novel of family dinners, when his biggest concern was how to avoid eating the sweet potatoes. In the kitchen, they found his mother sitting at the table in a flowered apron, head in hands.

"Alice, are you all right?" Joe asked, reaching out to her.

"Mom?" Dutch said with concern.

She saw them and rose. "Oh, there you are, sweet boy," she said, hugging her son. "I thought I'd forgotten to invite you. But here you are!"

Dutch hugged her and looked helplessly over her shoulder. His father smiled sadly and went back outside.

"I could smell dinner out on the street," Dutch said.

"Nothing's too good for *my* men," she said, busying herself at the stovetop. "Pour yourself an iced tea."

He filled a glass and sat watching his mother's back. She had always been the cornerstone of the family, the one they turned to when things got rough. Now she seemed lost.

"I had a call from Doctor Wingate," he said and waited for a reaction. When none came, he continued: "He says you're healthier than he is, but you should be taking it easy. Maybe we could get you some help around the house?"

She stopped stirring and stiffened. He rose and put his hands on her shoulders, now so thin. He could feel her sob. He turned her around and hugged her. She held on like he was a life raft and she was going under.

"You have to take care of yourself, Mom," he said. "We need you here with us."

She pulled back and dried a tear. "I try, Dilly. I truly do. But it's all…well, it's just so many things. But now, you go help your father and let me get this dinner together."

He poured another iced tea and brought it to his father, sweating in the sunshine over his shrubs. Dutch rolled up his sleeves and pitched in. After a while Joe spoke: "Sometimes she's aware and knows things are slipping. She just wants everything to be like it was." After a pause he continued: "She was always the strong one, you know. Even now she's most concerned about me."

"Maybe we could get someone to come in," Dutch said. "You know, help with the shopping and the cooking and give you some peace of mind."

"You're right, Son, but we have to find a way to ease her in so she doesn't feel useless."

As they stowed tools in the garage, Joe mentioned the upcoming retirement of a long-time employee, and they agreed on a restaurant for the traditional farewell party. Joe always insisted they treat retirements with gratitude and respect.

Then Dutch mentioned seeing Bud. "He was one of the Americans at Trinity with me. Called to say he just moved to town."

"I remember. You were there with old MacTone's kid, the professor on TV?"

"Ansel MacTone. Yeah, he was there, though he's changed his name to 'Tone.' How do you know his father?"

"Oh, now you're going way back. We did some business when we were both starting out. Jordan MacTone had a Chevy dealership then. I went to him for our first truck."

Dutch turned and waited for the rest of the story.

"Well, we bought the truck but I never went back to MacTone. He was the kind of salesman who wanted to do everything on a handshake, but his handshake wasn't worth too much."

Dutch nodded, not surprised. "Anyway, I got along with the son well enough."

"And now he's a star. Probably chases skirts too, like his old man. There were stories about how he used to step out on his wife, poor lady, before her horrible accident."

"What accident?"

"Oh, you must have heard about that. I guess you were just finishing high school. She went off the road one icy night. She was a frail lady; no one could figure why she was out driving in that weather."

His father's assessment of Jordan MacTone was unusually blunt, and might fit Ansel as well, but Dutch saw no sense bad-mouthing someone he hadn't seen in years. "I don't know," he said finally. "Not really my business."

Chapter 8

Molly gripped the kitchen counter with both hands and breathed deeply. Mondays were no time for morning sickness, at least not until the kids were off. But she'd been through this more than she cared to recall and knew she could hold it together for a while.

"Where's my Pumpkin?" her husband Pete sang out as he breezed into the room in a gray suit, carrying a briefcase.

"Almost done, Daddy," five-year-old Anna responded, looking up with an earnest smile minus one front tooth. "But can't I take Ratso?"

"Oh, don't call your bear 'Ratso,'" Molly said, exasperated. Her son Theo laughed so suddenly orange juice came out his nose.

"Ratso can't help his name," Pete said, handing Theo a napkin, "but he will definitely *not* be coming to school today. And you, young lady," he said, mockingly stern, "had better move your little behind or we'll be late."

After a momentary pout, Anna grabbed her jacket and a backpack covered with ladybug designs. Her father picked her up with one arm. They kissed Molly on both cheeks at once and were off.

"You too," she said to her son. He ran upstairs for a jacket. Molly switched slippers to sandals and led him up the block to the bus stop. When she got back to the kitchen, the morning sickness returned on schedule.

The rest of the day was better. She caught a yoga class, lunched with a friend and had time for a nap after another chapter of *The Handmaid's Tale*, finding dystopian horror a relaxing break from her routine. Then she was off to pick up Anna.

Walking Anna home from kindergarten was her favorite part of the day. She wondered whether all five-year-olds sparkled like her daughter. She couldn't remember Theo being that way. Was it because he was a boy or because, with him, there was always a little sister in the picture? And now he was a wise guy, eight going on fourteen, interested only in soccer and superheroes.

They walked through the park and whistled to birds. Molly's whistle was really a tweet and Anna's no more than bubbles.

"It's the tooth, sweetheart." Molly said. "Soon you'll get a new one and whistle like a pro."

"Like you, Mommy?"

Molly peered at her daughter but could detect no sarcasm. Anna just looked up, earnestly awaiting a reply. If only she could remain this age and never become a cynical eight-year-old like her brother! Molly took her in both arms and squeezed until she made a sound like a little sea lion.

Molly never wanted to be a stay-at-home mom, and even hated how that sounded, but things just went that way. She started a career at a big bank, where Pete worked and caught her eye. She was unused to attention from men, but he made his interest clear from the start. She was flattered and then flustered and then found she couldn't do without him. He gave her confidence; she had to hang on to that. Theo arrived a year after the wedding and Anna three years later. Then, just as they were discussing Molly's return to the workforce, a surprise Christmas present arrived, to be delivered in August. So, she'd get back to the real world eventually. For now there was nothing to do but savor her time with the children.

When Molly and Anna retrieved Theo from the bus stop, his shirt was torn.

"What happened to you?" Molly said.

"Ah, nothing," he responded and walked on.

"Excuse me, mister!" she said, hands on hips. She knew where this was heading and that it would ruin her karma. She also suddenly felt bloated and thought she had better get home without delay. Another suburban afternoon dealing with eight-year-old angst and bodily fluids; was it too late to trade in this life?

Late in the afternoon Molly sent the kids into the backyard to play. She was leafing through a cooking magazine, looking for a way to dress up chicken and potatoes and wishing she didn't have to cook. The phone rang. "Molly, is that you?" came a voice familiar yet hard to place.

"It's Bud," he continued. "from Trinity?"

"Bud Roberts! How are you? It's been…ages."

"Yeah, that's what we were saying. I just moved to Queens and had drinks with Dutch last week."

"Dutch! My God!"

"Yeah, well, so listen. What do you say to a reunion? You know, the McYanks—and whatever significant others have glommed on?"

She rested a hand on her midsection. "Yeah! It happens I've got a house bursting with significant others." She smiled; what a welcome surprise this was.

After the kids were in bed, Molly and Pete sat on stools finishing dinner. "Oh, yeah," she remarked. "I got a call today from someone who studied with me in Dublin junior year."

"Not the guy on the cover of *Time*?"

"No, not Ansel, though he might be there too. It was Bud Roberts. He was our 'social director.' He organized trips and parties, the kind of guy who told jokes and kept things lively."

"So, what did he say?"

"He just moved to town and wants to have a reunion."

Pete grimaced. He was not much for parties, especially with people he didn't know.

"So, remind me who they all are," he said cautiously.

She stroked his shoulder. "Well, Charlie and Tess will be there. You like them."

He smiled. She knew he gave Tess a pass because she was Molly's roommate for the famous year in Ireland. Her own view of Tess was more complex. Molly had a good life, but she fantasized about seeing the world from atop Tess's high heels. Molly spent her time working bake sales and watching soccer games, while Tess wore evening clothes to fancy restaurants. Granted, Tess *was* stunning, which opened doors for her. Then she ended up with a world-famous author, a house out of a magazine and a job that paid more than Molly could ever hope to make. Why did some people get that kind of life while others shuffled around in slippers and made lunch for the kids?

Molly shook her head to return to the conversation. "I know you found Charlie's book depressing, but you guys can always talk sports. And then there's Dutch; you met him at the wedding."

"Big guy, kind of quiet?"

"That's him. He gave us the wooden pepper mill. We also saw him once when we took Theo to the Thanksgiving Day parade."

"Yeah, I remember. He was a good guy."

"He's not famous like Ansel and Charlie." She paused thoughtfully and rubbed her thumb across her lips. "But he was always nice to me. Not like Ansel, who frankly was the type who'd say anything to get what he wanted. I could never understand what Tess saw in him."

"Wait. She married *Charlie*."

"Yeah, but later. Tess connected with him after she realized Ansel was a shit—forget I said that."

"Sounds like a terrific evening. But what about this love triangle? Did you tell me this?"

"Basically, Tess and Ansel met first term and right away were sleeping together, when they could get a room. That was sometimes a pain for me because we were roommates and Tess was so gone on him it felt cruel to deprive her."

There was a sparkle in her eye and she bounced playfully on her toes. "What?" he said, smiling.

"It's just that school: right in the middle of Dublin. The campus is out of a historical romance! Since the fifteen hundreds it was where landowners sent their sons. The Irish rebels all started out leading student rebellions there. The two debating societies stole paintings and ledgers from each other, and from Cambridge and Oxford. We got hold of this book from the seventeen hundreds. It was advice on how privileged Trinity students should brawl and drink and cut obscenities in the desks."

Pete laughed. "Well, I'm sure you guys weren't *that* crazy."

Her expression turned sheepish.

"I do believe you are blushing, Mrs. Peretti," he said. "And for a lady in *your* condition. Come on, fess up."

"Well, I did drink a bit that year and…carved my initials, a small thing, on a table. Oh, and I was in on a plot to paint a poem on a door to the Buttery—that's like a cafeteria."

Pete shook his head and smiled. "Good thing Theo isn't up. All he needs is juvenile delinquency tips from his mother."

"Anyway," she continued, "I loved the Irish accents and the pubs and the cobblestones. The campus was enchanting, almost wizardly. A hundred acres surrounded by a high stone wall. Late at night you're cut off from the world within all these stone buildings, big lawns, wooded squares. Tess and I called everything inside the walls the 'Candy Kingdom.'"

He smiled, seemingly infected by her moment to dream.

"Six of us in this history seminar," she went on, "including Ansel and Tess, lived on the same hallway, so we spent a lot of time together. It was so much fun. But yeah, at the end of the year there was all this strange stuff. Beyond my roommate's melodrama, one of the teachers wrecked his car in a race, and then there was a break-in where this sweet old man, a kind of guard, died chasing a burglar. Actually, that happened while we were all at Bud's last party."

"Makes *me* want to visit Ireland," he laughed.

She smirked. "Well, we didn't know about Digory—that was the old guard's name—until the next day, and it's not like what happened to him—or the teacher—had anything to do with us. It just happened all at once and it was so sad."

Pete smiled affectionately.

"I really liked the classes and rooming with those guys, and all the rituals. I loved going to chapel Sunday mornings and listening to the choir. Yeah, it was an important year for me."

She paused to think. It *had* been an important year, and she had always felt close to Tess in spite of the way men treated Molly like the homely friend of the beauty queen. That wasn't Tess's fault and she could be excused a touch of vanity, given her looks. She still felt like a sister.

Pete carried dishes to the sink and hugged her from behind. She nestled against his shoulder. "Well, any friends of yours…" he said.

On his way out of the room he added, "Oh, don't forget Theo and I have a game at ten on Saturday, and I told Arnie I'd ref the next two games."

"No problem," she said, loving the energy he put into coaching his son's soccer team. "Theo can stay down at the field with his buddies, and I'll take Anna to the farmer's market." Maybe she and Anna would shop in style, in matching designer dresses; maybe in her dreams.

Chapter 9

As Ansel listened to a report on the radio about the presidential race, there was a knock on the door. A woman named Hattie Richards arrived to apply for the nanny job.

She was a former schoolteacher in her sixties who came recommended by an associate of Leah's. With a substantial spread of hips, a matronly air and a gentle but firm expression, she seemed exactly what they needed.

Still, he hated giving a key to a stranger. She might show up at inconvenient times or stick her nose where it didn't belong. But he had to hire someone, and she agreed to come during the week to get True back and forth to school, make sure he was fed and spend afternoons with him until Ansel could take over. And she and Becca hit it off. Together they brought a degree of normalcy to his life, giving him time for his classes and his book.

On Wednesday afternoon Ansel took True to see his mother. Hattie made sure True dressed neatly and brushed his hair. When he and Ansel stepped out of the building, Henry was waiting by the SUV. "Professor," he said to Ansel and then turned his infectious smile on True. "And *little* professor."

In the car True was wide-eyed but silent. He ran his hands over the leather upholstery and gazed through the tinted windows. Ansel smiled softly, wondering what kind of life True led with his mother.

Florence had regained consciousness the day before and was eager to see her son. Ansel brought him to her room and then stepped aside for their reunion, relieved she was on the mend. Seeing their affection for each other brought back moments with his own mother.

"I'll be eternally grateful, Ansel," Florence told him when a nurse took True to the vending machines, "but I knew you wouldn't forget us."

He could only shrug, wondering how he deserved that kind of faith. "Just leave True to me," he said, "and concentrate on recovering." The more at ease she was, the faster she would go home and relieve him from babysitting.

* * *

Back at the apartment, True headed for his bedroom but Ansel put a hand on his shoulder. "How about a peanut butter sandwich?" he said.

True hesitated. He wanted to be by himself but he was hungry. "Yeah, okay," he said finally.

"Great. You go wash up and I'll get lunch together."

He didn't know washing his hands was part of the deal, but it was easy enough to just run the water while he played on his phone. His mother would know he faked it but not Ansel. It was kind of fun having a parent so easy to fool.

When he returned to the kitchen True saw sandwiches on two plates and realized he'd have to sit with Ansel. He decided to just eat fast. But then it worked out because Ansel got a phone call and went out on the balcony. Finally, True could eat without answering questions.

His mom asked him stuff all the time but that was different; she knew him and cared about him. Ansel and Hattie just talked. Still, his mom said to give Ansel a chance. She promised this would all be over soon and he could go home and be with his friends. He guessed he could stand Ansel and Hattie for a little while.

Ansel saw True's posture relax as soon as he excused himself. Getting food into that boy was like luring a wild bird to eat out of your hand, but at least he came to the table this time without whining, so that was progress. Florence must have said something to him.

Leah wanted to talk about Karla. Ansel turned toward the river and used the speaker phone so he could finish eating.

"It isn't good, Ansel."

He nearly choked. "What do you mean?"

"Well, I don't know if you remember her, but I'm guessing you do. She's attractive and well-spoken and serious. This is *not* someone we want to see in court."

"Court! My God, is she suing me?"

"Hold on. She's not suing, not yet, anyway. She showed me the term paper and a ream of research notes, and also your *Redux* book with pages highlighted. I didn't check every line, but it looks like you copied her."

"Oh, shit!"

"My reaction exactly. She also pointed to the acknowledgments, where you thanked a number of colleagues but omitted any mention of her."

"She was a student!"

"You took her work, Ansel. It doesn't matter that she was a student."

"Fuck! What do we do now? What does she want? Money?"

"I'm not sure, and I didn't press. She's mostly upset you didn't give her credit. Whether paying her would make it better, I don't know."

"Well, shouldn't we make an offer?"

"I'm not sure. She promised to think about how we could fix this and meet me again before she went public."

"Can we trust her?"

Leah paused. "Ansel, you're in no position to doubt *her* honesty. I think we can believe what she says."

"Look, I don't care what she thinks is right or wrong. We can pay her, but there's no way I admit to using her work!"

He hung up and sat for a moment, head in hands. When he looked up, True was just inside the balcony door, his face screwed up as if he were trying to understand what he just heard.

"How long have you been standing there?" Ansel snarled.

"I don't know," True said, looking away.

"Well, that was *not* your business. Someone should teach you not to eavesdrop on private conversations."

True ran into the office. It was so annoying having him underfoot all the time.

* * *

By early evening True was hungry again. Something smelled good in the kitchen. Hattie made pork chops and potatoes, and Ansel told him to come to the table. He ate looking down at his phone.

"Hey, dude," Ansel said, like he was friendly but he really wasn't, "let's put the phone away while we eat, okay?"

He pretended not to hear and kept looking at his game.

"True," Ansel said, louder, "put away the phone."

True scowled. "You can't tell me what to do!"

Before True could react, Ansel snatched the phone from his hand and put it into his pocket. "You can have it back when you finish eating," he said, like he was the boss of everyone.

True pushed his plate across the table, meaning just to move it away, but it crashed onto the floor. Now, he was really in trouble, but so what? He hated Ansel! Why did he have to stay here? He ran into his room.

"You little shit!" Ansel yelled after him.

Hattie looked alarmed and reached for a broom. Ansel bit his lower lip and watched her sweep. The kid could starve for all he cared.

"The boy is having a difficult time," she said.

He shot her an icy stare. "And it's hard for you, too," she added, "of course."

Ansel went into his bedroom and closed the door. He fished his cocaine out of a drawer. Then he sat back on the bed with a book on the psychological effect of propaganda. But he couldn't concentrate. His mind raced. Was it always like this between fathers and sons? True was lucky Ansel wasn't Jordan, who would have tanned his hide for a stunt like that.

He left the apartment to get some air and cool down, and stopped around the corner for a drink. Alone at the bar he thought about how this kid was wearing on him. What the hell did he want, anyway? He *must* see how he was turning Ansel's life upside down! Sure, he was young, but still. Florence had better get home soon and end this. And what would he do if she didn't make it? What a shit show that would be!

He stared at a faded photograph on the wall behind the bar. A guy with gray hair had his arms draped around the shoulders of two young men. They were all bright-eyed and laughing, and the pride in the father's expression jumped out of the photo. Could that be more than just a rare moment in a family relationship, or was fatherhood supposed to look like that? He couldn't recall any times like that with Jordan, certainly not since his mother died. That put an end to any hope he would ever be close to his father.

One bourbon turned into three, and he struck up a conversation with an advertising guy who recognized him from television. Then he walked back to the apartment, hoping for a quiet evening with no more fireworks.

Reaching for his door key, he felt True's phone in his pocket. That was for the best anyway; teach the boy his actions have consequences. He could do without video games for an hour.

When he entered the apartment, Hattie jumped up. "He's gone!" she said frantically.

"What do you mean 'gone'? Where did he go?"

"I don't know, Mr. Tone. I was cleaning up the kitchen and heard the door close and he was gone!"

"Oh, shit! Just what I need. Call the front desk. No, let me."

The doorman said he hadn't seen the boy but would check with the porters and the garage attendant.

Hattie was frantic. "Look," he said, "calm down. We'll go down to the street, in case he got out."

They left the door unlocked and took the elevator to the lobby. Ansel spoke with the doorman, and they were joined by the superintendent and a porter. The super said the garage attendant was sure no one had come down. He sent the porter to check the basement and laundry room and said he would go to the roof terrace. Ansel rushed outside to the sidewalk with Hattie, and they jogged in opposite directions around the block.

A half-hour later, Ansel sat in the apartment looking at his son's phone. Why had he yelled at him? What difference did it make if he used his phone? It wasn't like they were conversing anyway. Maybe it was the boy's only connection to his regular life?

True had taken his backpack but where could he go? He was too young to be on the street. This was all Ansel's fault! He wondered if he should call the police and what he could tell them. He didn't even have a picture of True. Then he remembered the Christmas cards! He ran to his dresser and pulled out a handful of envelopes, most unopened. He spread them on the bed and looked for the most recent, then ripped it open to find a snapshot of his son, looking the age he was now. He stared at the photograph, trying to imagine himself operating the camera and telling his son to smile. Sitting on the bed he opened each envelope, more carefully now, and lined up the photographs by year. The growth from one shot to another was startling, and he had missed it all.

The super knocked. They hadn't found the boy. He asked if Ansel had called the police.

"They won't do anything," Ansel spat out. "Not when the kid's only been gone a couple of hours."

The super went back to the lobby and Ansel stood in the hallway, looking at True's phone. Why hadn't he given it back? Then at least he could call. Pacing back and forth he found himself at the fire stairs and decided to walk down a floor. Maybe he should walk each of the floors to street level? He couldn't just sit in the apartment and wait.

When the fire door closed behind him, he heard a sound and froze. It was sobbing coming from above.

He leaped up the stairs.

True sat on a step with his head against the wall, clutching his backpack. Ansel lifted him to his feet and opened his mouth to yell, but his anger left him short of breath. Then he stopped, holding True by the shoulders. He saw himself as Jordan and recoiled at the image. This was no time for yelling. That was no way for a father to act. He pulled True in and hugged him hard.

"We were so worried," he said, surprised to feel a tear running down his face.

"Sorry," the boy sobbed.

"No, True. *I'm* sorry."

It felt like the sun had burst through the clouds.

Next afternoon they visited Florence again, and then Henry drove them to a theme restaurant near the apartment. Becca suggested a father-son dinner to help Ansel connect with True.

The restaurant décor had an outer space theme. They entered through a room where the seats shook, simulating a blast-off accompanied by vaguely scientific chatter. Ansel had trouble keeping a straight face but it was clear True loved the effects, and Ansel was gratified to see how they captivated his son. True's eyes were ablaze when they emerged into the seating area for his favorite meal of chicken tenders and French fries.

"This is great," True said, his mouth half full. "Can we come here every night?" Ansel recalled Becca's poster show for his lecture. It was amazing what a bit of special effects could do.

At home True knocked on Ansel's bedroom door and came in dressed in pajamas. "Ansel?" he said tentatively.

"What is it, True?"

"Will Momma get better?"

He could see the kid would believe whatever he said, which made him feel out of his depth. "Yeah, of course," he said, trying to sound confident. "She'll be good as new."

True lowered his eyes and his little mouth frowned. "You wouldn't lie, would you?"

Ansel was struck by the gravity of this conversation. "No, True. I wouldn't lie to you."

True seemed satisfied. Then his face clouded again.

"Is there something else?" Ansel said, feeling he was getting the hang of this fathering thing.

"You were on the phone before…."

"Before when?"

"You know, at lunch. You were outside and you were yelling you didn't care what was right or wrong. What did that mean? Is it about Mom…and me?"

"Oh no, kid. Listen, that call had *nothing* to do with you. It was a work thing. I have to work out a business issue with someone."

"Did you do something wrong?"

Ansel paused. He had just said he wouldn't lie. "No, True," he said, nonetheless. "It's just a disagreement about a book."

Ansel tucked True into bed and brought a drink out onto the balcony. The night was misty, the river a rough outline in the distance.

Raising a son was complicated, not just the logistics but also having this juvenile conscience nagging at him. What did the kid know about the world? Sure, he had no father growing up and that was less than ideal, but at least he didn't have a dad like Jordan blaming him for his mother's death, and everything else.

A jet flew over, beginning its approach into Kennedy. The roar of the engines triggered a vision of the theater at the space restaurant. There was something wondrous about seeing the world through a boy's eyes.

Maybe Ansel should give Karla credit for her work and a real share of the proceeds? He had cleared close to a million dollars on *Stick it to the Man* and got a huge boost in popularity. He might owe her some share in that success.

Chapter 10

Charlie drove Tess to the train station. "Looking forward to seeing the crew?" he asked when they slowed at the switchback.

"Sure, I guess." She seemed distracted by the view. "Molly's the only one I really miss. With her kids and my job, we don't see each other anymore."

"Yeah, but it'll be interesting being all together."

"I guess you're right. Bud was always fun and Dutch, well, he was always Dutch."

"Right," he laughed, noting her omission of Ansel Tone. Could she have lingering feelings for him? He dismissed the thought. It was twelve years ago, and she chose Charlie, after all.

"I guess I'll come meet you at your office," he said. He liked to show the flag in the Regis offices to discourage Mr. Carter or anyone else from pursuing his wife on those late work nights.

"If you like," she said absently. "By the way, I meant to mention a few things. You should fix the latch on the dog door; I'm sure Seusy will be eager to help. And then, we're running on empty and need groceries."

He rolled his eyes, resenting how she found "projects" to fill his day when he was fully engaged writing a novel. She acted as if she had a "real" job while he played at being an author.

"And," she continued, "oh, yeah, does it feel like the car pulls to the left? Maybe you should drop it off and have Kelly take a look?"

On a straight-away he wiggled the steering wheel. "I guess it could be loose," he said. "I'll check when I get home."

While he was eating lunch, *The Breakfast Club* came on television. He'd seen the movie before but watched anyway. He liked the ensemble acting and saw this as a case in point: the public wanted stories about young people. Also, the school setting was a perfect device to assemble a cast.

But, this movie aside, he was bored by teenage stories. Besides, he had covered everything worth telling from his early life.

The movie turned into a love story in its closing minutes. This confirmed another observation: people want stories about young romance. And then it struck him: the story of how he won Tess!

He jumped up, startling Odysseus. That was it! He would tell how he won the girl of his dreams. The story had a clear frame, a crisis and a happy ending! He could add some drama, adjust the facts, but it would make a great novel! It could even bring a spark back to the marriage.

To make the story real, he'd stick to the facts in describing the setting: the McYanks surrounded by Georgian buildings, statues of writers and rebels, high stone walls. In laying out a plot, he'd revise the history to spice up the story.

Charlie had never before belonged to a tight group like the McYanks, all smart and quirky. It was certainly nothing like high school, where he camped out in the library to avoid going home, or even college, where he kept his head down and worked hard, for fear they might send him back to Baltimore. Trinity was intellectually stimulating—which he might say to the McYanks but anyone else would think pedantic. And that was the point: those friends were extraordinary, or maybe it was partly being twenty-one, with no need to apologize for profundity.

One night the old security guy, Digory, said they should never walk through the high arch in the granite base of the Campanile, the copper-domed bell-tower inside Front Gate. "It is well known," he cackled, "that an undergraduate who walks *through* the arch, particularly when the bells are ringing, will *not* pass his exams—or maybe he won't even graduate, I don't recall which."

"Ah, we heard that blarney at orientation," Ansel croaked. "I can't see how it applies to us, since we won't graduate from Trinity."

A week later, Charlie led Ansel, Bud and Dutch on a James Joyce pub crawl. They drank Guinness and, to the annoyance of many fellow drinkers, Charlie recited *Ulysses* excerpts. He knew his friends would never read the book, it was too long and dense, but they seemed amused by small doses, set in context by Charlie, at each stop as they sorted who would buy the next round.

Returning to campus Ansel pulled a flask from his coat and waved it. "It's time to put the curse to rest," he proclaimed.

"I'm in," Bud said and walked with Ansel toward the Campanile. Charlie and Dutch looked at each other and turned to follow.

Ansel stopped on the path beneath the old tower. There was no one in sight. Front Gate was locked for the night and the campus was asleep. "So, I propose a fitting way to cap off a night well drunk," he said and sat heavily on the pavement, waving to join him.

With a bow of his head, he offered the first drink to Dutch, who took a swig and passed it along.

When the flask returned to Ansel, he toasted, "These pillars of history shall bear witness."

"Are you on again about Parnell and Wolfe Tone?" Bud complained.

"Sure, and I'm referring to *ancient* history, none of this recent millennium nonsense," Ansel slurred, "and you'll not be interrupting a man's toast."

Bud waved a hand dismissively. As long as the whiskey held out, Ansel would have a captive audience, but they were lost. Charlie asked: "What in the name of Robert Emmet and all the rebel ghosts are you on about?"

"The statues!" Ansel exclaimed. "The four figures guarding this venerable tower."

Seeing they were still confused, Ansel said in frustration, "The figures seated on the keystones of the Campanile are the Greek philosophers Homer, Socrates, Plato and Demosthenes. And, in fact, I have hit upon a brilliant idea! We shall each assume the role of a kindred predecessor."

He handed the flask to Charlie and said, "Charles Piedmont must be Homer, as he assures us his novels will surpass the efforts of mere mortals in relating the story of the age."

Charlie liked that, raised the flask and took a swig.

"Yeah," said Bud, "like Homer Simpson."

Charlie raised and tipped back the flask again.

Ansel threw a scolding look at Bud but gestured for Charlie to pass him the flask. "Buddy-Bobs here," Ansel continued, "will be Socrates, since that giant of ethics and philosophy left behind no writings, and our man is reputed to have finished two years of college without once handing in a paper."

"On time, you mean," Bud qualified and hiccupped. Ansel nodded.

"Well, only if we can agree the proper pronunciation is 'So Crats,'" Bud said.

"Brilliant!" Ansel said as they all nodded approval, recognizing the mispronunciation from a movie they had seen together. "Long as we're talking ancient history, we should go to a reliable source to get our facts straight."

Bud tipped the flask to each of them and took a long drink.

Ansel continued: "And then, Dilbert Gilroy…"

"Present," Dutch said.

Ansel shook his head sadly as Bud passed the flask. "Dilbert must be our Plato, given his spirituality, in that he is our only scholar to have attended chapel since orientation."

"Whoa," Dutch said, raising a hand. "Molly goes to chapel every Sunday."

"The only *present* scholar," Ansel said with annoyance and another hiccup.

Dutch bowed his head and took a drink.

"Which leaves me, of course, as Demosthenes," Ansel concluded, reaching for the flask.

"Easy for you to say," Dutch laughed.

"Hey look," Bud said. "Who is Demos...?"

"Demosthenes!" Ansel said in exasperation. "Haven't you blighters studied Greek history? Demosthenes, the master of rhetoric? The perfect orator? The darling of Athens? The carved head with the golden tongue!"

The nicknames stuck. Charlie found it hard *not* to greet his namesake, at least silently, when he walked past—or through—the Campanile. When drunk he sometimes referred to himself as "Homer" in the third person. It was obviously grasping to aspire to write his own *Odyssey*, but it seemed no more monumental than catching a lifeline out of Baltimore. Why not aim for the top? Composing a classic might require a broader frame of reference than he had at the moment, but he had time and talent. He just had to *do* it—and maybe enlist for the next Trojan Wars.

He was also enamored of his "Homer" nickname because he was reading *Ulysses* and worshiped James Joyce. He spent afternoons tracing the action of the novel, smitten with the concept of fictional characters walking actual streets in the course of the real June 16, 1904. This reality made the story come alive, feel real.

Charlie needed to infuse his own novel with actual life. He brought up mental images and typed scenes of a campus alive with youth, toasting ancient Athenians and arguing Kafka and Marx in pubs unchanged for hundreds of years. He described the cricket pitch in College Park and the resplendent reading room in the Old Library.

As to the characters, he would change the names and physical features, though Tess *had* to be a stunner and Ansel a movie idol to set up the story of the underdog winning the day. The hero would be a normal guy but for his tragic childhood in Baltimore. (Joan would kiss him for giving Penguin's marketing department a hook to *Against the Odds*.) These and the other three McYanks would be the focus, with Digory in a tragic supporting role.

Digory would be all the more tragic for being comical and lovable early on. He had been at the job long enough to know how not to be too accountable, which allowed him freedom to pursue his primary interest: telling stories, or "slinging blarney" as Ansel called it.

One evening in early fall Digory came upon Charlie, Bud and Ansel drinking whiskey in a common room. "So, this is how you Yanks repay your welcome," he said, wagging a crooked finger. New to the school, the boys feared they might be in trouble. Ansel met it head-on by offering Digory the bottle. Digory peered at Ansel as though he could see right through him, then a smile spread across his craggy face. "Well, a wee drink couldn't hurt, now could it?"

Digory stayed to share a few wee drinks and lots of college lore. "I'll wager," he said, scratching his whiskered chin, "that they never told you at the orientation about mounting the tower."

"The Campanile?" Bud asked incredulously.

"Aye, lad. *Three* times it was climbed, all in the dead of night, of course. The first climber placed a red top-hat on the peak."

"My grandfather told me about that," Ansel said, "though I didn't understand what the Campanile was."

Climbing campus structures, or "buildering," was not the only prank pulled off by Trinity students over the centuries. Ansel told them about a book in the Old Library called *Advice to the University of Dublin.* Published in 1791, it was one of the priceless volumes you couldn't touch, but they found a copy online. It was the comprehensive guide to how Trinity College members should best abuse their position in the academic and social hierarchy. It said the best way for boys to become men was by heavy drinking, fighting and carousing. One piece of advice that seemed to remain sound was:

> *You must cut your name on the table, together with any obscene words that occur to you by which you will transmit your memory to succeeding classes and give testimony of your genius.*

Ansel found his grandfather's name in Examination Hall and prodded each of them to carve their names somewhere in the old woodwork.

Charlie tried to remember where Ansel found that book. He could have heard about it from Digory. Or, it could have been the professor who advised him on his paper, the guy who had the racing accident. And *he* could be another tragic character. He was quite young and raced an old MG at a small track outside Kildare. Charlie would have to check the details of his crash. Ansel went to the races to help with the car; he'd know.

Charlie filled pages with character attributes and sketches of the campus layout, and then pulled up the old photos on his computer. It was lucky he had saved up for his first digital camera before going to Ireland and so had visuals to flesh out his descriptions.

They all looked so young! Bud was typically clowning and Tess was always gorgeous. Her hair was long then, before the sophisticated lawyer cut. He clicked on a closeup of her in a dark Aran sweater that matched her eyes, her long hair tied back but with two strands blowing across her face. He printed the shot and stared at it. Her expression thrilled him, even after all these years.

He flipped to mid-year, when Tess and Ansel were together. In one photo she leaned against him about to burst out laughing, while he wore his usual smirk. They looked like models in a magazine ad. Something tugged at Charlie's throat. The resentment and jealousy that tore at his insides all those months never really left him, even after he made Tess his bride. He thought he had deleted the shot of them together years ago, although the image was burned into his subconscious like a bad dream. He reached for the delete button, but then stopped. That photo stirred him in a way he should capture and try to translate on the page. He would channel his intoxicating rage into the novel. He loaded photo paper and printed a large copy. This was not some dead or hazy history; it was a real moment frozen in time. He would squeeze every bit of life out of it.

He read a lot of literary criticism in preparation for *Apostate Agonistes*. Milan Kundera described the novel's spirit of continuity, where each work answered the preceding ones. Charlie intended *Agonistes* as part of this continuum, although the effort failed when no one read the book. So now he would spit out a page-turner, but that didn't mean he had to lose touch with serious literature. He stuck his dog-eared *Tess of the d'Urbervilles* into his backpack to start rereading, although its protagonist reminded him a bit too much of his wife. Someday, he would craft an answer to the great books of the past, an answer meaningful to someone besides himself and his agent.

He dressed in his favorite tweed sports jacket for lunch with Joan. As he drove the Volvo to the train station, the steering *did* feel loose and he remembered he was supposed to check this. He should probably let Kelly take a look instead, but with Tess's car at the garage they would have to rely on the Jaguar, which he did not want to park in the train station lot. Better to bring Tess's car down to Kelly's after the weekend. If he left it Tuesday morning on his way to meet Joan, maybe they could finish it by the time he got back from the city, or else he could bum a ride at the garage.

Charlie walked from Grand Central Station to a small French bistro on a quiet block of West 52nd Street. He arrived just as his agent pulled up in a cab. "*Mademoiselle*," he said with a French accent as he opened her door.

She looked up with an eager smile. "You look rested," she said, leaning in to kiss him on the cheek. He tilted his head so their lips met instead. He often flirted playfully like that, and she seemed to like it. Behaving suggestively was a way of rebelling against convention, which any serious artist *must* do. Besides, as his most ardent supporter, Joan was also his muse and deserved a kiss of appreciation.

He looked her business suit up and down. "And you look ravishing and brutally efficient, as always," he said, offering his arm to escort her across the sidewalk. Meeting with her always felt like an assignation in a World War II spy movie. Maybe it was the way she treated him like the hero of his own story.

"So what good news have you brought down from the mountain?" she said once they were settled.

"Not just news," he said, "new life!"

She perked up.

"I have dug up a story that ticks all the boxes. It is as real as all Ireland is washed by the Gulf Stream, and it has sex and love and death and all the other detritus that sells to the unwashed masses."

"Wow, Mr. Piedmont, and when can Penguin and I hope to see some token of this cascade?"

"Soon, my literary angel. I am deep into outlining and will begin the actual writing tomorrow, or maybe even today. I will have a first chapter by next week to show you thoughts are translating to the page. It will give you a taste, and you know I can't show you any more until I have a whole draft."

"Understood," she said happily, holding up her glass.

"To pulp fiction," he joked.

Joan frowned. The expression echoed her plea that he not belittle his gift for reaching people, something for which most writers would sell their souls. He loved how seriously she took his work. She had published her own book of criticism of the works of Norman Mailer, so her opinion was erudite, and he was fortunate to have teamed up with her. If she had not tired of corporate publishing and hung out her shingle as a literary agent, she would never have met a young newspaper reporter with a horrific childhood tale. And without *that* stroke of providence and her indefatigable support, *Against the Odds* would never have been a bestseller.

Chapter 11

Ansel sat at his desk thinking about the final assignment for his Propaganda class. He couldn't transparently solicit research for a book, especially with the Canterwail thing and Ed Flagel's harping on students doing free research for faculty. He had to stay on Professor Flagel's good side to ensure tenure, and that was essential. The "professor" title sold books and Ansel needed the financial backstop for when book sales dropped off. Besides, there was nothing like molding young minds.

But the Canterwail mess kept distracting him. He called Leah.

"I think we need a copyright lawyer," she said.

"Damn it! I thought you were taking care of this? Shouldn't we just give her credit?"

"Be sensible, Ansel. We can't risk your reputation. If you copied some of this book, who could be sure you wrote any of it?"

She had a point. But, noticing True's sneakers on the floor, he wondered what kind of role model he would be if he dodged responsibility. Could this incident with Florence and getting to know the boy be a chance to earn his son's respect, and maybe self-respect? Was that ultimately what he wanted?

Leah continued: "So I spoke again with Karla and she made clear she is *not* just looking for a payoff. I'm concerned she may want something public. We need to know where we stand legally."

His pulse was racing.

"I've got a guy, a top-notch litigator," Leah said. "He represents big-name writers. How about I set up a meeting?"

Ansel knew what Jordan would say. His no-good son was soft. It showed weakness to care about making some shrew happy when she was throwing his life into chaos. And, if he asked Jordan for help, his father would add this to the list of times he pulled Ansel's ass from the fire.

"You think he'll be able to work this out," he said, "make everyone happy?"

"Well," Leah seemed to channel Jordan, "we don't give a damn if *she's* happy as long as she leaves us alone, and I think this guy is our best chance. I'll see if he can fit us in tomorrow."

Ansel was impatient. It felt sordid dealing with this legal process with True around. But that kind of thinking would get him nowhere. To put his mind off it, he downed a double-espresso. Nothing could slow him down.

After lunch Henry drove Ansel to the university. Ansel wanted to stop at his office in Fayerweather to check the mail. He snaked through campus to the building, tucked behind Avery Hall and St. Paul's Chapel. In the quiet courtyard, he paused to breathe in the scent of flowering trees and admire the familiar brick and concrete structure. It seemed appropriate the History Department was housed in this building, so prominent in '60s protests.

The mail was largely interdepartmental memos, "Flagel flotsam," which went directly into the trash. There were also letters from admirers, one enclosing a snapshot of an attractive redhead with a telephone number scribbled on the back. He saved the photo, thinking he might look up this aspiring historian next time he visited Chicago. There was also a solicitation to write a journal article on the Cold War and an offer to teach a symposium at the University of Bath. Florence and True would be back to normal soon, and as a tourist attraction for two thousand years, Bath certainly had historical chops. It was also convenient to London, where he could find all sorts of trouble. He stuffed the letter from England into his briefcase to pass along to Leah so she could run dates and look at the finances.

He checked the full-length mirror. Satisfied he looked sufficiently "professorial," he headed out of the building. But with the exit almost within reach, he ran into his department head, the last person he wanted to see.

"Ansel," Professor Edmund Flagel said enthusiastically, "good to see you." He was old school, from his white beard and bow tie to his tasseled loafers.

"Professor," Ansel nodded.

"We missed you at the departmental meeting last week. Did it conflict with your, uhum, personal appearance schedule?"

Ansel couldn't tell if Flagel's question was sarcastic. "Not at all, Ed. Personal matter, very last minute." Personal, as in he personally did not have time to snore through Flagel's meeting. There was no time for anything not directly related to the business at hand.

"Oh, I see," said Flagel, squinting slightly. "Well, I hope everything is, uhum, in order."

"Yes, yes. Crisis averted." Ansel would rather walk on hot coals than have to explain to Flagel all that happened last week. The professor wiped his glasses on a handkerchief but said nothing more, so Ansel added, "We should get coffee, Ed, but I've got to get over to Havermeyer for my two o'clock."

"Ah yes, uhum," Flagel said dryly, "mustn't keep our students waiting."

Ansel escaped out the front door and hurried to the chemistry building, its auditorium large enough for his Propaganda lecture. The popularity of his classes *had to* help when his appointment came up for consideration.

Entering the room he slid on his public face and strutted down the aisle. When the class quieted, he began: "We closed last week with an 'expert' saying propaganda aims to make people believe in dogma or accept an idea. But propaganda actually is meant to provoke action! Take Cuba in 1959. To show democratic support for the revolution, Fidel Castro incited the people through state propaganda to hold mass demonstrations in support of death sentences handed down by the courts. Propaganda helped him satisfy the people's blood lust while tying them to his government with the bond of their mutual crime."

The hour passed easily. He hardly glanced at his class plan until he addressed the final assignment. "We have focused on who uses propaganda and with what effect. And now history informs the present. The apparent front-runner among the Republican candidates has coined the term 'fake news' for a concept long familiar to autocrats: any fact contradicting the candidate *must* on that ground be false and made up to embarrass him. This is an ideal justification for supporters to adopt simple explanations and ready-made opinions and thus an ideal propaganda tool."

"In your materials, Jacques Ellul writes that, on the most complicated issues of the day, only those *most* informed or who pay the *closest* attention decline to express strong opinions, because they understand they lack sufficient information to pass reasoned judgment. The majority, in contrast, want only to espouse preconceived judgments. The ability to label any contradictory fact as 'fake news' helps the propagandist dictate these judgments, however unsupported and insupportable." He paused with a sincere frown. "But for all our sakes, let us hope facts still matter."

"For your final paper, you will assess the concept of 'fake news' in the context of how a historical regime manipulated its citizens' perception of their past and thus also their present and their future. You may use any historical period, other than The Great War, since that is the focus of our class. I am eager to see what you come up with. Enjoy your week and take some time to savor this wonderful spring weather."

He was disappointed the dark-haired beauty skipped the after-class discussion. Was he losing his touch?

Walking to the car he recalled that the Trinity dinner was set for Friday. He thought about sending his regrets but then conjured up an image of Tess twelve years ago, stretched like a cat on the cricket pitch. She was married to Charlie, of course, but Ansel was eager to see how the years had treated her.

Chapter 12

For Friday's meeting with Herb Drexler, Ansel showed up stone sober. This left him jittery, wishing he had a drink. Leah met him in the lobby of the Sixth Avenue high-rise. "Just tell him the facts," she said as they produced identification at the security desk. "He's on our side."

"Facts are overrated," he replied.

Drexler met them in a conference room with large abstract oil paintings on the walls and a wide southern view. He introduced Ed Gamber, a young associate apparently present to take notes and drive up the bill.

Paperback editions of Ansel's *Redux* books lay on the table. Drexler said he hadn't read them but had leafed through to become familiar with the genre. "Leah has explained the background," he said, "and described her two conversations with Ms. Canterwail. We don't yet have a copy of the term paper, but Leah saw the paper side-by-side with the *Redux: Stick it to the Man* book. We'll need to do a side-by-side comparison ourselves, but for now let us assume there is substantial similarity between the two."

"Not really," Ansel burst out. "Karla wrote a short paper for a class assignment. My book is three hundred pages taken from substantial research and *multiple* sources."

"Understood," Drexler said, "but the relevant similarity is between Ms. Canterwail's earlier work and any similar portion of your book."

"But what about the rest of the book?" Leah interjected.

"That the book also includes much that was *not* copied is irrelevant. Our concern is whether *any* original work was copied. This will turn on whether any of your words and sentences are substantially similar to Ms. Canterwail's. Also, Ed has turned up no registration in the Copyright Office."

"So she has no copyright?" Ansel said.

"Well, her copyright came into existence when she set down her work in tangible form, such as when she printed it to hand in."

"But she submitted it electronically," Ansel said hopefully.

"Tangible enough, and the copyright is automatic. But without a registration Ms. Canterwail has limited remedies. She must prove actual monetary damage in order to recover. Also, she cannot be awarded attorney's fees. While she could seek to enjoin further publication of the book, that is not likely her aim or worth the cost to litigate. For these reasons, we hope she'll be open to settlement."

"Our main concern," Leah said, "is reputational. We have to avoid any suggestion of plagiarism."

"First, let's not confuse concepts. Copyright infringement essentially means copying someone's original *expression.* This is a legal charge that could lead to an injunction or damages. Plagiarism is an academic or journalistic concept that means passing off someone else's work *or ideas* as your own. We are not concerned with whether Dr. Tone copied Ms. Canterwail's ideas or used the same research or whether he gave her credit, only whether he copied her actual words.

"Ms. Canterwail's lack of a registration makes it unlikely she'll find an attorney willing to take the case and, facing high litigation costs, she may have little choice but to negotiate—and we'll insist any settlement be confidential."

Leah said. "So what's next?"

"We'll do the line-by-line comparison, and then, do we know if Ms. Canterwail has retained counsel?"

"We don't think so," Leah said.

"Good. Let's keep it that way. Once the lawyers get involved, everything becomes harder to resolve. Could you let her know Ansel is taking the matter seriously and you hope to speak with her…let's say, by the middle of the week?"

Ansel kept seeing True's guileless expression and decided he should try to make things right. "I should talk to her myself," he said.

"No, Ansel, I can do that," Leah said. "Or shouldn't the lawyers talk with her?"

"Again," said Drexler, "we want to resolve this quickly and quietly. If your lawyer calls, she'll think *she* needs a lawyer, and then her lawyer will want to show he's earning his fee and we'll end up with a mess. Now, if Ansel wants to take this meeting, it's up to him, but that might look like we're making too much of the claim. We can always hold that back in case we need it."

Ansel agreed to let his representatives handle the matter. Leah looked relieved.

"Well then," Drexler said, extending his hand, "we should have a handle on this by Monday or Tuesday and be able to come up with a game plan. The important thing for you, Dr. Tone, is to know the matter is in our hands. Let us take care of it and get back to your usual business."

Chapter 13

For the McYanks reunion, Bud booked "Arobel," an artisanal restaurant in Hell's Kitchen. Dutch arrived twenty minutes early, as usual. He hated always being first to show up and then waiting for everyone, but far worse was the thought of ever being late himself.

To avoid awkwardness he strolled around the block. This was the first time he'd been out to dinner in months. It felt like sweeping aside the cobwebs, the pressure to do his job *and* his father's plus deal with his mom. He looked forward to relaxing and connecting with old friends, recreating what it felt like to be young. Maybe this could be a start. Maybe he could get out more, see these guys some, even find a woman to date more than once. Given his weekly overload of pot roast, he also hoped there was fish on the menu.

When he returned, a hostess showed him to a table set for seven in a semi-private room ringed by wine coolers. Bud was giving instructions to a waiter. He turned a big smile on Dutch and grasped his hand. Like Dutch, Bud wore a sports jacket and dress pants. "On time and looking good, sport," Bud said. "Hey, let's not wait for the rest." He waived to the waiter, who took their drink orders.

Just then Charlie and Tess arrived. "Disgraceful what riffraff they let in here," said Charlie, stretching out his hand to Dutch while Tess and Bud kissed on both cheeks.

"Hey, Homer!" Bud laughed, when Charlie turned to him.

"So Crats, you old bastard." Charlie grabbed his hand.

Dutch was unsure how to greet Tess, but she took hold of his forearms and planted a kiss on his cheek, so he reciprocated.

"You look good, Dutch," she said, eyeing him up and down.

"*You* look good, Tess," he said sincerely. Twelve years had brought maturity to her beauty without lines of age. A shimmery black dress showed off her slender figure. He was reminded how they all had once been a little in love with Tess. He still wondered how Charlie had pulled off marrying her.

She smiled, squeezed his arms again and turned to see Pete arrive with Molly, who rushed to hug her. Tess looked down at her belly and raised an inquiring look. "Everything going well?"

"Oh, you know me, a regular baby machine." Molly turned un-abashedly to hug everyone and accept best wishes on the impending event. She introduced Pete to those he had not met, and he also accepted congratulations.

"He's been busy," Charlie commented, nodding toward Pete.

"Someone's got to sustain the species," Bud rejoined.

"Someone other than me, you mean," Charlie said petulantly.

Bud held up both hands in a gesture of surrender. "Hey, sport," he said, "at least you've got a relationship."

Charlie play-punched Bud's hand. Dutch wondered what their exchange said about Charlie and Tess.

Bud suggested they take seats but married people could *not* sit together. Tess sat between Dutch and Pete. Charlie and Bud flanked Molly and the three started arguing the details of the "counter-ball" they held at school, a spoof on the annual black-tie Trinity Ball.

"It was at Mulligan's," Bud insisted.

"Ah, you're daft," Charlie said in a comical brogue. "Sure, and we were at Club Twenty-one for the main festivities, though we may have stopped at Mulligan's for last call."

"You were too tanked to remember," said Molly. "I recall that the *women* had to lead the way home."

Conversations crisscrossed the table. Hardly any of them had seen each other since Ireland. Molly wanted details about their careers, while they were all in awe of someone actually raising a family.

"Do they give you an instruction manual at the hospital?" Charlie asked.

"I'd love to have a kid," Bud boomed, "just couldn't handle having a wife."

Dutch thought he was the only one to notice the empty chair at the head of the table until the waiter arrived with drinks on a tray and Ansel at his heels.

Ansel arrived full of coke-induced animation. "Greetings assembled masses!" he intoned, spreading both arms in his Demosthenes, darling-of-Athens pose.

Everyone rose except Charlie and Molly, who were deep in conversation. Bud and Dutch looked delighted to see him and came in for back slaps. Pete introduced himself and held out his hand, which Ansel shook, looking past him. "Tess, my sweet," he said, stepping over to hug her close. "More lovely than ever." She fit so well against him. He sensed she was slightly breathless as she stepped back to take in his outfit.

"Nice suit," she said.

He smiled knowingly.

Tess continued to stand close. "We've followed your career. Do you have another *Redux* book in the works?"

He smiled, suddenly glad he showed up. "I'm honored you've heard of the first two. Yes, the publisher won't take the bit from my mouth until the public tires of those books."

"No accounting for the public," Charlie said, inserting himself between Ansel and his wife to offer his hand.

Ansel turned to survey Charlie, in a tweed jacket hanging on him like a sign reading "solitary novelist." He shook Charlie's hand and said with mock solemnity, "And if only I could leave behind pseudo-history for the creative heights of Charles Piedmont III."

"A literary giant in my own mind," said Charlie.

Ansel sat at the head of the table. Bud remained standing to propose a toast. "So good to be together," he began. "It reminds me, did I already tell my déjà vu joke?" He paused for laughter, but they rolled their eyes. "But seriously, folks," he went on, "to the McYanks Reunion Tour. Let the spirits flow!"

Bud suggested they order appetizers for the table.

"I'm up for that," Molly said, "although I crave certain foods and others make me gag."

"We want no childbearing untidiness," Bud laughed, "so we shall leave the choice of appetizers to the glowing mother-to-be."

Ansel leaned over to Charlie. "You know," he said, "I read *Apostate Agonistes*. The critics screwed you."

"You actually *read* it?" Charlie asked.

"Of course." Ansel had picked up the book in an airport but couldn't get through fifty pages. But, having paid retail, he felt justified saying he read it. Besides, it cost nothing to flatter the author.

"Well, you are of the select few. If only the reading public had time for such things."

"Buck up, my friend. What are you working on now?"

"The barbarians, by whom I mean of course my editor and my agent, have bludgeoned me back to fictionalized memoir. Apparently, I lack the ability to put across pure fiction."

"Tell me about it," Ansel moaned. "All my publisher wants is more one-dimensional research packaged as accessible history with an edge."

"Right, well I guess it's all in the packaging." Charlie sipped his wine and then continued: "Remember when we were going to change the world?"

"Right, like the Greek philosophers…and look what happened to them." Ansel clinked his glass against Charlie's.

Charlie sipped and leaned toward Ansel. "I've been wracking my brain for a real story worth telling in a novel. In fact…" He raised his voice to address them all. "Comrades, I've decided to make you all stars of a fictionalized account of our Trinity Term in Dublin."

Ansel did not like the sound of this.

This was the first Tess had heard of Charlie's plan for the new book. Her hands turned white as she gripped the table. Conversation halted. They all looked at him.

"Oh, God," Bud said, "you'll not be writing about that trip to Tralee?"

Charlie laughed. "Well, I'm not above a bit of comic relief. But don't worry, I'll change the names to protect the iniquitous. And it will be a novel and so entirely deniable."

Everyone looked dubious.

"And it was more than ten years ago," Charlie pleaded. "No one's going to hold us responsible for college pranks."

The mood lightened, but Tess remained wary. "Anyway," Charlie continued, it's basically a love story: how I won the woman of my dreams." He beamed at Tess. Her expression was icy.

Dutch raised his glass in toast: "To another bestseller!" Bud looked down the table at Dutch, laughing at his friend.

"Thank you, Mr. Gilroy," Charlie said, tipping his glass, "and thank you all. And be forewarned, I shall need help recalling the actual incidents, not *as* the story but as the *foundation* for the story. My memory is fuzzy about certain incidents."

Everyone but Tess and Ansel laughed. She watched Ansel from the corner of her eye. He looked like James Bond, an inscrutable expression atop a perfectly fitted suit.

"Welcome to middle age," Molly said.

"Like the hippies said about the sixties," Bud added, "if you remember our year at Trinity, you weren't really there."

Appetizers arrived. Tess seethed inside but tried to look calm. She tuned back into a story Molly was telling about her eight-year-old busting up a table in their backyard and getting caught because he and his buddy taped it on Pete's video camera.

Tess was pleased at how sure of herself Molly had become. She had always been sweet but kind of mousy. Having a living person inside seemed to open her up…and with two kids already! It was mind-boggling how she handled it all.

Molly concluded her story to general laughter and then added, "You guys don't know how *great* it is to be out with adults and not talking about lawns or grammar school."

They looked at her with curiosity and sympathy. "I wish," she went on, "we could all get together again before I start my next full-time job in August."

Everyone seemed agreeable. Tess looked at Ansel and then around the table and blurted out, "Let's do it at our place."

They turned to her. Charlie froze with his drink nearly at his mouth.

"We haven't had a party in way too long," she continued.

Bud raised his glass in support.

"Huzzah!" Dutch toasted.

Charlie seemed to gather himself. "Right," he said. "You all come up some Saturday. We'll cook out. And we have room," he said, leaning around Molly to look at Dutch, "for anyone who can't drive home."

"I am perfectly in control," Dutch said. "And a nice person from Uber will be conveying me home tonight, thank you very much."

No one pushed Ansel, who stared into middle distance. Tess wondered what preoccupied him. Did he realize her invitation was mostly to him?

Chapter 14

On a conference call Tuesday afternoon, Drexler confirmed Canterwail's copyright claim was viable. Leah reported Canterwail was insulted that Ansel didn't speak with her directly. "She rejected any effort to buy her off and said she'd consult her brother-in-law, some lawyer in town."

Ansel was frustrated. Maybe he should have asked his father to handle this? The morality would not bother Jordan. But asking for help would give his father one more proof he couldn't clean up his own mess. He could just picture the derision in Jordan's eyes. No, Ansel had to resolve this himself.

"Leah," Drexler said, "please assure Karla that Ansel wants to settle this quickly and quietly and her brother-in-law may help. Ask that he call me."

"But our plan?" Ansel said.

"This may work in our favor," Drexler said, sounding confident. "Let it play out. It won't help to get upset. It's just business."

"Just business," Ansel cursed as he hung up. It's not *his* reputation. He gets paid even when they run me out of town on a rail.

* * *

Things were going well for Bud. He had signed Helen Smith to a whole life policy and a variable annuity and arranged a steakhouse dinner with two new clients.

"Good week!" his secretary commented cheerily as she brought him a cup of coffee.

"You know it! Hey, Lois, can you pull up data on the restaurant supply business on Long Island? And check who writes policies on the top companies?"

"You got it, boss," she said, turning with a smile.

He crumpled a piece of paper and tossed it into the trash basket against the wall. "Nothing but net!" he said out loud. The day was turning his way. He wondered how to direct this good luck and then remembered the Trinity dinner.

The food had been good, a little pricey but a write-off. And it was great spending the evening with those fine people who did not yet know all the insurance they needed. Aljo was already on his list, but he added Molly and Pete's growing family. Also, Mountain House *had* to be underinsured, what with mudslides and forest fires and all the other hazards of living in the country. Finally, there was the one and only Ansel Tone: perhaps the biggest prize and the toughest nut to crack. Bud set up a page on his phone about all the McYanks and the policies he might push.

He recalled what Charlie said about his novel. He had forgotten that party where Ansel and Tess blew up. Ansel was Bud's roommate then, so he had to let him have the room with that American girl, but it was annoying putting up with his bragging the next day. They were Tess's friends, after all. He saw an image of Tess at their reunion dinner, so stylish and lost in thought. How could anyone pass on her for a one-night stand?

But it was time to push on. He checked local events, finding the first-place Orioles were coming to town to play the Yankees. He wrote the date and time on a pad and called to make sure he could get the firm's tickets. Over the course of the morning, he reached Dutch and Charlie and left a message with Ansel's assistant, inviting the guys to the game.

* * *

Dutch was thrilled to get Bud's call. It was a break from trying to make sense of his accountant's tax memo. He loved the Yankees but hadn't been to a game in years. And it would be a treat to spend a Saturday somewhere other than the office or his parents' house. First, though, he had to call home.

"Mom, it's Dutch. How are you feeling today?"

"Oh, Dilly, sweet boy, is it you? Oh, honey, it's so good to hear from you."

"Yeah, Mom, and it's great to talk to you. You are taking it easy, right, like Dr. Wingate said?"

"Dr. Wingate? Oh yes, of course." She laughed quietly.

He took a deep breath. He felt helpless talking to his mother over the phone. "Listen, Mom, I'm going to have to come out this week on Sunday instead of Saturday."

"Oh," she said and paused. "Have you got a date?"

"No, Mom, just going to a ball game with some friends."

"No nice young lady?" she said, obviously disappointed. "I'd think the girls would be lining up for a good man like you."

"Well, they're not exactly lined up. But I am looking forward to getting back to the stadium."

"Oh, well. You have a good time, and we'll see you Sunday. I'll make a pot roast."

These days he cooked only vegetables in his apartment to go with the pot roast piled in plastic containers in his refrigerator. "Okay, Mom. I'm looking forward to it. You get plenty of rest, okay?"

"Of course, sweetheart. Don't you worry about me. I am happy as a busy bee."

* * *

For Charlie the timing of the game was perfect, as he needed help filling in gaps in the Trinity story. Someone might know what happened with the Digory investigation. He remembered talking to the Gardaí afterwards; it must have been right after that party. They asked about his whereabouts, when he left the student paper offices, when he got to the party. But that was not why that night was etched in his memory; that night was important because, after a year of obsession, he finally connected with Tess. If only Molly had not been with them after the party, they might have made it official then, instead of waiting until two years later.

While he looked forward to the game, he couldn't think about the Orioles without reliving incidents in Baltimore he had long struggled to forget.

In his father's lucid moments he had sometimes talked about taking his kids to a game at Camden Yards, but it never happened, not once. Then, in fourth grade, Charlie finally got his chance. His class attended a matchup with the Blue Jays on a day that encapsulated his childhood. He had saved money from his paper route to pay for the ticket and spent weeks memorizing batting averages. He hung a newspaper photograph of Cal Ripken over his bed. But in a drunken spasm, his father tore down the photo, yelling that the tape would ruin the wall. Even at ten years old Charlie knew his father's anger was about drinking and hating everything, not the paint, but there was no fighting his rage. Charlie tried to scrape the remnants of tape off the wall, but in the process peeled away paint. Then he panicked. He tried to run away before his father saw it but never made it to the door. His father removed his belt and whipped the skin off Charlie's rear end.

The tears were long dried by game day, although it still hurt to sit down. Ripken played his usual great game and Mike Mussina pitched a masterpiece. Charlie was so elated he didn't want to leave the stadium when the teacher gathered the class to go. He carried the glow all the way home, bursting to tell his mother and sister about it. But, instead, he endured another shouting match between his parents and had to fetch ice for his mother's black eye. In later years he wondered why his mother stayed with his father and was sure she would have lived longer—and much happier—had she left him. He had to believe she only stayed for her kids.

His sister's answer to the oppression at home was to withdraw within herself and later turn to drugs. They called her death in high school an accidental overdose, but Charlie knew it was her escape. His answer was to keep his emotions bottled up and retreat into novels. He pored through books in search of worlds to inhabit in place of his own. And then in his junior year he lucked into Ms. Garfield's English class. By then his sister was dead and his mother a hollow shell. Ms. Garfield saw what Charlie faced at home and helped him submit an application to Cornell. She was the only one to see him off when he boarded the bus to New York, praying he'd never have to return.

Chapter 15

Ansel lowered his newspaper and watched True eat a bowl of cereal. This was beginning to feel natural, being comfortable with his son without needing to talk.

It occurred to him that sitting across the table like this was all Karla Canterwail wanted. It was not much to ask. He *had* used her work. He could own up to that in person.

Becca arrived, planning to show Ansel how to access his Medium.com account, but he asked her first to help True search for lost homework. She did a quick sweep of the living room and went into Ansel's office. True followed and immediately burst into laughter. Ansel looked through the doorway.

"What's so funny?" she asked, straightening on her knees with a snarling face.

"You're like a big dog looking for a ball!"

She frowned and bent again, stretching beneath the bed and coming up with a sheet of paper. "And I suppose this is not what you're looking for, wise guy," she said.

"You found it!" He snatched the page and squeezed past Ansel to stuff it into his backpack.

"Hey, no need to thank me," she said from her knees.

"Thank you," he called out in sarcastic singsong.

Ansel gave True a playful scolding look. True responded with a genuine smile for both Ansel and Becca. The kid was a real MacTone; he knew how to work a room.

"Hey, don't forget your phone," Ansel said, handing him the device.

"Thanks, Ansel," the boy said. "See you later."

With True gone Ansel returned to his bedroom. When he emerged, dressed for the day, Becca said, "Someone named So Crats called. He wants to know if you can make a game at Yankee Stadium on the twenty-third. He said 'Plato and Homer' would be going. You have an appearance that day, but I said I'd give you the message."

She grinned as if waiting for the punchline. When he said nothing, she added, "So, should we send your toga out to be pressed?"

His jaw tightened. The day was barely started and already he was dealing with this crap. Why did it have to be the twenty-third? Leah had set up a radio time slot that day, and he felt no driving need to see those guys again so soon. But he had to find out about Charlie's book and here was his opportunity. "Listen," he said, "I do *not* want to talk to him, but call back and say yes. I'll put off whatever I have."

She scrunched up her nose and tilted her head. "I hope Leah doesn't blame me that you're passing on NPR to play hooky with dead philosophers."

"Just do it!" he almost shouted. There was nothing funny about this.

Her smile vanished. She stepped out on the balcony to call. He went into his office, kicking True's sneakers out of the way. At his desk he pushed aside a faculty report and focused on Charlie's manuscript. He needed to find out what that dope was writing.

After Becca made the call, she told Ansel she'd be in touch later in the week and left for the subway. He was the boss and all but he could be such an ass. Why would he yell at her for making an innocent joke? How could he be so nice one minute and psycho the next? She had to find a way to parlay this job into something more stable, and soon.

On the street she checked her phone and saw her father had called. With headphones plugged in, she hit speed dial.

"Hi, Daddy. I see you called."

"That's right, sweet pea. Your Aunt Elizabeth is cleaning out the old house and asked if you want any furniture."

"Oh," she said and stopped to think. "I'd love some of that stuff, but I don't have any room, and who knows how long it'll be before I have my own place?"

"That's what I thought, but if there's something you really want, I could store it in the basement."

"You're the best," she said in her way of half-consciously wrapping him around her little finger. "I love her house. It's so sad she's moving." She thought for a moment and added, "I guess one thing is the big rocking chair. I remember sitting on Mom's lap in that chair."

"The oak rocker from the sunporch? Yes, I told her you'd want that, although I think your memory comes from the snapshot." Becca's mother had passed away when she was five, so memories of her mostly grew from photographs and her father's stories. It was odd, but comforting, how her mind played tricks on her, transmuting photos and bedtime stories into what seemed like real memories.

"Well, it's important to me anyway," she said. "Beyond the chair, I'd have to think about it, or is there a list?"

"Not to worry. I'll help her put together an inventory and we can talk later. And you *are* coming home in August, right?"

"Yeah, I plan to come for the week up through Caitlin's wedding, since I'm a bridesmaid *again*, assuming work doesn't interfere."

"And how is it working with the professor?"

"Mostly he's nice, and I'm getting good at online marketing. Working for him opens doors to all sorts of places and people."

"Mostly," he said, homing in on that word with the fatherly insight that never ceased to amaze her.

"Well, yeah. I mean he pays me well, he values my advice, and…"

"And what?"

"I don't know. He's moody, and sometimes he has a temper."

"You're watching out for yourself, right?"

"Yes, Dad." Yes, except for when she let him seduce her like some country bumpkin.

"Fresh Air? Exercise?"

"I run along the river—which is when I miss Wolfy most, by the way—and might join a softball team."

"Do they know you're a ringer?" he laughed.

"Right, when I was eighteen maybe. Anyway, Dad, I've got to go. Everything's fine. New York is colossal. I'm going into the subway now but I'll call you over the weekend."

"Okay, sweet pea, or sooner if you need to."

On the way to Brooklyn, Becca pulled up a photo of her dad and her dog and made it her phone's new home screen background. She then scrolled through text messages, which reminded her she had a life away from Ansel. He was obviously good at what he did, and he could turn on the charm, but deep down he was a jerk. She wouldn't let his behavior mess her up. Self-pity was not the answer. She needed to be strong and smart, learn from her mistakes. She simply would not let the miserable interlude that afternoon affect her.

Caitlin, her best friend from home, had replied to her text about Ansel: "So sorry. He sounds like a complete pig. But, as we know, all men are pigs, other than my Jeremy, of course."

She smiled. Caitlin and Jeremy had gone out since high school, and now they'd be married. It was good there were genuine people like them in the world, and Caitlin always brought her back to earth.

Chapter 16

On Saturday Dutch headed for the subway in the Yankees cap he wore to the office on weekends. He had always followed the team but lately he barely caught an inning or two with his dad or skimmed the box scores.

It was easy to pick out other fans on the 4 train headed to the Bronx. One little boy in a Yankees jacket smiled at him. A man in an over-large "Jeter" jersey wrapped his arms around his girlfriend and a pole.

When the train emerged from underground, he watched out the window to glimpse the field. It always thrilled him to see that slice of the outfield when he had taken the subway up with his father. But he had forgotten the new stadium was north of the old site, so the subway didn't pass the field until after his stop. There was only a moment to pine for the past, though, as the doors opened and nearly everyone hurried off. He was carried along with the crowd, infected by the general eagerness for an early-season matchup with the first-place team.

Down on the street hawkers pushed pennants and hats and posters. People moved in all directions across the sidewalk and the streets snarled with traffic.

"Ice cold water, water, one dollar! Ice cold water!" a vendor shouted.

"Tickets? Who needs two?" said an insidious voice.

"Let's go, Yankees!" three teenaged girls chanted and laughed as a train rumbled overhead.

Several police vans were unloading officers with casual efficiency into the plaza around the stadium. Merchandise booths were doing solid business. Banners picturing Babe Ruth and Lou Gehrig hung from Yankees' lampposts. A muffled drone from the public address system inside filled the air. Two cops stood on a corner, one checking his phone while the other eyed the crowd through mirrored sunglasses.

The Yankees never put players' names on their jerseys, so *real* fans would buy a jersey with a number but no name: "5" for Joe DiMaggio, "15" for Therman Munson. But Dutch smiled at fans of all shapes and sizes, who cared more about displaying their heroes' names than about authenticity. He had forgotten how exciting it was coming to a game. It seemed he had hardly taken a whole day off since Jennifer left. It was great that Bud was in town to get him out for things like this.

His ticket was for Legends Seating. At a folding table, an officious young woman checked his ticket a second time and snapped a red plastic bracelet around his wrist. This was new, but clearly a good thing, as it opened the way into a cavernous hall full of free food. He was glad he had skipped lunch. After gorging on this spread, he'd be skipping dinner as well.

They offered all kinds of food but the smell of hot dogs transported him back to games with his dad at the old Yankee Stadium. He grabbed one with lots of mustard and headed through a short passage to the field.

Outside he froze, awed by the sunshine, the crowd, the almost too-green field. So much open space! He was just to the side of home plate, seemingly within reach of the players warming up. Brett Gardner was thirty feet away talking with an umpire. Mark Teixeira stretched against a wall, laughing with fans. Dutch had seen plenty of games at the old Yankee Stadium, but this was incredible!

An usher showed him to his seat, where he found Charlie and Bud. Bud waved a hand at the seats and the view. "What do you think, sport?"

"This is amazing. Thank you so much!"

Bud smiled. "The game should start in a few. Order any food you want; it's free. And order a beer as well; they're on me."

"Oh, no," Dutch said. "*I'm* buying the beers today."

Bud tipped his head in appreciation and nodded toward his companion. "So, Homer here has a literary question for us."

Dutch looked at Charlie, who said, "As I told you guys, I'm basing my book on our year in Dublin, mostly Trinity Term. We all remember the shit that went down at the end of the year, with Digory and all, and before that, what was the professor's name who had the wreck?"

Dutch looked at Bud. "Was it McDoodle?"

Bud laughed. "No, I honestly don't remember."

"Ansel will know," Dutch said. "the guy was *his* advisor."

"Anyway," Charlie said, "I'm focused on the personal story of the hero, who would be me, and the romance with the Tess character, which of course also involves Ansel."

Dutch squinted, trying to remember details.

The PA system crackled overhead. "The New York Yankees welcome you to Yankee Stadium, home of the New York Yankees. Introducing today's starting lineup…"

"But at the year-end party…" Charlie began again.

"Is this where the swells sit?" interrupted a voice from behind.

While Ansel's entrances always demanded attention, Charlie was clearly eager to get back to his question. "As I was saying, before I was so rudely interrupted." He cast a stern look at Ansel, who threw up his hands. "I'm trying to pin down details, especially about the year-end party. Now I know *you*, particularly," he looked at Ansel, "may have a different perspective, and the facts don't really matter because I'll alter them to make a better story, but I want to start with what *actually* happened. That way it all makes sense—and my publisher insists it's the only way I can write a bestseller. Also, this is basically a love story and your character," looking again at Ansel, "unfortunately has to be the villain."

"Play ball!" came the umpire's shout. Dutch had never sat close enough in a big-league park to hear the umpire so clearly.

"What?" Ansel exclaimed, distracted by the batter coming to the plate. "Why do I have to be the villain?"

"Strike one!"

"Well, first of all, I'll change everything around, so your character will not really be you. But there has to be a conflict to resolve and you—call him 'the guy who loses the girl' rather than the 'villain'—you get the biggest role, after the hero, of course."

"Okay, I get it," Ansel said, unamused.

"Strike two!" The crowd clapped in unison before the third pitch.

Charlie continued: "So, while I know what my character saw, I was late to that party and heard conflicting stories."

The batter smacked a pitch high in the air. They turned with the crowd to watch it sail. Aaron Hicks tracked the ball in straightaway center and caught it for the first out. The crowd applauded, and the next batter walked toward the plate.

They turned back to Charlie. "Well, all right," he said. "To start, Bud, you organized the thing, right?"

"Batting second, third-baseman, number thirteen, Manny Machado."

"Who else, sport?" said Bud. "Yeah, I talked our way into a room at the GMB and got you and Ansel to collect money for beer. Dutch helped set up, along with some other kids."

"Ball one!"

Dutch nodded. "I think Molly and Tess brought food from the Buttery."

The crowd in the bleachers began a rhythmic roll call to Yankees players in the field. They stretched or squashed each player's name into four syllables to fit their chant and kept it up with each name until the player acknowledged them with a bow or a wave.

"Right, yeah," Bud said, turning back to the conversation. "And the Australians showed up early, of course, thinking we might have already tapped the keg. I remember one cute blonde from Brisbane I was trying to chat up. Anyway, the thing got going about six. That guy from Kilkenny brought his stereo and decent CDs, and somebody had some skunky weed, if I remember right."

"Ball two!" The crowd became tense and started rhythmic clapping.

"Okay," said Charlie, "and hopefully this doesn't stir up bad memories, Ansel, but what happened at the party between you and Tess?"

Ansel rubbed his finger across his lips. "We had had a fight," Ansel said.

"Strike one!"

"Actually," Ansel continued, "we hadn't gotten along for weeks. She—no offense, man; you said you wanted the real story—had been getting clingy about the end of the year and what would happen when we got home, *ad infinitum*. She was also giving me a hard time about other girls, getting jealous if I even talked to someone. So, by the time of the party, I was pretty fed up."

The crack of bat on ball drew their eyes to the field. Machado made it to first base on a blooper over the leaping shortstop.

Charlie kept looking at Ansel, whose attention slid to the waitress in the aisle. "Can I get you gentlemen anything?" she asked, fluttering her eyelashes at Ansel.

Dutch asked what kind of beer they served. Ansel ordered sushi and Bud a pretzel. Dutch asked for a quesadilla and four IPAs. Charlie waited until she typed in their order and then glanced meaningfully back at Ansel.

"Batting third, center-fielder, number thirteen, Adam Jones."

Ansel looked at the field and then turned back to Charlie. "Well, there was this girl from California. She was traveling around. She was hot, and I was ready for some fun without the drama."

"Strike one!"

Charlie was growing impatient. "So what happened *at the party*?"

Ansel looked at the field and then back at them as if he'd forgotten what they were talking about. "Oh, right, the party. Well, like I said, Tess was giving me grief, and so I told her we were through and found a new friend."

"Strike two!"

They looked at him, expectantly. He added with a leer, as if he should not have to say it, "You remember, Bud, you cleared out of our room for the night?"

"I guess," Bud said tentatively. "Dutch and I finished a bottle of whiskey while we straightened up the party room and I ended up…in *his* room?" He looked over for confirmation.

"Right," said Dutch. "You collapsed on Charlie's bed, and he never came home."

"Ball one!"

Charlie was following this closely. "Right, I crashed on the floor between Tess and Molly," He paused and grimaced as if trying to recall the details, "though in my novel Molly will find somewhere else to spend the night."

"Wait, I know her!" Dutch blurted out.

Jones singled, advancing Machado to second and putting the crowd on edge.

Now Ansel seemed more interested in the conversation than the game. "You know who?" he asked.

"The California girl! You remember, Bud. While we were cleaning up, we found that phone in a fuzzy pink cover? I had talked with that girl; her name was Reilly. Her family owned a diner I'd been to near UC Santa Barbara."

Another crack of the bat drew their eyes to a long fly ball caught by Aaron Judge on the warning track. The runners returned to their bases.

Bud waved his hand and said, "And what has this got to do with…"

"Well, we found the phone and I took it to turn in to lost and found. But next day I remembered talking with that girl. I saw her leave the party with Ansel but had no idea where she was staying, so I must have asked you, right?" He looked at Ansel, who shrugged his shoulders.

"Batting fifth for the Orioles, designated hitter, number forty-five, Mark Trumbo."

"Well, I must have," Dutch said. "But she was gone by then, and you didn't know how to reach her. Then I remembered the diner and emailed about the phone. And then I had to keep the phone in case they replied, so I took it home to New York."

Trumbo fouled off a pitch into the stands.

Bud shook his head. "Only *you* would think it was your job to do that for some chick you'd never see again."

"Ball one!"

Dutch was embarrassed. "You're right, I know. But anyway, a month after I got home, I heard from her and sent back her phone. Actually, she was really happy to get it, and we emailed for a while. She was nice. Last I knew she was living in LA."

"Strike two!"

Charlie and Bud chuckled.

"She was cute," Dutch said defensively. "Ansel, you remember."

"Hey sport," Bud said, poking him with an elbow. "You should give her a call."

"Yeah, maybe," Dutch said sincerely, "but she's in California."

Charlie chimed in, "You know, people *sometimes* travel between New York and LA."

Ansel seemed anxious, but Dutch was grateful he didn't join in the kidding.

"Crack" came from the field. Starlin Castro snagged a screaming line-drive at second and tagged the runner, retiring the side.

In the top of the fifth inning, Baltimore made it seven to two and put the game out of reach. The cheers were subdued as the Yankees came up in the sixth. Dutch and Bud went inside for food and Ansel turned to Charlie. "So how far along are you with the manuscript?"

"I've outlined the whole thing and I'm most of the way through. It's going really fast, but I'm still filling in spaces."

"What comes next?"

"When I'm happy with the draft, I'll send it to my editor…."

"Wait," Ansel interrupted. "Does anyone see it before that?"

"Not the whole manuscript. I'm pretty antsy about that. I dribble out a chapter or two to my agent so she can show the editor the book is real. But those are rough drafts."

"Okay, so it goes to the editor…."

"Yeah, and she'll do a developmental edit, which will require more work on my side, and then she'll pass it to an underling for a line edit. After all that, we round up beta readers."

"You mean volunteers?"

"Yeah, friends and colleagues, anyone who hasn't seen the book before and is willing to read it and comment."

"My books go so quickly from the editor to the distributors that I never get a chance to have friends read them."

"Maybe it's the difference between fiction and nonfiction. Anyway, I think the beta thing is new, sort of like crowdsourced editing."

"Well," Ansel said, seeing an opening, "*I* could read it for you."

Charlie's eyes went wide. "Wow. I wasn't fishing for help. This is pretty much below your pay grade."

Ansel laughed, trying to seem nonchalant. "Hey, it's what friends do, right? You think that other Homer finished the *Iliad* without suggestions from his drinking buddies? In a couple of weeks, I'll be grading papers and pushing out *Son of Redux*, but I have time right now…if you think it might help."

"Help? It'd be great, so long as you understand it's pretty rough. I mean, I normally won't let anyone see a book at this stage, but if this is my one chance to get *your* input, I could give you the draft. Would you want a print copy or should I email it?"

"I prefer to hold a book in my hands." Ansel thought fast and added, "You know what clse? I'm driving an incredible car these days, and this weather has me itching to take her into the country. How about I come up your way on, make it Tuesday morning? I could pick up the manuscript and also get a look at this famous Mountain House—and the Jaguar."

"That would be *too* good. I can't believe it! And the *Jag* is my real passion. Your dad sells luxury sports cars, doesn't he?"

"Absolutely. I grew up tinkering with cars. My father always said there was motor oil in my veins. And wait till you see the Zagato!"

As the home team went down in order, the others returned and Ansel moved next to Dutch. To a scratchy recording of Bessie Smith singing *God Bless America* during the seventh inning stretch, he asked, "So Plato, how's your love life?"

Dutch snickered at the "Plato" nickname. "Had a long-term thing two years ago," he said, "but it didn't work out."

"So, you're going to beat the bushes in LA?" Ansel said, as if that were the most ridiculous idea he had ever heard. "Haven't you heard of Tinder?"

"I tried those sites; they're just not right for me."

"Well, that babe in LA is probably married with three kids by now."

"Oh, I know, but you guys are right: what have I got to lose?"

"Strike two!" Ansel glanced at the struggling batter. With two strikes, he was flailing at pitches. Ansel felt his pain.

"Let me think about it," Ansel said. "I'm sure I know some woman firmly within the Yankees fan base."

Later, Ansel fended off Bud's attempts to talk about insuring against defamation claims by pretending to be distracted by the game. Bud gave up the sales pitch and joined him in focusing on the field.

But Charlie turned to them all again. "One more thing. Did they ever arrest anyone for that thing about the old security guy?"

Ansel tensed.

"Strike three!" The side was retired again.

"Digory!" said Bud. "Who could forget him?"

"Right," said Charlie. "He fell from the Arts Block while we were all at the party."

"Wait," Ansel said. "That wasn't the same night."

"Sure it was," said Bud. "There was a mob of Gardaí the next day. I remember the flashing lights took my hangover to a whole new dimension."

"Did they find out why it happened?" said Dutch. "Didn't they think someone was trying to steal books from the Old Library?"

"Oh God, I don't know," said Bud. "But wasn't that old guy a hoot? Remember his story about students lifting a trolley car to the roof of Examination Hall? We didn't believe him, but it turned out to be true."

Dutch and Charlie laughed. "That's exactly what I need!" said Charlie. "I mean, not necessarily *that* story but details about the year, about the crazy shit we did, and how tame it all was compared to Digory's stories of riots and bonfires."

"And tales from Mister Trinity-tradition-back-to-Wolfe-Tone here," Bud said, nudging Ansel, "about the original hooligans."

"I *know* you don't mean to insult my ancestor," Ansel sneered. "Give the guy his due. He led the rabble at Trinity, and then the Irish people, and died in prison for his pains."

"Ball one!" the umpire shouted, pulling their attention to the field, where the Orioles were up to start the eighth inning.

"The Digory story I liked best," Bud said, "was the one about the guy who insisted on being provided a mug of porter during an exam, the 'refreshment' cited in the old college rules. The assistant dean had to bring him the porter but then threw him out of the exam because he wasn't wearing his sword and so violated the gentlemen's dress code."

A wild pitch was called ball two.

"That was funny," Charlie said, "but hardly credible. Fake news. And hey, I just remembered another mystery. We can't remember the name of the professor who wrecked his racing car. You know," he said, turning to Ansel, "your advisor? We all went to one of his races in Kildare."

"Strike one!"

Ansel coughed. "Um, yeah," he said, trying to seem unruffled. They were all looking at him and there was no sense hiding the name, since Charlie would find it on his own. "Doogan," he finally responded. "His name was Brandon Doogan."

"Right, thanks. I wonder who would know when he came out of

his coma," Charlie mused as he typed into his phone. Ansel saw no reason to share Doogan's sad fate.

The Yankees surged in the eighth. They focused on the field—or in Ansel's case stared at the field lost in thought. He was encouraged to find a way to review Charlie's manuscript before anyone else, but he would now have to divert Dutch from looking up that girl in California.

Chapter 17

Tess found a plate of currant scones and the Sunday *Times* laid out on the terrace, with a yellow wood poppy in a bud vase. Charlie was in the kitchen squeezing orange juice and slicing melon. Mellow saxophone played through the outdoor speakers.

"How nice," she said, standing with tousled hair in big slippers and a chenille robe.

"Have a seat," he called from the kitchen. "Coffee's on."

She pulled up a chair and sipped orange juice while she perused the paper. Charlie handed her a section folded to the front-page article on the Paris Climate Agreement, signed that week. "Perfect setting to wonder if we're in time," he said, waving toward the view.

She nodded noncommittally. It was fine for her husband to worry about saving the planet; she was more interested in the Business Section report on her deal. It was exciting to do work that made news. She pulled out her tablet and texted congratulations to Tom Carter on the press mention. She then showed Charlie the article.

"Way to go, babe. So, are you done now?"

"Oh, we've just signed the agreement. Now we have to get ready for the closing next month."

He looked deflated, so she continued: "But we'll be on a regular schedule. No more late nights for a while."

He brightened again and took a seat. She hoped her smile didn't look patronizing. He was such a child. He didn't understand—or even care—how business worked.

"I was thinking," he said, sipping his coffee, "we might go up to that new Italian place in Beacon for an early dinner."

"What," she said absently. "Oh, sure, whatever you like."

Charlie quickly became engrossed in the Sports Section. She looked out over the valley and daydreamed. Seeing Ansel at the restaurant had awakened long-forgotten feelings. He was even better looking than she remembered, and his suit was impeccable. Charlie wore nothing that well-tailored. She pictured the first time she and Ansel made love—in his room in Botany Bay—and sighed.

"Did you say something?" Charlie asked.

"Just savoring the breeze and the view…and a *damned good* cup of coffee."

He returned to reading. She thought again of Ansel. Their breakup had been so harsh and public; she was fortunate to escape.

He finished his article and picked up a clipboard, a familiar tool for his editing. Thinking of his book made her grimace. She didn't want to see herself "won" in print. Besides, he didn't *win* her at school or at any other time. What was she, a prize calf? And why did he have to bring this up in front of Ansel? He told them all he wanted the *real* story? Well, the biggest event of the year was their breakup.

That was a little cold; Digory died that night. But who knew if his accident would even make it into the novel, with Charlie focused on his grand love story?

She could see he would now slip into his "great author" persona, where everything took a back seat to his writing. And his agent would facilitate that attitude, encouraging him to neglect everything else, except Joan herself. She imagined it was hard for an ego run wild to resist that kind of veneration.

Charlie's alter ego had already reared its head. The prior weekend, he was in his den when it came time to drive Odysseus to a vet appointment. Tess knocked on the door.

"What is it?" he snapped.

"Sorry. It's time for Seusy's appointment. You said you wanted to take him."

"Right," he said, the frustration in his voice ratcheting down. "I'll be down in a minute."

He apologized on his way out the door, but it was hard to overlook his reaction. Could he be so absorbed in writing that real life was an intrusion, sometimes almost an assault on his efforts?

"Charlie," she ventured that evening, "do you *have to* write about us? I mean, don't you see it makes everyone uncomfortable?"

He looked at her like she had lost her mind. "Babe, Joan says Penguin insists the book be based on real life. What else is there?"

She frowned. She was tired of hearing what Joan had to say.

He went on, "Besides, it makes a great story in a remarkable setting. And no one will know who the models were for the characters."

"I'll know, and so will the rest. I just don't think it's fair to use us as material."

"Damn it, Tess! You've been on me to do something productive. Now that I've got an idea that's real and promising, you shoot it down. I can't believe you!" He rose angrily and went upstairs.

She watched him mount the steps and turned back to the view. What perverse twist of fate left her on this lonely mountain with the self-absorbed artist in the frumpy tweed jacket?

* * *

Ansel sat on his balcony. True and Hattie were at True's classmate's apartment, so everything was quiet. He watched a sailboat on the Hudson. Its wake quickly disappeared, leaving only a faint impression, just the way actual events not recast into history were lost.

So much was upended in his life. On one hand the semester was winding down, the new book underway and the radio interview coming up. But he still had to resolve the Canterwail thing. And then he had

Charlie and Dutch dredging up the past, like a bad dream each time he slept, if you could even call what he did these days "sleeping." He was so tired some mornings he needed coke to get going. Why could Charlie not write fiction like a real novelist? Digory died; that was sad but why relive it? Sure, he was a funny old coot. Ansel enjoyed his stories more than anyone, since he grew up hearing those stories from his grandfather. But what good was there in going into all that again? It was bad enough when the accident happened. A guy too old for the job slipped and fell. Period. The police didn't arrest anyone. They never even confirmed there was a break-in. Anyway, the history of Trinity was full of students sneaking into buildings. This was no different.

But now Ansel had to make sure Charlie wouldn't bring attention to that old shit. And Dutch, too; Ansel had to keep him from contacting that girl in California. The past had to stay in the past. The fix was doable—those guys would be easy to manipulate—but it was such a bother.

It was hard to miss the irony. Charlie espoused a kind of re-visionist history—improving the facts to make a better story—while unknowingly threatening the revisionist historian with the facts. It was ironic but not funny. Ansel would have to make sure he set the "real" facts in stone.

And on top of it all was the mess with Florence and True. Having the boy and his nanny at the apartment cramped his style. He couldn't bring women home. He had to be careful about drug paraphernalia. Worse still, having True with him was messing with his head. Two weeks ago he would have sicced his father's lawyers on Karla Canterwail until she squealed. Now, all of a sudden, he felt like he had to play fair.

The night before, True had told him he had to do a presentation for school on the early settlers in Roanoke. "I suck at drawing," he complained as he got into bed.

"I'm sure you can glue some photos and maps to a poster board without much drawing," Ansel said.

"But I still have to label stuff, and I'll make a mess; I always do. Could you help me?"

"No worries. You get the pages ready, and I'll help paste them on and write the labels."

"Thanks, Ansel," he said and turned toward the wall.

Ansel was impatient for True to go home, but moments like this grabbed him. His feelings toward the boy were different from how he once felt about Florence or how he ever felt toward anyone. Lovers came and went but True would always be his son. It made no difference if he was a prodigy or a fuck-up, or that Ansel had deserted him for ten years or even how the boy reacted to him now. He reached his hand toward the sleeping head but stopped at the pillow and slowly pulled it back.

Chapter 18

True had gone to school and everything was quiet when Ansel's phone buzzed. It was a text from Becca: "POSTER VIDEO WENT VIRAL!" Another text added: "1.2 MILLION VIEWS!"

He stared at the messages. He wanted exposure on social networks, and she got it done. He had done well in hiring her. But he didn't want to engage in a conversation now, even by text. He left his phone on the nightstand and walked out on the balcony.

Watching a tanker power up the river, he thought about Charlie's book. Once he got hold of the manuscript he could assess the problem. Then there was Dutch, who couldn't get a date without dredging up that girl from California. Ansel needed to find someone closer to home to keep the big lug's attention.

The landline rang. He always ignored this, but a voice too loud to tune out came through the answering machine: "Ansel, it's Leah. You're not picking up your cell!"

He was sick of hearing bad news and yet here was Leah to start his day. He answered, "What's up?"

"Ansel, good. So, Drexler spoke with Canterwail's brother-in-law. The guy is *not* a copyright lawyer or a litigator—I think he does real estate—and Drexler explained the facts of life to him. He thinks the guy will bring Karla around to accepting a payment and maybe some kind of credit."

"I admit she wrote part of the book?"

"Not exactly. Drexler suggested you revise the acknowledgements. Tip your hat to her in the e-book and in future print copies. No one will notice but her. I can work with the layout people and pass it off as an oversight. Also, I rebooked the NPR appearance for May 7. But Harvey is having a cow about the outline."

He promised her the outline and then sprang into action in the more urgent matter. First, he called Aljo and reached Dutch. "You know," he said, "I was thinking. If you'd really like to meet a nice young lady, you're so in luck!"

"Ah, I don't know if I have the time. Anyway, would I be right for one of *your* friends?"

"Oh, absolutely. Matter of fact, I know someone you'll flip over."

"I appreciate the thought but…"

"Don't give me 'but.' You'll be doing me a favor. She's a really nice girl, but she's on her own in the city and a little homesick. She's also quite pretty. You guys will be great together. I'll set it up for Friday night and send you the details."

Next, he reached Becca. "Remember that new Asian Fusion place in TriBeCa you told me about?"

"Wait! What about the video? Did you see those numbers?"

"Yes, you did a fantastic job. But about that restaurant?"

She didn't miss a beat. "AzaFuz?" she said. "I've got the website up."

"Yeah, that's it. How'd you like to go there Friday night?"

"It'd be impossible to get a reservation." She paused. "And what do you mean 'go there'?"

"Well, I've got this friend, great guy, salt of the earth. You two would really get along."

"You want me to go to dinner *with your friend*?"

"I *need* you to go to dinner with my old friend. This is very important. Listen, you don't have to do anything you don't want; just have dinner and spend some time with him."

"Spend time doing what?" She sounded angry.

"Oh, I don't mean you should sleep with him or anything. Just have a nice dinner. Whatever."

"What's going on, Ansel?"

"I can't explain now, but you *have* to do this for me. Friday night, eight o'clock. I'll make the reservation in my name. The food will be great, and you can take a day off next week to make up the time."

* * *

Becca was livid. It was bad enough Ansel had seduced her and tossed her aside like an old newspaper. Now he was pimping her out to his friends!

Her roommate, Roxy Smith, was sprawled over the edge of the sofa painting her toenails. "Is that steam coming out of your ears?" she said playfully.

"Could be. My boss just set me up with a date."

"And that's a *bad* thing? Maybe your date has a friend for me?"

It was not like Roxy needed help attracting men, with her figure and come-hither smile, but she was always open to possibilities. Becca wished she were as dauntless as Roxy.

"So, let's see," Roxy continued. "Your boss is how old, like thirty-five?"

"Yeah, about."

"And so this "friend" is probably the same age, say ten years older than you?"

"What's your point?"

"Oh, nothing. Just thinking you've got nothing to fear from a guy with a walker who wants to buy you a fancy meal. He's probably too old to chase you around the table."

"Very funny. No, this is bad. Maybe I should get a job in an office, with normal people."

"I'll trade places if you can stand being a sales assistant. That boss of yours is dreamy!"

Becca looked at her with a crooked smile, and they broke out laughing. Roxy had been her roommate in college and had found the Brooklyn apartment and lined up the third roommate. It was comforting having her there when Becca needed to vent. About the tryst with Ansel, Roxy said she would have stuck around out of curiosity, but she understood Becca's anger. At any rate, they agreed she couldn't leave one job before lining up another—and they had both sworn off waitressing. Taking the moral high road would not put food on the table, and going on this date promised *excellent* food, at least for one night.

"I think I need a good run," Becca said. "Sweat out all the crap."

"Better yet, come to practice with me. You said you'd think about it. It's only sixty bucks for the season. The girls are chill and pretty good, but we could really use a clean-up hitter."

Becca tilted her head, thinking it over.

"I saw you play at school," Roxy said. "You hit better than most of the guys."

Becca smiled with closed lips. She had thought about playing softball in college but knew a varsity sport would take all her attention, while she wanted to try new things. Intramural games had filled some of the gap, though, and let her be a monster on the diamond.

"I don't know, Rox," she said. "I need to focus on finding a real job. Anyway, now I need to clear my head."

She ran along the East River, only occasionally looking across at Manhattan. She mostly lost herself in a playlist streaming through her earbuds, all songs selected for tempo that matched her strides. After a shower she visited job sites and updated her resume, always cathartic activities. Her current position was easy to spin: "Global Head of Social Media for Internationally Renowned Author."

* * *

Ansel later called Leah. "How's my favorite agent?"

"I've been trying to reach you, Ansel. Why don't you ever answer your phone?"

"It's a long story, darlin', which I shall spare you."

"Ansel, Harvey wants the outline. We *need* the outline. You are pushing this, and me particularly, too far!"

"Peace! Please! I called to thank you for getting me through the Canterwail thing, and for juggling the NPR appearance. Sorry about screwing that up; I had to take care of something. I also promise to get you the outline next week."

"Like when next week?"

"Wednesday, latest. Promise."

"I will hold them off until Wednesday but that's it, Ansel. This is a firm deadline."

"*Sprioc-ama*," Ansel said under his breath.

"Is that some kind of Gaelic kiss-off?"

"No, just an inside joke. But, oh yeah, there is one more thing...."

"Yes, Ansel, what is it?"

"I need a reservation for two at AzaFuz on Friday."

"That new Joey Bernard place? It just opened!"

"I know, but it's important."

"Important, as in you're pursuing a new woman?"

"You always think the worst of me. In fact, I'll be staying home with True to eat popcorn and watch monster movies. This is for a dear friend who needs to get over a woman emphatically wrong for him."

"Right," she said doubtfully.

"Great. So, any time is okay. Use my name. You're the best."

He put aside his phone with a self-satisfied smile. A few quick calls and his life was pumping like a finely tuned V12. Next day he'd get an early start to Mountain House so he could make it back in time for his lecture. Then he'd figure out the name of that brunette.

Chapter 19

For the first time in weeks Ansel felt in control. He took the elevator to the garage beneath his building. A grizzled parking attendant helped him remove the canvas cover from his lion red Aston Martin Zagato.

"She's a beauty, Professor Tone," the old guy said with a big smile showing one gold tooth.

"That's right, Mack. Sheer perfection. Let's see how she sounds."

He climbed into the driver's seat and turned the ignition. The engine rumbled. Ansel stepped out and listened, hand on the hood.

Mack watched excitedly. "Sounds A-OK to me," he cackled.

"A cylinder's misfiring," Ansel said, more to himself than to Mack.

Mack shook his head. "Well, you're the professor."

"I'll take her in over the weekend. She'll be fine for today." He pulled out his phone. It was not easy being Jordan MacTone's son, but it had its perks.

"Carlo," he said to his father's head mechanic, "I need to bring the Zagato in for a quick tune-up. Can you give me a hand Saturday?"

"Sure, sure, Mr. Ansel. You come late morning, say eleven?"

"Perfect. And hey, there's *no* chance the old man will be in, is there?"

"Ah, Mr. Ansel, you know Mr. MacTone, he don't let me know when he'll be where. But you come. We take care of you."

Ansel hung up and headed north, loving the feel of the steering wheel through his driving gloves and the engine through the seat of his pants.

Dealing with Charlie shouldn't be hard. If there were issues, Ansel could fix them before anyone else saw the manuscript. It was really not worth worrying about. He sought distraction in imagining a road trip with the brunette from Propaganda. He really hoped she'd show up for his office hours. She'd make a fine picture in the front seat of the Zagato with a scarf blowing around her neck.

* * *

Tess had gone to work early, as usual. After breakfast Charlie straightened his den and the garage. He was not sure if he was prouder of his new book or his car but both would be on display. It pleased him *the* Ansel Tone was driving up to see him, and he stopped to wonder why he and Tess never entertained anymore. But now, at least, they had the Trinity party to plan.

Late morning he heard a car on the road below the house and went out front to watch it pull into the driveway. He commanded Odysseus to sit and opened Ansel's door. The dog waited while the two shook hands and then lunged when Ansel made a face at him.

While Ansel petted the dog, Charlie stepped backed to view the car. "Sweet," he said. "Looks brand-new."

"Better than new. One of the very few 2012 Zagatos. Still had the classic style."

"Wow. Does it take a lot to keep it on the road?"

"Some. But I've got an *artiste* of a mechanic from the old country. We do a lot of the work together."

"You're kidding! You work on your own car?"

"Call it a guilty pleasure. The old man always said: when it comes to a high-performance automobile, you can't trust your life to some yahoo at a gas station."

Charlie went into the garage to roll out his car.

"Very nice!" Ansel said. "An XKE should always be British racing green."

Charlie nodded proudly. "It's a '75, last year for the model. Runs like a dream."

"Let's see this V12."

Charlie smiled and opened the hood. They talked about the engine, and Charlie pointed out the car's single-shell construction.

"*Monocoque,*" Ansel replied. "Supporting the structure through the external skin was a French concept."

So, the historian knew more about the Jaguar than he did. Charlie tried not to look impressed.

"And I see the dual disc brakes?" Ansel said.

"That's right." Charlie wondered if Ansel was patronizing him.

"It's not *all* original?"

"A few replica parts. Hell, a complete survivor from 1975? My advance wasn't *that* big."

"I hear you. Aston Martin is looking into 3-D printing for factory-made replacement parts, which will undercut the value of a car but may actually improve performance."

"I have to admit, old parts have their off days."

"Them and me both," Ansel laughed. "But as to cars, you can't beat the originals, even the upholstery." He lowered his head and breathed in the smell of the Jaguar's leather seats. "It was never quite the same after Connolly Leather went under. When was that, 2002?"

"You'd know better than me," Charlie said, accepting that he could not compete with Ansel's knowledge of sports cars. "Anyway, how about a drink?"

"Think I'll pass. I'm hoping to find some open road before I head back to town."

"Coffee then?" Charlie said, leading the way into the house.

As they sipped coffee on the terrace, Charlie said, "For a rousing drive, you can't beat this mountain. The road out front's a dream, from foot to peak. There's almost never any other cars. I can show you a hidden turnoff that leads along the ridge that no one ever uses."

Ansel bowed his head graciously. A minute later Charlie said, "I'll go get the manuscript."

"You know," said Ansel, "as one writer to another, I'd love to see where the work is done."

"Absolutely," Charlie said, flattered. He led the way upstairs. The den was his sanctuary; hardly anyone other than the dog ever visited. Two walls were floor-to-ceiling bookshelves. A laptop rested on an oak desk. An overstuffed chair surrounded by piles of books faced big windows opening on the view. Odysseus dropped to the floor in front of the windows, head on paws, and watched them.

"So, you write on the laptop, obviously," Ansel said.

"Yeah. You know, some scribbling on pads, but the writing has to be on the computer."

Ansel shrugged. "But what about backups? Aren't you afraid of crashing and losing work?"

"The machine backs itself up, and I dump everything onto a remote drive every couple of weeks." He opened a drawer and held up a hard drive, its short cord dangling.

Ansel nodded. "And you don't send it to your editor, or anyone, until it's finished?"

"No. No copies to anyone. Well, I'll have to give my agent the first chapter or so, so the publisher thinks I'm earning my advance. Oh, and I do print a copy every few weeks, just in case." He pointed over his shoulder at pages bound with binder clips on the cadenza.

"Which brings us to the present," Ansel said.

"Right." Charlie handed over a large manila envelope. "Now, this is rough, and there are chapters missing. I'm hoping to get more details at the party. You're coming, right?"

"What? Oh, yeah, yeah. Wouldn't miss it."

"So, don't get hung up on proofreading; the publisher has earnest young things in thick glasses to find typos, and the words will change anyway. I'm looking for big-picture suggestions and help on the setting."

"It will get my prompt attention," Ansel said sincerely.

When it was time to go, Charlie showed the way over the mountain. They left in convoy, two muscular engines roaring together. Just before the crest, Charlie stopped and Ansel pulled up behind him. Charlie then turned sharply onto a narrow road hidden behind an outcropping. He reached a rise and then floored the Jaguar along the ridge. Ansel loved this! He tore after Charlie. The release of letting the Zagato run was orgasmic.

Where the road started to descend, Charlie stopped and walked back to Ansel's car. "That's my favorite bit," he said. "No one knows it's here so you can really fly."

"I'm stoked!" Ansel said, stepping out of his car and breathing in the fresh air. "In fact, *everything* about this mountain gives me a tremendous hard-on."

Charlie flinched. Crude remarks didn't bother him but this was different. In declaring his sexual feeling took in *all* of the mountain, it almost sounded like Ansel meant to include Tess.

Ansel seemed oblivious to Charlie's reaction and went on, "You may find me on your mountain all the time now."

Charlie felt like punching Ansel in the nose but shook it off. He couldn't have meant his comment the way it sounded, yet he still wore that pompous expression. Charlie decided it was best to end the conversation. "I turn back here," he said. "You can see the road north. Across the bridge Route 84 leads to the Thruway and back to the city… or up to Newfoundland."

* * *

Ansel descended the mountain. Breakneck Road would be exhilarating after a stimulant but that would violate one of his few hard and fast rules: never drive the Zagato high because he wouldn't be able to hold back. Even though he had to hurry to class, he wanted no trouble with traffic cops—who tended to pay attention to the bright red car. He held close to the speed limit.

He smiled, thinking how proud Charlie was of his Jaguar. The E-type was not much of a racer. Its V12 didn't put out enough power and made the car nose-heavy. Still, it was undeniably a beauty, which was what mattered most to Charlie.

In the city Ansel went directly from garage to campus. He strode into a full auditorium a few minutes late and launched into distinguishing vertical from horizontal propaganda, but he couldn't keep his mind off Charlie and Ireland. Veering from the class plan, he said, "How can propaganda mold facts? Trinity College in Dublin is a school steeped in tradition. Since its founding, clubs and student societies have been central to campus life. In 1770 students established a debate club called the Historical Society, known generally as 'the Hist.' Some seventy-three years later, the Philosophical Society, or 'the Phil,' was established, and since then the Phil and the Hist have competed for primacy on campus. One thing on the Hist's side, however, was its pedigree; it could lay claim as the oldest student society at Trinity."

"That was…until the 1990s, when the Phil's president discovered that in 1683 one William Molyneux formed the Dublin Philosophical Society or 'DPS.' Some DPS members went on to form the Royal Dublin Society, which exists to this day.

"But the Phil's president was not concerned with the facts. Instead, like a true propagandist, he made up his own facts, revising history to fit his needs. He claimed, with no evidence, that the Phil was the natural successor to the DPS. This set the 'historical' founding of the Phil in 1683, eighty-seven years *before* the Hist. The president simply revised history for his own purposes and he, and the Phil, never looked back."

Walking home Ansel regretted going off track in his lecture, when it was so important to make everyone forget his time in Dublin. What was he thinking? Next week he'd get back to World War I and weave in fake news—with no more mention of Ireland.

But that would have to wait. Directly after he got home he had to dig into Charlie's book. If it took all night, he had to get through the manuscript and gauge his problem. Hattie could feed the kid and get him to bed.

Hattie was ladling out pasta for True when Ansel arrived home. "Will you eat, Mr. Tone?" she said.

"Save me a plate, Hattie. I have to get to work and may be at it all night. I'm also going to need you to keep True occupied, see that he gets to bed, etcetera."

"Sure, Mr. Tone," she said matter-of-factly. "I can do that."

He was surprised by True's distraught look. "But you'll still do the labels on my poster, right?" True pleaded. "And glue the pictures?"

"Ah, not tonight, buddy. I have super-important work to do. But hey, we can do the poster tomorrow. I'm good at letters."

True looked at his feet.

"What is it?"

"It's due tomorrow."

Ansel shook his head. "Sorry, man. You know what? *Hattie* will help." Seeing this didn't satisfy his son, he improvised: "She has quite an artistic eye."

Hattie laughed, looking flattered. True stamped his foot and ran into his room. Ansel shrugged, grabbed an apple from the counter and stepped into his bedroom with Charlie's manuscript. The kid could fuss all he wanted. Ansel needed to get this done.

* * *

At dinner, Charlie told Tess about his afternoon. After years of ignoring the fact that Ansel lived and worked so near her office, she felt her heart speed up at the thought of him visiting her home. And she marveled that Charlie had shared his manuscript; he never let *her* see anything until after the editors worked on it. She wondered how Ansel would react to the sweeping "love story." Clearly, it was too late to convince Charlie to write about something else.

She kept seeing Ansel at the restaurant in his dazzling blue suit and thinking how she lost her breath when he hugged her. Did he hold her tighter than was called for? Did she imagine sparks flying?

She wondered how recent years would have gone if Tom Carter or some other Regis partner had Ansel's allure. But no one ever affected her like Ansel. Still, he dumped her in the end, and she was better off for it. She needed to rein in her fantasies.

* * *

By morning Ansel had finished the manuscript and buzzed with caffeine and nerves. That sap Charlie would sink him! It was not so much how he played up his romantic lead—which was predictable—but how he wrote about seizing his opportunity with his rival out of the way. "Stephen" (the Charlie character) worked late at the school paper the night of the party, and when he stopped at the dorm to change clothes, he saw "Evan" (the Ansel character) return to the dorm *alone*. Even worse, Stephen then saw Evan quickly leave his room and head across campus—in a dark hoodie! Damn! He had been so careful disposing of that sweatshirt.

This was a catastrophe, and *so* unnecessary! It would be easy to "correct" those details without affecting the romance or the story. Charlie should just write that Stephen saw Evan go into his room *with* a girl. That would clear the way for Stephen's move on the Tess character and establish that Evan was not sneaking around campus!

Why did this shit have to haunt him?

True was eating breakfast, trying not to look at Ansel, but he was frustrated his father didn't notice. Ansel looked angry at everyone. His eyes were red. He didn't even ask to see the poster, rolled up against True's backpack.

Then Ansel went to take a shower. He didn't say he was sorry. He didn't say "good luck" or anything. He acted like True wasn't there. Mom had asked him to give Ansel a chance, that he really wanted to be a good father, but that wasn't how it felt.

Chapter 20

Becca tried on the dress she wore on the rare occasions she went out dancing. Going to a hot new restaurant, she also wanted to borrow Roxy's red heels, but decided she better wear flats. While she bristled at Ansel lending her out to his friend, there was no sense making the guy feel insecure about his height.

She had had her share of boyfriends, but since coming to New York went out mostly in groups and romance wasn't often on her mind. She could always drag someone out to explore the city and hooked up with guys occasionally though not lately. Guys her age seemed more interested in beer pong and fantasy football than acting like grown men. She was better off focusing on her career.

She arrived a few minutes before the reservation, assuming her date would be late since he *was* the boss's friend. But when she approached the hostess, a big guy in a suit and tie tapped her shoulder.

"Hi, is it Becca?" he said. His disarming smile looked almost shy.

"Yes," she said. He reminded her of a big friendly dog, not at all what she expected. "And you must be Dutch."

He handed her a bouquet of white gardenias. "I guess this is corny," he said, "but I know Ansel probably sprung this on you and, well, I'm just glad to meet you."

She smelled the flowers and looked up at him like he was from another planet. His face was too big and square to be called handsome, but he had a good head of hair and certainly was tall. She wished she had borrowed those heels.

The restaurant was elegant, ultra-modern glass and stainless steel with chefs performing behind clear panels. The diners were dressed to impress: women in designer dresses; men in expensive suits or meticulously distressed jeans.

Dutch was quiet at first. But they were soon laughing at the menu's descriptions of unusual dishes, trying to keep quiet so no one would notice, which caused them to laugh more. Their waiter, an impossibly thin aspiring actor, took pity. He brought a vase for the flowers, helped them order sake and walked them through the menu.

Dutch seemed genuinely interested in what she had to say. Over appetizers they covered hometowns and schools and siblings. He told her he loved baseball and classical music. She said she was living her dream in New York and hoped to become an art photographer. But Ansel had set this up, so she was wary of what Dutch might expect. She was determined to bolt for the subway as soon as dinner was over.

Dutch lapped up her stories about her golden retriever and her father and growing up in a small town. He critiqued the wine coolers along one wall and said he sold restaurant equipment with his dad, which was good but sometimes challenging.

When she asked if his mother was still alive, he turned serious. She was afraid she had made a faux pas, highlighting their age gap or something, but he shook it off. Before she could make a joke of it, he blurted out, "This is such a cool place. The food is incredible, and you…"

"And I?"

"You…have such a healthy appetite."

Despite the mood-lighting, she was almost sure he blushed. She screwed up her face and smiled, wondering what he had intended to say. This guy was so earnest he could almost be from Wisconsin.

They discussed the recent Academy Awards and found they were both partial to old screwball comedies. And he knew much more than she did about the current presidential campaign.

"Growing up in the Midwest," she said, "I feel a little dopey about things like how much to trust the media."

"Well, clearly you shouldn't believe something just because it's called 'news,' but at least an established source like *The Washington Post* or *The Wall Street Journal* has standards. They fact check and corroborate. They don't always get it right but they're a hundred percent more reliable than, what did Trump call him, some three-hundred-pound guy sitting on his bed somewhere?"

"And *that* guy," she said. "He certainly commands attention."

"The three-hundred-pound guy?"

Becca laughed.

"Oh, you mean the candidate! He's an old story in *this* town, an old sordid story. You were fortunate to miss it, growing up in the Midwest."

"Oh, we saw him on TV, and he's rich, which carries weight with people who don't have much money."

"Yeah, *maybe* he is, or maybe that's just another part of the con."

They left off politics by agreeing none of the comical cast of Republican candidates would likely beat Hillary Clinton, even though they wished the Democrats could come up with a candidate with less baggage and a little more charm.

"She should make appearances with a dog," he said, "some breed that loves everyone, even her."

She looked down wistfully.

"I'm sorry," he said. "Did I hit a nerve?"

"Oh, don't apologize. I just miss Wolfy. He's my best friend and designated listener."

He looked at her thoughtfully. "I considered getting a dog," he said, "someone to share solitary moments, you know, without demanding much."

"Exactly! I talk to Wolfy in a language all our own, and he *always* gets it."

"A conduit to self-communication," he suggested and for a moment their eyes locked, but the waiter broke the spell when he appeared to top-off their sake.

As they pondered the proper way to eat their complicated entrees, she said, "I'm a little surprised you're such good friends with my boss."

"You *work* for Ansel?"

"Yeah, didn't he tell you? I do his social media."

"He didn't tell me much. And, honestly, we attended the same college, but I really only spent time with him over one year in Ireland. Until recently we spoke maybe twice in ten years."

This caught her by surprise. Why did Ansel set her up with this guy? She really didn't understand him at all. She shrugged. "I'm actually glad to hear that, Dutch. Because you know—and I'm trusting you to keep this to yourself—he is not always the nicest person."

He started to speak, then stopped, and they both laughed. "Well," he said, "I'm glad he arranged this dinner, anyway."

"Right," she agreed. "Without him, I don't know how I would have satisfied my yen for king crab amazu ponzu."

On the sidewalk after dinner, he said, "Can I see you home?"

"Oh, no, but thanks. You're Upper Eastside and I'm out in Brooklyn. But would you walk me to the subway?"

She was scrambling for an excuse not to give him her number when he asked. He was nice and the evening had been fun—like getting together with an old friend—but she wasn't looking for a relationship, and it would be cruel to lead on a straight-forward guy like him. Still, she liked having him walk beside her, the way he filled the sidewalk.

She also assumed he would kiss her goodnight, which would be okay as long as he didn't overdo it. At the subway stop, he handed her the bouquet from the table. Then he surprised her by holding out his big hand to shake. "Thank you, Becca," he said, gently taking her hand. "I can't remember when I've had such a good time."

In a crowded L train, she listened to quiet music through her headphones. It was funny, after all her apprehension, that she almost felt disappointed Dutch had not kissed her, or at least asked for her phone number. One way or another, dating always confused her.

Lowering her face to the gardenias, she marveled at how they blocked out the smell of the subway. It was just like how Dutch's guileless smile blocked out all the "beautiful people" trying so hard to be noticed. Who knew there were men like him in this city?

Chapter 21

Early Saturday Ansel opened the door to his office. True was sleeping, his sheet and blanket in a tangle mostly on the floor. Ansel stepped in quietly and covered him. It almost caught his breath seeing the little face pushed into the pillow.

He picked up a pad from the floor. True had drawn a black SUV with Henry smiling out the window and a hand waving from the back seat. Ansel had filled notebooks with sketches of cars when he was a kid. He wondered if the automobile obsession was genetic. He would have to see how True handled a socket wrench, he laughed, but then turned serious. Had life turned out differently, would his days be filled with moments like this?

He made coffee and popped a frozen bagel into the toaster. The newspaper was outside the door, but he couldn't focus on it. He had to get past this thing with Charlie or his world would come crashing down.

To take his mind off his troubles, he went into his bedroom to finish his last bit of cocaine. But the buzz made him obsess even more about Charlie's book. All he needed was one small change—and to make sure Dutch didn't reminisce with that woman about what happened after the final party. That, in any event, was something he *could* control. He walked out on the balcony and hit Becca's number.

"Hello?" she said hoarsely. He looked inside and saw it was seven o'clock. He had to stop getting high so early in the day.

"Oh, sorry, sorry," he said. "It's Ansel. Hey, I was headed out early but wanted… You know what, we can talk later."

She sighed and her voice livened up. "It's all right. I'm up. Everything okay? Something happen with True?"

"No, really. I just wondered how your dinner went. Good place?"

There was silence, then she said cautiously, "Yeah, it was nice. Great food. Pretty expensive."

"He *paid*, didn't he? You know he runs his own company?"

Now she seemed to come wide awake. "No, he didn't mention his company, other than he works with his dad. But yeah, he paid for dinner." She paused and then added quickly, "He was a perfect gentleman."

"Oh, I didn't doubt it for a minute." He tried to think of something else to say. "So, are you going to see him again?"

"I…" She hesitated. "I mean, *we* didn't talk about it. I guess we'll see."

"Oh, I just wondered. He's a great guy."

"Yeah, you said. Is there something else?"

"No, no, you go back to sleep. Sorry for calling so early. We'll speak Monday."

Ansel was not reassured. That chump didn't know what to do with a pretty young thing gift-wrapped and left at his door. He'd have to force them together again…maybe at the Mountain House party?

Before anything, though, he needed more information, and he needed to slow down. Too much coffee. He poured himself a short glass of bourbon to take the edge off the cocaine high and then tinkered with his *Redux* outline, making no progress.

When True woke up he was still angry about his Roanoke report. But Ansel had no patience for pouting and just put cereal, milk and orange juice on the table and let True watch cartoons in the living room while he ate breakfast.

Ansel returned to the balcony to call Dutch. "Hey, buddy," he said. "How was the date? Pretty hot babe, huh?"

"Yeah, she's nice," Dutch said reluctantly. "Thanks for setting it up."

"Will you see her again?"

"Oh, I don't know."

"Okay, well I thought I should pass on that she had a really good time. She asked if she could come to Charlie and Tess's party and maybe run into you again. Don't tell her I said anything, okay? She's a little shy."

"She said that?" Dutch sounded surprised. "No, I won't say anything. I'd like to see her, too."

After he hung up, Ansel looked in at True, hanging upside down off the edge of the sofa. What could he do with the kid while he took the car to Queens? He couldn't risk True meeting his grandfather; talk about Armageddon.

Then Drexler called. "Ansel, good morning. Have you got a minute?"

"Sure," he said, plugging in headphones so True wouldn't hear the *whole* conversation this time. "Is there news?"

"I've spoken to Ms. Canterwail's lawyer. I explained the litigation hurdles she would face. He seems close to talking his sister-in-law around to a financial settlement and a correction of the acknowledgments, but she's resisting. She wants an apology from you."

Ansel gritted his teeth. The last thing he wanted was to meet with that woman.

Drexler continued. "I'm sensing you've changed your mind about a personal meeting?"

"You sense right, counselor." It was time to get past this crap and focus on important matters.

"Well, I have another idea. What about a letter of recommendation 'to whom it may concern': something she can use looking for work?"

"Do you think she'd go for that?"

"She might. We'll put together a letter and an insert for the book and send them to Leah today. If you approve, I'll put it all before Ms. Canterwail's lawyer. And, as to money, he asked about profits from the book but I convinced him the accounting is so convoluted it makes more sense to just talk turkey. You gave me authority up to a hundred thousand, so I offered thirty. He came back with a hundred. I'm sure we'll split the difference, sixty to seventy-five."

"Okay. Good. Let's get this done."

Having arranged the budding romance and given instructions on settlement, Ansel felt free to plan the morning. He needed to bring the car to his father's shop, but what could he do with True? Hattie had gone to her sister's house for the weekend, and he couldn't call Becca again after waking her up on a stupid pretext. If only he knew a neighbor, but befriending building residents had never been a priority.

He would have to bring the boy along. There was no reason for Jordan to be at work on a Saturday. Carlo would be quick, and then Ansel would take True to see his mother and maybe on a drive to check out the car.

True got over his disappointment about the school project when he saw he was going on an adventure. He was surprised Ansel's car lived under a canvas cover, and amazed when it came off to reveal the sleek red automobile.

"This is *your* car?" he said in wonder.

"It is," Ansel replied with pride, although it belonged to Jordan's company. "So, hop in."

True looked confused. "There's no back seat."

"That's right, little man. Today you ride shotgun."

True ran his hands over the seats and looked around like he was in a spaceship.

"Is it fast?"

Ansel smiled. "Very, but speed is only one advantage of a world-class automobile."

Carlo was at the shop. His short-cropped graying hair contrasted with bright, dark eyes. His "MacTone Motors" jumpsuit was immaculate. Ansel knew cars, but the native Italian was a magician.

"Mr. Ansel," Carlo laughed, reaching out both hands to shake. At one time Ansel thought of asking Carlo to call him "Professor Tone," or even just "Ansel," but it was hard to break a habit in place since he was a kid.

"Carlo, my friend," Ansel replied. "So good to see you, and I hope Mrs. Righetti is well?"

"Ah, Mrs. Righetti, you know, she is fat and healthy and keeps me on my toes."

Ansel smiled at the ritual exchange. Carlo turned friendly eyes on the boy. "And who is this handsome young man? You have brought maybe an expert to watch over my work?"

True beamed, and Ansel smiled uncomfortably. He'd forgotten to concoct a cover story. "Ah, this is True, uhm, my driver in training." He handed the boy a couple of dollars and turned him by his shoulders toward the vending machines. "Why don't you see what kind of candy bars they've got?"

True raced off clutching the bills. The men watched him go, and then Carlo turned a questioning look toward Ansel.

"I'm taking care of him while his mother's in the hospital. But you've got to keep this to yourself, okay?"

"Whatever you say, Mr. Ansel. But he *is* a handsome boy."

Ansel nodded. "So listen, Carlo, I haven't got a lot of time. I took the Zagato upstate this week and got a chance to open her up."

Carlo raised an eyebrow.

"Well," Ansel admitted, "I don't mean 'opened her up' like on the autobahn, but I got in a good run on a winding mountain road…like the Amalfi Coast without the tourists."

Carlo nodded eagerly.

"And we need to check whether the cylinders are firing perfectly."

"I see," Carlo said, suddenly serious. "Fabio!" he shouted into the garage, "take Mr. Ansel's car into the bay number one."

Carlo turned back to Ansel. "You like maybe an espresso?"

"No, Carlo, thanks. Let's get under the hood."

Once Fabio drove the car into place—and True returned with a candy bar to join the inspection—the booming voice of Jordan MacTone pierced the noise of the garage. "Do you know what it costs to tie up my senior mechanic all morning?"

Carlo stood up slowly, an obsequious smile in place. Ansel pulled his head up so fast it hit the underside of the hood. True looked around in confusion. Before Ansel could speak, Jordan strode over, bristling.

"Having your picture in a magazine doesn't entitle you to monopolize my shop," Jordan said to Ansel. "And you," he spat at Carlo. "Aren't you supposed to be on the Maserati?"

"Yes sir, Mr. MacTone," Carlo responded. "Luis and Jose are running the analytics now. We'll have Mr. Hyde's car ready in plenty of time."

"It was me," Ansel interjected, hesitantly.

His father turned, focusing steely eyes within a reddened face.

"I asked Carlo to take a quick look at the Aston. A cylinder is misfiring."

Jordan peered at Ansel, then turned his attention to the boy. "And this is?" he snapped.

"Ah, yeah," Ansel stuttered, "this is True. We're spending the day together while his mother recuperates from an accident."

"True?" Jordan said in a mocking tone, as if that could not be a *real* name. He scrutinized the boy, who stepped closer to Ansel. Ansel met Jordan's gaze with only a slight flinch.

Jordan shrugged and turned to the car, crowding out his son to look at the engine. He had no patience with people but he did value an exceptional car, especially a rare model he had pulled strings to purchase. Jordan nodded for Carlo to continue and watched the mechanic work.

When Carlo told Fabio to start it up, Jordan listened for a moment and then turned abruptly to Ansel. "With me," he said and walked off. Ansel looked desperately at Carlo, who nodded and placed an arm around True's shoulder.

Ansel followed his father to a glassed-in office at the end of the garage. Jordan growled at a woman at a desk that he needed the room and she scurried through a door. Ansel stood silently, hands crossed in front of him.

"What is this I hear," Jordan growled, "about you *not* attending my reception in Newport?"

"I..." Ansel began.

"The dealer hosting this cotillion does more high-end business for us than the rest of New England put together. For whatever reason, the codgers up there—or their old biddy wives, I don't know—find you an attraction, probably because of the promo shots of you with the Aston I so generously leave in your care. You *will* make an appearance."

"I'm sorry, Father. My publisher set up a book tour."

Jordan stared until his son turned away. "You'll *make* the time. Fly in and out the same day; I don't care. But I *need* you there for dinner and the presentations."

"Yes, Father."

"And beyond this tune-up," Jordan continued, "the Aston is performing?"

"Oh yes, sir. She is all we hoped she would be." His father had taught him to refer only to the finest automobiles as "she."

"Good. Send your itinerary to Marcia, and this time be mindful of the audience if you *must* bring a date."

Two years earlier Ansel had made a long weekend of his trip to a similar reception in Charleston, escorting an exquisite singer from Argentina. The local gentry assumed her flawless dark skin indicated a multi-racial background, which upset their bigoted sensibilities. Ansel got grief from his father for months afterward.

"Yes, sir," Ansel said. "I won't bring anyone."

"Better yet," Jordan said. "That's all."

Ansel turned toward the garage, but Jordan spoke again. "And who is this kid you're carting around?"

"Ah, there was this woman..."

"I thought so. Always the same with you. And she's got you watching her brat?"

"Well, she's in the hospital, so I offered to help out."

"You're soft, Ansel. Some woman crooks her little finger and you become a nanny."

Ansel wanted to shout, "He's your grandson, you old shit!" but he kept quiet. Nothing good could come from Jordan getting his hooks into the boy.

Jordan stared at his son in a way Ansel used to call "x-ray eyes." Ansel could not be sure what he was thinking but was certain it followed a standard theme: Ansel the fuck-up, or Ansel the cause of his mother's death. Jordan never let him forget his mother's accident. It would not have happened if Ansel had not been so stupid; that was true. But Jordan refused to acknowledge he shared the blame.

It was Christmas break during Ansel's last year in boarding school. If Jordan had only given him a reasonable allowance, spending money wouldn't have been an issue. Instead, he had to scrape by and so came up with the plan to buy a pound of weed in the city, bring it to school and sell it as half-ounces. The markup would get him through to the summer.

Bringing Jayne along made sense, too. She had been standoffish on their first date but was dazzled by the idea of playing desperado. He was sure they'd hook up afterward on sheer adrenaline. She'd also provide cover if they were stopped.

After sampling the weed before he bought it, they should *not* have smoked more driving home. But they did, and when her giggles distracted him and he missed a stop sign, Sergeant Delio appeared out of nowhere. He stepped back to avoid the cloud of smoke when Ansel opened his window and spotted the bag of weed in plain sight.

Thankfully, Delio knew Ansel's father. He didn't book them; he just called Jordan. Then, after the tragedy with Ansel's mother later that night, Delio disposed of the weed and any charges against Ansel. Instead, the conscientious public servant offered his sympathy—while starting to plan the security company Jordan would help him launch after he retired. Jordan made clear *that* expense went on Ansel's account.

Their housekeeper later told Ansel about a loud argument between his mother and father that night. The cops took Jayne home right away, but Jordan told them to hold Ansel until morning, to teach him a lesson. His mother rarely stood up to his father, but she was frantic to get her son out of jail. Finally, she slipped out and drove to the station house on her own. She had poor eyesight and never drove at night. She should not have been behind the wheel in her state of mind, and on icy roads. Her accident was Ansel's fault—since she was coming to spring him—but Jordan shared the blame for letting her go alone.

Back in the shop, the Aston hummed like a rare old violin. Ansel said "*Grazie*" and gestured in helpless apology. Carlo shook this off.

"Thanks for showing me how it works!" True said to Carlo, oblivious of the tension around him.

Carlo bowed, offered his hand to True and sent them off with a salute. Ansel got True out of the garage fast, fearful his father might return.

When they reached the hospital, Florence was sitting up in a chair, more alert than on their last visit. True ran to smother her with hugs. She laughed in a way that brought back happy memories, as she gingerly guided the boy away from the casts on her arm and leg.

"What have you guys been up to?" she asked.

Ansel started to speak but True cut in. "We drove Ansel's really cool car to this huge place with all these other cars, and this guy who talked funny but was nice looked under the hood, and then this big, loud guy wanted to talk to Ansel, so the other guy showed me how the motor works...."

When True ran out of breath, Ansel summarized: "We took my car in for tune-up, and True met Carlo. You remember him?"

"Of course! The Italian with the fat wife," she laughed.

"Right. Some things never change."

"And the big loud guy?" She raised an eyebrow.

"You got it," Ansel sneered. "The devil himself blustered through. I didn't fill him in about *anything*."

Florence nodded her understanding and turned to muss True's hair and hug him again. Ansel went down the hallway for coffee and caught up with the doctor.

"All indications are that Florence is on the mend," the doctor said.

"She is strong and willing herself to get up and going so she can care for her son. She should be on crutches within days and able to go home, assuming she can arrange for some help over the next few weeks."

"That's great," Ansel said sincerely. "We'll get someone in."

He thought for a moment how True had grown on him. It was not fair to the boy or himself for him to live outside True's life. Strangely, having the boy around also changed how Ansel felt about other things. But it was time to focus on what was most important: getting True home and finding a way to revise Charlie's book. Nothing could get in the way of fixing the story of Dublin; otherwise, he would be no good as a father or anything else.

They headed out on Long Island. Ansel wanted to check the car and True seemed to enjoy the drive. Ansel wondered again if he had inherited some of that motor oil in his veins. He smiled at the image of True and Carlo with their heads under the hood.

They took Grand Central Parkway and the Meadowbrook south to Jones Beach. It was still cool, and the big parking lot was nearly empty. They took off their shoes and hiked across the beach to the water. True was mesmerized by the waves and kept standing too close until the water splashed his rolled-up pants. After a while they sat together watching two teenagers bodyboard in wetsuits.

"I want to be a surfer when I'm bigger," True said.

Ansel smiled. "You can do anything you set your mind to."

True looked up as if these were wise words. It surprised Ansel that anyone would take such platitudes so solemnly. Then he thought about the truth of it. Had he succeeded by hard work, his own work? Was the Canterwail mess his fault for not doing all of his own work, and was this the underlying source of all his problems? The mess in Dublin, after all, stemmed from the same thing.

"Who was that big man?" True asked.

"You mean at the garage? The guy with the huge head?"

"Yeah. He wasn't nice. Do you know him?"

"I *do* know him. He owns that place, and he gets excited about cars. He's just a big potato head." He puffed up his cheeks and framed his face with his hands.

True laughed. Then out of nowhere said, "Why don't you and Mom live together?"

"Oh, it's a long story, True. You'll understand when you're older."

"But then she got in an accident and you came to help."

"Well, yeah. You see, your Mom and I aren't together but we still share some things. Mostly, we share you. I couldn't leave you on your own. You're my *son*, and a father doesn't desert his son."

True thought hard. "I'm glad," he said.

Chapter 22

Sunday morning Tess was gardening on the terrace when her phone rang.

"Morning, Tess, it's Molly. Pete took the kids to the park and I could actually sit down for a minute, so I thought I'd give you a call."

"Hey, Momma. So glad you got a break." Tess plugged in headphones and continued pruning.

"I wanted to check: you really want us to bring the little monsters to your party?"

"Absolutely! Your kids will liven things up."

"That's what concerns me. I'm worried about white carpets and fragile sculptures."

"Molly, get real. Everyone wants to meet your kids, and I'm sure they're angels. Besides, we live with a hundred-and-thirty-pound slobbering child who bumps into everything and spreads hair everywhere. Whatever is Seusy-proof will certainly be child-proof."

"Well, I tried. You know, seeing you all the other night reminded me how I miss adult conversation."

"Well, *honest* conversation. I see people at work but everyone's always busy or posing. It's different with people who knew you as a kid. They know who you are, so you have to relax." Tess thought about Ansel and decided maybe "relax" was not the right word.

Molly asked about her job and the partnership process. Tess said she was on track for promotion, but her boss could be just stringing her along to buy a few more years of slave labor.

"But you like what you do, right?"

"Well, it's intellectually challenging and the money's good, but the hours are rough and, frankly, corporate deals at my level can be a little dry."

"What do you mean 'your level'?"

"It's not like I come up with the idea or make the deal. The decision makers are always two guys—yes, two *men*—Frank and Harry or whatever—and their teams have to negotiate all night so Frank can sign and take off on his sailboat or because Harry wants to announce the deal before quarterly results."

"And here I pictured you poised in stilettos and a tailored suit, dazzling with your confidence and your style."

"Right. That happens too." They both laughed.

"So, what about you?" Tess said. "*Another* kid? You trying to build a whole basketball team?"

"Oh, I know. It's crazy, certainly not what we planned. I don't look forward to a hot summer of tender breasts and being tired all the time. But I'm trying to savor it this time, sure to be my last. Luckily, there is something life-affirming—well, obviously life-affirming—but really something magical about it all."

"I envy you."

"Oh, how could *you* envy *me*, with your career, your fabulous house and your author husband?"

"Well, they're not all they're cracked up to be," Tess said, thinking she could improve on each of those points.

"Listen, hon, I know we don't talk enough, and it's none of my business anyway, but I got an uneasy feeling at our dinner party and when we talked last week. Are things all right, between you and Charlie, I mean?"

Tess looked out at the valley. A flight of geese flew toward the horizon in a wobbly vee-formation.

"You don't have to say anything," Molly continued. "I just, well, our year in Dublin meant so much to me, and you, particularly, meant a lot. And, I wanted you to know I'm here and you can talk to me."

Tess felt a lump in her throat. "I can't tell you how much that means to me, Molly. You're so right, and it seems like I never *really* talk to anyone. I just don't know what to say about Charlie and me. I really don't."

"It must be hard with your long commute and the ups and downs of publishing."

"That's part of it. I don't know. At one time I admired how hard he worked, how dedicated he was, but lately…."

Molly was silent.

"Well," Tess went on, "when things went off the tracks with the last book and the movie, he got sullen and self-centered. Everything was about *him*, and everyone was out to get him. He never thought about how it all affected *me*. And then he gets down on me for working late or thinks I'm messing around with my boss, which is insane. You'd have to meet my boss: rep ties, ridiculously conspicuous comb-over. I don't know. I think Charlie even suspects I still have feelings for Ansel."

"Oh, *that's* not true, is it?"

"Of course not! I haven't thought about him in years, not until dinner the other night."

Molly hesitated. "That sounds like you *have* been thinking about him *since* our dinner."

"No, not at all! I just meant getting together again, I don't know, brought back memories." Her explanation sounded unconvincing, but what could she say? She couldn't stop thinking about Ansel in that blue suit.

Molly paused. "Well, anyway, Charlie is excited about the new book."

"I guess. Even so, I wish he'd find a subject that doesn't involve me and the whole mess about my breakup with Ansel."

"You know, I never could understand what you saw in him."

"Well, let's see: he was exciting and gorgeous and rich, oh, and did I mention he was great in bed?"

"Yeah, a few dozen times. Of course, he was also full of himself and a bit sketchy. You were lucky you got rid of him."

"I know, but it's hard to shake the vision. Ireland and all; it was so enchanting. I guess Charlie can't compete with a memory, but I never went head-over-heels for Charlie the way I did for Ansel."

"You're talking about a fairy tale. We were twenty years old, Tess, living in an enchanted city; our whole lives were fantasy. But now we're grown up, and you've got a great guy, and you married him."

"Yes, Charlie was there when I needed something constant in my life. I don't know. We just kind of got swept up into marrying."

"Listen, he's a solid guy, and it's clear he loves you."

"I know." Charlie loved her, though not as much as his own creative genius. "Ansel is just the same as always, and you were always my voice of reason."

Molly paused. "You haven't seen him since our dinner, have you?"

"Ansel?" Tess said, caught off-guard. "No, of course not. When could I have seen him?"

Tess heard commotion at Molly's end. "Theo, take off those muddy shoes!" Molly shouted. "Listen, hon, I've got to help Pete herd the wild animals. Can we pick this up later tonight?"

"Oh, not tonight. Charlie wants to go out to dinner and I've got an early morning." She stared at the sunlight dappling the valley. "Everything's fine; don't worry about me." She could always retreat into her fairy tale.

Chapter 23

Ansel came out to the kitchen as Hattie and True were leaving for school. When they reached the door, True ran back to hug him. When they left Ansel felt as if part of himself was straying beyond his reach, beyond where he could keep it safe. He hadn't reckoned on fatherhood involving this kind of vulnerability.

Becca showed up a half-hour later, all smiles. "How's my favorite guru?" Ansel asked.

"On the job, boss, and we're trending on Twitter."

"Oh yeah, my department head saw the poster video on YouTube and reminded me we must discourage students from posting lectures. I mentioned it might bring attention to the fall classes, but he wasn't convinced."

She shrugged her shoulders.

After they reviewed the hits on various apps, they discussed misinformation posted on Ansel's Wikipedia page. "What can we do about it?" he asked.

"We could revise the article ourselves, but better to post a comment to the editor. We just explain it's *you* asking for a correction."

"And they'll fix it?"

"As long as we improve the page. They want to get the facts straight."

"But how does misinformation get there?"

"Fake news," she said with a smile.

He looked up in frustration but the sparkle in her eyes stopped him and he smiled as well. He was definitely getting soft.

* * *

Ansel was on the stationary bike in the late afternoon when Leah called, so Becca took the call. "I finally found him the right date for the Met Gala," Leah said.

Becca was pleased Leah was confiding in her but a little confused. "Why doesn't he just take one of his girlfriends?"

"Oh, we couldn't leave this to him. This event is too big a deal. He's focused as always on who he can get into bed, but we have to think about his image."

Becca winced. Leah saw Ansel's predatory nature as obvious and pitiable, which reminded Becca how blind she had been. But, like Roxy always said, there was no point dwelling on the past.

"This is the premiere event of the fashion season," Leah continued, "so his date has to make an impression. And, fabulous agent that I am, I lined up Kat Tiergarten. She's the young actress in *Graduation Day*."

"I saw that. She was the younger sister?"

"Right. The movie was a hit, not to mention she is quite attractive, so she'll draw attention. Ansel is amused they won't meet until the night of the event."

"Like a royal marriage."

"Something like that. Anyway, he's seen the movie, and Kat presumably knows who *he* is, so they should both be happy with their date of convenience. For PR photos we'll have to rely on the fashion press, and Kat's ability to wear a skin-tight dress without bending over. Anyway, Ansel will have a glamorous date on his arm."

"And for once he won't stand out in a crowd," Becca said, wishing she could attend this event. She could hold her own in that crowd if she could borrow the right dress. She saw herself sipping champagne by the Temple of Dendur, some tuxedoed hunk on her arm.

"That's right, honey, but don't let him hear *you* say it."

Becca smiled. She was starting to like Leah, or maybe it was respect. Leah didn't care about stylish clothes or whether people thought she was pushy. She just dug in and did her job, and you had better get along or get out of her way. It was funny: people back home thought Becca so tough and fearless just to be living in New York. She didn't feel tough. She'd match up better against the fashionistas at the Met Gala than against Leah.

"So what's next?" Ansel said, wiping his forehead with a towel. Becca turned from the vision of her sequined gown to her ideas for the website launch. She had loaded a program to animate the cover photo so one photograph melted into another. She thought this communicated the revisionism theme and he liked the idea, so they sorted through photos to use with the cover image: Ansel with gorgeous women, Ansel with television personalities, Ansel with his car.

He mentioned he'd be attending a party in a few weeks at the house of the author, Charles Piedmont III. "It's called 'Mountain House.' It's up the Hudson in Cold Spring and really stunning. I thought you could drive up with me in the Zagato."

Her warning antennae shot up. The house sounded interesting—and she loved *Against the Odds* and would like to get her copy signed—but she needed to understand this invitation. Was this some kind of weekend getaway? Was he looking for an escort?

"I should come along as what? Your employee? Your date?"

"Oh, don't get me wrong. I'm talking about a nice afternoon with friends and dinner at a fabulous house overlooking the valley. Think of it as a reward for your good work. We'll drive up and back, no strings attached. And there'll be interesting people there. Dutch will be there."

So *that* was it. He was still pushing her at the big appliance salesman. She should have known he wouldn't just be nice. After having been fixed up with another hapless friend of a friend over the weekend, she recalled how much she had enjoyed dinner with Dutch. Still, she was not going to keep working for Ansel if he thought he could tell her who to date. It didn't matter what a plum job it was.

"Hey, no pressure," Ansel said. "I think he liked you, but he's got a lot going on, and he's not the type to push anything. There'll be other people you'll want to meet, too. And it'll be a day in the country."

"Let me think about it, okay? My roommates have been talking about going to the beach, and I sort of said I would go along." She realized her response sounded like treading water, but he didn't push, so she left it there.

* * *

Early in the afternoon Ed Gamber arrived with the settlement papers. Ansel signed the agreement and the recommendation letter. Leah would wire sixty-five thousand dollars to Drexler.

Before dinner Ansel pulled True aside. "Can you come with me for a second?" he said, leading the way into his office. With the Canterwail mess resolved, he thought he should direct some effort toward being a father.

When the boy was seated in the desk chair, spinning back and forth, Ansel dialed his phone and put it on speaker.

"Hello," a woman's voice answered.

"Karla, this is Ansel Tone."

"Oh," she said, obviously surprised. "I didn't expect to hear from you."

"I know, and I'm sorry I didn't reach out sooner. Do you have a minute?"

"Sure, Professor, whatever you say."

"Oh, no need for the 'professor' stuff. I don't deserve it." He paused to collect himself. "I want you to know I have my young son here listening because I think it's important he hear his father admit to making a mistake and try to make amends. You probably know I signed the settlement papers. You should already have the payment and the letter."

"Yes, my brother-in-law sent everything over this afternoon."

"Well, you can count on me recommending you for employment at every opportunity, but more than that I want to offer my sincere apology. You did excellent work and I used it without your consent and gave you no credit. It was wrong of me, and I am truly sorry."

"I'm touched, Professor, a little surprised but mostly touched. Thank you for calling."

He hung up and looked at True, whose face was frozen in confusion and amazement.

* * *

True was happy when Ansel joined him for dinner. Hattie made hamburgers and French fries, and Ansel said he didn't have to eat the salad.

"How come I can't come to the party?" True asked.

Ansel laughed. "Oh, you wouldn't like it. You have to get dressed up and stand around while the ladies have their pictures taken."

"Sounds *boring*. But what about the dinosaurs?"

"No, that's Natural History—we'll go there sometime. This is the Metropolitan Museum of Art."

True thought about this. "But do they have stuff to eat?"

"Well, they do," Ansel responded, tossing a French fry into the air and catching it in his mouth. "But when you're all dressed up, it's bad form to stuff your face with jumbo shrimp."

"Shrimp! Gross!"

Ansel laughed. "Right, or little French snails."

True moaned and plugged his ears.

After dinner True sat on the bed and watched Ansel put on his tuxedo. "Do you always wear such fancy clothes to parties?" he said.

"I do for this event. My date is a movie star, and she'll be wearing a beautiful gown." He pulled out his phone and showed True a shot from Kat's movie, where she looked about sixteen years old.

True had no interest in girls, but he'd seen this actress on one of his shows and she was pretty, even if she *was* old. He wondered at how amazing Ansel's life was. His car, his apartment, the clothes he wore, that girl he was going out with: it was like a video game, where you could do whatever you wanted.

"Are you driving the red car?" he asked excitedly.

"No. Henry—you remember him, right?—he'll be driving us."

"In the big black car?"

"Right. I don't want to park at the museum, so it's better for Henry to drop us off."

"When I grow up, I want Henry to drive me in that car."

Ansel paused in tying his bow tie and noticed how the boy's eyes seemed to fill his face. He wondered if he was overdoing it, introducing his son to this glamour when he would soon return to his little Chelsea apartment. But there was nothing to be done about that now. He'd talk to True later.

Ansel emerged from the building feeling like he was born in a tuxedo. Henry was leaning against the SUV. "Looking sharp, professor," he said, his smile a mile wide.

Once Henry pulled away from the curb, Ansel asked about the cocaine.

"Oh, Professor mon, I am so sorry but the man, he is gone from town until later in this week."

Ansel chewed on this and decided he'd make the most of the evening anyway. He went into the hotel lobby to escort Kat to the car. In the back seat, he focused on her like a laser. She seemed nervous and grateful for the attention. He got a kick out of performing with Henry watching through the mirror.

The gala was over-the-top, as expected: strutting overdressed women, cameras clicking. Even the photographers were dressed up for this event. Only a few women stuck to the *Manus x Machina* theme of man-made versus machine-made clothing in the age of technology. Most focused instead on promoting their best physical assets and an attitude of entitlement.

Ansel's date stopped on a landing to pirouette beneath his raised arm in a spontaneous dance move that brought hoots from the photographers. Then Ansel stepped aside so Kat could be photographed alone. He smiled genuinely. She could not be more than twenty years old but had parlayed high cheekbones, cat-like eyes and a great stage name into early success. He'd give her a go tonight, depending on how the evening progressed. But then he remembered he had no apartment! He needed for Florence to go home and give him back his life!

At any rate, this is where he belonged, among the rich and famous. With the beauty on display, he would normally have worked the room. But decorum kept couples linked, and he must help Kat maneuver so she could be admired—and appropriately appreciative later in the evening.

The museum was festooned with walls of red roses, purple lights and drapes: backdrops for more photo ops. There were so many entertainers, models and athletes that Ansel had an unusual feeling of anonymity and had to admit he was a little star-struck. No one would look for his autograph in *this* crowd. In a way it was liberating, and he thought he really would gorge on the crab cakes if he didn't have to stand by to keep Kat upright. He could only snag hors d'oeuvres and champagne from passing trays.

An hour and a half on crazy-high heels left Kat ready to collapse. Ansel saw this as good fortune and called Henry. They had put in their appearance; there was no need to prolong the show.

In the car heading downtown, he suggested a quiet nightspot, but all she wanted was to return to her hotel and get out of her dress. "I support that idea," he said, thinking the evening was looking up.

But she didn't even recognize his advance. She asked for the phone he carried for her and texted her handlers. They met her at the hotel door, where she kissed his cheek absently and said they should get together again soon.

He returned to the car shaking his head, then met Henry's expression in the rear-view mirror. "Pleasant evening, Professor?" Henry said, in quiet amusement.

Ansel did not like being patronized, especially by a teenager. But this was Henry, and things with the young actress were stacked against him from the beginning. "Home, Henry," he laughed. He'd take another at-bat with Kat in a few years, when he was not encumbered with a son and she had matured into a twenty-three-or-four-year-old sensation.

Sitting on his balcony with his jacket off and bow tie undone, he sipped bourbon on the rocks. He was pleased with where things stood. True was asleep, Canterwail was resolved and tenure was within reach. The *Redux* books had legs to go on for years. Florence would be home soon and everything would go back to normal. He just needed to complete his maddening dance with history.

Chapter 24

The doctors were sending Florence home. Ansel offered to pick her up and hired Hattie to help Florence and True at their apartment.

Henry drove them all to the hospital. Florence was wheeled out but immediately pushed herself up on crutches. Her beaming smile reminded Ansel of their early days. Her energy was the best thing for their son. And through it all she remained ethereal, like she could raise her arms and twirl out of sight.

True stuck by his mother's side like a border collie. At the apartment, Ansel and True helped her while Henry carried bags and Hattie took over the kitchen and brewed tea. Ansel then sent Henry home but stayed himself to help get things settled. Neighbors dropped by, including Helen, who had taken True in after the accident. It made Ansel easier knowing people like her were nearby.

When he stopped by the boy's room to say goodbye, True said, "Does this mean I won't see you anymore?"

"Are you nuts?" Ansel said, making light of the question so real for them both. "You think anything could keep me from my favorite son?"

"I'm your *only* son."

"Right, and I told you a father does not desert his son. No, I'm sorry for the time we've missed, really I am. I'll show you. We'll get together lots. Tell you what: we'll go back to the beach, and I'll show you an even cooler part. Not this weekend—you should be here with your mom—but let's say the *next* Saturday for sure."

"Promise?" True said, eyes alight.

"Absolutely, we'll make a day of it." Ansel held out his hand to shake. True tried to grip hard like his father taught him.

Ansel added, "And I'll buy you a boogie board, and maybe it'll be warm enough to swim."

"Oh, man!" True shouted.

"I'll work things out with your mom. But remember, you're the man of the house, and your mom will need your help getting around."

"Don't worry, Ansel. I'll take care of her."

* * *

Bud arrived at Aljo's office Thursday wearing a pressed suit and salesman's smile. He pitched various insurance policies to Dutch and his father, and then Dutch walked him out.

"How do you think it went?" Bud asked.

"No worries. Dad always tries to seem aloof at the start of a deal. He thinks it makes him a good negotiator."

"Is he still active in the business?"

"Well, I suspect that meeting will conclude his business for the day."

"I get it. Hey, did I hear Ansel was fixing you up with a date?"

"Yeah, and he did. How did you know?"

"I heard him at the game. It sounded like he really didn't want you calling that girl in California."

"Yeah, I thought the same," Dutch said, eyebrows furrowing.

"You ought to tell Ansel she's coming in for a visit and ask if he wants to get together."

"I don't even know if that's funny. Something about how he acted, and this thing with Becca, make me pretty sure he doesn't want to see Reilly again. I wonder what happened between them that night."

"It always comes back to that night, doesn't it?"

Chapter 25

Having the apartment to himself was liberating but Ansel found that he missed True. Having the boy with him gave him a strange kind of strength, as if his son set a foundation, made sense of who Ansel was.

But he had to get things moving. First, he called Charlie.

"You finished the manuscript already?" Charlie asked in amazement.

"Like I said, I have time now but soon I'll be buried. Can you get down to the city to talk about it?"

"Absolutely. I'm coming in Tuesday to meet my agent. What about then?"

"I've got a class and then office hours, but I could meet you in Midtown at say…six-thirty?"

"Perfect. I'll finish up and meet you at the Shakespeare. It's on 39th east of Madison."

Ansel hung up and checked his watch. It was almost time for the monthly departmental meeting. He looked wistfully at the bottle on his bookshelf but decided not even a slug of excellent bourbon would make the afternoon palatable.

In a Havermeyer conference room, Professor Flagel was gathering papers at the head of a large table. Small talk centered on when, if ever, the Second Avenue subway would open. Ansel took a seat and checked his phone. Leah had texted that Harvey wanted to see a completed outline. Old news.

"Uhum, yes, let us begin," Flagel said, swiveling a look around the room. He ran through dates for evaluations of teaching assistants and summarized a budget report. He thanked two colleagues for their seminar on pre-Soviet Russian history and asked those remaining in the city for the summer to let him know if they could help interview for a new ancient civilizations position.

Ansel blocked out the drone. He could only think about the manuscript. There was no way to convince Charlie he was mistaken about what he saw, but he *could* suggest a plot twist. The real facts didn't matter, like Charlie said. It was only important to engage the reader. The best story would tell what *should* have happened, not what *did* happen. Ansel's idea would improve the plot (and only incidentally omit incriminating details).

As for Dutch, it didn't matter if Becca was actually interested in him. As long as she strung him along, maybe he'd forget about that woman in California, or Ansel could find someone else for him, someone more his speed. Maybe Leah could scare up some lonely, four-eyed copy editor?

When the meeting broke up, Flagel pulled Ansel aside. "So," he said, "about that video uhum, on the internet. Do you have suspicions about the source?"

"You know, Ed, it's so easy to shoot video these days. Everyone's got a phone and half the kids use them during lectures. I don't think we'll to be able to track this down."

"I suppose, uhum, it's partly the classicist in me holding the ramparts against the modern world. Still, we must control what goes online from our classes. Do you know Jim Klein? He teaches computer science and said there is often some kind of 'watermark' that identifies the source of a video. I might follow up just to see where that leads. There's probably not much we could, or would want to do, but I am curious."

Ansel couldn't believe Flagel was pursuing this. Had he nothing better to do? And could someone actually trace the video back to Becca and then to him, after he had denied knowing its source? That would certainly sink Ansel's promotion.

His publisher, his agent, his ex-wife, his idiot classmate and now Edmund Flagel: they were all conspiring to muck up his life. Why couldn't he just teach his classes, write his books, screw that brunette in Propaganda and be left alone?

Next day Ansel checked with Becca whether anything could tie them to the video. She doubted it but said she'd ask a friend who designed software.

With True gone, Ansel was able to finish the *Redux* outline. It was thin but connected the dots between "fake news" and authoritarian regimes. This would get Harvey off his back. Charlie and Dutch also should be easy to steer, which would squelch any incriminating stories about Dublin. Maintaining composure was all it took to wrap up everything and move on. For the moment, he would let it ride and find some diversion for his weekend.

At Thursday's office hour, three students from Ansel's Communications in Politics class showed up, confused about their assignment, so he concluded his instructions had been unclear. He was drafting an email to head off more lost students when there was a soft knock on the door.

It turned out the brunette from Propaganda was named Georgia Howell. She spoke in a slow southern accent and was even better looking up close than she had been in the auditorium: dark piercing eyes, more curves than any one girl should have.

She had a question about the fake news assignment. He offered her a seat, struggling to keep his eyes on hers. But she wore a tight black sweater that made his mouth water, and when she stretched to look at a book on the shelf, his gaze was drawn to her breasts like light into a black hole.

When she looked back at him, his eyes snapped up to hers. She smiled, knowingly. "So, Professor, if information is an essential part of propaganda, and the 'fake news' label undercuts the legitimacy of information, doesn't the public's acceptance of the fake news concept undermine its susceptibility to propaganda?"

"I see you've been paying attention," he said, thinking this was too easy. "Well, propaganda can't distort local facts, where its recipients can see the distortion. But propaganda *can* effectively assail a larger or more remote fact. In 1958, Khrushchev labelled previous agricultural production figures as 'false,' so he could claim greater gains under his own stewardship. Denouncing 'a lie' meant he *must* be telling the truth. In the same way, Donald Trump labels any embarrassing fact as 'fake news' and so his followers believe it must be false, despite any evidence to the contrary."

She looked impressed and eager, but he had to be cautious. There was no explicit university policy against faculty relations with students, but that was the trend. It was hard to see the harm, though. Georgia was grown up enough to know her mind, and her body drove him to distraction. "My new book will address this question," he said. "I'd like to hear your thoughts."

She smiled, absently tracing slightly parted lips with a blood-red fingernail. "I'd love to help any way I can," she said, stretching out the word "love."

"Well," he said, glancing at the clock, "the office hour is over, so how about grabbing a bite?"

They continued talking at a quiet restaurant a few blocks west. She was from a wealthy Atlanta family and found New York City "stimulating." He suggested they take the evening to explore its wonders. But she had studying to do for an early class. With little prodding, however, she said she would cancel her date for Saturday so they could drive upstate to a farmhouse restaurant.

Friday morning Ansel was feeling great when he got a call from Florence. "How are you feeling?" he asked with genuine concern.

"Better each day," she said brightly. Walking well with a cane. I'll be dancing any time now."

"That's so great to hear, Florence. And how's True? I bet he's glad to be back in his own room, with all his friends."

"Oh, he is. But I have to say, Ansel, you really stepped up. He's had a rough time in a lot of ways, and he's not an easy kid to get close to. But you reached him. He said he's glad he has a dad now, and that you told him you'd stick around for him."

"You know, in a way I'm grateful this all happened, not that *you* had to suffer but that True and I had time together. I'm sorry I've been gone from his life for so long."

"Well, that's in the past," she said. He wondered at how easily she forgave him for ten years of neglect. "So," she went on, "our surfer boy is all excited about your big beach trip tomorrow. What time should I have him ready?"

"Oh shit, Florence, I forgot all about that!" He pictured True's earnest expression, but then he saw Georgia with her hair blowing back and the seatbelt separating those enormous breasts. "I've got a meeting tomorrow with one of my seminars. It's the last of the year so I can't miss it."

She was silent for a moment and then in a flat tone said, "I understand. But *you'll* have to tell True. He hasn't stopped talking about your trip since I got home."

"Hi, Ansel!" True shouted into the phone. "Did you get my boogie board? You should get one, too!"

"Yeah, hey buddy, listen. I messed up the dates. We're going to have to do the beach some other time, okay?"

True dropped the phone and ran into his room. From his bed he could hear his mother say, "He's a little upset but it'll be all right. I'll talk to him. Just don't forget him, all right?"

True squeezed the leather bracelet his mom had helped him braid to mark their surfing adventure. This was just like his Roanoke project. Ansel said he'd help and then forgot. He always said he'd do something but never did!

He had thought he finally had a dad, like other guys, and his was really cool with a fancy car. But he was wrong. Ansel didn't care. He only was nice because he had to be. It was only True and his mom, just like before, just like always. He threw the bracelet into the trash can and buried his face in a pillow.

Chapter 26

Charlie had a late lunch with his agent and stopped in the main public library before walking to the Shakespeare, a pub one floor below the street. A side room looked colonial, with small tables and etchings hanging on red wallpaper. But he chose the main room, with a bar of dark wood and plank flooring. He was sure Ansel would approve of the draft English beers, soccer on television and genuine British bartender.

It seemed like such a wild ride to go twelve years without seeing Ansel and then have him so present all at once. More importantly, it was amazing to have a writer of his stature help with the manuscript.

When Ansel arrived, they took pints of cask beer to a table. Ansel complimented the pub and they talked beer. Then Ansel said, "Before we get to the manuscript, I'm still curious about the process. Say we talk and you—not to say you would or should at all—decide to take a suggestion from me." He stopped, seeing Charlie wanted to break in.

"You're helping me out, man," Charlie said. "I can't say I'll incorporate *every* comment you make, but I want to see them. You'll probably show me where I got it completely wrong. So, please—sorry to interrupt—go ahead."

"So, I know this is picky and personal to every writer, but how do you make your edits show up in all versions? You know, so you don't confuse drafts."

"There are always printouts of early versions. As to electronic copies, I just replace the document on the computer and the remote hard drive. Any other versions, emailed or on a thumb drive, don't matter because I know they're outdated."

They ordered food and more beer. Ansel handed across a manila envelope. "You'll see minor comments throughout," he said. "Some typos. Some question marks where I lost the thread. And then I *know* I can help with one plot point."

Charlie put down his glass and gestured eagerly.

"Okay, when Stephen, your leading man," he grinned, gesturing at Charlie, "comes back to the dorm before going to the party...."

"Yeah?"

"At first he thinks Evan," gesturing at himself, "is at the party with the love interest, and Stephen is all sad he had to work late and maybe doesn't even want to go to the party and see the two of them together...."

"Yeah, you're tracking the book *and* the facts."

"Right, but when Stephen sees him at the dorm, Evan shouldn't be *alone*. He should be with the other girl! Then the hero sees the villain is occupied and the way is clear to the love interest."

"Sure, just the way it happened."

"Yeah, but you wrote Stephen sees Evan *alone*, and then Evan goes out again. So Evan could have just run back to the dorm for something; the Graduates Memorial Building is right across the yard. He could have been heading right back to the party. You see?"

"Yeah...I guess."

Ansel shrugged. "Well, that's what happened—not that the actual facts matter."

Charlie was confused. Although it was years ago, seeing Ansel going back to the dorm was etched into his brain because it meant Charlie's way to Tess was in fact clear, and he took advantage of that. "What do you mean 'that's what happened'?"

"I mean *you* may have only seen me, but the girl was there too. We left the party together—ask anyone—which is what finally did me in with the "love interest." And I know I didn't go out again, certainly not for a couple of hours. I don't remember that chick's name but I do remember this exotic thing she did with her tongue."

Charlie laughed. "Man, I've always wondered what it's like to be you."

As they left the pub, Ansel got serious. "You've got the envelope?"

"Right here," Charlie said, patting his shoulder bag, grateful for the camaraderie and the concern of a fellow writer.

"And you'll make that change?"

"Oh, yeah, like I said, we'll see how it fits."

On the way home, Charlie leaned against the window, lulled by the rhythm of the train on the tracks. It was strange about Ansel's comment, not the idea itself—which might make sense—but how he insisted it was what really happened, like it was crucial to know what was true. Maybe it was just the historian pinning down the facts. Then again, Ansel's field was *revisionist* history, which was perfect given that he was always rewriting the story. Charlie laughed out loud, remembering how Ansel had talked them out of a jam when a porter caught them all painting a stanza from "Over the Wall to the Trinity Ball" on a door to the Buttery. He was so convincing in pleading they were victims of circumstance that even the other McYanks half-believed him.

So now the historian sought to revise a random moment in history, or maybe it was *his personal* history and maybe not random. Also, he seemed to have no interest in Reilly, so why did he care if Dutch called her? What was Charlie missing?

His smile faded, thinking how Ansel referred to the "love interest" rather than "Tess." Did Ansel's view of that night differ from his in some way involving her? He pictured the two of them at Arobel. It seemed almost out of line the way he hugged her when they greeted, while everyone else—except the expectant mother—exchanged polite kisses on the cheek. And what about her reaction? She looked out of breath and then seemed almost to avoid looking at Ansel the rest of the night.

At Trinity he never felt like he could compete with Ansel, and had been surprised Tess chose *him* in the end. But what was going on between them now? Could they have been seeing each other in New York? He'd have no way to know that. What did it really mean that Ansel was back in their lives?

Joan called the next day while Charlie was working on his book. "Charles, I've got incredible news! Are you sitting down? Or better yet, pop a bottle of champagne."

"What? What is it?"

"Resurrection Pictures picked up the option!"

"They're going to make *Against the Odds*? What happened?"

"Who knows how Hollywood works, and who cares? The point is they want to make the movie now, *and* they want to talk with you. They may want you on the screenplay! Is this unbelievable?"

"Joan, I love you!" Charlie whooped and kissed the phone. "This is fantastic!"

"So listen, I've got to run. You deserve this, Charles. I'm so happy for you. Clear your calendar for next week. I'll book you a flight to LA for Monday and email the details."

Charlie was ecstatic. He immediately called Tess, but she was at a meeting. That stung. She never seemed to be there to share his life when it most mattered. But he was jazzed nonetheless and couldn't sit still. He rolled out the Jag and tore up the mountain and across his secret road.

When Tess came home from work, Charlie and Odysseus were wrestling in the great room. "You guys will destroy the room," she laughed.

He rolled off the dog, who continued to push his big snout against Charlie's leg. But when Charlie lay flat, catching his breath, Odysseus plopped down next to him, tongue reaching the floor.

She reached down a hand, just like the old Tess. What had he been thinking? When she helped him up, he hugged her.

"Yuck," she laughed, "dog hair!"

He just smiled.

"What's going on?" she said.

"A producer picked up the film option! I'm flying out Monday to meet with them."

"What? I thought that deal was dead! Oh, my God!"

On the terrace he opened a bottle of champagne and they toasted. She took only one glass, as she had work to finish. But he didn't mind finishing the bottle on his own, feeling indomitable, like the lone hawk he watched slice across the darkening sky.

Next day Charlie went through his notes for turning *Against the Odds* into a movie. He wished he could send the Trinity manuscript to Joan as is, so his editor could start working on it, but he had to finish the draft. Maybe after the party he could fill in the blanks. Thinking the man-uscript might also make a good screenplay, he wondered about moving Digory's accident to the Old Library; its ironwork staircases and barrel-vaulted Long Room would be more dramatic than the modern Arts Block. He decided to try out this idea at the party.

Friday afternoon Ansel called to ask if he could bring a friend to their get-together. "Of course you can bring a date," Charlie said, relieved Ansel had a girlfriend.

"Oh, she's not a date. She works for me, but she's really nice and a big fan of yours."

"All the better!" Charlie said. It didn't matter what Ansel called his companion as long as she diverted his attention from Tess. "And hey, man, I got some news. I'm flying out to Hollywood to talk about making the first book into a movie."

"That's terrific!" Ansel paused. "I guess that'll shift your focus from the current book?"

"Oh yeah, I can't think of anything else right now. I may just send off the manuscript and deal with revisions later."

"Yeah," Ansel said, "I can imagine you need to shift gears."

"But hey, I'll get back to your comments, for sure. Don't think your time was wasted...really."

"Oh, no worries. So when do you head out?"

"Flying to LA Monday early. I'll get back Wednesday evening to help set up for the party. And who's this woman you're bringing?"

"Oh, her name is Becca Howard, a young woman from Michigan

or Minnesota or somewhere. She does web stuff for me. She and Dutch have gone out."

"Dutch? You're kidding."

"No, really. They seem to like each other. Anyway, I'll let you go. See you next week."

Charlie didn't know what to make of Ansel's call. Why was he bringing a woman who was dating Dutch? He shook this off and started a to-do list for the party. They needed charcoal for the grill, beer, some kind of fancy soda for the kids. He checked the bar to make sure they had the basics. He kept wondering why Ansel was so intense about getting the facts straight in his book, or not "straight" but bent to fit some alternate reality. He couldn't shake the feeling it somehow involved Tess. This unsettled him. He went back over his conversation with her about Ansel's visit. Did she react strangely? Was she *too* interested in the details? Something was unspoken there. She had surprised him by inviting everyone to the house; was she just hoping to see Ansel again? That was far-fetched, even crazy. But one thing was certain: having Ansel in the picture unsettled everything.

Chapter 27

Ansel watched the river, thinking about his weekend with Georgia. She had loved the Zagato and showed she was no innocent by packing a toothbrush for their dinner date. He couldn't get enough of her languorous southern drawl, like when she said, "I just knew you'd own a *powerful* car, Professor." He only regretted he couldn't show her its real power, with state troopers behind every embankment.

Dinner at the farmhouse restaurant was enchanting, and she seemed game. "So," he asked, "have you any plans for tomorrow morning?"

"As it happens, Professor, I find myself free. I was hoping you might buy me breakfast."

He tried not to look too carnivorous. "Let me make a call," he said and pulled out his phone.

"Sanctuary Inn," a man answered.

"Yeah, hi. I was wondering if you folks might have space tonight for my little lady and me."

"Ansel, you old dog!"

"Hey, Jake. Long time. I am, in fact, in the neighborhood and looking for a place to hide out for the night."

"Oh, come ahead. You've got our best room, and we are nothing if not discrete."

"Knew I could count on you, buddy. And I'm curious to see what you've done with the place since last year."

"Hey, that was a time, right? We haven't changed much; expanded the dining room a bit."

Ansel looked up at Georgia. "Turns out a *very* old friend runs a small inn near New Paltz. It's a short drive, just made for the Zagato."

Jake Hadley was Ansel's closest friend from boarding school. Together they had broken just about every rule at Swinmore Academy, which got them into loads of trouble but also bred intense loyalty between them.

When Ansel and Georgia stepped out of the car, Jake hugged Ansel like an old comrade. "I see you're still going with the top of the line," he said.

"Have an image to keep up," Ansel replied with a delayed smile, recognizing Jake was referring to Georgia as well as the Zagato. "Can I ask a favor, though?"

"*Mi casa...*"

"Is there someplace under cover for the car?"

"Sure. Pull it into the barn around back. It'll be safe there, although you did, you'll recall, say I could drive it next time you came."

Jake showed them to their room and left them a bottle of wine. Georgia joined Ansel in a toast and in exploring ways old and new to imbibe his coke purchase. They emerged so late the next day they would have missed the locally sourced breakfast had Jake not kept the kitchen open for them.

"You never could keep time," Jake said and pulled back a chair for Georgia.

"Oh, we've been *making* time," Ansel responded.

Jake sat with them over coffee and then left while they ate. It was everything Ansel needed after the last few weeks: bacon and eggs and a ripe Georgia peach. She may have had the ulterior motive of helping her grade, but Ansel was willing to be used and she clearly enjoyed the sex as much as he did. When he dropped her off at her apartment Sunday, all was right with the world.

But now he had to review Charlie's new information. His movie deal could be dangerous; he might send along his manuscript without making Ansel's revision. But maybe the movie would distract Charlie enough for Ansel to slip in the change. He could surreptitiously improve the plot while the future screenwriter was busy preparing his Academy Award speech.

Looking across the room, he noticed a picture True had taped to the wall. There were two figures standing on a beach, one tall and one short. He had always scoffed at children's "artwork" displayed in offices, but this was different. True's picture touched him like an image from his own dreams.

He reconsidered taking his son to the Mountain House party. Molly's kids would be there, so he'd have someone to play with. But Ansel had to see his plan through, and he needed Tess's help to access Charlie's computer. Meeting True for the first time would *not* help Tess focus. Anyway, there would be no room in the Zagato with Becca along, and it was important to put her together with Dutch. No, this day was too important to bring True. Still, he wondered how the boy was getting on. He dialed True's cell phone and left a voicemail.

Later he met Leah and Becca at the studio of a high-end photographer. Leah wanted a new headshot for book publicity, and Becca would post video of the shoot. Leah instructed the photographer in every minute detail. He bristled at being ordered around his own studio but did what he was told. Nobody stood up to Leah.

On a stool in front of a neutral backdrop, Ansel struck his "Golden Boy of Popular History" pose. "My social media expert says we should try a three-quarter profile," he said, nodding toward Becca.

Leah shot a caustic look at Becca, but the photographer agreed to try it and the results were good.

Over the course of the morning, Becca revealed her fascination with photo equipment. She also demonstrated a natural fluency with online technology, which even Leah acknowledged. Still, it was clear his agent could not believe he was keeping his hands off the young woman with the impossibly Midwestern smile. Well, he had *mostly* kept his hands off, and their relationship would be professional going forward. She was too wholesome for him, anyway. You expected her any moment to pass around home-baked biscuits.

On a break he found a private room and called Regis & Kessler.

"Hi, Ansel," Tess said, sounding excited, "What a surprise."

"How's my favorite lawyer?" he said brightly. "You know, counselor, I find myself in your neighborhood, and I wondered if they let brilliant young attorneys out to eat."

"Yes," she said, "every once in a while. I mean sure, we can have lunch. Do you know a place?"

He looked with a smirk at the hotel sign across the street, thinking what a shortcut that would be, but shook his head. "How about Luigi's on 59th near 9th? I'll walk over now and try to wrestle us a table."

The lunchtime crowd was sparse, and a booth toward the garden afforded them privacy. Ansel turned on the charm, complimenting the sapphire earrings that matched an ordinary business suit and feigning fascination with her work. He was self-effacing about his *Redux* series. "And why they let me come on TV to promote those books is a mystery to me," he said.

"Well, you are successful *and* fairly presentable. And I recall you can be amusing."

"Oh, you remember, do you?" he said with a sly smile. "And I guess I should thank you for the 'fairly presentable' comment."

She smirked.

They passed on wine. Tess ordered only a large salad. "I see," he said lasciviously, "how you've kept that spectacular figure. You look in better shape now than when we were in school."

He was pleased to see she still lapped up compliments about her looks; that should make things easier.

After the plates were cleared, they each ordered an espresso. But the waiter returned first with glasses of limoncello and tiny cookies on a plate. "Mr. Luigi," the waiter said with a southern Italian accent, "he sends his regards to the professor and his lovely lady."

Ansel spotted the portly owner leaning on the bar. Luigi raised his glass in toast, striped red suspenders stretching over the bulging midsection beneath his jacket.

"Seems your reputation precedes you," she said, tipping her glass toward their benefactor.

"It's not me, Tess," he said, raising his eyebrows, "it's you. Luigi's Italian, so by nature he worships beauty."

He wondered if he should have thrown in a reference to Rome and Venus, the goddess of love. But he preferred the Greek gods and none of them had anything on Tess. She was herself an ideal. Her dark sensuous eyes, her full lips, the gentle lines of her face; it would be hard to overstate her stunning looks. In any event, his comment obviously pleased her.

Lunch stretched on. She finally checked her watch and said she had to get back to the office for a meeting. He walked her toward her building. On the way he said, "Tess, I could really use your help with something."

She stopped and looked at him, nodding.

He took her arm and continued walking. "It's not all that impor-tant. Or, I suppose it's important to me for personal reasons, but it's no big deal."

"What is it?" He could feel her arm tense beneath his hand. He slowed so they almost stood in place.

"Well," he said, trying to look embarrassed. "You know, maybe it would be better if we talked about this later. It'll take some explaining, and you've got to get back."

She screwed up her face as if to ask when "later" could possibly be.

"What if I drove up tomorrow evening? I have to meet someone in Newburgh and I could swing across the river on the way home to see you and Charlie."

"I don't know if that's a good idea. The movie mogul's out of town."

"Oh, that's too bad. But it's not *about* Charlie, anyway. Or it is, but not really about *him.* It is, well…it's complicated and there is some urgency. Anyway, it won't take long, and I'm sure Charlie won't mind."

"I..." She paused. Looking into his eyes, she felt herself slipping into a cataract and couldn't see the bottom. "I guess so," she said. "I'll be home around eight."

Back at the apartment, Ansel had a productive meeting with Becca. They crafted a LinkedIn response to a German historian and went over how Ansel could participate in a podcast on American culture.

Becca seemed more at ease than she'd been since their afternoon encounter. He deserved the blame for that debacle—should not shit where you eat and all. And she was good at her job, which was more important than an afternoon's diversion. At a break in the work, she said, "My calendar cleared for the 28th, and I'd be happy to join you, as long as they don't mind if I shoot some photos. I found an *Architectural Digest* spread from when Mountain House was built and I'd love to see it myself, especially after it's been lived in."

"Great. They expect us early afternoon. We'll work out the details later."

She put the date into her phone and looked up. "And how's your son doing now that he's home?"

"True?" He realized he hadn't heard back from the boy. He'd have to give him another call when he got a minute. "Oh, he's great. Everything's good."

Everything *was* good. Ansel was hitting on all cylinders, like his finely tuned Zagato. He was sure Tess would help with the manuscript. Becca was a team player, even if she was unaware of the game. Dutch— poor sod—would forget all about the woman in California if he thought Becca might be interested. The semester was done except for grading, and he was sure he'd get excellent reviews from his students. The appearance schedule was picking up. Now that his apartment was his own again, he could arrange "student conferences" with Georgia. Her term paper added nothing useful to his research, but she'd be pleased to hear "class participation" had earned her an A for the semester.

Chapter 28

Back at Regis & Kessler, Tess attended a meeting about the purchase of a drug store chain and then hurried to her office and shut the door. What was she getting into? Life with Charlie had been rough but he seemed to be coming out of his funk, with the movie and all. Maybe she should make more of an effort. They *were* married, after all.

But every time she thought about Ansel, her heartbeat quickened. She could feel it; the reaction was physical. He was an egotist—Molly was right—but he was also an enchanter, and Tess could not forget how he made her feel as a twenty-one-year-old lover. Tess had been lucky to get rid of him, but here he was again and here she was. She should not have invited him to Mountain House while Charlie was away but that was just how the timing worked. She'd simply have to hear him out and send him on his way; she hoped she could.

After an early train home, she straightened the house and tried on outfits. She decided on a maroon sweater that hugged her frame and pants that fit like a second skin. He had last seen her in a boxy business suit, and there was no reason she should not look her best.

He arrived early in the evening in a gorgeous red sports car. She heard him round the switchback and waited in the driveway. Her Volvo was parked by the front door and she waved him toward its space in the garage. They had nothing to hide, but there was no sense advertising his visit if someone happened to drive by the house. It was hard to miss that car.

He came out of the garage wearing his confident smile and a jacket of black leather that must have been made for him; it looked like it would melt in your hands. He tussled with Odysseus and then kissed her cheek, gently holding her elbow. She showed him in and joined him in a bourbon, an unheard-of liberty for a work night. He complimented the gardening, prompting a tour of her plantings. She asked how the *Redux* book was coming, but he turned the conversation to what *she* was accomplishing at Regis & Kessler. She was charmed by how diffidently he spoke of his own success. They sat on the terrace watching two falcons soar on air currents in the last of the sunlight and she wondered: why had he come all this way? Ansel never did anything without a reason.

He poured a second round of drinks with a heavy hand.

"You're trying to get me drunk," she said with a smirk, accepting her glass.

"I plead nolo contendere, counselor."

She was chilled by the breeze. He draped his jacket around her shoulders. She snuggled into the soft glove-leather and breathed in its smell, earthy and slightly sweet. He settled in his chair, pulling so close their knees almost touched. "Tess," he said, "there's something I need to say. I'm just afraid you might take it wrong."

He seemed almost bashful. She wanted to bundle him up in her arms, if only that were possible. "You can tell me," she said softly.

"In a way, things couldn't be better: the money, the travel, life in general. But there's something fundamental missing. I have no one to share it with who matters to me and cares about me."

She looked up in alarm and anticipation. It was clear where this was headed.

"I can't help how I feel," he said, looking at the valley. Then he turned his gaze on her. "I didn't realize it until I saw you again, but I never got over you."

She tried to calm herself by gulping her drink. "We shouldn't go there," she said urgently. "We...what's done is done. It was nobody's fault." She struggled to catch her breath, looking into the valley to avoid his eyes.

"It was *my* fault," he said forcefully. "We were young and had so much to accomplish, and I was scared we were getting too close. I couldn't get you out of my head."

She looked around, searching for a way to divert the conversation. But he continued: "I can't shake the image of you in that loft room. You remember, when we drove through Kerry and found that hotel on the coast with the squeaky bed?"

She struggled *not* to remember making love in a sun-soaked room, passion sweeping over them like salty gusts from the sea, but the image was vivid.

With a start, she realized their knees were touching. She turned again toward the view. He put down his glass and reached for her hand.

In a moment they were standing and kissing. She lost herself and leaned into him. He ran his hands up her sides and over her breasts. She panted as he kissed her neck. Their ardor ran through the house. It felt like the climax after a dozen years of foreplay.

When they were spent, they lay on the big bed, curtains wide open to the valley, her fingernail drawing lines across his chest. Then they slept, wrapped in each other's arms.

* * *

Making love with Tess would have been well worth the trip. It reminded Ansel that all the chemistry he learned in college had *not* come from textbooks. They were great together, always had been, but twelve years apart had made her voracious in a way that almost made him forget why he was there.

When he heard gentle sleeping sounds, he got up. Wearing only the pajama bottoms Tess had loaned him, he mounted the stairs, entered Charlie's den and closed the door. He turned the desk lamp on low and took a seat. The laptop was gone; obviously Charlie took that with him.

He found the hard drive in the drawer and held it up to the light, its short cord dangling. Would this be password-protected? He needed to plug it into a computer to see if it would open. He absently stuffed it into his pocket and sifted through the manuscripts on the cadenza.

He found a printed draft, dated March 7, and flipped pages looking for the scene at the dormitory, but then he looked back to check if this was the most recent printout.

Tess woke and sensed Ansel was gone from bed, but felt warm and sated and drifted back to sleep. When she woke again it was pitch-dark and he still wasn't with her. She pulled on her robe and went out to the kitchen. Maybe he was hungry after their workout?

He wasn't in the kitchen or the living room or on the terrace. She stood still to listen, hearing only a breeze. Odysseus had risen heavily and followed her from the bedroom to lay by the doors to the terrace. He looked at her lazily and closed his eyes.

She saw light beneath the door to Charlie's den. This made no sense but it had to be Ansel. She stepped quietly up the stairs and opened the door. He sat with his back to her, bound pages in his hands. She couldn't make any sense of this scene and reached for the light switch.

He spun around, shock splashed across his face.

"What the hell are you doing?" she said forcefully, waving her arm to take in the room.

"I..." he said and hesitated. "I was looking for the last version of Charlie's book. There's a change I wanted to check."

She cocked her head. "No, really! What are you doing? This isn't right. Charlie would flip out if he saw you in his papers."

"But he gave me the manuscript!" He rose from the chair and approached her with both hands out. "He brought me the book last week!"

It was hard to miss the hard drive in his pocket. "And this is?" she said looking down at his pocket.

"Right. No banana in my pocket. Just kidding."

She saw nothing funny. This was wrong!

He placed the hard drive on the desk and sat in the easy chair, bolt upright. "Look, I'll be straight with you," he said sincerely.

She remained standing and waited. She wanted him to convince her it was a mistake. She couldn't lose him so soon after they had reunited. She had to hold on to the dream of some other kind of life.

He went on, "So this is the real story. You remember that rough patch we had in Dublin at the end of the year? I mean, physically it was always amazing, but we weren't talking anymore, and then we were arguing about…who even remembers?" He paused, with a sideways look of remorse.

She eyed him closely. He avoided her stare as if embarrassed, which she could not help but find endearing. "Then," he continued, "at that party, I just, I don't know, lost my head. I thought you didn't love me and I wanted to make you jealous, maybe as a clumsy way of holding on to you. So, I left with some girl. I don't even remember her name. I took her to my room and we would have slept together, but I… well, for the only time in my life, I couldn't do it. I kept thinking how I loved you and it was wrong."

She heard only the "love" part. Could love explain what he was doing here? In the middle of the night? What was happening to her?

He kept his eyes on the floor. "So, she went back to her hostel and I returned to the dorm alone. I guess that's when Charlie saw me. And now he's written about seeing me alone and realizing I wasn't at the party, so he could mount his glorious assault."

She grimaced. "I was hoping he wouldn't go overboard with the grand seduction. I wasn't interested in him at all then."

"Well, that too. But you know he'll write himself in as the romantic hero. Thing is, I pointed out it didn't matter what he *thought* he saw, because his story made more sense if he saw my character *with* a girl."

"But what difference does it make to you?"

"Maybe it's ego. But I really was trying to help him. He *is* my friend, you know, despite everything. But he's a famous author and people will find out the character is based on me and, well, it's kind of the burden of being a pop star to a bunch of undergrads."

"Oh, come on! You honestly think anyone would care?"

"I don't know. Call me crazy, but I thought…since a revision would improve the story anyway, and it was such a small thing, and changing it would make my agent and publisher happy—they always push this insipid image thing so hard."

She pondered this with a long sigh. Cheating on her husband may not be right, but allowing someone to mess with his work was worse. The writing mattered more to him than anything, certainly more than her. But how was *that* fair? It seemed they married "for better or for worse," except when it interfered with publishing deadlines. Those deadlines and satisfying his publisher and his agent—must *not* forget Joan—were all that mattered to him, besides convincing the world he was a literary giant. He didn't care about her, not really, so why should she care about his writing?

He raised doleful eyes and reached out his hand, so forlorn. "I hate this damned book," she said. "I begged him not to drag up this old stuff, but he wouldn't listen." She paused, looking at Ansel's bare shoulders. "But it does no good to change old copies when Charlie carries the current version with him. And he'd notice, anyway."

"Oh, I know," he said resignedly. "And the hard drive, and his computer: they're sure to have passwords."

She pondered this. She and Charlie shared a master list of essential passwords to use in case of emergency. Ansel's problem was not an emergency but he seemed to think it was. Could she let Ansel make his revision, such a small thing but so important to him, and then have things continue as before? It would not do any harm, and Charlie would never figure out she'd done it. "Well maybe that's not a problem," she said.

His eyes flashed as he rose. "You mean you'll help?" He threw his arms around her. "My guardian angel!"

His enthusiasm took her by surprise. "Look," she said, pulling back and peering into his eyes, "I don't want to hurt Charlie. But you're right: making this change will help the book and also help us, by which I mean you."

He squeezed her arm. "So how do we do it?"

She tingled at hearing him ask for her help. She was finally in control. "Well, the timing might be perfect. He's so wrapped up in the movie now, he'll probably send off the manuscript pretty much as is, and when he notices the change, he'll think the editors did it and he'll like it."

Ansel nodded eagerly. "So, how?"

Tess pondered a moment. "I'll get the passwords; we have a list... somewhere; I'll have to dig it up. Then, when we're all here Saturday, I'll lead everyone off and give you time in the den. You can make the change on the electronic copies and that will be the end of it. But you have to *promise* you'll use the passwords this one time only, and only for what you described. I mean it, Ansel! And you can't tell anyone about this...*ever*."

"Oh, absolutely. You have my word." He pulled her against him. She melted in his arms. They returned hand in hand to the bedroom, to lose themselves in each other again.

Chapter 29

The day of the party, Charlie opened his eyes and looked through a gap in the curtains at the valley, dappled with golden sunlight. He closed his eyes again and thought about his book, focusing on the night the McYanks introduced their Irish hosts to beer pong. He didn't want to drift back to sleep and forget this incident, so he sat up and typed a note into his phone. Then he noticed Tess wasn't beside him.

He rose to join her in the great room, excited about the party. She was preparing food and handed him a cup of coffee.

He took his cup to the bar to confirm all he needed from the liquor store was scotch, but was surprised they were nearly out of bourbon. This was odd, since he preferred scotch and Tess hardly touched anything but white wine.

"Do you remember when we drank the bourbon?" he said.

"No idea. Maybe for hot toddies after that snowstorm in January?"

That might make sense, except he thought he had checked the bar when he started his to-do list before the LA trip. "Well," he said, "I'll get a high-end bottle for Ansel; show him we travel in lofty circles."

"Why do you care about that? This isn't a competition."

"You've lost me, Tess. What are you talking about?"

"Trying to impress people with expensive liquor: is that necessary? Ansel's just an old friend. Relax and enjoy the day."

"Right," he said, thinking how lately Ansel found his way into all their arguments. "Well, we're nearly out of bourbon and need scotch, so I'm off to the liquor store."

"Fine," she said, and paused. "And you can also pick up the cake."

"You ordered a cake?"

"Yes, I did. Molly's kids will be here, so I asked the bakery do a chocolate cake with a princess for Anna and Spiderman for Theo. I didn't order it until yesterday, but they said it would be ready by ten."

Charlie smiled at Tess acting all motherly about Molly's kids. "No problem," he said. "And I think I'll take your car. I want to check that steering."

Driving down the mountain he found the steering *was* loose. After shopping, he stopped at Kelly's, where a mechanic said the boss should check it on Monday. But Charlie didn't have time to leave the car. He arranged for a tow truck to pick it up after the weekend.

Tess was arranging chairs when he stepped onto the terrace. "I've got some bad news," he said, "and some worse news. Which do you want first?"

"Just hit me with both," she said impatiently.

"Well, the garage is sending a tow truck Monday to pick up the Volvo. The steering is worse. I barely made it home without dropping off the cliff."

"Oh, damn. Well, I'm glad you checked."

"Then," he continued, grimacing theatrically, "the *really* bad news is the cake wasn't ready. Some baker didn't show up and they were backed up with orders. We can pick it up after three."

She screwed up her lips. "Well, no matter. You can buzz down with one of the guys. It'll give you a chance to show off your car."

He brightened.

"And you know what?" she added. "Bud's a fisherman, right? You could pop over and show him that spot along the river."

"Brilliant! We could get the cake, check out the 'troutskis' and be back here in forty minutes."

A half-hour later, Bud and Dutch arrived in quick succession. "That's some driveway," Bud said. "Glad I didn't have to walk it."

"It's dramatic in the Jaguar," Charlie said. "I think that road is my favorite part of living here."

"Have you ever raced the Jag?" Bud asked.

"Not in an organized race but taking those switchbacks is a thrill. As a matter of fact, you'll see for yourself if you're willing to do a little chore with me later on. And there's a secret fishing hole on the Algonk River...."

Bud's eyes lit up. "Trout? I'm your guy. I was planning to take a prospect there in the fall but we settled for golf."

In the great room Charlie prodded Dutch. "I hear you made a conquest with Ansel's assistant."

"So he says, anyway. I met her once—her name is Becca—and she's really nice."

"Oh, I get it: nice personality but face like a squid."

"No, not at all! She's like the dream girl next door. But, I mean, what's the point? She went to dinner with me as part of her job."

"Hey man, don't sell yourself short."

Molly and Pete pulled up, and everyone went out to meet them. The kids had unbuckled and burst out as soon as the minivan door slid open. But they pulled up short when they saw Odysseus, his collar tight in Charlie's hand.

"He's all right," Charlie said. "He's just affectionate, and I didn't want him to run you over."

Anna stepped forward cautiously and then looked to her mother. Molly nodded, and Anna shyly held out her little hand, which the dog licked with his enormous tongue. Theo took his cue from this, and both kids wrapped their arms around the dog's thick neck.

"Looks like Seusy's made some friends," Charlie laughed, letting go of the collar.

The two women hugged like long-lost sisters.

"Seusy, as in Doctor Seuss?" Pete asked Charlie, one eye on his children and the dog while shaking hands all around.

"I guess that works, too," Charlie laughed, "but it was a nickname for Odysseus, part of a long-running Greek philosopher joke. But then the full name doesn't fit; he's such a pushover."

The men took turns kissing Molly. Charlie took her arm to lead her into the house. The dog and kids scampered through the door in front of them.

"Remember what I said!" Molly called after the children, and they returned vague assents. Inside, Charlie accepted a bottle of wine from Pete and took it to the kitchen. Pete wandered out to the terrace, whistling in admiration of their panorama.

Tess watched Molly take in the wide-open great room, separated from the kitchen by a high wooden table. "Oh, Tess," Molly said, "this is dazzling! And what a view!"

"I can't believe we haven't had you here before," Tess said, taking her arm to begin a tour.

After covering the rest of the ground floor, they ended in the master bedroom suite. "Sorry for the mess," Tess said, picking up clothes. "My 'lord and master' has trouble finding the hamper."

"I know all about that, times three," Molly laughed, though with little humor. "But more important: things in general have settled down?"

"Sure," Tess blurted out, and then realized Molly was asking about her marriage. This was awkward, given how everything had changed since Tuesday night and in light of the caper she and Ansel planned for the day. "I…yeah, Charlie and I are okay. We're fine."

Molly looked surprised, or was it concerned? This was not what Tess needed. She'd have to watch her tone if she was going to carry on an affair. She turned quickly toward the master bath. "This bathtub was a big selling point for me," she said, annoyed at how transparent this change of subject sounded.

Molly's heart went out to Tess. She could always see through the smiles when her friend was troubled. There was something very wrong here. She said gently, "Do you want to talk about it, hon?"

"No, or not now. Everything's fine. I'd better go check on the food."

Molly stayed behind to use the bathroom. Mostly she wanted a moment to think. What was wrong with Tess? How could she have *so* much and still be miserable? Was there something going on between her and Ansel? That would be so messed up.

Molly thought of how secure she felt with Pete and her kids. She looked at her pregnant body in the mirror and smiled. It was a laughable picture, that was certain, but then it was also the opposite of laughable. It was the circle of life, something Tess would never understand. What seemed most comical at that moment was that she had envied Tess all these years.

When Molly returned to the great room, Charlie said, "Can I get you a cold drink, or a pillow, or whatever else you pregnant ladies use?"

"You're such a dope, Charlie," she laughed. "But I can see why Tess keeps you around."

The rev of an engine announced Ansel's arrival. Charlie was eager to join Bud in stepping outside to get a glimpse of the young assistant.

Ansel jumped out of the car and strutted toward them, gave each a back slap and waved toward Becca. She was a luminous summer day, in a red-striped sundress that matched the car. Charlie took in the vision but could make no sense of it. Why was Ansel delivering this woman to Dutch? She was certainly pretty enough to be with him and everything would be so much more settled if Ansel had a date. Could this woman be a beard, so Ansel could focus on Tess?

"Thank you so much for inviting me, Mr. Piedmont," Becca said, reaching out long fingers and turning up cornflower-blue eyes. "I loved *Against the Odds*."

"Oh, this one can stay," Charlie laughed, shaking her hand. "But you'll have to drop the 'Mr. Piedmont' stuff and call me Charlie, like everyone else."

"Charlie, then," she said and turned to shake hands with Bud. "And you must be the insurance mogul."

Bud laughed. "Is that what Ansel calls me? Just for that I'm going to hit him up for a policy on his publishing empire."

Dutch listened to the commotion out front but hung back. He chided himself for thinking he had a real chance with Becca. And did he even *want* a chance? She was nice but his life was complicated enough.

Regardless of what he thought best or achievable, he could not get those blue eyes out of his mind. As a distraction, he got down on his knees to help the kids try to make Odysseus roll over, to the great amusement of their parents.

Tess stood by the door. She kissed Ansel perfunctorily on the cheek and took Becca by the arm to lead her into the house. "It's so nice to meet you!" she said.

"Oh, thank you for inviting me. What a beautiful setting for a home."

While Becca gazed around the room, Tess looked her over. "We're so glad you were able to come," she said, casting a suspicious glance at Ansel.

Tess showed them out to the terrace and introduced Becca to Molly and Pete, just as the kids and dog took off down the wooden steps to the clearing.

"And you know Dutch?" she asked, as he rose from his knees to hold out his hand.

"Oh, we're old friends," Becca said, shaking his hand with a quiet smile. "Hey, Dutch. Long time no see."

He smiled at her and said almost imperceptibly, "Seems like a long time."

Becca looked up with a start, just as Anna returned up the stairs to tug at his shirt. "Come on, Uncle Dutch!" the little girl pleaded, "We have to see if Seusy will fetch!"

Molly called timeout to introduce Becca, which held her daughter's attention for barely a moment. Dutch turned a resigned look at Becca and was led down the steps by the five-year-old to where Theo and Odysseus were cavorting.

Tess pondered the connection between Dutch and Ansel's assistant. Did she see something there? That would be a good thing; she needed no competition with the edge of youth. She returned to the great room, where she and Ansel exchanged comments on the fine weather and how Charlie and she had furnished the house.

As he took drink orders on the terrace, Charlie watched Tess talk with Ansel. Their stiffness concerned him. If they were just old friends, like the rest, they'd be at ease with each other. But they looked stilted and careful, as if conscious he was watching. Still, it would be self-defeating to look suspicious. He would instead appear confident and energized. Tess was *his* wife, and Ansel would have to get over it. He was just a horny old hound dog who needed to be slapped down.

Charlie apologized and asked Pete to repeat what he wanted to drink. He brought Molly a mineral water and Pete a summer ale, pointing out the tub for refills.

Becca accepted an iced tea and complimented Charlie on the house. She mentioned the *Architectural Digest* spread. "Do you mind if I take a few photos?" she asked. "You know, not personal stuff or with people; just the house."

"Oh, you may shoot away, and by all means include our distinguished guests, as long as you send me copies."

Tess was pleased with how she had orchestrated the afternoon. The children never tired of playing with the dog. Bud got Pete onto the subject of homeowner's insurance. Ansel dutifully answered Molly's questions about his celebrity friends. Dutch and Becca seemed acutely aware of each other while avoiding direct contact.

Tess moved into the kitchen to arrange hors d'oeuvres on a tray, and Becca followed her. "You have such a lovely home," she said. "May I help with something?"

"No, but thank you. Everything's under control."

Charlie appeared. "That's right," he said, "and *you* are a guest."

"Oh, I like to help," Becca said.

"Becca's a photographer," he said to Tess, affectionately putting his arm around his wife's shoulders. "She's going to shoot a party montage and update our architectural photos."

Tess frowned. "You're *not* putting her to work?"

"Oh, no," Charlie and Becca said together and both laughed.

"No," Charlie went on. "This is wholly voluntary and, in fact…" he grabbed Dutch's arm, "I am assigning her a bodyguard for the outdoor shots. You know how treacherous those woods can be."

Becca looked up in concern, but Charlie laughed. Nonetheless, he ushered the two of them out the front door and closed it behind them. Tess applauded Charlie's initiative, though she was confused why he wanted to separate Ansel from his assistant.

* * *

Finding herself on the driveway with Dutch, hearing only the sounds of birds in the trees, Becca smiled at him. "You've got some interesting friends."

"They can be a little pushy."

"Even so, they think the world of you—and each other."

He dismissed this with a good-humored shake of the head and followed her to Ansel's car, where she retrieved her camera.

"You know what?" she said, removing the lens cap. "Before I do the house, I should take some shots of the cars; that'll make Ansel happy."

"The cars?"

"Well, not *your* car, Dutch. No offense, but Ansel is kind of particular."

"Here," she went on as she opened the Aston Martin's door, "why don't you get into the driver's seat?"

"He won't mind?"

"Of course not, long as you don't spill anything."

Dutch left his beer on the ground and squeezed his big frame into the seat. She reached in and adjusted it to give him room, then backed away and photographed him from several angles. Then she got him to pose in the Jaguar. Since it was in the garage, she zoomed in for closeups with a blurred background so it would look like he was driving.

"You're an excellent actor," she laughed.

"You should see me sing and dance," he replied, carefully extricating himself from the car.

He accompanied her as she set up photos of the house. There was a pang in his bad knee when they scampered down the hill behind the garage, but he focused on making sure *she* didn't fall. It was clear he need not have been concerned, though. She took the slope like a mountain goat and looked strong enough to carry him.

At the lower clearing he turned his attention to the kids and the dog. When he turned back, Becca lowered the camera pointed at him. She checked the viewfinder and showed him the image.

He smiled at the photo, and when he looked up her warm expression washed over him. She pronounced, "My Instagram caption will be 'Little Boy, Big Man.'"

* * *

Tess caught up with Ansel behind the bar. "Your husband stocks some respectable liquor," he said, cracking open a bottle of Old Bones.

"He bought that for you," she said and lowered her voice. "Charlie is going to town to pick up a cake. The way the bakery is backed up, it'll take half an hour, or more if they stop to see the trout stream. Here are the passwords." She placed a folded napkin on the bar. "I'll keep everyone else occupied."

"You make an enticing Mata Hari," he said quietly.

She was thrilled Ansel had placed himself in her hands. "Just do it fast, okay? And get out if you hear the car. He always revs it in the driveway before he shuts it off."

He palmed the napkin and turned, speaking in a louder voice. "What a guy!" he exclaimed. "Where is he?"

He caught Charlie's eye and strode over to him. "Didn't expect to find Old Bones in your liquor cabinet," he said, tipping his glass forward in toast. "You've outdone yourself."

"Only the best for the McYanks," Charlie said without enthusiasm.

At two-thirty, Tess said: "Everyone, Charlie and Bud have to head off on a brief mission for chocolate cake."

Theo and Anna cheered. Odysseus added a rare bark.

They all went out to the driveway. Becca saw the opportunity to photograph Ansel and Charlie by the Aston Martin. Neither of them wanted to pose, but she pleaded with Charlie and he convinced Ansel.

After the Jaguar disappeared down the mountain, everyone returned to the great room and Tess announced: "So, poor Professor Tone has some stodgy work call to make. But the rest of us are in for a treat."

They looked up in anticipation.

"Off the clearing below, there is a short and *gentle*," looking at Molly, "path to the most breathtaking view on the mountain. It won't take ten minutes to walk there and Seusy is eager to lead the way."

Odysseus, tired by his playmates, was stretched out on the floor. He raised his eyes lazily at the sound of his name and everyone laughed.

Pete dutifully took his wife's arm to help her down the steps, and Tess herded everyone else after them. She wore a private smile of self-congratulation at how flawlessly her plan was unfolding.

Odysseus took off along a wide dirt path, stopping to mark trees and sniff the entrance to an animal's lair. Theo pranced after him. Becca photographed Anna stooping to smell a flower. Dutch walked with Molly, so Tess took Pete's arm and encouraged him to talk about camping he had done in these mountains before he had a wife and kids.

Ansel waved from the terrace and, as soon as they were out of sight, rushed up the stairs. He sat in the desk chair, for a moment feeling wrapped by the bookshelves in a layer of silence. In a strange interlude, he realized Charlie's books were *not* arranged by size and color, like those in his apartment. Novelists had no design sense. But he had to hurry and so opened the laptop and pulled from his pocket marked pages from the manuscript. Using the password on the napkin, he pulled up the book and started revising. This was going to be a breeze.

* * *

Bud held on as Charlie took the sharp curves in the road. "I've got to get me one of these babies," he said. He saw Charlie's life—the car, the gorgeous wife, the house—as the target, and ultimately attainable. It just took ambition and drive, and he had plenty of both. He'd keep churning contacts for all the insurance they'd swallow. It was true everyone might not need so much coverage, but it was his job to sell, not to decide what someone should *not* buy. Soon enough he'd have it all, and then he could let up on the sales pitch and start being everyone's best friend.

"I assume you've got substantial coverage on the car," he said.

"You know it, brother: appraisal value. But the best insurance is this." Charlie twirled the small silver coin hanging by a chain from the rearview mirror.

Bud reached for it. "It looks ancient."

"So Crats, you do not disappoint. It is, in fact, an ancient Greek drachma, Thracian Kingdom, to be precise."

"Ah, still batshit crazy over the Greek philosopher thing."

"Well, I don't call myself 'Homer' out loud."

Bud laughed. "But you stole an ancient coin from some museum."

"No, I bought it at the same time as the car. It's not *that* rare, but it *is* my talisman. It keeps the Jag secure. It's my safety insurance."

"Right, well I guess it works," Bud laughed. "I wonder if I could sell 'safety' coverage? But as to real-world insurance, what about other risks: house, life, the book business?"

"My broker worked through the other stuff."

"Did he put you into whole life policies, you know, to build equity?"

"Well, for me, yes. Tess has this huge term life policy through work; pays a million and a half. We also get all our medical and dental through her job."

"I'm impressed. Disappointed but impressed. Most people are babes in the woods about protecting what they've got. Trust me, though, I'll think of some other policy you need."

Charlie laughed. "Well, could be, and I'm no finance guy. I don't even do my own taxes. But writing comes with time in the doldrums when I'll turn to practically anything for distraction, so I look at investments, insurance, that kind of thing."

The bakery was a short drive from the bottom of Breakneck Road, and the cake was ready when they arrived. The missing baker had shown up after all. Outside, Charlie asked, "Ready to see the secret fishing spot?"

"I really *would* like to see it," Bud responded. "I love fly fishing more than just about anything. But I'd rather get back to the party. We get together so rarely." He wanted to find out about Ansel's publishing coverage. He imagined writing books about recent history risked defamation claims, and a lead on the professor's business would help in writing off those expensive Yankees tickets. "And honestly," he continued, "what I'd love more than anything would be for you to let me drive back up the mountain."

Charlie breathed in through his teeth, momentarily looking anxious, but then handed over the keys. "It's all yours, brother," he said graciously.

They buckled in, Charlie offered a few words about the five-speed shift, and the engine came to life. Bud lit up. There was definitely a car like this in his future.

* * *

Ansel checked to make sure he had put in all the changes. It was simple: "Stephen" now came back to the dorm late, saw "Evan" go into his room *with a girl,* recognized his opportunity and headed to the party to lay siege to the woman of his dreams.

He saved and closed the document, but then a nagging thought occurred to him. Was there a mention of someone kidding Evan about striking out and not spending the night with that girl? He opened the document again and skimmed the next chapter. He must have imagined that. He closed the document again and plugged in the remote hard drive from the drawer, checking the napkin for the second password.

* * *

Bud was seeing a payoff to this get-together. Not only did he have a lead on selling a homeowner's policy to Pete, and an invitation to his weekly poker game with other potential clients, but all this talk of cars made him wonder if he could get Charlie to replace his coverage on the Jaguar and maybe write a policy on Ansel's car as well, which would make for high-end policies on two of the most expensive cars he ever saw.

And speaking of unreal cars, this ride was fantastic! The mountain road felt alive beneath the Jaguar, nothing like when he arrived in his Fiat. This was radical. He took the turns slower than Charlie had but itched to push it faster. Too soon they reached the switchback below Mountain House. He let up on the gas, relishing the last few moments, and coasted into the driveway.

"You've made my day, sport," Bud said, shutting off the engine.

Charlie was confused by the quiet when they entered the house. Where was everyone? Bud raised an eyebrow in question. Charlie shrugged his shoulders and set the cake box down in the kitchen. He gestured Bud toward the tub of beer and began looking around the house.

There was no sign of life in the bedrooms or the TV room. No one was on the terrace or in the clearing. He looked up the stairs and saw the den door was closed. Tess would not have brought everyone up there while he was out, or at all, and how could they all be so quiet if they were there?

Bud had settled in on the terrace. Charlie moved to join him, but then hesitated, turned back and quickly mounted the stairs.

He swung open the door. Ansel sat before Charlie's laptop.

"What the fuck?" Charlie shouted, eyes blazing.

Chapter 30

"What the hell are you doing?" Charlie barked.

"I'm…okay, just listen."

Charlie strode into the room.

Ansel moved from behind the desk. "Please," he said urgently, "let me explain. I needed to join a conference call and Tess offered this room. Listening to the endless drivel, I noticed your laptop. The thought sprang on me that you wouldn't have time to fix that plot point."

"What plot point?"

"You know: what we talked about, where the hero sees the villain without a girl?"

"We talked about it, yeah, but that doesn't explain this."

"Well, I misunderstood…obviously. I thought you agreed it would help the story. Anyway, that's what I thought. So, I scrolled through the document while I sat on the call and made the change. It was only a few words."

Charlie stared at him, trying to see into his mind.

"Look, I overstepped. I see that. But I was trying to help. I know how publishers nag when they're waiting for a manuscript. Obviously, you'd change it back if you didn't like it."

Charlie wondered how he could have left the manuscript open. This was too strange.

"Listen," Ansel went on. "I know you can't focus on minutiae when a new opportunity turns up."

"Charlie, are you up there?" Tess called from downstairs. They heard people on the terrace.

Charlie called down. "Yeah, babe. Where were you?"

Tess appeared in the doorway. "We walked to the overlook. We saw those two falcons." She looked past Charlie into the den. "Everything okay?"

"No worries," Charlie said. "We'll be down in a minute."

While Charlie turned to close the door, Ansel slipped the napkin with the passwords into his pocket.

Charlie turned to him again. "So, what? You figured you'd make the change as a surprise, like it came out of the ether?"

"Oh no, man. I was going to tell you later, a parting gift after we put a dent in the Old Bones. Look, I'm sorry this upset you."

"Upset me! You broke into my computer and fucked with my book! And what else have you been fucking with, Ansel?"

"What do you mean?"

"Don't play innocent."

"Charlie, look. I was trying to help! Of course I was going to tell you. It was a favor. Scrivener's services, *you* know." He cocked his head with a sad smile.

Charlie seethed.

"Man, I'm sorry. What more can I say? You asked for help."

Charlie let out a deep breath. This was *so* wrong. This bastard took liberties with his book *and* was toying with his wife; he was sure of it. But Ansel was right that Charlie asked for his help. Was it possible he was telling the truth, at least about this?

He pictured kicking Ansel down the stairs and jamming him into his damned Aston Martin, head-first would be best. That would feel great, but then everyone would see Charlie as the monster, and it would be the end of the reunion and the McYanks.

No, he had to calm down. The insult burned into him like a hot brand, but Ansel was right that any harm could easily be fixed. It was more of an insult than actual damage. As to Ansel inserting himself into Charlie's marriage: this was not the time to squelch that, not with everyone here. He would sort it out later, after he calmed down, but he *would* sort it out! For now he had to keep his cool. He could not let Tess see he was upset; she would think he was just jealous.

He looked once more at Ansel, who stood motionless. "Look," he said, "this is *not* okay. But it's easy to undo and we're not getting into it now." He turned to open the door. "Come downstairs," he said stoically.

Tess met Charlie at the bottom of the stairs and said in a low voice, "Anything wrong?"

"Nothing, babe. Just book stuff. We're all straightened out."

He hoped he was right. He would just reverse Ansel's changes. Whatever his friend was up to didn't matter. He'd always been an arrogant son of a bitch. Now that he was famous, he was worse. But Charlie would not act angry, not in front of everyone. Everything was fine. The book was on track, the movie was underway, he and Tess would get back to their first days and for now they had a house full of old friends to entertain.

Straining to hide a feeling of foreboding, Charlie handed Ansel a drink and poured one for himself. He then moved out to the terrace, where everyone was laughing at Bud's stories about Red Sox fans at Fenway. Sunshine filled the valley with warm light. The sky was clear but for thin clouds in the distance. The kids had wound down. Odysseus slept in a corner. A soulful Miles Davis tune caressed the air.

Charlie sat in a wicker chair, waiting for his pulse to slow down and for Bud to finish his stand-up routine. "So my drug test came back negative," Bud said, before a theatrical pause. "My dealer's got a lot of explaining to do." He stopped short at a stern nod from Molly toward her son.

"Yeah," he stammered. "Sorry about that. Like they say, when life gives you melons, you might be dyslexic."

Theo looked questioningly at his mother. She grinned and then started to laugh.

Bud could see Charlie had something to say, and concluded,

"Thank you, folks. Don't forget to tip your waitress. And now, I give you our gracious host, Charles Piedmont III."

Charlie smirked at Bud and turned to the rest of them. "So, beyond wanting to host you all in our home, we had an ulterior motive in inviting you. I need help remembering facts from Trinity, as building blocks for my novel. The book is fiction, but it's important to understand what *really* happened before I craft our history into a story."

"A fair price for the soiree," Bud said, holding up his glass.

"Absolutely," Dutch toasted.

Ansel looked straight ahead and sipped his bourbon. Becca picked up her camera and started taking candid shots.

Molly looked around and laughed. "Are you kidding? What better subject could there be? But just so we understand, you're only interested in spring term?"

"Well, no, I'll use the first part of the year as an introduction, but the action will center on third term."

Molly nodded thoughtfully.

"So who remembers," Charlie began, "how we found that book *Advice to the University of Dublin*?"

"Yes!" Bud shouted. "The mayhem playbook!"

"Right. The worst we ever did was tame compared to the student riots of the eighteenth century. But how did we find that book? Was it your advisor, Ansel?"

Ansel sat deep in his chair, intent on his drink. "What," he said, as if he hadn't been following. "No, I think it was my grandfather."

"No," said Molly definitely, her hands pausing from braiding her daughter's hair. "I remember you pointing out Professor Doogan and saying he told you about the book. What a tragedy about his accident!"

"And I had a question about that too, Ansel," Charlie said. "Doogan crashed at a race in Kildare, right? Didn't you go along to help with his car?"

"No," Ansel said abruptly, then he paused. "I went to some races in Michaelmas Term, mostly to watch. You remember: you all came along once in October or November? I couldn't go to that last race, finishing up with school and all."

Charlie pondered what schoolwork would keep *Ansel* from an auto race. On top of which, the term was over. It was so hard to pull the truth out of anything he said.

As the others shared Trinity anecdotes, Ansel wished his own story was innocent and magical like the others. But this noxious attention to twelve years ago threatened his future! He struggled for a solution. What was Charlie's problem? Why wouldn't he just fix the story? Did he suspect Ansel had seduced his wife? He wasn't devious enough to exact quiet revenge. If he suspected them he would beat his chest and throw Ansel off the terrace. No, he was not smart enough to figure out what he had—or recognize what he did *not* have. He had just fumbled for a story and stumbled into the muck. And then Ansel had also just fumbled, big time. There had to be another way to stop Charlie.

Dutch was paying closer attention than the others. He couldn't make out what was going on with Ansel; one moment he seemed miles away and then suddenly he was arguing details like a historian. And why did he say schoolwork made him miss Brandon's race? Of course, Ansel was always making things up. But the more he thought about it, the more it seemed Ansel was concocting a defense, but a defense against what?

He looked up to see Becca pointing her camera at him and struck a silly face to make her laugh. She was so sweet, and it occurred to him she might really like him. He glanced at her again and saw her turn shyly away. He was not imagining this. It was time to forget about the whole mess with Jennifer. Just because she left was no reason to distrust *all* women. Having Becca in his life could change everything.

"Okay," said Charlie, "so who knows what happened to Professor Doogan? When did he come out of his coma?"

Bud pulled out his phone and worked his thumbs. As the conversation turned to Digory's accident, he interrupted. "I found an article. Professor Brandon Doogan died from his injuries in 2005. Damn, I don't remember hearing that."

The mood darkened. They were quiet until Tess appeared in an apron, a cheerful smile on her face. "Duty calls," she said to Charlie.

He was annoyed she had interrupted talk about the book, but he rose to man the grill. Ansel followed Tess to the kitchen and returned to carry out a platter piled high with flank steak and salmon.

"Very retro, charcoal instead of gas," Ansel said, handing Charlie the tray.

"We're just an old-fashioned couple," Charlie said with a sharp edge to his voice intended as a warning.

Ansel winced but recovered. "I'm glad you're not angry."

"Look, man," Charlie said, intensely but so only Ansel could hear, "just drop it! I'll pull up the prior version. I…well, just forget it."

Tess couldn't understand how Ansel had still been upstairs when the men got back with the cake, but she'd been unable to get him alone to ask what happened. She hoped he and Charlie had worked it out, whatever it was. She wished even more that Charlie would give up on this book, which was causing trouble for Ansel, who might implicate her for helping him.

She had almost gagged when Charlie announced *we* had an ulterior motive for inviting everyone to the house. He clearly meant *he and Tess* wanted help with the Trinity story, but *she* had no interest in his book. She had only been thinking about Ansel when she blurted out that invitation. But Charlie would never suspect that. He was too wrapped up in his book and his movie to see anything else. It all made her want to scream, or get away. Maybe she should take his precious car for a run over the peak? That would show him.

Charlie carried the grilled food into the kitchen and carved the steak. Tess and Becca spirited hot and cold dishes to the table and everyone took seats. When he sat down, Charlie swallowed his anger and focused on the convivial scene.

"Your table's lovely," Molly said, settling into a chair. "We usually eat off plastic or in shifts."

Once Tess joined them, Charlie tapped a fork on his wine glass and rose to propose a toast. "I'd first like to give credit where it's due, to my lovely wife, without whom dinner would have been pizza and chips."

Everyone applauded. Tess seemed poised between embarrassment and impatience.

"And on a more serious note," Charlie continued, "the Greek philosopher So Crats," nodding toward Bud, "left behind no writings, but one verse of his has come down to us through oral history, and I recite it in sincere toast to the McYanks of Botany Bay:

> *I left at five, and glad to survive,*
> *Some never recovered at all.*
> *For no one stayed sober the night we went over*
> *The wall to the Trinity Ball!*

They all laughed, other than the kids, who at least enjoyed clinking their milk glasses in toast. Charlie knew they'd all remember the stanza from the poem the McYanks had been caught painting on the wall of the Buttery, perhaps the closest they came to creating genuine mayhem on campus.

Conversations sprang up, none lingering on Trinity. Charlie noticed Ansel still looked distracted. He clearly was embarrassed about the altercation, which was just. Could he actually also be contrite? This was Ansel, after all.

After a couple of glasses of wine with dinner, Ansel went to the bar for a fresh bourbon. Charlie desperately wanted to keep the party on track and so poured himself a bourbon as well.

"*Sláinte*," Charlie said, toasting with a deadly serious expression toward Ansel, who raised his glass feebly and echoed the Gaelic toast.

* * *

After dinner, Becca picked up her camera and looked for subjects. She wanted to thank Charlie and Tess for inviting her by capturing some candid shots. Theo was showing Tess and Molly a magic trick in the great room. Ansel was pouring himself a drink and offering one to Pete, who opted for coffee. With a second wind, Anna was chasing a bewildered Odysseus around the house.

"So how did the architectural photos turn out?" Charlie asked.

"Well, let's see," Becca said and held up the camera. "Here they are." She handed the camera to Charlie.

"You've got a great eye," he said, flipping through the photos.

"Thanks!" she said. "There are some nice ones at the overlook, as well, if you back up a few. I'll send along the whole set once I delete the duplicates and edit the rest."

Becca left Charlie to take his time with the camera and wandered onto the terrace, where Bud was talking with Dutch. As she approached, Bud asked, "Becca, have you noticed anything odd about your employer? He seems to be drinking pretty hard."

She shrugged. "It's part of my job not to notice when Ansel acts oddly."

"What does *that* mean?" Dutch said abruptly.

She was taken aback by how protective that sounded. "I mean," she said, "he's had a lot on his mind, especially with his son showing up."

"His son?" Dutch and Bud exclaimed together.

"Oh fudge," she said. "Didn't you know about True?"

Dutch and Bud looked at her in shock, saying nothing.

"You're such old friends," she said painfully. "I assumed you knew."

Bud looked at Dutch for confirmation and then turned to Becca. "No, this is breaking news. How old is he? Who's the mother?"

"Look, I screwed up," she said, embarrassed. "It's Ansel's business what he tells people about his life. You've got to promise you won't say anything. He'll definitely fire me."

"Oh, come on," Bud said. "You can't leave us hanging!"

Dutch looked ponderous, but held up a hand to stop the conversation. "It's okay, Becca. It won't go any further. We're just…amazed is all." He seemed genuinely concerned about repercussions she might feel for revealing Ansel's secret. He really was a noble sort.

Charlie flipped through Becca's photos of the house and the party. She had a talent for catching personality in unguarded expression. One picture showed Molly in a single glance both warning and embracing her son. An outdoor shot caught Dutch's eyes alight while he watched the kids play with the dog. Another…another was a punch in the gut: Tess sipping wine with a longing look clearly directed at Ansel. What was this shit? This wasn't right. And under his own roof! He set the camera down and mounted the stairs to the den, where he sat staring at the valley. Ansel was messing with his work *and* insinuating himself into his marriage. This could not go on!

Ansel needed a new plan. He decided to make them all think he was drunk, in case this opened up an opportunity. Maybe he would stay overnight and fix things. He took his full glass to the bathroom, where he flushed most of it down the toilet. It was a sin to waste good bourbon but he had to do something. He made up for the lost liquor with a couple of coke lines, limiting himself to avoid looking too bright-eyed.

He couldn't object to what Charlie did with his own book, regardless of whether the change would improve the plot. And now there was no way to fix the problem; Charlie would resist just to be obstinate.

Everything was closing in. He had to head this off. There could be no discussion about Dublin. Not now, not after all these years. All it took was one damned book by one hack author—who just might sell a million copies—and people would put two and two together. He could picture Ed Flagel pontificating on how the History Department must avoid any whiff of scandal. Then who knew what else might come out, like about Georgia and the other undergraduates he dated. He really had to clean up his act, but most important was to stop Charlie's book!

After they had digested dinner, Molly announced she and Pete had to get the kids home. Pete found Theo mesmerized in front of a monster movie in the TV room. Anna sat on a sofa rubbing her eyes with the back of her hand. "She's *too* cute," Dutch said, carrying her out to the driveway, her tiny arms around his neck.

"We can't thank you enough," Molly said, hugging Tess and reaching out a hand to Charlie.

"I'll text about poker next week," Bud said, shaking Pete's hand. Ansel set aside his glass long enough to mumble goodbye and then returned shakily for a refill.

Pete pointed the minivan down the mountain and everyone went back inside to lounge over chairs and sofas in the great room. The house was eerily quiet with the children gone and the dog asleep. Charlie put on a mellow Wes Montgomery disc.

"Oh," he said suddenly, "I meant to ask if you guys have ideas for a book title. I was thinking maybe *Mayhem and Magic*."

"How about *Over the Wall*?" Bud suggested.

A half-hour of discussion apparently produced no keepers. Ansel thought about suggesting *How I Screwed the Historian with His Own History*, but said nothing.

Charlie finally said, "We've got several empty beds, and you guys are *not* driving home tonight."

"Oh, I'm okay," said Bud and, looking at Dutch sipping a cup of coffee, added, "and the big fella's solid as a horse, as always."

They all turned to Ansel, sunk deep into a sofa with his eyes closed and a glass balanced on his chest.

"Well, *one* of you will be staying over," Charlie said, clearly relishing Ansel's incapacity.

On cue, Ansel sat up. "What? Me? Oh, I'm fine." He stood and purposely stumbled and spilled his drink and then sat again. He opened his eyes wide and looked at Becca. "You know what, my es-tim-able social guru, I think maybe I *should* have a wee nap. Maybe old Plato boy here will drive you home."

She turned to the rest of them in confusion. Dutch pointed a thumb at himself. She looked at Ansel, annoyed, then back to Dutch. "Would that be okay?" she asked apologetically.

"No problem," he said. Ansel laughed to himself at succeeding in pushing Becca and Dutch together again. They were both so guileless, maybe they *were* a good fit? More importantly, he had bought himself a way to remain on site and think of what to do about Charlie.

Ansel went partly limp as Bud and Charlie helped him to the guest room under the den. Tess brought a folded towel and pajamas into the room. "I just washed these things," she said, setting them on the dresser. "I'll leave them in case he wants them."

The guys lowered Ansel onto the bed, removed his shoes and left him on top of the covers.

Left alone, Ansel wracked his brain for how to stop Charlie.

* * *

In a few minutes the guests were gone, and Tess was in bed. Charlie locked up and sat on the terrace with Odysseus to finish his drink.

"You've had a busy day, old fella," he said, scratching the dog's ears.

He would kick Ansel out in the morning and then make calls about the movie. But something was nagging at him. He couldn't put his finger on it but was sure it concerned Ansel and Tess. Lately, they were all he could think about.

He kicked off his shoes and considered whether to change into pajamas. Then it struck him: she said she had just washed those things! He jumped up and went to the guest room, quietly opened the door and retrieved the pajamas Tess left for Ansel. Back in the great room, he held them under a light. He knew precisely the last time he wore these pajamas because it was the last night he and Tess made love. That was two months ago. How could she have "just washed them"?

Something was wrong. The missing bourbon when he only drank

scotch. Tess's look at Ansel in Becca's photo. His pajamas needing to be washed. And the password! Thinking about it now, there was no way he left his manuscript open. The laptop turned itself off. What was the setting, an hour? Ansel could *not* have found the document open, which meant he had the password. Charlie never left passwords lying around, so Ansel must have gotten it from Tess!

"Damn her," he growled and threw his glass over the railing into the woods. It all fit. They chose each other to start and they were at each other still. The only question was whether this had been going on all along, or if they started up only after the dinner at Arobel. In agony, he thought of the times lately he had left town, clearing the field for that bastard, and of the fact that they both spent their days in the city. How could he be so dense? And how could she betray him?

He shut off the light, and Odysseus followed him into the master suite and collapsed on his dog bed. Charlie looked long at his sleeping wife, wondering if she had ever really been his.

Chapter 31

Becca was grateful for Dutch's caution driving down the mountain. As they approached the main road, orchestral music hummed from his pocket. He handed his phone to her and asked her who was calling.

"It says 'The President.'"

He pulled over and took the phone. "Hi, Dad. Everything okay?" He paused. "Is it bad? I mean, of course it's bad. What hospital?"

He hung up and gripped the steering wheel with both hands.

"What is it?" she asked.

"It's my mom. She burned herself. She's, well she's starting to have trouble, you know, remembering things."

"Oh, I'm so sorry. Where's the hospital? Can we go there?"

"It's out in Queens. I'll drop you first at your apartment."

"No way. We're going *straight* there." Having lost her mother at an early age, Becca thought nothing was more important than family, even if it wasn't hers.

She nodded in response to his questioning glance and he threw the car into gear. They drove in silence. She watched him, intrigued by determination that reminded her of her father. She also saw the confidence of a man who ran his own company. It was clear you could rely on this guy.

They crossed the bridge to Long Island. She recounted the day: the kids, the fabulous house, that great dog and those people! She wished she could have studied abroad, like them, and they were all so interesting and successful. Well, hopefully she'd have a career by the time she was their age.

When they parked at the hospital, she began to get out but dropped her phone and bent to pick it up. When she sat up, she saw that, even in his distracted state, he had walked around the back of the car to open her door. She couldn't suppress a smile. He was a real throwback.

Inside they approached a nurse at the reception desk. "Are you family?" she asked officiously.

"I'm her son, Dilbert."

"And this is your wife?" She nodded toward Becca. He turned to her, looking helpless. She responded to the nurse with her best sad smile and took his arm. The nurse gestured toward the elevator. Side by side on the ride to the third floor they shared a tight-lipped smile.

They found Joe in the room with Alice. Her arm was bandaged and she looked tired. She perked up when they entered.

"Here's my sweet boy!" she said, reaching out her unbandaged arm. Dutch took her hand and leaned in for a hug. When he straightened, she looked past him at Becca, trying to stand out of the way by the door. "And he brought an angel."

"Oh, Mom, Dad, yeah," Dutch said, "this is Rebecca Howard. We were driving home from a dinner party when I got your call and she insisted we come straight here."

"It's so nice to meet you, Mrs. Gilroy," Becca said, stepping forward to take Alice's hand. "I hope you're feeling better."

"Oh, sweetheart," Alice said, "you light up the room! Isn't she pretty, Joe?"

Joe had stepped back to make room but now smiled and shook Becca's hand with both of his, obviously relieved at their arrival. There were tears in his eyes.

Dutch stepped in and hugged his father in greeting, gently turning him toward the window and giving him a chance to collect himself. Smoothly done.

Before long the nurse came by and said Mrs. Gilroy needed to sleep. They could return in the morning, when she'd be released. In the parking lot, Joe apologized for dragging them to the hospital and said they shouldn't bother returning the next day.

"It was no trouble, really," Becca said.

"I'll pick you up at ten, Dad," Dutch said, "and we'll bring Mom home together."

Joe hugged his son, nodded politely to Becca and climbed into his car. As they watched him drive off, she slipped her arm through his. It took a moment for him to notice, but he didn't let go.

She liked how it felt hanging on to this man, strong in his core and attuned to things outside himself. The handsome bartenders she schemed to attract, the basketball player with the beautiful body, even her dreamboat high school boyfriend, all thought so much of themselves. But Dutch was different. He paid attention to what other people felt and needed rather than how he looked in their eyes.

On the way back to the city, he turned on the radio. Orchestral music filled the car. "Oh, I'll get that," he said and pushed a button to change the station.

"No, I like Mozart," she said, switching it back. "It's the 40th Symphony. I played cello when we butchered that in middle school."

He looked at her with a sideways smile. "So you're a musician, too?"

"Too?" she said, wondering what else she was supposed to be. "No, I'm no musician. My dad could never get me to practice, so I wasn't any good. And then I did the music world a favor and gave it up for sports. But I love the passion of a symphony…by a *professional* orchestra."

The detour to the hospital had stripped away any awkwardness. They talked like teammates after a victory, about photography and baseball and living in New York City. She was touched by his affection for his parents, that he felt more blessed to have time with them than put upon dealing with his mother's condition. He planned to get tickets to more Yankee games and she said she'd join him, as long as she could wear her Brewers cap.

He looked her up and down, as if he were assessing an athletic prospect. "Do you play anymore?" he asked. "Baseball, I mean."

"My roommate's trying to recruit me for a team in the 'Bitches Softball League.' I just have to work out if I have time, and get my dad to send my glove."

After a few minutes he said, "And what about Ansel? I'm not sure it's great for you to work for that guy."

"You sound like my dad," she said, thinking that was not a bad thing. "But it's a good job and, at my level, I need the experience."

She thought about her regrettable afternoon with Ansel, a few weeks back and a lifetime ago, and how angry she was when he brushed her off. There was no way she would tell Dutch about that; he might break Ansel in half. Why did Dutch see him for what he was, while everyone else made excuses for him? There was perception in those deep blue eyes, perception and a kind of dignity.

Talking to Dutch gave her confidence she'd make it in the city after all, but what it meant to "make it" was changing. It was not so important any more to attend the Met Gala or drive an expensive car, but she *would* find some way to make a living at photography or marketing, and money would be nice as well. Maybe Leah should be her role model. And the guy behind the wheel? He was no matinee idol, but in real life pretty boys could only carry the conversation so far. He was someone who could surprise her and challenge her. The strength obvious in those hands steering the car didn't hurt either. There was a primal attraction in a man who could lift her up and beat off the wolves.

He looked over at her, amused or maybe just curious.

"I wonder," she said thoughtfully, "if something's going on with Ansel. Lately, he's been on edge for no reason."

"You know, it all seems to tie back to Trinity. In fact, I think he set up our dinner because I mentioned looking up a girl we met there. Ansel went off with her when he broke up with Tess. I assume you know she went out with Ansel before Charlie?"

"I didn't, but I can believe it. She's so stunning, just Ansel's type."

"Well, as far as I know, he never saw this other girl again, but she and I kept in touch for a while. A couple of weeks ago the guys kidded me about calling her, which made Ansel look like his head would explode. I think that's when he decided to introduce us, like you'd take my mind off her."

She smiled cautiously, wondering if Ansel's plan was working.

Then he added: "I think I'll call her. We need to find out what happened that night."

Chapter 32

Ansel stayed in bed until he heard activity in the house. He knew they'd push breakfast on him but he wanted to leave as soon as possible. With his hair and clothes disheveled, he shuffled out to the kitchen.

Tess, emptying the dishwasher, looked up with a sympathetic smile. "Ready for coffee?" she said brightly.

Charlie was carrying a chair across the room. "Well, if it isn't the life of the party."

Odysseus licked Ansel's hand, angling for a scratch.

Tess insisted on cooking him bacon and eggs. He acquiesced, squeezing the bridge of his nose to ease his hangover, which was only partly an act. Charlie put two aspirin and the empty bourbon bottle on the table, next to Ansel's orange juice. "Well, we polished off the Old Bones," he said.

Ansel half-smiled. "I'm glad you said 'we.' I was afraid I did that all by myself."

He looked at them both. "Look, I'm sorry about last night. I don't know what came over me. Just a lot of things with my book deadlines and the university. I don't remember anything after Molly and Pete left, like how I ended up in the guest room, but I hope I didn't embarrass anyone."

"Not to worry," Tess said. "You faded away and the men put you to bed. I hope you slept well."

"Like the dead. It took the smell of coffee to wake me."

Charlie and Tess continued to straighten the house while he ate. Although he was hungry, Ansel only picked at his breakfast. He could see she wanted to take care of him but that could not happen, and Charlie was clearly eager to see him gone. As soon as he could, without seeming to hurry, he bid them goodbye, thanking them for the party, the bed and their understanding. He said he hoped they would all get together again soon.

He took it easy driving down the mountain, enjoying the view. Wind through the open windows helped clear his head. He regretted things had not gone the way he hoped. If Charlie had just changed the book himself!

* * *

With all the guests finally gone and the house put together, Charlie retreated to his den. The manuscript printouts behind his chair were mixed up, which must have been Ansel's doing. Damn him! Why was the book so important to him? Obviously, he had a public image to manage, but why would a fictional romance based on his college days matter to anyone? It had to be something related to Tess. She hated the idea of the book, so maybe that was a clue. He slammed his fist on the desk, breathing heavily.

When he had calmed down, he dialed the phone. "Joan, it's Charlie."

"And a bright good morning to you."

"You said they hired Milo Channing to direct, right?"

"Yeah, that was after you met the producers in LA."

"Right, and you also said he was visiting Baltimore to scout locations?"

"That's right. Why?"

"I was thinking. If I could meet him and show him around, it might help get me the job writing the screenplay."

"You're right, Charles. I should have thought of that."

"So, can we arrange it?"

"I'll get on it right now."

Charlie hadn't planned to ever go back to that hell hole where he grew up, but this was a great opportunity.

Joan called back an hour later. "We're on," she said. "Sunday evening we'll meet Milo for dinner and then visit a few indoor spaces, and then he asks if you can show them some outdoor locations early Monday, before the city's quite awake. The lawyer will be there as well so, if all goes well, we *could* bang out a contract. Fingers crossed."

"That's fantastic! It's really time for a new start, for the movie and everything else."

"What else? You mean the book?"

"Yeah, the book. Anyway, I'm sure I can show them places to shoot; I *do* know the story pretty well."

She laughed. "You so deserve this, Charles. I'm proud of you."

"Thanks, Joan. I'd be adrift without you."

"So, I'll book seats for late afternoon and send you the information. We'll stay at their hotel. Hopefully, we wrap everything, celebrate at a dinner Monday and fly back Tuesday morning."

Charlie was ecstatic about the movie. But the weekend still loomed over everything. He couldn't escape thinking Ansel had designs on his wife, or that they had been meeting behind his back. He wondered what everyone at the party saw and who he could even ask. Molly was too close to Tess. Bud never paid attention to anything. That left Dutch, who wouldn't speak harshly about anyone but who at least would be honest. Charlie also had an excuse to call.

"Hey, Plato," Charlie said. "Just wondering how the ride home went."

Dutch was with his dad at the hospital, waiting for his mother to be released. He stepped outside to talk. "Thanks for the party. It was outstanding. But enough happened afterwards to fill a couple of chapters."

"You didn't…"

"Oh, not that, you dog. No, I drove Becca home but we got sidetracked because my mom went to the hospital."

"Oh, no! Is she all right?"

"Well, yes, for now. She's not really *all right*, but that's a long-term thing. Anyway, Becca was amazing! Her being there did more for my mother than the doctors and all the rest of us."

"That's no surprise. And hey, she's a keeper. I hope you two can get clear of Ansel's shadow."

"Yeah, maybe. It *is* an ominous shadow."

"Funny you should say that. We had a run-in at the party when I found him in my laptop messing with my book."

"You're kidding! How is that possible? Isn't there a password?"

Charlie didn't want to look foolish or appear as if he suspected Tess. "Yeah," he said, "but I've got it set to stay open, apparently just long enough for Ansel to get in."

"You know," Dutch said, "he acted so weird about Reilly. I should call and see what she knows."

"You *should*. He's hiding something and it all goes back to Dublin and, damn, the night of that party was when Digory died! What he changed in my story was where I saw him come back to Botany Bay alone and then go off again toward the Buttery, but he could have known some back route to the Arts Block."

"Where Digory fell."

"Exactly. Listen, I'm going to pull out all his changes to the manuscript and see if there's more to go on. Let's talk later."

"Okay, brother."

"Oh, my God!" Charlie said.

"What is it?"

"I just thought…" He stopped. "Ansel also acted like he couldn't remember Professor Doogan's name, even after working with him the whole year."

"Right, with the races and all."

"And the professor was his advisor on his paper, the only thing that mattered to him."

"But what has that got to do with anything? Should we call Bud, or the police?"

"Not the police! We don't want them sniffing around. Anyway, New York cops won't care about something that happened in Ireland. But Bud might know something. Ansel was *his* roommate."

"And what about asking your wife?"

"Oh, I don't think so," Charlie said, suspecting she might alert Ansel. "We'd better keep this between us and Bud until we know what's up."

Chapter 33

Dutch wondered what was wrong between Charlie and Tess. Then he thought about Becca. Ansel was his friend, but she was too good a person to get caught up in his crap. The way she took Dutch's arm at the hospital and how they connected on the ride home made him believe he *could* deserve her, that he *did* deserve her. There was nine years difference between them, and she was way better looking than him, but there were more important things in the long run. Maybe this was where life took a turn for the better?

He called Reilly's old number.

"Reilly, it's Dutch Gilroy. You know, from Dublin?"

"Dutch Gilroy! What a nice surprise! It must be what, five, six years? I think it was me who dropped the ball."

"Oh, no matter. How are things?"

"Married a guy from work, second son is six months old, so everything's upside down here. But we love it."

"That's great. I'm so happy for you." He hesitated. "Listen, I won't keep you, but…"

"You sound concerned."

"It's just, well, some strange things have come up lately about Dublin. It's about that night we met at a party on campus and you lost your phone."

"I was traveling with my friend Carol. Some Irish guys invited us."

"Right. Well, here's the thing. We—my American friends who spent the year there—were talking about that party. I don't know if you heard, but a security guard died that night."

"Oh, no! I had no idea. Carol and I left for Galway early the next morning and all I heard after that was when you sent back my phone and we emailed."

"Yeah, I know, and this has nothing to do with you. It's just, well, Ansel Tone is the guy you met at that party."

"I definitely remember him! Dark wavy hair. Is he Ansel Tone, the writer?"

"Yeah, or he *became* Ansel Tone. But what do you remember about him?"

"Well, he was hot and Carol and I had been watching him. It looked like he was with this dark-haired girl, very attractive. But then he came up and asked me to dance, and well, he didn't act like he was with anyone. And then later he and the brunette had this loud argument, and she stormed off. Then we danced and he was all over me, or we were all over each other. I was twenty."

"Oh, don't worry; this is ancient history. But what happened *after* the party?"

"He invited me back to his room. He said we could be alone, and I was up for it. So I let Carol know and we left the building."

"Did anything odd happen, anything you can remember?"

"That's an understatement. He made a big exit from the party, shouting out and shaking everyone's hand. People looked at us strangely. But when we were outside it got really weird. As we crossed that fantastic campus, he suddenly said he didn't feel well and would put me in a cab back to my hostel. I thought he was nuts, but he got this intense look so I didn't argue. He walked me out to the street and hailed a taxi. I remember distinctly because he told the driver the address of my hostel, kissed me goodnight and handed me twenty euros. No one had ever done that before. And it was way more than the fare. It felt like he was paying me off."

"So that's the last you saw of him?"

"That's right."

"And do you know what time you got back to your hostel?"

"I don't know exactly, but well before they locked the door. I stayed up for a while but was still asleep before Carol got back. You know, I'd pretty much forgotten about this, but it *was* strange."

"Thank you, Reilly. This is helpful."

"Is he in trouble, that Tone guy?"

"Ansel? Yeah, I think he might be."

* * *

Charlie printed all the manuscript pages showing Ansel's changes and replaced the doctored version on his computer with the last one saved.

Then Dutch called. Charlie reported, "Ansel was focused on what I saw at the dorm. That's all he changed."

"Well, I got hold of Reilly," Dutch said. "She remembers leaving the party with Ansel to go to his room, but instead he sent her home in a taxi. So he *didn't* spend the night with her and he *did* go back to Botany Bay alone. It sounds like that was his plan all along."

"And he didn't want you calling Reilly and discovering he set the whole thing up. He also got rid of Bud so no one would check on him before morning. He set up a perfect alibi for whatever he was up to." He stopped for breath. "It might make a good novel, if we could find a motive."

"Do you think he broke into the Arts Block?" Dutch asked. "But how, and why?"

"As to how, don't you remember how Ansel always knew the back ways into buildings, which doors were unlocked? Remember the night he led us up to the roof of Examination Hall to smoke weed with those Irish guys?"

"Oh God, yes! But that was just a goof. Why would he break into an office building?"

"I think the Gardaí were concerned someone might have been after the valuable stuff, like the illuminated manuscripts."

"Yeah, but they're all in the Old Library. Digory fell off the Arts Block."

"Well, there's some kind of antiquities museum there and…"

"And what?"

Charlie let the question hang for a moment. "Well, stay with me on this. Doogan was the advisor on Ansel's paper and wrote his recommendation…."

"Yeah, so?"

"And someone broke into the building where Doogan's office was…."

"Right," Dutch said thoughtfully.

"And that was after Doogan had his accident."

"I'm with you so far, but why would Ansel break into his office? It doesn't make sense."

"What if there was something in Doogan's office that Ansel wanted?"

"And the professor was in the hospital," Dutch said and paused. "Ansel could have broken in to 'set things right.' But what would be so important in that office, and why wouldn't he tell *us* about it, get our help for God's sake?"

"I don't know. But if he *did* break in, and Digory died chasing him, Ansel would cover it up. He wouldn't want anyone to know, even us. The last thing he needed, with his father and all, was a scandal."

As if in a bad dream, he recalled Ansel hugging Tess at Arobel, wearing his familiar smirk, and then how guardedly they treated each other at the party. He felt in his bones that Ansel was no good, not for anyone. "I've got to go down to Baltimore this evening," he continued, "but I'll be back Tuesday afternoon. You talk to Bud, and then we'll figure out what to do."

"Right. I'll reach you on your cell if he has something to add. It's been twelve years; a couple more days won't matter."

Charlie would know after checking Tess's phone whether a couple of days mattered. He just had to remember where they kept their emergency password list.

Tess glanced at the door to the den, which had been closed all morning. She wanted to finish vacuuming but Charlie would throw a tantrum at the noise. She hoped at least he was working on the movie and would make a success of it. In a perfect world, he'd become a "player" in Hollywood, and she and Ansel would have space to get to know each other again and maybe move toward the life they should have had all along. It would be best to think about that later, though, after the movie was in production and Charlie published his novel. For now, she was content to see Ansel whenever she could.

She decided to make sandwiches from the leftover steak and hazarded a knock on his door. He wasn't angry at being disturbed and they returned to the kitchen together and ate at the table.

"Oh," he said, "I forgot to tell you. I have to pop down to Baltimore later."

She looked up questioningly.

"It'll be a quick trip to meet the director and scout locations. Joan is coming along to negotiate the contract, we hope. There also will probably be a dinner with some investors, so I'll be back Tuesday morning."

"Joan is going?" she said harshly.

"What do you mean?" He sounded annoyed.

Joan would go with him, of course. For a "literary agent," she really went the extra mile. And where would he be without his devotee? Tess could almost see her picking out a short skirt and high heels to impress the Hollywood guys and help them close the deal. She wondered what other surprises Charlie's little friend would pack for their two nights in Baltimore.

But she was letting her emotions get away from her. She forced her expression to soften. "Nothing," she said. "I didn't mean anything.

It sounds like things are really moving forward for you. How will you get there?"

"We'll fly down from Stewart."

"Should I drop you at the airport?"

"Oh, don't bother. I'll get the service to take me over. You stay and enjoy some quiet time. Oh, and remember to leave the keys in the Volvo so the tow truck can pick it up in the morning. You'll have to use the Jag to get to work. And for now, I'm going to take Seusy for a walk in the woods. See you in an hour."

She watched the two of them descend the steps to the clearing, hating how she immediately jumped to the thought of seeing Ansel while Charlie was gone. But Charlie *was* going with Joan, so Tess had no reason to feel guilty. As soon as he had disappeared down the path, she called Ansel. There was no answer. She didn't want to leave a message or a text and so decided to call back.

When Charlie returned Tess was finishing a workout on the terrace. She looked great in yoga pants but Charlie found she no longer attracted him. It had been too many years and he had spent too much effort. Unless he could be sure about her, what good was it to keep pretending?

"I'm due for a long soak," she said, rolling up her mat.

"Excellent idea. You relax. I've got a few things to wrap up before I go."

* * *

Bud was sprawled on his sofa watching golf on television when Dutch called.

"This is *Ansel* we're talking about," Bud said. "You know the normal rules never applied to him." He wanted no part in a conspiracy theory. It could only hurt his chance of selling Ansel coverage for his super car or his apartment or maybe even getting a shot at Jordan's business. And what difference did it make, really, after all these years?

"Are you saying he shouldn't be held accountable if he caused Digory's death?"

"No, not that. Look, I was messed up about what happened to Digory; he was a cranky old coot but soft inside and funny as hell. If Ansel did break into that building, I'm sure it was some kind of prank between him and his professor."

"You remember, don't you, that Doogan was in the hospital at that point?"

"Oh yeah, right. Then it does sound, I won't say suspicious, but a bit off." Dutch was right. Something must have happened, but why should they care?

"Man, we're just concerned. There is a right and a wrong here."

"And you're sweet on his assistant."

"Well, yeah, I am. But even if I weren't, I'd be worried about her working for Ansel if he's involved in something. I know you think this is none of our business, but I really could use your help; we *all* could use your help. If Ansel was involved in Digory's death, that has to come out."

Bud chewed on that. He had never heard Dutch speak so forcefully about anything, or so definitely about a woman. And then there was that night in the alley outside the pub. He owed his health and maybe his life to this guy and, so far, had repaid him only by targeting his company as a client. Maybe Dutch deserved more.

And what was pushing Charlie? Could he suspect Ansel was sniffing around his wife? That would not be far-fetched; she was an eyeful, and Ansel respected no boundaries when it came to women.

"You still there?" Dutch asked.

"I'm with you, big guy. Thinking it out a bit, Ansel *did* flip out at the game when I said you should call that girl in California. I was just giving you a hard time but he acted like I told you to go club baby seals."

"More of the same. And like I said, Reilly was clear he never intended to take her back to the dorm."

"Right, and he made such a point about it being his turn to entertain in our room, and then was so cocky about it the next day."

Dutch paused. "So if it was a prank on the professor, which would not be even remotely all right, given that he was close to dead, why would he go to such lengths to hide it from us? He normally would brag about putting one over on the university."

"Right," Bud said, although he still wanted to avoid stirring things up. "But it all makes sense only if there was something he wanted in the Arts Block."

"And that's where we hit a wall. If he had no reason to break in, the rest of it could just be coincidence."

"Exactly. If there were a reason for Ansel to break in, I'd be convinced. Look, keep me posted, will you?"

"Sure, just sit tight."

Bud hung up and stared absently at the television. None of these suspicions and ulterior motives would move him toward his goal of selling enough insurance to earn his house on the hill. But Dutch was coming down the tracks like a locomotive and there was no slowing him down. And his friends? Did he owe them an obligation as well, just because they spent a year together long ago? It was an unaccustomed feeling, but it felt like he did.

* * *

Charlie's overnight bag stood by the door. He checked to make sure Tess was soaking comfortably in her bath and then went to the kitchen, entered her code into her phone and checked her recent calls. There were two to Ansel while Charlie was out with Odysseus!

That was it. There was no doubt. Tess had left him behind; it was just like when his sister and then his mother abandoned him.

He stuck his head into the master bathroom and asked, "Are you good? Can I get you anything?"

"No, Charlie. I'm content to soak the afternoon through."

"Okay, well, I'm packed and the car will pick me up in an hour. I'll be out in the garage. I want to tighten a loose mirror on the Jag before you drive it."

Chapter 34

Tess looked through her closet. It had been too long since she wanted to look sexy for anyone. She picked out a short black dress she bought for a party in New Haven, when Charlie and she were at least playing at being lovers. She got lots of attention at that party, and not just from her husband. Ansel was going to eat this up.

She tried calling Ansel again but he still didn't pick up. Where could he be? Charlie would be back in two days! Ansel didn't know he had left town, but why wasn't he answering his phone?

There was no telling, really, where it would all go with Ansel, but their night together made clear she needed more than a life with Charlie. At least for now, she wanted to be with Ansel, kiss him, talk to him, *be* with him. And he felt the same. But this was their chance and he was unreachable!

In the morning she called again, but he still didn't answer. She couldn't imagine what was wrong, but she decided not to worry; she'd get hold of him during the day. They couldn't pass up this opportunity.

She poured double the normal food into Odysseus's bowl, since he wouldn't be fed again until Charlie got back Tuesday. She also checked that the dog door was unlatched, but saw it was still broken and wouldn't close. This was concerning but home security could wait; she ached in anticipation of seeing Ansel.

To avoid any mix-up with Charlie calling the house, she texted him: "Timing worked for once. Late night ahead. May stay in the city. See you tomorrow."

She left the keys in the Volvo and the garage door open. When she started up the Jaguar and felt it hum, a smile seeped across her face. She had to admit it was exhilarating to drive this car. How long would it be before she got a chance to try the Aston Martin?

She left the house early so she could park in a garage by the station. But, sitting behind the wheel, she found she had extra time. "And this big boy can make time," she said out loud.

Instead of heading directly to the station, she turned *up* the mountain. The Jag roared. Its sleek body clung to the road. She almost squealed with excitement, leaning into the sharp curves.

In a few exhilarating minutes, she reached the overlook. She hit the brakes hard to skid on the gravel turnaround, because she knew this would irk Charlie *and* it made her feel unfettered. She needed that. She ached for pure release almost as much as she desired Ansel.

But why had she needed to pump the brakes? They were usually responsive. It would be just their luck to have a problem with the Jaguar when the Volvo was already in the shop. And how could she tell Charlie to have his brakes checked without admitting she was skidding his precious car? Could she say a kid ran out into the street or she had to brake for a deer? At any rate, this was no time to worry about brakes. This car was made for going, not stopping, and there was just enough time for a fast run to the station, followed by a maddingly slow train ride and day at the office, and then a lusciously endless night.

For a long moment she breathed in the mountains, full of trees and soil and vast expanse. Ribbons of cloud laced a clear blue sky. She was filled with ardor for the fields, cut like exotic continents in the deep-green forest. Her passions overflowed in all directions.

She put the car into gear and threw up gravel turning back down the mountain. The road was free of traffic, as always, so she could really fly. Punching the speed and then downshifting, cutting perfect arcs on the curves, there was no doubt she was a better driver than Charlie.

She pumped the brakes and slowed as she approached the house. But then she remembered there was no need to stop at home; she had everything she needed for work and a night of bliss. She pictured Ansel's confident smile and could almost feel his breath on her cheek as she accelerated past the driveway. Bypassing Mountain House felt like leaving her old stolid life behind and barreling into the intoxicating unknown. She was finally headed to where she was meant to be. She and Ansel would again be the couple everyone envied, this time on the biggest stage.

At the switchback below the house, she downshifted and hugged the curve in the oncoming lane.

But a truck was bearing down! She was going too fast!

The truck filled her vision! She slammed the brakes to the floor but the car didn't slow. She swerved to her own lane and grabbed the emergency brake! The guardrail splintered. The car launched into the air, the only sound was the wind, and time slowed and then stopped.

Chapter 35

Charlie's visit to Baltimore was going well. He showed Milo potential locations for the film Sunday night and agreed to continue the tour the next day. Over an early breakfast, Milo offered him the screenwriting job. Then, while Charlie and Milo visited locations, Joan would negotiate the contract with the studio lawyer because she had to leave early to fly to Detroit; her mother had gone into the hospital after a fall. But then a call came on Charlie's cell phone.

A cop told him Tess had died in a crash.

Dead? He felt numb, as if he couldn't move. How could everything change inexorably in one moment? Was that possible? What would life be without Tess? If he just kept staring at nothing in particular could he freeze time, or unwind it?

Joan knocked on the door. "Charles," she said with concern, "everything okay?"

He told her. Her expression convulsed. She hugged him close and then backed away, her face overflowing with concern.

"I'll make arrangements to get you home," she said softly. "Is there someone I should call for you?"

"I don't know." He handed her his phone. "Just tell Bud Roberts; he'll know who to call. And her mother; tell her mother."

* * *

Bud was enjoying the morning. Sales figures looked good and Lois had brought in a box of doughnuts. Then he got the call from Joan.

When Lois came into his office to remind him of a meeting, he was staring through the blinds. She touched his arm, which wrenched him into the present.

"I've had some news," he said. "Please cancel my meeting and hold my calls."

Lois backed out of the office. Bud continued to stare. Then he called Molly. She wailed like a wounded animal.

* * *

Dutch was shocked by Bud's call but took it like a soldier. He strode into his father's office to tell Joe he'd have to hold down the shop while Dutch drove up to Mountain House.

"I'm really sorry to hear about this," Joe said, "but this is a woman you haven't seen for years?"

"That's true, Dad, but this connection, to Tess and to all of them… It's hard to explain but I feel like they represent the best of me. Anyway, her husband will need someone and I'm not sure there is anyone else."

No one answered the bell at Mountain House, but Dutch found the door unlocked and entered. Odysseus pushed his snout against his hand. Charlie sat in an Adirondack chair on the terrace staring at the valley.

"Man, I'm so sorry," Dutch said, squatting by Charlie's chair. "It feels like anything I could say would be a cliché."

"Dead prose and rotting poetry," Charlie said, seeming almost amused.

"What?" Dutch said, but realized Charlie wasn't talking to him. Even in his distraught state he was reciting literary quotes, but this one made no sense.

Dutch went back into the house. He answered phone calls, filled the dog's water dish, checked arrangements with the funeral home and made a lunch Charlie wouldn't touch.

* * *

Ansel had told Becca to come in early Monday morning. She took this as a sign he wanted to get some serious work done and showed up at eight, excited to show him photos from the party. She thought they should post one of the whole crowd, kids and dog included, with some clever Trinity College caption, maybe in ancient Greek. There was also a great upper-crust shot of Ansel and Charlie by the Aston Martin. Ansel loved pictures of himself with celebrity friends or his car, and this was both.

"No pictures from the weekend," he said firmly. "Post *none*."

She was stunned. Then he added, "Any trouble getting home from the party?"

She tried to recover. "No," she said, "Dutch brought me home. It was fine."

He turned away and she retreated to the kitchen for a cup of coffee, mostly to get away from him. What was his problem? It was her job to take pictures, and those shots were amazing—Roxie even volunteered that when she saw Becca editing. But a voice inside said maybe she was fooling herself, maybe she was a shit photographer and no good at her job.

She texted Roxie to vent. Her roommate responded: "He's an idiot. Doesn't know what he wants. You're a badass photographer and those pictures rock." Buoyed, Becca collected herself. With a determined smile, she returned to Ansel's office to discuss the new website content and interactivity. The weekend did not come up again.

Later in the morning Ansel jumped at his ringtone. "Hey, Bud," he said in his distracted telephone voice. Then, urgently, he said, "Oh God, no! What, what happened?"

Becca looked up.

"Charlie? He went off the road?"

Ansel's expression flashed from violent emotion to deflation. "Tess?" he said softly. With a dazed look, he handed the phone to Becca.

"Bud, it's Becca," she said breathlessly. "What happened?"

"It's Tess," Bud said. "She crashed off Breakneck Road. She's dead."

"Oh my God!" Becca held the receiver to her chest. After a moment, she gathered herself. "Thank you for calling, Bud. What can we do?"

"Nothing, Becca. Just keep an eye on Ansel, will you?"

"Of course."

She hung up and turned to him. He mumbled and pushed his thumbs into his eyes. She closed her laptop and gathered her things on the kitchen counter. What could she do for Ansel? When she returned to his office, he was on the speaker phone. She heard Bud saying, "Ansel, I'm on with Dutch, just…"

"She was driving?" Ansel interrupted, his voice full of anguish. "Volvos are supposed to be safe!"

"Calm down," Bud said. "I don't know more than I told you. The rest doesn't matter. I have to go."

Ansel opened his laptop and began typing but cursed and slammed it shut.

"What can I do?" she said, wondering at his intensity. "You need something?"

"No. Yes, I wanted to see if there's anything about the accident. A photo or something."

"On it," she said and slunk into a stuffed chair, fingers tapping fleetly. In a minute she showed him a report from an online news site. It was short on details, identifying the victim only as a local homeowner. There was a photo taken from a helicopter through the trees: police technicians around the carcass of a green car.

Ansel stared at the photo and shut the laptop hard. He rubbed the back of his hand across his face. Then he burst up in anger, kicking a chair across the room. She put the kitchen counter between them.

When he slumped into a chair, she made him a cup of coffee, thinking it might calm him. She wondered again how to help him, and

Charlie. She had really liked Charlie and Tess; they had such a perfect life. People dying too young always made her think of her mother, but this was no time to think of herself. She wanted to help. Who was with Charlie now? Then she thought of Dutch; he'd know what to do.

She stepped out on the balcony and pulled out her phone. Thinking back to their walk to the subway after dinner at AzaFuz, she wished *she* had asked Dutch for *his* phone number. But that was easily remedied. She looked up the number for his company and reached a young man who said Mr. Gilroy had been called away on a personal matter. "But I would be happy," he said, "to pass along a message or transfer you to the appropriate person at Aljo."

"Thanks, but this is really personal. I'm…a friend, and I know things are difficult for Mr. Gilroy right now. Could you please tell him Becca called and asked if there's something she can do?"

"You…you're the woman from Wisconsin?"

She was confused. That was hardly how anyone would describe her. "Yes, I'm from Wisconsin. Do I know you?"

"Oh, I apologize, miss. My name is Michael Devers. I'm Mr. Gilroy's executive assistant. I handle his calendar and happened to recall that detail. Perhaps I spoke out of turn."

"It's okay. You just surprised me. So, could you please give Dutch, uh, Mr. Gilroy my message as soon as you can?"

Devers paused. "Listen, miss, I'm not supposed to give out cell numbers, but Mr. Gilroy could use a friend right now. Have you got a pen?"

When Becca hung up, she paused. Why would Dutch's assistant know where she grew up? But that was unimportant; she dialed his number, which went straight to voicemail. She hung up and called Leah to let her know Ansel would miss their meeting and ask for help. Leah had worked with Ansel for years but had never heard of Tess, though he *had* mentioned knowing Charles Piedmont III.

"Stay with him," Leah ordered, "so he won't be alone. I'll come by this afternoon."

* * *

Dutch spoke with the fire department and the police. He called Tess's firm. He tried to reach Joan Munchin but her phone went right to voicemail. He coordinated with Tess's mother, who would make burial arrangements, "since the plot was already paid for." He asked Kelly's Garage to send another tow truck for the Volvo. He drove Charlie to the morgue to identify what was left of the body, through scraps of a suit and a sapphire earring. He was helping Charlie sign papers when his phone rang.

"Dutch, it's Becca."

"Becca? Hi." It felt like someone had opened a window to let in a fresh breeze.

"Listen, I don't want to be a bother. I'm just so sorry about Tess. I know you're busy, between this and everything else, but I'd like to help."

A smile touched his lips for the first time all day. "Thank you. I'm just keeping Charlie company and dealing with the calls. There's not much else to do. I think Bud's driving up tomorrow."

"Okay. Well, this is my number just in case."

When he hung up, he saved the number as a new contact but also copied it onto an old receipt in his wallet.

Chapter 36

Dutch heard a car pull up and opened the door. A tall man in a rumpled brown suit showed his badge. "I'm Detective Crosby," he said, "with the Cold Spring Police." Waving toward a younger, dark-haired woman at his side he added, "And this is Detective Miller. Are you Charles Piedmont?"

"No, I'm Dilbert Gilroy, a friend of the Piedmonts."

"How do you do, Mr. Gilroy?" Crosby said, shaking his hand. "Is Mr. Piedmont here?"

Dutch showed the detectives in. They sat with Charlie and Dutch in the great room. Charlie confirmed the Jaguar was *his* car, and Tess was only driving it because hers needed repair. Miller copied down the number for Kelly's Garage and details of Charlie's visit to Baltimore, where he stayed and who he saw.

"She was the same as always when I left Sunday night," Charlie said. "We had just finished cleaning up after a party, and I took a car to the airport for a meeting Sunday evening and Monday."

"You always take a car service to the airport, as opposed to driving yourself?" Crosby asked.

"We both did. It's so hard dealing with the traffic and parking. You can contact the service. I've got the number on my phone."

"Wait," Miller said. "You flew to Baltimore? What airport did you use?"

"We caught a regional flight out of Stewart."

"That's what," Miller asked, "like a half-hour drive across the bridge? Why didn't your wife drive you?"

"I didn't want Tess to bother driving over Sunday evening."

"And you said 'we' got a flight?" Crosby said.

"Right, my literary agent and I went together."

"And his name is?"

"*Her* name is Joan Munchin. Do you want her number?"

Miller wrote down numbers for the service and the agent and then looked up. "In Baltimore did you and Ms. Munchin stay together, in the same hotel?"

"Yeah, of course. I mean, we didn't stay 'together' but we both stayed at the airport Marriott, where the movie people were. She was there to negotiate my screenplay contract. Then she had to leave separately to deal with her own family emergency and I flew home alone."

"I see," Miller said with a quick glance at Crosby. Dutch saw this silent communication. It almost looked like they found something wrong with Charlie's answers. How could that be? He worshiped Tess!

Crosby returned to his fatherly tone. "And so, let's back up. You say you had a party?"

"Yes, on Saturday. Just a few people, old friends from school." Charlie stared blankly. "Tess was her usual self. Everyone had a great time."

"We'll need the names of those who attended, and their phone numbers," Crosby said.

"I can write those out for you," Dutch volunteered.

"Oh, were you at the party?" Crosby said.

"I was," Dutch said and pulled a pen from his pocket. Miller handed him her pad.

Dutch understood that the detectives needed to gather the facts, but their questioning was insensitive to a guy who had just lost his wife. And something about Crosby's easy, friendly tone unsettled him. It seemed to leave open no possibility of refusing to tell him everything you knew, while he revealed virtually nothing. And it almost seemed like they suspected *Charlie* of doing something wrong. That was ridiculous; he loved that car, and his wife!

And why did they care who was at the party Saturday? The accident happened Monday! They should be examining the road. This couldn't be the first time somebody went off the cliff at that turn. Or they should talk to the truck driver who almost crashed into her, or the mechanic who serviced the car. Surely, Charlie didn't work on the Jaguar himself.

"Mr. Gilroy?" Crosby said.

Dutch realized he'd been off in his thoughts. "Yes," he replied. "Sorry."

"What impression did you have of Ms. Piedmont at the party?" Crosby repeated.

"Tess, uh, Ms. Piedmont was…the perfect hostess: elegant, gracious, happy to be entertaining old friends."

"I see. And did you notice anything unusual at this party?"

"No. Like I said, it was just a few old friends, a nice afternoon."

"Thank you, Mr. Gilroy. And thank *you*, Mr. Piedmont. We are both very sorry for your loss. We'll be in touch when we get the report on your car. By the way, it was quite a distinctive car, I believe?"

"Yes, detective," Charlie said almost wistfully, "a 1975 Jaguar XKE: a classic."

"The car is being transported for examination. We'll let you know what we learn. And again, Mr. Piedmont, we are very sorry. Please understand we'll have to ask you to stay in town for now."

"What? Yeah, sure. I'm not going anywhere."

Dutch showed the detectives out. "One more thing," Crosby said on the driveway, "did you see the Jaguar Saturday?"

"Yeah. It was in the garage. I'm not a car guy but we had quite a display here, between that and Ansel Tone's English car."

"Right," Miller said, checking her pad. "And I presume you mean *the* Ansel Tone, the writer?"

"Right. He drives an Aston Martin."

Miller and Crosby exchanged looks, and Miller added this to her notes.

Dutch wondered why Ansel's car was important and tried to remember if Charlie had ever mentioned his agent.

* * *

Ansel's phone rang and Becca picked up. She walked into his office with the receiver covered. "It's the Cold Spring Police," she said. "Are you here?"

He took a deep breath and reached for the phone. "Ansel Tone," he said with authority.

"Mr. Tone, or should I say 'Dr. Tone,' this is Detective Miller of the Cold Spring Police. We are looking into the accident this morning on Breakneck Road. I assume you know about this?"

"Yes, detective. I got a call. What a tragedy! Charlie and Tess are, or were, old friends."

"And you attended a party at their house Saturday?"

"Yes, ma'am, I did, and I slept over as well."

Miller paused. "Say again, Dr. Tone. You stayed Saturday night at the house?"

He panicked. Had he given something away? No, obviously they would know he spent the night. There was nothing wrong with that. "Yes, Detective," he said in a measured tone. "A bunch of college friends got together after many years. I'm afraid I overdid it and didn't want to drive home."

"Always best to be safe, sir. So, when did you leave the house?"

"Ah, right after breakfast on Sunday. I guess about ten?"

"And in the morning, or at the party the day before, did you notice anything unusual in Ms. Piedmont's behavior?"

"No, I can't say I did."

"One more thing: we understand you drive an English car?"

"Yes, an Aston Martin."

"Like James Bond?"

"Right."

"And did you see Mr. Piedmont's car while you were there?"

"Yes, I did. He has a beautiful old Jaguar."

"Well, he *did*."

"Right. I mean he *had* a beautiful Jaguar."

"Well, thank you, Dr. Tone. We'll be in touch."

Ansel felt more alone than he had since his mother's death. He realized he had cared more than he knew for Tess, but it was more than that. It was how everything had gone wrong, starting with Brandon and Digory and now Tess. Why did Charlie have to bring Trinity back to life? Why couldn't he keep his wife happy? Why wasn't *he* driving that damned car?

And why did the police ask about the Zagato? James Bond? They had to be kidding!

* * *

At the police station at the end of their long day, Crosby asked Miller to compare notes on the Piedmont case. "So what do we have?" he said, biting into a ham sandwich left from lunchtime.

"The report on the car should come in tomorrow. It took some time to reach it in the gorge and cart it up an old logging road."

"Is there much left to examine?"

"The guys in the garage seem to think so. Guess we'll see."

"Right, so we've got a happily married lawyer, driving her husband's car to the train station because *her* car needs repairs, while he's been called out of town on a trip with his female agent."

"Yes," Miller said. "He's a successful author. She was a corporate lawyer, big firm in the city. No priors on the husband or wife. Nothing from toxicology, though the body was badly burned so that's inconclusive. The party was on Saturday, and we don't know much about Sunday other than Tone had breakfast there and later Piedmont flew to Baltimore."

"He seemed attached to that car. I don't picture he'd use it to off his wife."

"Not to mention they were the perfect couple, according to everyone we've spoken to. And she, by the way, was quite a looker." She pushed a head shot of Tess across the table.

Crosby whistled. "Wow, Mr. Piedmont must be a *very* successful author, or he was punching above his weight class."

"Maybe it was his sparkling personality."

"Right. So, the Piedmonts threw a wingding Saturday with the old college chums, and we've spoken to all of them?"

"Not yet, but so far the same story: Ms. Piedmont was charming and cheerful and the life of the party. Mr. Piedmont was happy about a movie deal and a new book. Everyone was jolly. They drank cocktails and sang *Kumbaya*."

"And one distinguished guest drank himself stupid."

"Well, there's that." She stopped and pondered as Crosby watched her. Miller was developing a real instinct for this work. It was helpful, in any event, having young brain cells on the case.

"The one mother in the group," she said, checking her notes, "Molly Peretti, seemed closest to the deceased. She said back in college Ms. Piedmont and Tone were an item." Again, she checked her pad. "He was then known by his family name: MacTone."

"Are we seeing a current connection?"

"No, but we're checking. Are you thinking there might have been trouble in paradise and the beautiful Mrs. Charles Piedmont III was stepping out with her old boyfriend?"

"A jealous husband? Wouldn't be the first time, right? We also need to get a read on this agent, Ms.," he checked his notes, "Ms. Munchin. Anyway, first things first. Let's see about the car."

Crosby sniffed at his sandwich and threw it in the trash can. "And let's see what else Ms. Peretti can tell us."

Miller nodded, but her attention was on her laptop. "Hey, Crosby," she said, "you'll like this. This Tone guy doesn't seem the type to pine for a college sweetheart." Miller turned the laptop to show a shot of

Ansel before a "step and repeat banner" with a striking, olive-skinned woman.

"Well, either she's tall or he's pretty short," he said.

Miller laughed.

"Right," Crosby said. "So we'll pick this up in the morning, and let's check the insurance on the Jaguar."

Chapter 37

Dutch checked in with Michael at the office, and with his father. "Of course," his father said. "you take all the time you need. You have to take care of everyone; it's your nature and why we love you. We'll be fine. Tell your friend he's in our prayers."

Dutch got a bottle of seltzer from the refrigerator and planted himself on the terrace, scratching the dog's ears and breathing in the forest and the wide-open sky. He decided to stay over. He could give Charlie a hand and enjoy the spectacular view. It was amazing how the passage of twelve years didn't seem to matter; the recent reunion filled a gap in his life and left him back in school, helping out a roommate.

Late in the morning he heard a car in the driveway and jumped up, hoping it was Bud. He opened the door with Odysseus at his side. His grateful expression swelled into an expansive smile when he saw Becca climbing out of the passenger seat.

"I know you said not to come," she said quickly, "but Bud offered a ride. Anyway, I figured you were just being polite."

He shook his head. She was a wonder.

"I can make meals," she said and started to count on her fingers. "I can take calls; I can find *anything* online...."

"Okay," he said softly, trying to suppress a smile.

"I can walk the dog," she said, raising her eyebrows at Odysseus and still counting, "I can change sheets...."

"Okay! Okay, you got the job." He loved her earnestness. She smiled but avoided his eyes as she walked past, Odysseus close at her side.

With reinforcements on hand, Dutch crashed on a lounge chair on the terrace, thoughts veering between Tess's accident and cornflower blue eyes. Bud went up to the den to sit with Charlie. With Odysseus at her side, Becca set about straightening things in the great room.

"It was really nice of you to be here for your friend," Becca said through the doorway.

There was no response. She walked onto the terrace, drying a bowl with a dish towel. He was asleep and looked like she couldn't wake him if she tried. She pulled out her phone and shot a photograph. Maybe she should start promoting Dutch on Instagram? She would title this one: "Deserved Rest."

She made a pot of coffee and then heard Bud on the stairs.

"Tell me again," he said. "Where is Ansel?"

"He had meetings, and…" She stopped short. He was shaking his head.

"Right. He said I could come up but he doesn't want to do anything."

"Well, that does *him* no good. The way this happened right after our party, he must feel what we all feel." He pulled out his phone.

"Wait," she said, pressing a button and handing him her phone. "If you're calling Ansel, he'll answer from this number. It's our 'Batphone.'"

He held it to his ear. "No, Ansel, it's Bud. Listen, we're all here at Mountain House, or all but Molly and Pete, and Becca's taking care of us. You should come up."

"Yeah, I know," Ansel said, feeling pressure behind his eyes. He was breathing too quickly and tried to slow it down. "I got a call from a detective who said the same thing. I just have to take care of a few things, and I'll see you all later."

At one o'clock Henry would drop off a package, essential to keeping Ansel sane over the next few days. While he waited he drank too much espresso, stopping only when he felt his hands shake. He had to slow down to call Ed Flagel about classes for the fall. A tenure decision was likely in August. There could be no missteps at this point.

At least he could coddle Flagel by phone and didn't have to meet with the old toad. "Ed, it's Ansel," he said, friendly and professional. "I hope you're finding time to take a break. I called to confirm I'll take the Tuesday Propaganda class and the new History of Mass Communications on Thursdays. Also, I'd like to join the diversity committee you mentioned."

"That's fine, Ansel. I'll add you to the committee list. We should have a first meeting right before classes. Thank you for getting back to me."

"My pleasure, Ed. You have a good break."

"Oh, and about that video, uhum, of your class…."

"Yes, Ed." Flagel was like a dog beneath a treed squirrel, howling and running around the tree. It was unnerving.

"Well, our computer science people say there's little chance of identifying the source from the video itself. But Harley Mudd, over at the law school, says we could subpoena records on the IP address."

"Do you think it's worth the time and expense?"

"I wonder. Harley says we should let it go, although he tells me this video has been seen more than a million times. I don't mind the publicity, uhum; I'd just like to control the message. As our resident expert on propaganda, I'm sure you can appreciate that. Anyway, I'm having lunch with Mudd and the university counsel next week. We'll do the diligence and, uhum, decide how to proceed."

"Okay, Ed. Let me know if you want my help on getting the word out to students. Obviously, we have to keep things from getting out of control."

It was Flagel who was out of control. Somebody should give that muttonhead real work to do. He devoted so much time to enforcing rules, often his own random rules. Why should he care about a video on YouTube? It was free advertising! Was he threatened by Ansel's popularity or just an old salt lost in the sea in social media? Ansel thought about adding something to his Propaganda lectures about universities striving to "control the message."

Anyway, this thing could not touch him. Even if they traced the unsanctioned video to Becca, he would just say she was young and overly ambitious and didn't know the rules. Obviously, *he* wouldn't have posted the clip, not after Flagel discouraged this.

Last, he needed to talk with True. They hadn't spoken since the cancelled beach trip. While that weekend with Georgia had been just what he needed at the time, it now felt like he should have been with his son instead. He was coming to see that parenthood came with obligations. He would need to adjust his actions if he hoped to build a real relationship.

He called True's phone, but it went to voicemail. He then tried Florence. "How is everything?" he said energetically. "How's the leg?"

"Much better, thanks. I'm using a cane but can get by without it."

"That's terrific. And how's True? I can't seem to reach him."

She paused. "Yeah, I meant to call about that. I think you've got some ground to make up. He cried for, like, two days after you cancelled the beach trip, and he hasn't seen you since. I told him you're a professor and really busy at the end of the semester but I'm afraid he isn't buying it."

"I'm so sorry, Florence. I wish I could explain it all. But, I have missed him and I'm determined to make this right. You'll see; you'll *both* see."

"Look, Ansel, as far as I'm concerned, you showed up when we needed you and I really appreciate that. It was a life-saver. As to True, you just can't promise him things and then back out. He hangs on every word you say and needs to be able to trust you."

"You're right, Florence. Everything you say is right. I'll fix this. I will."

Chapter 38

Dutch woke to the trill of a house finch. Dark clouds drifted over-head.

He suddenly realized where he was and sat up. He remembered stretching out, but must have fallen asleep, and who covered him with a blanket? He yawned and rubbed his neck.

Everything was quiet. The light was on in the den, so he walked to the stairs but stopped on the bottom step. He heard voices too soft to make out. He didn't want to interrupt, so backtracked toward the kitchen.

Footsteps pounded up the wooden stairs from the clearing. Odysseus rounded the corner from the terrace to the great room followed by Becca waving at his tail and making cattle driving sounds. At the top of the stairs she stooped over to catch her breath. When she straightened, she saw Dutch watching. In the midst of the gloom, she brimmed over with life. She looked away, blushing, and smiled as she squeezed past him.

He wondered why she took the time to come to the house. She didn't share the McYanks' history, which bound them in a way difficult to explain. But she fit in seamlessly, maybe because she worked for Ansel or because she had a role in the tragedy by attending the party. Or maybe, partly and possibly, she was there for Dutch.

* * *

About three o'clock Becca let the detectives in. They arrived with a patrol car and a van carrying three technicians in white coveralls. They ran police tape around the garage and then donned gloves and cloth covers over their shoes. This was not looking good.

The detectives wanted to speak with all of them together, so Becca gathered them in the great room.

"We've got some disturbing news," Crosby said.

They all tensed.

"Someone tampered with the Jaguar. That's apparently why Ms. Piedmont lost control: the brakes failed."

Charlie sucked in air, his fist over his mouth. The rest were wide-eyed and silent.

Crosby continued: "We've already cordoned off the garage, but we'd like your consent, Mr. Piedmont, to search the garage and the house."

Bud jumped up and Dutch started to object, but Crosby held out a hand for calm. "It looks like there's been a murder. We can get a warrant but that will just delay things. I know this is a difficult time for you all, and it's a total pain, but it has to be done, and it has to be done *now*."

"Whatever you need," Charlie said resignedly.

"Thank you. Oh, and could we take a look at your phone?"

Charlie put in his passcode and handed his phone to Miller.

"Thanks again, Mr. Piedmont. We'll give this right back. We're all looking for the same thing here, and your cooperation is a big help. Now, we will need to talk to each of you about the weekend. And we'll need the other three adults." He raised his eyebrows to his colleague.

"We've got Dr. Tone on the way," Miller said, "and we need to meet with the Perettis, the couple from Long Island with young kids."

"So you think one of us at the party was involved?" Bud said incredulously.

"That's nuts," said Dutch.

Charlie was grim. Becca sneaked looks from one to the other, all looking as baffled as she was.

"Why don't you all relax for now?" Crosby said. "The crime scene people will begin in the garage and upstairs. I will ask the rest of you to remain in this room and try not to touch things. Also, please keep the dog here with you." He looked at Odysseus, asleep on the floor. "Ms. Howard, you and I should start out on the deck? And Detective Miller will begin with Mr. Roberts at the other end, okay? By the way, is there any way to get a cup of coffee?"

Becca sat with Detective Crosby. She said everyone at the party got along; they were mostly old friends. "And, specifically," Miller said, "what about Dr. Tone? I understand you work for him."

"Yes, I do. Well, he was a little moody, but that hasn't changed since I met him six months ago. But the last few weeks have been odd."

"Can you give me an example?"

"Well, part of my job is to take publicity photos to post on his social media accounts."

"Like Instagram?"

"Right, and there are always new apps. I'm supposed to keep him current."

"I understand. Go on."

"Well, I took loads of photos at the party, some of the house and a bunch of candid shots. I thought they were really good. But when I tried to show him, he said forget it; he didn't want me to post *any*. He didn't even look at them."

Miller looked interested. "Can *we* see these photos?"

"Absolutely. I just finished editing."

"Actually, we'd prefer to see *all* the photos *before* any editing."

"Oh," Becca said, confused for a moment. Then she understood they were looking for evidence, not art. "Oh, of course. I'll email the file when I get home."

"Good. That may be helpful. But go on, please. You work for Dr. Tone and that's why you came to the party?"

"Yeah. Ansel just introduced me to these people, and they were all really nice. Oh, actually he set me up to meet Mr. Gilroy a couple of weeks ago. We had dinner."

"Was that unusual, for him to arrange something like that?"

"Well, he never did it before, but one day he asked me to meet his friend. Mr. Gilroy thought it was weird, too, and that it might have something to do with a girl they all met in Dublin. It made no sense to me."

Miller scribbled notes and looked up, gesturing to continue.

"I can't imagine any of them hurting Tess, particularly not Charlie. He was crazy about his wife; you could see it in everything he did."

She confirmed Ansel had no trouble finding dates, and as far as she knew had not seen Tess since they were in school together. As she rose, she paused. "Something else: Ansel nearly went into shock when he first got the call. From seeing them at the party, I didn't get the sense he was closer to Tess than the rest of them. I have no idea what that means."

"Thank you, Ms. Howard. Is there anything else you'd like to share?"

"Just one more thing. Ansel got *really* drunk at the party, which I had never seen before; he was always so in control. But even so, his eyes looked almost paranoid. Drunk people I've been around were always kind of dopey, but he was alert. I asked myself if he could be putting on an act so Mr. Gilroy would have to drive me home, more pushing us together. But then I thought I must be imagining things."

* * *

Bud took his turn with Detective Miller. "The Piedmonts were happy," he said. "They had it all."

"Did you observe any disagreements at the party?"

"No, none. Charlie and I drove the Jaguar to town for a cake. He let me drive it back and there was nothing wrong with the brakes. That car handled like a dream. We pulled up just before everyone came back from a hike, and I didn't notice Ansel again until he was pounding his chest against some fancy bottle of bourbon."

"Thanks, Mr. Roberts. Another thing: Ms. Howard said she

thought Dr. Tone was trying to push her together with Mr. Gilroy. Do you have any insight about that?"

Bud rubbed his chin. "Yeah, I guess. At a ball game a few weeks ago, Dutch said he still had a number for this woman, Reilly, who we all met in Dublin. She was a tourist who hooked up with Ansel. But when I kidded Dutch about giving her a call, Ansel got this wild look. Then I guess right after that he set Dutch up with Becca, like maybe as a distraction? Anyway, Dutch said he called Reilly a few days ago, but I'm sure she has nothing to do with Tess's accident."

* * *

Dutch watched Detective Crosby relishing his steaming mug of coffee. The man seemed to know how to make himself at home. Without prompting, Dutch then began: "I don't know the details, you should ask Charlie, but Ansel did something at the party to Charlie's manuscript for his new book, like went into the computer and made changes. There was some kind of quiet blow-up between them, but they resolved it and were friends and we all had a nice dinner. But then, yeah, Ansel got loaded and almost passed out. He stayed over to sleep it off, and I drove Ms. Howard home."

"So, Dr. Tone was drinking more heavily than the rest of you?"

"By far. The rest of us mostly had wine or beer but he was pounding away at the bourbon. It seemed like he was going for a refill every time I looked up. It was no surprise he couldn't stand by the end of the night."

"And was there anything else? Any drugs?"

"Ah, not that I saw," Dutch said uncomfortably.

"Mr. Gilroy. We are not from narcotics. We only need a clear picture to help us solve a homicide."

"Right. Well, we were friends in college, and it wouldn't have been odd for someone to light up a joint, but Molly's kids were there and no one would smoke in front of them."

"That's helpful, Mr. Gilroy. And one more thing: how was the marriage, you know, between the Mr. and Mrs.?"

"I'd say not all it could be, maybe, but I figured that's how artists are."

"What makes you say that?"

"I don't know. Charlie seemed to keep a close eye on Tess, and she was clearly unenthusiastic about his new book, like she wished he wouldn't write it at all."

"So, you think there was trouble in the marriage?"

"No idea, not any more than what I've told you."

"One more thing," Miller said, stepping over to join them. "Could you tell us about a woman named Reilly? Mr. Roberts said you spoke with her recently?"

"Yeah, sure," Dutch said, surprised. "It was twelve years ago. I didn't think she was relevant."

"No telling what might be relevant," Miller said.

"All right. So, we all—Ansel, Tess, Bud, Charlie, Molly and I—spent a year at Trinity College. We studied together and roomed together and all became close. At the end of the year we had a party. We were all there, except I think Charlie was late. So about the time we were all feeling the liquor, something happened between Ansel and Tess. Oh yeah, I should have said: they were a couple then. Anyway, Tess stormed out and Ansel left with that girl, Reilly. It was shocking because he and Tess had been together all year. Given their looks and their kind of entitled air, they were like celebrities, with everyone other than us, I mean. But then, I guess, it all fell apart at once."

"So none of you knew Reilly?"

"No. She was an American tourist. But I found her phone and eventually got it back to her. I still had her number and last week, when Ansel was acting so strangely, I got hold of her."

"And?"

"And it was odd but she said Ansel dumped her in a cab as soon as they left the party and she never saw him again."

"And this was odd why?'

"Well, he acted like he spent the night with her, which pissed off everyone because we were all Tess's friends. It seemed callous. But if he *didn't* sleep with Reilly, we couldn't make any sense of it, unless…"

"Unless what?"

"Unless he was covering up something else. And the scary thing was a campus guard died that night chasing a burglar. Still, that's an old story. Tess's accident couldn't have anything to do with that."

* * *

The technicians were ready to focus on the great room and the terrace, so the detectives took Charlie upstairs and everyone else waited in the TV room.

Crosby made sure Charlie was comfortable. "Now, Mr. Piedmont," he began, in the same friendly tone as when they first met, "we apologize again for turning the house upside down, but now we have a few specific questions. When did you first plan to go to Baltimore on Sunday?"

"Well, a producer is making my book *Against the Odds* into a movie and I wanted the job of writing the screenplay. But first I had to meet the director. Then I found out Sunday he was coming east to scout locations."

"So your trip was planned spur of the moment?"

"Right, it was arranged Sunday morning."

"And you spoke with…"

"My agent spoke with the director's assistant, I think. Her name is Marci something."

"I see, and this Marci reached out to ask you to meet the director in Baltimore?"

"Right. Like I said, we had to meet about the screenplay."

"And with your wife's car out of commission, you knew she would use *your* car while you were out of town?"

"Right, yeah."

"And she wasn't able to drive you to the airport in that car?"

"Well, no—I already told you—we always took a car service to the airport. It's so much easier than driving and parking."

"Although, if she dropped you off, she wouldn't need to park."

"Right, yeah, I guess that's right."

Charlie had the feeling the detectives were suspicious of him. But why? Everyone knew he worshiped Tess!

"Another thing, Mr. Piedmont. You were aware your wife's life was insured through her employer, right?"

"What? Yeah, I guess. I'm pretty sure she signed up for a policy when she first took the job."

"And you were the sole beneficiary?"

"That would make sense. There's no one else."

"Do you know how much the policy pays?"

"Ah, not exactly. It's been years."

"Would it surprise you to know it pays a million and a half dollars for accidental death?"

"No, that sounds right; she got the policy when she started working several years ago." Charlie was starting to perspire. Did they suspect him?

"Okay, Mr. Piedmont, let's leave that for now. Did you harbor suspicions your wife might be involved with Dr. Tone?"

"What? No!" Charlie looked neither detective in the eye. "No," he continued. "We were *happy*. She hadn't seen Ansel in years, not since Ireland."

"But they were a couple then, right?"

"Yeah, *twelve years ago*. But we were kids. We all moved on from there. We have careers. Tess and I were married! There was nothing between them anymore."

"Okay, Mr. Piedmont. We're just checking all the angles." Crosby shifted his tone to sound business-like. "Now, can you tell us about the incident at your party with Dr. Tone and your manuscript?"

"How do you know about that?"

"It's not important how we know. Please just tell us what happened."

"Well, I had to drive to town to pick up a cake and took Bud

Roberts along. When we got back there was no one here, but I saw the door to my den was closed and went up to see why. I found Tone at my desk in front of my laptop. I had given him a copy of my manuscript to read the week before, but there was no reason for him to access the manuscript on my computer."

"Here," Charlie said, holding papers out to Crosby. "These are the changes he made."

Crosby and Miller leafed through the pages. "Mr. Piedmont," said Miller, "it looks like Dr. Tone was trying to divert attention from a character called Evan, something about skulking around the campus. Is that right?"

"Exactly."

"And is Evan modeled on one of your classmates?"

"On Ansel Tone."

"I see," Miller said, scribbling a note. "So, you weren't suspicious when you saw these changes?"

"I was mostly angry he messed with my manuscript. But as to the specific changes, the odd thing was not that he suggested the revision, but that he insisted his version was what actually happened. I had told him I would change the facts to improve the story, but I was crystal clear about the actual facts. For some reason he wanted to change history."

"To be clear, Mr. Piedmont, you are writing *fiction*?"

"Yes, but a type of fiction based on real events, in the same way I based my first book on my childhood."

"I see. Okay, so there was a break-in that night on campus?"

Charlie stopped being surprised at how much the police knew. "That's right. Someone broke into a building and a security guard died trying to catch him."

"Him?" said Miller. "Do you know the burglar was male?"

"Oh, I don't know that. I just know Ansel left the rest of us and concocted a story about where he was, and then I saw him head across campus."

"So you don't really know...."

"And, yeah," Charlie interrupted. "The building with the break-in held the office of Ansel's advisor, the guy who wrote a recommendation Ansel needed. Still, we couldn't explain why he would break in."

"When you say 'we,' Mr. Piedmont, who are you talking about?"

"Dutch and I talked about this, about how Ansel had been mixed up with something in Dublin."

"I see," Crosby said. "And did you two confront Dr. Tone?"

"No, we were still trying to put the pieces together."

Miller got a call and excused herself. When she returned ,she pulled Crosby aside, who then returned to Charlie. "Mr. Piedmont, I'm afraid we have to return to an awkward subject. Based on conversations with your wife, Ms. Peretti suspects there was something current between your wife and Dr. Tone...."

"Look," Charlie burst out, jumping from his chair. "If there was anything between them, *I* didn't know about it, so how would Molly know?"

The detectives looked at Charlie closely. He sat back down and sank into his chair.

Miller opened a folder and pulled out a photograph of Ansel and Tess, looking young. "This photo was in your desk, Mr. Piedmont," she said. "I assume this was taken while your wife was seeing Ansel Tone back in college?"

"That's right."

"And you saved this photo from that time, that is from 2004?"

"Yes. I use visual aids to help me describe people and scenes. I found that print among a bunch of old notes and pictures from Trinity. I have all sorts of clippings and photographs like that."

"So this is just one of several old photographs you used in writing the novel?"

"That's right. At the beginning of the year, the Ansel and Tess characters are together. That creates the tension in the story."

"I see. Oh, and one more thing: Ms. Howard said she had never seen Dr. Tone drink so heavily and wondered if he might be acting drunk so Mr. Gilroy would have to drive her home."

"Oh, he was drunk, all right," said Charlie, and then he stopped to think. "He might have tried to drive but we wouldn't have let him. He and I were past the book incident by then—I was, anyway—and we were concerned about him. But he seemed content to spend the night. I'm not sure what was going on with Becca and Dutch."

"And that's the last you heard from Dr. Tone?"

"Yeah. We all went to bed and I didn't see him until morning."

"And, generally speaking, Mr. Piedmont, does your dog protect the house, you know, bark at strange noises in the night?"

"Seusy?" Charlie laughed. "He's no watchdog."

"But that night, did he bark at all, wake you up?"

"Molly's kids ran him ragged all day. I don't think he would have woken up if a train came through the front door."

"And one more thing. Dr. Tone drives an expensive automobile. Would you say he is familiar with car maintenance, you know, the mechanics of the thing?"

"Absolutely. His father sells cars and he grew up working on them. In Dublin he helped his advisor with a race car. He knew way more about the Jaguar than I did."

"And how would someone with that kind of knowledge disable brakes, if you know?"

Charlie gave a start and then collected himself. "I'm not sure exactly; never thought about it. I guess he would cut the brake lines, maybe under the chassis?"

"Or under the hood?"

"I guess so, yeah. There's probably some way to do that. And damn it, Ansel knows everything about cars! Do you think he rigged the brakes?"

Crosby rubbed his hand over the back of his neck and turned to Miller. "We've got to make sure Dr. Tone shows up as promised."

Miller called on her radio for a patrol car to escort the red sports car when it arrived at the mountain.

"That's all for now, Mr. Piedmont," Crosby said.

"Uh," Miller interrupted. Crosby looked at her. She held up Charlie's phone, and Crosby nodded for her to take over.

"Sorry, Mr. Piedmont," she said, "but I'm curious about this last text Ms. Piedmont sent you the morning of the accident. It says she expected to have a late night and might stay in the city."

"Yeah. So?"

"Did she often spend the night in the city without you?"

"She works…I mean *did* work on big corporate deals. They sometimes worked all night."

"And was she working on a big deal this week, as far as you know?"

"No, come to think of it. They had just signed a deal. She said her hours would be regular for a while. I guess something came up."

"We have spoken with Regis & Kessler about the insurance, but can you give us a contact there who would know about her workload?"

"She worked for a corporate partner named Tom Carter. I don't have a direct number."

"Oh, we'll find it. Thank you, Mr. Piedmont. We're done for now."

"Hey, whatever you need. I'm going to stay up here for a few minutes. This has all got me a little shook up."

"Understandable, Mr. Piedmont," Crosby said. "We'll be downstairs."

With the door closed, Charlie thought about Ansel. That bastard came back into their lives and now everything was screwed. But he couldn't be allowed to talk his way out of this. Then he thought of a way to rattle Ansel so he might make a mistake and bury himself. He dialed Ansel's number.

"Oh hey, Charlie," Ansel said, "I'm so sorry. You know we all thought the world of her. This must be a shock."

"Thanks, Ansel. That means a lot, especially from you."

There was silence. Ansel resumed, "I'm on the road up. How are you dealing with it all?"

"Oh, you know, it sucks…but it's life. I'm sure *you* can put yourself in my shoes. Crazy how we all didn't see each other all these years, but right away you guys feel closer to me than anyone I know."

"I feel the same. It's as if we were meant to help each other through the rough times."

"I agree. It's like when Digory died when we were all together; well, except I guess you were off with that girl from California."

Ansel did not respond.

"You know, you mentioned her at the Yankees game and Dutch remembered her name?"

"Yeah. Funny, the big guy would still know her."

"What's really funny is he talked to her last week. Did he tell you?"

Chapter 39

Ansel hung up, stunned. He turned on to a side road and pulled over. His mind raced. Charlie and Dutch knew about Reilly! That left one small step to link Ansel to Digory's accident.

Who had they told? The police? Dutch wouldn't say anything, but Charlie was incensed about the book, unless…unless he also found out about Tess and him! That would put him over the edge. And there were a hundred ways he could have found out about his night with Tess. Any way you looked at it, he was fucked. There was no way out.

He put the car in gear and pulled a U-turn. He'd go back to the city, get Leah to set up a trip, go somewhere they couldn't reach him.

But he pulled over again, stopped and turned off the car. There was no sense running; it would just make him look connected with Tess's accident.

He had no reason to hurt Tess, but Charlie…that was a different story. The police might think Charlie was holding him hostage to his history, or that he was after Charlie's wife. And it didn't even matter whether they charged him with Tess's murder; an investigation would lead to Dublin and the Gardaí would pile on. Was there a statute of limitations for manslaughter in Ireland? Did it even matter? Once the story got out about Dublin, he could kiss tenure goodbye, and Wiley would pull the plug on the *Redux* books.

He needed to calm down before he talked to the police. Maybe he could pull Charlie aside and talk to him. They were friends, old friends.

He thought of True and their drive to the beach, seeing the world through innocent eyes. If he could just put this mess behind him, he might have a chance with the boy. He could learn to be a father. But this was now and he was on the precipice. One stumble and he was lost.

He needed relief and reached into the glove compartment. Breaking his own rule, he laid out cocaine on a folded map, spilling some on his legs. "Damn!" he shouted and tried to brush it off his pants.

He sat back against the headrest and closed his eyes, seeing tracers like a laser show. He needed time. He tried to focus on the feel of the steering wheel in his hands. The Zagato; he should think about what a joy it was to drive. He just had to get his head straight. A quick run up Breakneck Road would clear the cobwebs before he met the cops.

He started the car and cranked up heavy metal. The coke and the music emboldened him. He was the Golden Boy. Things would work out.

He turned toward Cold Spring. There was nothing to worry about. His friends wouldn't turn him in. He just had to answer a few questions about the party and he'd be free. He tried to get into the music, mimicking the screams and grunts in the wall of sound filling the car. No one would catch him.

He kept telling himself to take it slow until he reached the mountain, then he could cut loose. He was coming to help. There was nothing to fear. He was a professor, an author and a father. He was Demosthenes!

A vision came to him of his father, with seething red eyes. Jordan had reason to blame him for his mother's accident but Ansel had loved her! She may be the only person he ever loved…until True. And it was not as if his guilt needed prodding. He had spent a lifetime trying to undo that day. But Jordan made sure he wouldn't forget; he used the accident as an excuse to manage Ansel's life. When Ansel got to Dublin, it was Jordan who tagged Brandon Doogan as his target. Brandon was barely ten years older than his students and had a passion for racing. The young professor could hardly resist a Columbia exchange student eager to study propaganda, who knew *everything* about sports cars. Helping keep Brandon's MG in shape was not only easy for Ansel but fun, and this made it child's play to ingratiate himself. They were soon spending evenings in Brandon's garage or over pints at the pub. In the end Ansel should have spent more time on research and less on his mentor.

But he *had* put in a lot of time on his paper, sorting through news accounts and interviewing faculty members. But then he happened on that book in an old shop. It had been published in Australia in the eighties and was out of print, but it was a goldmine. He could not in ten years have duplicated the research on British press accounts of events in Ireland. And the book was obscure; no one else would find it. So what if he borrowed bits of text and research? Who was he hurting, when that book was buried on the back shelf of some shabby bookstore?

Brandon gave the paper an excellent grade and wrote the recommendation Ansel needed, in terms glowing enough to satisfy even his father. But then there was their final meeting for the term. He showed up at Brandon's office and everything seemed fine…until Ansel saw the Australian book on Brandon's desk.

"What have you got to say?" Brandon asked, nodding toward the desk.

"Ah, yeah. Good book. Helpful on the background."

"Not what I mean, Ansel. You obviously fancy the book. But why did you omit it from your bibliography and why does it look like you copied research and, dare I venture, some of the writing?"

"Ah, I wouldn't say 'copied.' Sure, I read it and parts overlapped with my research. My paper may sound similar because I addressed the same facts."

"Look," Brandon said, apparently pained, "I haven't done a line-by-line comparison, so at this point I'm most troubled that you may have used research without attribution. So, leave it at this: I'm gone for the weekend, but Monday morning you will show me your backup research, everything you've got. Show me your paper is original. This is serious, Ansel. I like you; you know that. I think of you not only as a student but as a friend, and I want to see you succeed. But convince me on Monday, and that deadline is *firm*. Call it your *sprioc-ama*. There will be no delay and no reprieve."

"I..." Ansel said and hesitated. Brandon looked up in both sympathy and disappointment. "I'll gather my notes. I'll show you."

"For your sake and the sake of our friendship, I'll count on it. And you should understand...." He placed on the desk a signed letter. "If I'm *un*convinced, I will have to deliver this letter, dated Monday, to the Faculty Dean and the History Department Head. It formally requests that the college change your grade to 'incomplete' and withdraw my letter of recommendation."

Ansel panicked. This was the end! He'd never get into grad school. His father would disown him. He'd end up working in a garage.

He wandered aimlessly across campus and found himself sitting on the grass in College Park. He stared vacantly at the bronze sphere in front of the Museum Building and screamed inside for a solution. But nothing came. Brandon would be racing Sunday while Ansel stewed in this mess. He couldn't talk Brandon into letting this go. There was no way to fake the backup research. His grade, his recommendation, his career were all in the shitter.

But then news came Sunday evening that Brandon had crashed at his race. He was unconscious in the hospital. People were saying he might not make it.

He felt terrible about Brandon but recognized this could be his salvation, or at least put off his fall. If Brandon wasn't there to change the grade, Ansel could be home free. But the letter! What would happen to the letter? Someone could go through Brandon's desk and find it! He would have to get into Brandon's office.

But that was simple. He would just break in after hours. For hundreds of years Trinity students had snuck into campus buildings. His grandfather told stories about stealing paintings from one building to hang in another, just for fun.

He needed the McYanks and anyone else who knew him to be all in one place. He mustn't be recognized on his way to the Arts Block, in case there were complications. But he could run into students anywhere. Except…except when there was a party! And Bud was setting up the last party of the year! Everyone would be there and paying attention only to drinking and dancing.

He also needed an excuse to leave the party but have an alibi, make everyone think they knew where he was. The solution to that was simple too. He had grown tired of Tess's jealousy. He could pick a fight with her, when everyone was roaring drunk, and go off with someone else, some stranger. He'd tell Bud he needed the room. Then no one would bother him all night and he could take care of business.

Grandfather had not passed along any secret way into the Arts Block because the building was too new. But he *had* told Ansel about a backdoor to the Buttery that led through to the Chapel, which would be a way to cross campus out of sight of the party at the Graduates Memorial Building. The Arts Building itself would require a bit of climbing and an open window but that would be easy.

The plan worked flawlessly. There were some American girls passing through the city and one was cute. He caught her eye and she played along. Actually, she and Tess both stuck to the script. Tess stormed off, he left with the girl and then ditched her, changed clothes and had no trouble sneaking across campus and gaining access to the building. The lock on Brandon's office door took ten seconds to pick. He found two copies of the letter in unsealed envelopes, stuffed them into his pocket along with the Australian book, turned out the light and stepped into the hallway.

"Aye, you! What are you doing there?" a janitor called out.

He ran. He couldn't be caught with the letters in his pocket!

The janitor shouted after him. As Ansel rounded a hallway, an alarm sounded. He feared they'd cut off his escape on the ground floor and so bounded up the stairs. He found his way onto the roof, ran to the back of the building and lowered himself over the parapet.

"You there, stop!" shouted a voice Ansel recognized. It was Digory. He was too slow to catch Ansel but would recognize him if he got close.

Ansel climbed down one story and jumped onto the grass, tumbling over into a run. Looking back he saw Digory step over the parapet. But then he slipped. He fell! He bounced off the building and landed in a heap.

Digory was a good old guy, but he shouldn't have been climbing around rooftops. Ansel couldn't go back for him. Someone else would call for help. He retraced his steps and shut himself in his dorm room.

With the exit for Cold Spring approaching, Ansel opened his window wide, trying to clear his head. The cocaine, combined with the caffeine overdose and the tension, made his heartbeat race. Beads of sweat ran down his face. He tried breathing deeply. He had to slow down and go over the details of the weekend before he talked with the police.

There was no dispute he drank heavily at the party. Charlie and Bud practically carried him to bed. He got up during the night to use the bathroom but didn't see or hear anything. Then, when he got up in the morning, he ate breakfast and went home. That was the whole story.

But someone would tell them about the confrontation in Charlie's den. How could he explain that without turning attention to Trinity? Or would Charlie just casually, and vindictively, mention that? If Charlie knew about the affair, he'd take his revenge, as if Tess's death weren't enough to punish them all. If only *he* had been driving the Jaguar, that would have solved everything. But this was reality. The world would go on with Charlie and no Tess, and once the Gardaí got wind of it all, everything would crumble.

Ansel shook his head to come back to the present and keep his eyes on the road. He was practically there. No one would make the connection with Dublin. He had to stop obsessing. He had to move on. First, he needed to get this interview behind him, after a fast run over the mountain. He downshifted and turned up Breakneck Road, ready to hit the gas. But a patrol car was parked at the turn.

Chapter 40

Becca wondered why Charlie stayed upstairs when the detectives came down. She started to ask about this but Crosby cut her off. "Mr. Piedmont wanted a moment alone," he said.

Dutch said, "So what happens now?"

"We're just waiting for Dr. Tone to arrive," Crosby replied.

Dutch and Bud exchanged looks. Becca watched them both. They seemed to share some secret. She couldn't understand why everyone was so focused on Ansel when they should be concerned about Charlie.

Charlie looked shaky when he finally came down from the den. Becca offered him a mug of coffee. "Thanks," he said distractedly.

Miller stood by the front window, looking out. Crosby stepped out on the terrace to make a call.

"Detective?" came a crackly voice over the radio in Miller's jacket.

"Go ahead, Duncan," she said, holding the radio to her mouth.

"A red sports car just turned up Breakneck Road from the west. We're following at a distance."

"Keep our friend in sight and escort him into the driveway."

Bud and Dutch jumped up and started asking questions. Becca rose silently. The detectives' grim expressions scared her.

"Folks," Crosby said, holding up his hands. "Please sit tight and stay in the house."

"Are you going to arrest him?" Bud asked. "For what?"

Miller went outside. Crosby stopped in the doorway and turned back to them. "We just need to speak with Dr. Tone," he said. "We don't want anyone getting excited."

The patrol car fell in behind Ansel. What was going on? He was helping! He drove all the way up here! Why were they following him? His pulse raced; he shouldn't have gotten high. He turned off the music to concentrate.

"Subject is picking up speed," came over the radio.

"That's okay, Duncan," Detective Miller replied. "Just keep him in sight."

The detectives and officers stood to the sides of the driveway with their eyes on the road. In the house, everyone pressed against the windows.

Ansel wiped a drop of sweat from his forehead. In his rear-view mirror he still saw the police car. He pressed down on the gas, taking turns fast and gunning it on straightaways. The cop couldn't keep up. But what was the point? They knew where he was going.

"We've lost sight," Miller's radio blared, loud enough to hear in the house. "No way to stay with that car."

"Understood," Miller said. "Keep behind him. Check any turnoffs before the house."

"Oh no!" Dutch said, nodding toward Crosby, who eased his service revolver out of its holster and held it behind his back. They all stared, frozen in place.

Why were they following him? Ansel went over everything again. They all saw at the party he was too drunk for anything but sleep. Was it the calls from Tess? He hadn't answered but maybe they knew she tried to reach him? How did she not know better? And now *he* would take the fall for it!

The curves in the road started to make his head spin. Digory. Brandon. Canterwail. The lecture video. *Sprioc-ama*. And now a patrol car on his tail!

No one forced him to drive here. He could turn around and head for the airport. Leah could line up something far away. Maybe he could take that job in Bath. They would have to wait if they wanted to talk with him. And no way his father would stand for this. Jordan's lawyers would protect him!

He didn't see the police car any more but it was sure to be following, so he couldn't turn around. They knew he was coming now; taking off would look bad. How did he end up in this mess? If that idiot had just have left the fucking past in the past! And now Charlie knew about Reilly and probably about Tess and had turned him in. He was nailed. There was no escaping the past.

He downshifted at the last switchback and approached Mountain House. "It's all right," he said out loud. "It has to be. They can't tie me to Digory. Charlie didn't rat me out."

He slowed to turn into the driveway.

Then he saw a patrol car, and a police van. A uniformed cop stepped forward. A guy in a suit held his hand behind his back. Ansel touched his brakes. Everything was closing in. They knew it all! They were there for him!

At the edge of the driveway he looked Crosby in the eye and saw him start to pull something from behind his back and shout. There was no time.

He spun the wheel and hit the gas. The Aston Martin vanished up the mountain in a cloud of dust.

Crosby jumped into his car, shouting for a roadblock. Miller joined him and they sped off, spraying gravel.

Everyone rushed from the house and stood in the dust from Crosby's car, which fell like snow in shafts of sunlight. The chase car sped by the driveway. Dutch grabbed Odysseus by the collar when he looked like he would run after the car.

Bud put his hand on Charlie's shoulder. "They'll never catch him," Charlie said somberly.

Dutch released Odysseus, whose attention turned to a sound in the woods. Becca reached for his hand. He looked down at her as she leaned her face against his shoulder.

A voice came between bursts of static: "Breakneck Road east closed off. No sign of subject."

The Zagato flew. If only he drove fast enough, Ansel could put this behind him. There was no way they would keep up if he could get to open road. He quickly reached the top of the mountain and turned onto Charlie's secret racetrack. Before the police knew it, he had descended the mountain and sped north on Route 90.

When Ansel didn't appear at the roadblock, Detective Miller called in an all-points bulletin. An officer driving south on Route 90 saw the car headed north and gave chase. The Cold Spring operator passed on the alert to Beacon and an officer there reported Ansel had taken the bridge over the Hudson. Miller called the State Police. Dispatch put through a trooper, who reported, "Subject in red sports car headed west on I-84. Too fast to get a license plate. He's really moving."

By the time Crosby and Miller reached the bridge, they heard: "Red sports car took the Thruway north but I've lost sight. Speedometer's off the dial. Only thing going to slow him down is the road."

Ansel let the Zagato run with no thought of speed traps. He needed to put miles between himself and the mountain. He couldn't talk to the police now, not until he came up with a story. There was no time while they were chasing. Later, after he lost them, he'd arrange the facts. It was what he did. He was the "Golden Boy." The *Redux* history of this mess would make him the hero.

He passed cars like they were standing still, flashing his headlights in the passing lane. The speed had a calming effect on him, and the world seemed to slow down. He took stock of the situation. Why did he run? Charlie may have told the police about Dublin, but would they arrest him? It suddenly made no sense. But here he was with the police after him.

There was no question of a patrol car catching him, but he had a different problem. It was at least fifteen miles to the next exit, at New Paltz. Could he make it before they closed the road? There was no way to get off the Thruway before the exit, so he'd have to push on.

At an overpass two patrol cars joined the chase, but he sped by them so fast they were quickly out of sight.

With the New Paltz exit ahead, he saw no flashing lights. The road looked clear. He took the exit and headed west. No one seemed to be following.

But it was just a matter of time. He couldn't keep running. He had to keep near the speed limit now but people would still notice the car. Then he thought of Jake Hadley. He turned onto a side road and pulled up the Sanctuary Inn on his GPS. It was barely two miles away. He covered the distance in a flash.

He pulled directly into the barn out back of the inn. As he got out of the car, a screen door slammed and he saw his friend walking toward him with a confused smile.

"This is a surprise, Ansel. What's up?"

"I need your help."

"Anything, bro."

"Okay, look, the less you know the better, but I need to stay."

"No problem, man. Come on in."

The chase and a hot shower sobered Ansel. Wrapped in a towel, he contemplated himself in the mirror. What the hell was he doing? This was insane. He pulled out his phone and hit speed dial. "Father, it's Ansel."

Chapter 41

With Ansel gone and the cops in pursuit, Dutch led everyone into the house. Charlie went up to the den and closed the door. Bud poured himself a drink.

Dutch sat Becca down. She looked shaken. He tried to put himself in her place. "It's hard," he said gently, "to think someone close to you could be mixed up in something like this. It's especially tough on you, since you have to untangle yourself from your job on top of it all. I wish there was something I could say."

"Oh, don't worry about me, Dutch. Charlie's the one we should be concerned about. And in a strange way, I'm even sorry for Ansel. He can be self-centered but I can't believe he'd kill someone. He's just not that kind of guy. And who could possibly want to hurt Tess? She was so nice and smart and beautiful."

"I agree it makes no sense."

"What will happen to him, do you think?"

"Well, I don't know, but his running off is pretty damning. I'm sure they'll catch up with him eventually, no matter how fast he drives. Then he'll face the truth, whatever that is."

"This is one mess even his father won't be able to fix," Bud said.

"Do you guys know his father?" Becca said. "Ansel never spoke about him, but his agent said there was bad blood."

"The old man's a tyrant," Bud said. "He probably deserves the credit for how his son turned out." With a sardonic laugh, he continued: "Demosthenes, the golden-tongued darling of New York. He'll have a tough time talking his way out of this."

As evening approached, Dutch found pasta and a jar of tomato sauce in a cupboard. Becca put water on to boil. Bud sat in the TV room nursing a drink.

"Guys!" Bud yelled. "Come in here, quick!"

A news conference broadcast was underway. The screen identified the speaker as a major of the State Police. Dutch picked up what he was saying mid-sentence: "…and local police in Putnam County are seeking to detain and question Mr. Tone, a teacher and writer, in connection with the alleged murder in Cold Spring of Theresa Piedmont, an attorney and wife of the author, Charles Piedmont III. Mr. Tone fled the scene of the investigation this afternoon in a red sports car. The police gave chase but Mr. Tone eluded capture. He was last seen in the vicinity of New Paltz. We ask that anyone with information about Mr. Tone's whereabouts contact our office without delay."

"Wow," Bud said. "How did he get past the roadblock?"

"I don't know," Dutch said. "And why did he run?"

Becca returned to the kitchen and set out four plates of pasta. Dutch and then Bud joined her. Becca went up and knocked on Charlie's door but he didn't answer. The others ate in silence.

Dinner over, Becca put Charlie's plate in the refrigerator. Dutch checked with the officer in charge, who said they were free to go but to stay in touch. Dutch offered to drive Becca home. Bud said he'd stay with Charlie for a while.

* * *

"So what will you do now?" Dutch asked Becca as they headed south.

"Just go home and take a long bath. I assume I'm out of a job, but I'll call his agent and see if there's anything I should do to close things up. He may need public relations help more than ever now but I doubt he'll keep me on the payroll, and I have rent to pay. This is going to be so hard on his son! The poor kid just got his father back and now he's lost him again."

"I don't know what to say about the boy; never actually met him. As to your job, why don't you come help Aljo with our website and the social media stuff. It would tide you over until you find something permanent, and we could really use the help."

She looked at him tenderly. "That's sweet, Dutch, but I'll be fine. I've got a little saved, and I'm sure I'll find something."

"You misunderstand. We really need help with this. I've been thinking of hiring a tech person for this exact job. And it will be a consulting thing, for as long as it takes. Really, you'd be doing us a favor."

She looked at him closely. "Okay," she said and smiled. "I happen to have seen your website and have a few ideas."

He smiled. "I'll call my assistant and have him set it up. Consider yourself Aljo's new head of communications—after you negotiate a fee with our president, that is."

"Oh no! I hear he drives a hard bargain."

They shared a muted laugh.

* * *

True came into the kitchen. Florence was listening to the radio while she made dinner. "They just talked about Ansel," he said in a scared voice. He had been in his bedroom when he heard someone say the police were chasing Ansel Tone. "What happened? What are they talking about?"

"Oh baby," Florence said. "I'm so sorry you heard that." She turned off the radio and turned back to him, looking hopeful. "I don't know what happened. I'm sure it's a mistake. Your dad would never hurt anyone."

He looked at her doubtfully. Things *never* made sense with Ansel, but then they were always true. If the radio said he was running from the police, then he was running. But the radio said he got away. Maybe his car was so fast no one could catch him.

His mother looked into his eyes and reached to hug him. "Don't you worry, Ducky," she said in the musical voice that always soothed him. "We'll find out what's going on. I'm sure your dad is okay."

* * *

Bud knocked on the door. "Hey, Homer, want some company?"

Charlie looked up from a clipboard, and Odysseus raised his head from his paws. There was more emotion in the dog's sleepy eyes than his friend's.

"Ah, thanks. I'm just trying to straighten things out, you know, keep the engine humming."

"Sure, sure. Oh, yeah, your agent Joan called to make sure someone was here with you. Something about her mother taking a fall. She said the screenplay contract was ready to sign when you're ready and she'll see you at the service. I'm going to nail down the funeral date with Tess's mother. Looks like it will be Saturday, and I'll get the word out. Let me know who I should call, besides Tess's firm. You should take the train down to the city and we'll drive out to Montclair together. Anything else I can do?"

"Thanks, Bud. I'll be fine."

Charlie's phone rang and he picked it up. "Oh, hi. Yeah, I'm fine. It was unnerving. He just took off. Listen, I have someone here. Sure, I'll call you back."

Charlie hung up and turned to Bud. "You guys have been great, all of you. I don't deserve it."

"Oh, no problem, sport. We McYanks have to stick together, right? So, you having company this evening?" He nodded toward Charlie's phone.

"Oh, no, that was just my agent. She watches out for me. She's apologizing for being away. I had to convince her not to cut her trip short."

"Glad to hear it. And so, listen, I'm going to take off. We'll see you Saturday?"

"Right. I'll check the trains and tell you when I get in to Grand Central."

Bud went out of his way to take the Taconic Parkway home, because he loved the winding road and needed time to decompress. The wind blew his hair back from his face. His thoughts drifted to Dublin. Was there something off about Ansel, even then, that they all missed? But then he also remembered—although it would be hurtful to say now—how Charlie acted like a jerk the day after the Trinity party. He had slept in Tess's room, sure, but with Molly there and only because Tess was a mess. Yet, Charlie had crowed about it like he and Tess were suddenly a thing. It was childish and not even true. Well, he did marry her in the end, so maybe it was Bud who had it wrong.

Anyway, he felt for the guy. One moment he was married to Aphrodite the goddess of beauty, and the next he was living alone with a big dog. He may have been a twit at times, but he didn't deserve this. No one deserved this.

As to Ansel: he heard what everyone said about him, that he was smug and egotistical. But no one remembered the other stuff: that he was funny and smart and a pretty good friend, and he did have that golden tongue. What kind of world was it where Ansel was a murderer?

Chapter 42

Detective Crosby emptied the coffee pot into his mug and sipped. It was bitter and full of grounds. He sneered but still carried the mug to his desk. Detective Miller sat across from him, focused on her computer screen.

"Highway Patrol sent over E-ZPass records on Tone's car," she said without looking up. "We can trace him crossing the Newburgh-Beacon Bridge and up the Thruway to New Paltz. After that he's gone."

"Could he have ditched the car? Maybe caught a bus or a train?"

"They've got that covered. The story is all over the news and social media, making Tone out to be some kind of desperado. That has really embarrassed the State Police; there's no way he can travel in New York, not unless he's hiking over the Catskills."

"He may be able to drive faster than us, but I don't see the professor escaping through the woods." He sipped the coffee and put it aside; the bitter taste matched his mood, and he wanted no more of either.

"Oh wait," she said. "The printout shows Tone took the trip north on the Thruway two other times in the last month and then again last week. And this is something: before the party he drove north on Tuesday evening but didn't return south until Wednesday morning."

"Wasn't that…" he said, checking his notes.

"Exactly! That was when Piedmont said he was in California for a meeting about his movie."

"Well, isn't that interesting? I wonder where Dr. Tone spent the night? We better tie up the loose ends so we can nail this sucker once we catch him."

"I'll line up interviews with the couple on Long Island. Piedmont's agent isn't answering her phone."

"We have to find her, if only to eliminate her as 'the other woman.' In fact, let's have one more go at everyone from the party. Oh, and what about those photos Rebecca Howard took; did she send them?"

"I just got the file. I'll see what we've got."

* * *

"Father, it's me," Ansel said desperately. Jordan had been expecting this call.

"I made a big mistake, and the police are looking for me."

Jordan shook his head in disgust. "I know, Ansel. I saw it on television, like *everyone*."

"What do you mean?"

"You're a celebrity. When you kill someone and lead the police on a high-speed chase, it's news."

"But it's not true! You have to help me! You have to get me a lawyer."

His son simply could not take care of himself. He chased women, he cut corners, he acted like nothing could touch him because Jordan would always save his hide. His mother had coddled him too much.

"I don't *have* to do anything, Ansel," he said. "I told you I was done cleaning up after you. Now you've scandalized the family *and* the business. I only wish that, when you changed your name, you made it into something *completely* different from mine…and your poor mother's."

"Father, please! Could you not bring Mom up right now! I'm telling you, damn it, I didn't kill Tess Piedmont! It's a mistake!"

"Mistake!" Jordan laughed. "Calling *me* was a mistake."

* * *

Ansel leaned into the wall, the dead phone against his ear. Jordan had hung up on his life. He looked up but could see no light. His job was sunk; there would be no more books; he would lose the apartment. He might go to prison.

Jake knocked softly. "Hey Ansel, should we talk?"

"Come on in, brother."

Jake took a seat. "Okay, to start, let me say I'm here for you. I saw the news, so I know about the chase. Your car is out of sight. No one saw you come in, unless they noticed the car on the road."

"Aren't you going to ask if I killed that woman?"

"No need, man; I know you. Besides, you've always had *my* back. Shit, I wouldn't have been able to buy this inn without you cosigning."

"We agreed never to mention that."

"You're right, but you knew I wouldn't forget. And so now it's my turn. Just tell me how to help."

"Well, I need to let it out. Have you got a bottle of something? This will take some time."

Jake grabbed a bottle of rum and two glasses. He poured and Ansel told the story, the *actual* facts, from plagiarizing the book to losing the cops. When he got to the part about colluding with Tess to revise Charlie's manuscript, he almost became lost in the story, the film noir version of his life.

"But," he said, speech slightly slurred, "the best thing I ever did was to have True. I was too stupid to know it at that time. I had this perverse sense of what fatherhood meant. Now I look at the kid and understand what I should have known all along."

"So what are you going to do?"

"Turn myself in. I just have to take what comes. And my life… well, I'm sick of living this way."

After Jake left, Ansel removed his shoes and collapsed on the bed. He had drifted off to sleep when his phone woke him.

"Yes," he said, clearing his throat.

"It's your father, Ansel. Don't talk; just listen. I don't know if you're guilty or not. Maybe it's my fault you've been reckless your whole life, and this is where it's landed you. But I made a call. Give me your address and first thing tomorrow a criminal lawyer out of the city will be there. Her name's Nora French. She's a shark. You stay put and don't talk to anyone. When she gets there, do what she says."

"I will, Father, and thank you. I think…I think I know where I'm going now."

Chapter 43

Ansel woke early. He showered and shaved. Jake brought in breakfast so he wouldn't be seen in the dining room.

"I don't know how to thank you," Ansel said.

"Now, don't get all mushy on me," Jake responded with deep concern. "I'll show the lawyer in when she gets here. Get some food inside you. Those scones are to die for."

The food and coffee revived him. It was the first he had eaten in almost a day. The tastes and smells were more intense than any he could remember.

Nora French arrived just after breakfast. She looked the part: dark suit, severely pulled back hair, no-nonsense expression. She immediately took charge. "The news says you're wanted for the murder of Theresa Piedmont."

"That's nuts! I wouldn't hurt anyone, especially not Tess."

"Well, let's explore that to start. I've seen her photograph and done a little background on you. One potential theory would be this was an affair gone wrong. She jilted you and you killed her."

"That's ludicrous."

"But you *were* having an affair?"

Ansel paused. "I can talk to you, right? I mean, you're my lawyer so our conversations are private?"

"I can only help you if you tell me everything."

"Okay, yes," he said. "Tess and I were together in college, and recently we met again and had one night together."

"And did Charles Piedmont know?"

"I'm not sure what he knew or suspected. Tess and I didn't talk about that. We hardly had time."

"Well, I understand the police can put you at the murder scene, with extensive knowledge of cars and a possible motive, and then you led them on a chase across three counties. Tell me you can explain that."

Ansel talked about his relationship with Tess but avoided saying anything about Dublin. Nora looked frustrated. "The case against you," she said, "seems to be entirely circumstantial. They've got you at the scene with a motive and all the knowledge you needed to get the job done, but I haven't seen any direct evidence tying you to the Jaguar. Still, you better come up with a better explanation for your flight."

She called the police and agreed Ansel would surrender himself at the Cold Spring station. She would drive him there and Jake would keep the Zagato in the barn until Jordan sent someone for it.

* * *

Detectives Crosby and Miller were waiting in an interrogation room. Crosby greeted Ansel and Nora. He knew the lawyer by reputation and had cautioned Miller that she was very good and they had to make certain their case was airtight.

Miller started the recorder and Crosby began. "Dr. Tone, we understand you attended a party at the home of Mr. and Ms. Piedmont last Saturday and you stayed over until Sunday morning."

"Right. I told that to the detective over the phone."

"Uh huh. Well, did you see Mr. Piedmont's Jaguar while you were there?"

"It was parked in the garage, but I didn't go near it."

"Not otherwise during the party or later that night?"

"No."

"You are an aficionado of sports cars, correct?"

"What? Yes, I guess I am."

"But you had no interest in a…" he checked his notes, "1975 Jaguar XKE?"

"It's not that I had no interest. I visited Charlie weeks before and he showed me the car, and I've seen plenty of Jaguars. I was at the party Saturday to see friends, not spend time in the garage."

"I see. Well, to back up a little, you not only drive an expensive sports car, but you are quite knowledgeable about the XKE and about automobiles in general; isn't that true?"

"Yes," Ansel replied in frustration, "I have worked on many kinds of cars, and am familiar with the XKE."

"So you would know, strictly from a mechanical sense, how to ensure the brakes would fail?"

"Detective Crosby," Nora interrupted, "has Dr. Tone been charged with anything related to Mr. Piedmont's car?"

"At this point, counselor," Crosby replied, "no charges have been filed, but we need to understand the facts."

Nora nodded for Ansel to respond.

"Sure," he said, "There are ways to do that, if I had a reason to."

"For example?"

Nora nodded again. "Well," Ansel went on, "you could simply cut the brake lines under the hood and tape them up so they'd blow when the brakes were pumped and spray the engine with brake fluid."

The detectives waited. Ansel shrugged. "Of course, that would be hard to hide. To cause an accident without evidence you'd do better to jam debris around the brakes so they'd overheat and boil the brake fluid."

"I see. And this would be hard to trace?"

"Impossible, I would think, in a wreck."

Crosby scribbled a note. "But you never did those things to Mr. Piedmont's car?"

"Of course not, damn it! I'm telling you, I didn't go near his car!"

"Okay. Let's go back to Saturday night. You drank a lot at the party?"

"I did."

"And was this typical? Do you often drink too much, Dr. Tone, and need to sleep it off before you go home?"

"No, it's not *typical*." He paused, collecting his thoughts. "I had a lot on my mind and, I don't know, found the bourbon near at hand and got carried away."

"And needed to be helped to bed?"

"My friends helped me, yes, but I'm sure I could have gotten to bed myself."

Crosby pondered this. "Do you ever black out when you drink, Dr. Tone? You know, forget what happened?"

"This is not a habit with me! I don't normally drink that much, and I have never blacked out!"

"Fine. So, you remember everything about that night?"

"Basically, yeah."

"Did you get up during the night?"

"I think," he said and paused. "Yeah, I think I went to the bathroom. It was dark. I don't know what time that was."

"But you didn't go outside, or visit the garage?"

"This is nuts! I told you I didn't go near Charlie's car!"

"Okay, going back to why you drank that night: what was so heavy on your mind?"

"The pressures of work, whether I would be make tenure in my teaching job, publishing deadlines for my book, and…"

"And your affair with Theresa Piedmont?"

Ansel was stunned but recovered. "Yes, I was concerned about that, too."

"Just to help us paint the picture, when did this affair begin?"

"Tess and I were together twelve years ago. We recently resumed our relationship."

"Did Mr. Piedmont suspect anything?"

"I have no way to know that."

"Okay, then, Dr. Tone…"

"Except," Ansel broke in. They stopped and looked at him. "Except one thing—I just remembered. It was a couple of weeks ago when he showed me his "secret road" off the top of the mountain. I said something crass about everything on the mountain exciting me."

He paused. Nora looked stoic. Miller smiled. Crosby gestured impatience.

"Right, so I made this kind of crude comment, taking in the road, the house *and* his wife, and promptly felt a cold wind from Charlie's direction. It was stupid. I was boasting about sleeping with his wife but was sure he wouldn't get the reference. But I underestimated him. I think he was close to clocking me one."

"So that was it?" Miller said finally.

"Yeah, one moment I thought he'd hit me and the next he turned for home, and I went on my way."

The detectives exchanged glances and Crosby continued. "Okay, Dr. Tone, we've also heard conflicting stories about a certain party you attended in Dublin and an incident there with Ms. Piedmont. What can you tell us about that?"

Ansel looked at Nora and shook his head. "Detective," he said finally, "I have told you Tess and I were together twelve years ago. We were kids in college. At the end of the year we all went our separate ways and Tess and I broke up. That's all there was to it until we met again a few months ago in New York."

"All right, Dr. Tone," Crosby said. "One more detail stands out, something about a woman named Reilly, someone you met at Trinity College. You told your friends you spent the night together after a year-end party, but in fact you didn't?"

"Detective, I was twenty; I met lots of girls. What has that got to do with Tess's accident?"

"Frankly, Dr. Tone, we were hoping you could tell us. We don't much care about what happened twelve years ago, except that it suggests a motive to cover something up. You will have to give us a clearer picture."

Ansel remained silent, concentrating on keeping his expression steady.

"And then," Crosby went on, "there is your behavior yesterday. Why did you run? Why did you hide out?"

"Like I said, Detective Crosby, I had a lot on my mind."

"Yes, but can you give us something specific because, honestly, Dr. Tone, it doesn't add up."

"I was high," Ansel blurted out.

Nora spoke up. "Let's be clear here. You do not intend to charge Dr. Tone with drug possession or impaired driving; is that correct?"

"Correct, counselor. This is a homicide investigation. Dr. Tone will have to answer to the State Police for his driving."

"Well, so," she continued, "it seems Dr. Tone had deep concerns, had experienced a recent tragedy and his self-medication harmed more than it helped; taken together, it could well explain paranoid flight."

"Well, it might, counselor, but a lot of people feel work pressure and use recreational drugs without leading the police on a high-speed chase." He and Miller rose. "Ansel Tone, I am charging you with the murder of Theresa Piedmont. You will be held in this station house jail and arraigned on Friday."

* * *

A guard returned Ansel to his cell. He stared at the grey ceiling. How could they think someone like him, a professor and famous author, would try to kill someone? He hoped True hadn't heard about this; the kid had just started to trust him.

He needed to keep calm and be careful about answering questions. They couldn't connect him with the accident and no one really cared about Trinity.

"So, we got ourselves a hot shit celebrity," came a gruff voice from the next cell, out of sight behind a wall.

"Hell, yeah," a deep voice answered. "Professor with the car."

Jordan told Ansel he had been on the news. It seemed the story had reached even into lockup. Ansel said nothing and the voices died away.

Late in the afternoon, the guards moved the prisoners to make room for new arrivals. In a brief walk down the hallway, another prisoner tripped Ansel. His ankles were shackled, so he fell hard. The other prisoner laughed, and Ansel ended with a sprained wrist and a broken nose. The doctor put his arm in a sling and said he was good to go, but added: "Of course, you may not be posing for any more magazine covers."

In the morning the big guard came by Ansel's cell. "Something delivered for you," he said, pushing an envelope through the bars.

The slit-open envelope held one sheet of paper folded inside another. The outer page said in neat script: "Ansel, we saw the news. True would not be consoled. He said a father doesn't desert his son, and a son can't desert his father. But they say we can't visit until after the arraignment, so we'll be back. Take care of yourself, Florence."

The inside page combined messy cursive with printed letters: "Dad, we came to see you. I know you did not hurt someone. True."

Ansel read True's letter again. "Dad?" he said out loud. Then, clutching the page with his eyes closed, he recited his son's message. That was it. This all had to change.

After lunch, a police van transported him to court. He met with Nora in an empty jury room. She was outraged when she saw his swollen nose and the arm sling and said she'd complain to the judge.

"If you think it'll help," he said. "But the only thing that will *really* help is to get me out of that place."

She looked at him sympathetically, and then abruptly opened her briefcase. "Okay," she said, "first things first. We will go before the judge to hear the charge and enter a plea. You stand quietly and I'll plead not guilty on your behalf. Then the judge will set bail."

"I understand. But one more thing: I want to tell them why I ran."

"That's smart, Ansel. You can't be worried about what happened in Ireland when you've got a murder charge hanging over you. But this is not the time. I'll set up a meeting with the detectives."

The arraignment began as Nora had described. Ansel was charged with first-degree murder and the judge accepted his plea. But the prosecutor argued he should remain incarcerated awaiting trial because he was a flight risk.

"But, Your Honor," Nora pleaded. "This was a first offense and Dr. Tone is a respected member of the community and the Columbia University faculty. He also voluntarily surrendered to the police. What's more, your Honor can see for himself the injuries inflicted upon Doctor Tone over his two days in lockup."

The judge looked at Ansel and then at the prosecutor, who said, "Dr. Tone has already cost the State substantial resources in connection with his very public flight at," he checked his notes, "157 miles an hour—the trooper was not certain the radar was accurate at that speed. Dr. Tone has shown not only the desire to avoid arrest but a unique ability to elude capture. And this is a capital charge of premeditated murder, Your Honor."

"I appreciate the government's position," the judge said, "and am aware of the publicity this case has generated. Ms. French, you will acknowledge this case is unique, and I am determined to proceed with no further drama." He banged his gavel. "I order the defendant held without bail pending trial. The defense may reapply on this issue when court is back in session Monday."

* * *

Detectives Crosby and Miller were waiting at the station house. Miller started up the recorder. "The floor is yours, Dr. Tone," Crosby said.

Ansel breathed in carefully to avoid the sharp pain in his nose. He wished he had a shot of bourbon to dull the ache, but he recoiled at his own weakness. He told himself to stop whining; it was time to perform.

"Okay, this is a bit involved but it's time I got it out. I am to blame for lots of things, but I did *not* hurt Tess Piedmont."

The detectives sat silently.

"Right. Well, there was an incident twelve years ago in Dublin. I attended school there for a year. I got a good grade on a major term paper, but my professor discovered I had plagiarized." He recounted the facts up to Digory's fall, and his disposal afterward of the letter, the Australian book and the sweatshirt he wore that night. "The police investigated but nothing came of it. The semester ended and we all went home."

"So, twelve years later Charlie decides to write a novel based on our time together and starts digging into what everyone remembers. His memory from that night threatens my alibi, so I suggest a way to change the story and improve the plot—and keep my secret. I see a way to make the change on Charlie's laptop so he won't notice or, if he does, maybe he'll keep the change. And yeah, I spend the night with his wife and she gets me the password to his computer. But he walks in on me fixing the manuscript and is pretty understandably disturbed. I'd say he is *very* disturbed."

"Violently disturbed?" Miller said, "like his unease could lead him to violence?"

"No, I wouldn't say that. He calmed down quickly, even offered me a drink."

Miller nodded and Ansel continued. "As to why I took off. First, I noticed a patrol car trailing me up the mountain, then I saw all these police vehicles at the house and you, Detective Crosby, pulling out a gun. I snapped. I put the gas to the floor and lost all sense of what I was doing. When I went to ground, I knew I had to turn myself in."

* * *

The detectives spent the rest of the day and the next morning checking financial records, talking with the Dublin police and Trinity College administrators, and calling the party guests.

Toward quitting time Miller sat at her desk covered with papers. Crosby paced, chewing a cold slice of pizza. "Do we have the right guy?" Miller asked.

"Well," said Crosby, "let's review. We have a guy who has built a successful teaching and publishing career, who is scared to death people will find out he cheated in college and, in trying to cover that up, he may have contributed to an accidental death. He finds out his old school chum is going to out him in a novel, so tries to get the novelist to change his plot. Along the way, the professor resumes a relationship with the novelist's wife, possibly to help him change the book.

"Meanwhile, our novelist has everyone over for a party, where the professor sneaks into his computer and tries to revise the novel. But the novelist catches him. There's a row, but everyone pushes this under the rug for the sake of the class reunion.

"The professor then gets falling-down drunk—possibly—and sleeps at the novelist's house. He has extensive knowledge of cars and admits he could easily have done the deed, if he had a reason to, and it happens he did have a strong reason to want to shut the novelist up. But his knowledge of cars told him cutting brake lines could be detected in a wreck, while jamming the brakes would be undetectable. We should check with the guys in the garage and see what they think about that.

"The novelist is then summoned to Baltimore to meet with a movie director about a possible job and leaves his prized sports car for his wife to drive while her car is being repaired. We don't know for certain whether he suspected the affair with the professor, but we do know he loved his car and all indications are he loved his wife, almost to the point of distraction. He stands to profit from the life insurance but had only vague knowledge about this. Did we check for insurance on the car?"

"I'm waiting on that," Miller said. "I'd guess he had plenty."

"Well then, we have the victim: a beautiful lawyer married to the novelist; her close friend thinks there may have been problems in the marriage, and we *know* she was fooling around with her old boyfriend, the professor.

"As for forensics, we have the husband's fingerprints on everything, as would be expected, and none from the professor that can't be explained by his attending the party."

"Piedmont's prints are on most of the tools in the garage," Miller said. "There are no prints at all on the hacksaw used to cut the brake lines."

Crosby pondered that. "So," he continued, "we have no eyewitnesses and no confession. The dog in the house apparently didn't notice anyone getting up to tamper with the car in the middle of the night, on top of which our professor may have been incapacitated by drink, although this was out of character. There were no traces of brake fluid on the professor's clothes."

Miller added: "The police in Dublin are reopening the case of the security guard's death, but they point out that the evidence is stale. They found an electronic copy of the letter Tone's advisor wrote about his plagiarism. The letter was dated the day *after* the racing accident, which would have been when the advisor was in a hospital. This fits with Tone's story."

"At any rate," she continued, "Mr. Piedmont refuses to admit there was anything between his wife and Tone, while he does paint Tone as desperate to see the novel revised. And the victim sent her husband a text about working late and staying in the city while he was out of town. Her boss says work had calmed down after a big deal was signed, so she may have been covering her tracks to spend the night with Tone."

"And what about Ms. Piedmont?" Crosby asked. "Could she have found herself stuck between her husband and her lover and looked for a quick way out?"

"Why would she cut the brake lines to drive off a cliff?"

"So, then, what's the answer?"

"Answer to what?" Miller replied.

"Your question: do we have the right guy?"

"Well, we still need to catch up with the agent who went to Baltimore with Piedmont. She hasn't returned our calls. We sent someone by her apartment, which is also her office, but there was no one home. We're trying to confirm the phone number. We also need to follow up with the other partygoers, to see if it all lines up."

Chapter 44

Tess's mother arranged a memorial service in Montclair. Dutch and Becca arrived early and stood in front of the church until Bud and Charlie pulled up. The four of them found Molly and Pete inside, along with Joan Munchin and Tess's colleagues from Regis & Kessler.

Tess's mother would have put Tess in the ground with no fuss, but her neighbors expected a ceremony. It was painful to see how she didn't interact with Charlie at all.

When the service ended, Bud suggested a proper send-off back in the city. Charlie was amenable, so Dutch and Becca agreed. Joan had to leave for a meeting.

"Pete and I also have to get home," Molly said, directing a chilly glance toward Charlie.

They were all upset about Tess, but Molly seemed to hold it against Charlie. It wasn't fair.

They arrived in quick succession at Charlie's favorite pub, and occupied a table. "So," Bud said, "I understand they caught up with that bastard. He won't be able to change the facts this time."

"Facts," Charlie said, absently ripping apart his beer coaster. "I was the one who wouldn't admit to what stared me in the face."

"Oh, you're too hard on yourself," Becca said.

Charlie let out a mocking laugh. "Not nearly hard enough. Tess and Ansel? I was such an idiot from the start."

Dutch kept quiet. They had all heard about Ansel and Tess having an affair and trying to change Charlie's book. When that failed, Ansel apparently snapped and sabotaged Charlie's car, only killing Tess by mistake. Now their "friend" was the star of a car chase video that went viral without any help from his web expert. Ansel and his Aston Martin outrunning the police proved irresistible on social media. The "Golden Boy" became the "Bad Boy" and drew followers around the world.

"You all knew, right?" Charlie said, "or suspected, at least? And then there was me, Homer channeling Odysseus, whose Penelope was faithful to the end, faithful until Ansel snapped his fingers, anyway."

Becca looked away, clearly distressed. Dutch shook his head. "No, Charlie. No one else knew anything about them, not since school."

Bud added, "Honestly, man, I envied your life. I had no idea."

Dutch wanted to change the subject. "So, what's up with Molly?" he said. "She sure didn't want to stick around."

"Give her a break," Becca said. "She's about to give birth and just lost her close friend. Jeez."

"She holds it against me," Charlie said. "Who knows what Tess told her about her brute of a husband?"

"Oh, Charlie, don't say that," Becca pleaded, covering his hand with hers.

Charlie shook his head and took a swig of beer. They drank in silence. Then Bud asked Charlie, "So, what about the book? Are you going forward?"

"Yeah, sure. I mean, I'll have to turn my attention to the movie, but the book won't take much more work, on the writing end, anyway. Oh, and speaking of irony—were we talking about irony?—I revised the plot like Ansel suggested, which does make a better story than the real facts. So, it only caught up with Ansel because of his paranoia. He'd have gotten away with Dublin and there would have been no reason for Tess to die." He paused. "He should have just bided his time."

"Well," Bud said, "maybe there's some justice in the revisionist historian failing to revise history."

* * *

Five years ago Charlie's worst fears were of losing Tess or of publishing books sold on the checkout line in the supermarket. Now he had lost Tess one way *and* another, and he was writing a novel designed, not to uplift and inspire, but simply to sell.

He wondered if he'd ever write the Mountain House story. His jumble of emotions would take time to sort out, and he'd have to rearrange the facts, but maybe writing about the tragedy would bring a catharsis, like *Against the Odds*. He could call it "Editing Is Murder."

But then, it would probably be better to put Tess and all this mess behind him.

"So, are you going to stay at Mountain House?" Dutch said.

"No, it's too big and lonely with just Seusy and me. I'm going to put it up for sale—and may use some of Becca's architectural photos." He nodded gratefully to her. "I want something smaller and closer to the city. But then there's Seusy; I've always loved that big hairball but now *we* are all we have, and I need a place he can run."

"Packing up will be a lot of work," Becca said. "Let us help."

"Thanks, but there's no hurry; have to sell it first."

"And what about the movie?" Bud said. "I read they signed that hot young actress."

"Kat Tiergarten," Charlie said. "Yeah, if there were girls like her in Baltimore, I would have stuck around."

They all laughed.

* * *

Becca was conflicted about Ansel. He could be a jerk, she knew that first-hand, but he was audacious, not vindictive. He obviously had an unhappy family life, and that messed up his moral compass, but he also had a gift, a way of making people sit up and take notice. And True's appearance seemed to make a difference; Ansel was softer, much more patient, and he seemed to be trying hard with the boy.

"So what's up with you?" Bud asked her.

"Well, Aljo hired me to redesign the company website, and set up social media accounts."

"How's that going?"

"After *one* day I'd say they've got good people who only need direction. And when the project is done, Dutch's father assures me he'll find me something permanent in photography or marketing. I'm not really sure what I want, but definitely something with a little less drama than my last job."

"I wonder if the infamous Ansel Tone will come up in your interviews," Bud said.

"There isn't much else *on* my resume. People will hopefully be more impressed by his celebrity than put off by his criminal record."

"No such thing as bad publicity, right?" Charlie sneered.

"But so," Bud said, looking at Dutch and Becca, "*you* two: that's one good thing coming out of this, right?"

Dutch laughed. "That and I got a spot on the staff of the Greenpoint Giants."

Charlie and Bud looked at him quizzically.

"Becca's softball team. The very proper ladies from Brooklyn dubbed me 'Bitches Batting Coach.' Only one practice so far, but our girl hits like Miguel Cabrera, and she's a gazelle in center field."

Becca blushed. "Well, it's not a very competitive league."

"Yeah, right," Dutch said. "I can't wait to see the opposition chasing balls she hits over their heads."

Becca said nothing but she was proud, not so much of how she hit a softball but of how she looked in Dutch's eyes. He made her feel like a superstar, like she could accomplish anything in the world, or in New York, which felt like pretty much the same thing.

Dutch asked, "So, what about you, Bud? Now that you're on your way to becoming a power broker, you in the market for a trophy wife?"

"No way, sport," Bud laughed, "although I was wondering about Becca's roommate...."

Becca smiled knowingly. "Well, *that's* interesting," she said. Bud had met Roxy when he picked Becca up on the way to Mountain House.

Dutch and Charlie shared a grin at Bud's eagerness. "Roxy's in big demand," Becca said thoughtfully, and then added, "but we *may* be able to work something out."

"Did I mention how glad I am you two got together?" Bud laughed.

* * *

Bud was relieved to hear Charlie talk dispassionately about Ansel. He also found himself pondering his own feelings, an unusual pastime. Friends were good for business, but there was more. He found that caring for this lost tribe of his youth made his world richer, gave him context, a place in a shared history.

He was glad the drama was over and he could focus on building a business. Dutch assured him he'd land the Aljo account, which would help him network with other local companies. The poker games with Pete were sure to net a few homeowner policies. He was planning a scuba-diving trip off Belize that should land him a big client. And, even though the commissions from these sales might enable him to move into Manhattan, he decided to stay in Queens, which was pretty cool after all.

Dutch said, "So I guess we should plan the next reunion for Pete and Molly's christening."

"Well, a reunion for everyone but the Golden Boy," Bud said. "I think he'll be tied up."

"I understand he's revising the history of Ansel MacTone," Charlie said disdainfully, "to correct certain inaccuracies in the record."

Becca said, "It's like writing those books and teaching propaganda mixed up his sense of truth."

"Well," Bud declared, raising his glass again, "here's to proving the victors don't *always* get to write the history."

Dutch suggested they call it a day with one last toast. The waitress left the check and Dutch reached for it, but Charlie beat him to it. "On me, folks," Charlie said. "You guys have stuck with me through this nightmare, and I find more and more that loyalty means everything."

When Charlie reached into his jacket for his wallet his keys fell to the table. Bud caught them backhand before they bounced onto the floor. He looked around for acknowledgement of his excellent reflexes, but no one had noticed. He shook his head with a frown and handed the keys to Charlie, who stepped up to the bar to pay the bill.

They parted ways on the sidewalk. As Bud walked alone toward the subway, something troubled him, something about Charlie's keys.

Chapter 45

Detectives Crosby and Miller returned to Mountain House Sunday. Charlie was not expecting them.

"Detectives," he said, opening the door to invite them in. "What can we do for you today?"

"Oh," Crosby said, noticing Joan. "I hope we're not disturbing anything."

"No, no. This is my agent, Joan Munchin."

"Ah, yes. We've had trouble reaching Ms. Munchin, so this is fortunate."

"I apologize," said Joan. "I lost my phone while I was traveling and kept thinking I'd find it. I guess I need a new one."

"Oh, no problem, Ms. Munchin. It's more conducive to speak in person, anyway."

"Why do you need to speak with Joan?" Charlie said. "Isn't the investigation wrapped up?"

"Strictly speaking, Mr. Piedmont, until an indictment comes down, nothing is really 'wrapped up.'"

Charlie showed them to seats at the dining room table and offered coffee.

Crosby looked pleased. "Never turn down a good cup of coffee, I always say."

Steaming cup in hand, Crosby continued. "So, let me get to the point. We, Detective Miller and I, have sorted through the evidence and had additional conversations with the people who attended your party, and we need to fill in a few gaps."

"Fire away," said Charlie. Joan watched from the arm of a sofa.

"Before we start," Crosby said, "could we make clear your role, Ms. Munchin? We understand you are Mr. Piedmont's literary agent, but you also work as a kind of business manager, setting up meetings, making arrangements...."

"Yes," Joan said, looking uncomfortable. "Charlie and I have teamed up on the literary *and* business end of all his projects."

"Excellent," Crosby went on, turning toward Charlie. "So, it was Sunday when you first made plans to go to Baltimore?"

"That's right."

"When the director's assistant contacted Ms. Munchin?"

Gilroy and Miller turned to Joan. Her eyes grew wide but she said nothing.

"Ms. Munchin," said Crosby, "who called you to set up the meeting?"

"Actually, it was Charlie's idea. The book is based on his life and we thought that showing the director actual settings from the book might help convince him to hire Charlie to write the screenplay. So, I called Milo Channing's assistant, Marci Gerber."

"No," Charlie barked, then spoke calmly but firmly to Joan. "Don't you remember, the producer said I would have to meet Milo?"

"Sure," Joan said. "That's right, yes. That's what we did. Charlie showed them places mentioned in his book, and I negotiated with the studio lawyer."

"But..." Crosby said and paused to sip from his cup. Charlie hung on this unfinished thought.

"Ah, that is fine coffee," Crosby said. "And as to the meeting, you see the thing we are most interested in is who *suggested* the meeting that would put you in Baltimore." He looked at Joan and then Charlie. "And it seems, Mr. Piedmont, that *you* were the one to ask your agent to call the director and suggest a meeting in Baltimore the day your car's brakes failed and killed your wife."

"So what? Are you saying I'm a suspect? You already arrested the killer!"

"Mr. Piedmont, like I said, we generally try to stay on a case until it all adds up. You know how that is, right? It must be the same when you set out a plot for a book."

Crosby smiled all around and went on. "So now we'd like to turn to some financials. When we last spoke, you were unaware of the amount of your wife's life insurance; is that correct?"

"I think I said it was a term life policy she got through work. I didn't know the details."

"Right, well that raises an odd point. You see, we spoke with Mr. Roberts. We understand it would be an understatement to call him 'an insurance salesman.'" Crosby paused for laughs but got only a patient smile from Miller. "Well, Mr. Roberts recalls speaking with you about insurance the day of your party. He said you had an unusual grasp of your needs and coverages, much to his chagrin. He said, in particular, that your wife's policy through her firm paid a million-and-a-half-dollars. Do you recall saying that, Mr. Piedmont?"

"I believe the policy pays a million and a half, yes. I guess that slipped my mind when we spoke."

"Mr. Roberts was also impressed by the policy on your Jaguar; he called it 'appraisal value.' I assume that means you will collect what the car would fetch at auction?"

"Yes, more or less."

"So, you lost the car you loved, but you'll have money to buy another if you want?"

"I suppose."

"Or not. Anyway, I guess you can see how these things make the picture more confusing. Because now the husband making sudden plans to be away stands to gain financially if his wife has an accident in his car."

"This is outrageous!" Charlie shouted and rose from his chair.

"Sit down, Mr. Piedmont. We're just getting started."

Charlie sat, feeling like a hunted animal.

"So, we should talk about what we found in the house."

Charlie eyes grew wide but Crosby seemed distracted, brushing something off his jacket sleeve. Finally, he continued, "You have a variety of tools in the garage. Would you say you use most of them with some regularity?"

"How can I answer a question like that? I use a tool when I need it."

"Of course. So what about the hacksaw? Have you had occasion to use that for anything recently?"

Charlie's jaw tightened. "I don't recall the last time I used the hacksaw. Why is that important?"

"Oh, just that we believe that saw was used to cut the brakes, and we found it completely clean of fingerprints, as if someone had wiped it down."

"Well, the killer probably did, right? What's that got to do with me?"

"Just covering the bases, Mr. Piedmont. And the Jaguar: I know you didn't buy it new—what would that be, over forty years ago—but did you have an owner's manual for the car?"

"Yes, I bought it online several years ago."

"And where did you keep it?"

"I…" Charlie looked upstairs. "I think it's in my den."

"That is *just* where we found it, in a bookshelf organized roughly by author's nationality, in between *Middlemarch* and *Persuasion*." He looked at Charlie as if awaiting an explanation. Charlie shrugged his shoulders. "Well," Crosby went on, "it *was* a British car, so I suppose it belonged with the British novels, but why was it in the house rather than in the car? I keep my manual in the glove compartment in case something comes up while I'm driving. Can we take it you recently referred to your manual in your den and forgot to put it back in the car?"

"I don't recall. A vintage car always needs something. I may have been checking parts."

"I see," Crosby said. He nodded to Miller, who pushed across the desk the black and white photo of Ansel and Tess that Charlie printed weeks before. "We found this in your desk."

Charlie shrugged his shoulders. "I explained this: real people are models for characters in my books."

"Right," Miller said. "And it's a terrific shot, but it's just something you said. I'm kind of a photography nut, always printing and copying photographs."

"What did I say?"

"When we asked the first time, you said this was an *old* photo you found with maps and notes and whatever from your time in Ireland."

"Right," Charlie said. "Tess was a beautiful girl and took a great picture. I think I can even remember when I blew up this print; while they were still dating, obviously."

"Well, this is where my photo-geekiness comes in, because we checked and this photo came from the printer in your den and quite recently. We can understand you having an old photo of your wife and Dr. Tone but we have to wonder why you would make a new print."

"I meant the picture was old, but yeah, I made the enlargement as a tool for writing the book, a couple or three weeks ago."

"It makes us wonder when you print a photo of your wife with her former lover and then lie about it."

"Lie about it? You think I'm lying? What reason do I have to lie? Have you got nothing better to do than pick at little details?"

"Details, Mr. Piedmont," Crosby said, "are the foundation for theories and we need a consistent theory of the case. You see, in our minds, this recent photo in your files suggests you may have been fixated on your wife and Dr. Tone, almost like you printed it to put up on a dartboard. You insist there was nothing between them, but Ms. Peretti believes something *was* going on. And, well, we have Dr. Tone's admission, and of course *he* would know. Apparently, he spent the night with your wife in this house, just days before your party."

Charlie sprang up. "What does it matter what that bastard says? And what is he hiding about Trinity? He's been no good the whole time we've known him." He walked to the bar, poured scotch and took a gulp.

"And one more thing," Crosby added, "Dr. Tone said you had a conversation while you were out driving together weeks ago, something about his being excited by everything about your mountain? He said he meant that oblique reference to include your wife but was surprised you picked up on it. He said you seemed quite angry."

"Who says I was angry?" Charlie snarled. "Did he say I hit him? Or yelled at him?"

"Just that you reacted as if you grasped the meaning of his remark."

"I don't know what he's talking about, but you can be sure he'll say anything to divert suspicion from himself."

"Well, maybe so but, like I said, it's hard to ignore one detail after another, especially…" He trailed off and seemed lost in thought.

"Especially what?" Charlie demanded.

"Especially when we get to the smoking gun."

"The what?" Charlie snapped.

"Sorry, Mr. Piedmont," Crosby smiled. "Just a term of art."

Miller handed Crosby two more photographs. He placed them backside up on the table. Charlie eyed them anxiously.

Crosby went on. "I'd like to ask about the car itself."

"The Jaguar? What about it?"

"Well, you know, my Mazda is full of stuff adopted over the years, clutter that almost becomes part of the car."

Charlie felt dazed but said nothing.

"For instance, we've got this old dreamcatcher hanging from the mirror. My daughter bought it years ago on a trip out west, and my wife has insisted it follow us from car to car ever since. She's sure it keeps us from having accidents."

Charlie stared.

Crosby shook his head. "Yeah, my wife… It seems a little inconsistent but she's also an observant Catholic, God bless her, and so we have a St. Christopher statue on the dashboard. She had me glue it in place."

Charlie said nothing.

"You know, St. Christopher? The patron saint of travelers?"

"Detective, could we please get to the point? Ms. Munchin and I have work to do."

"Oh, absolutely, Mr. Piedmont. Well so, we understand you own a kind of good luck charm, something you call your 'safety insurance.' Can you tell us about this?"

"Yes, Detective, if you really think it's relevant. I studied ancient Greece and I own an old Greek coin."

"And you always kept it in the Jaguar?"

"Well, not necessarily."

"Like when, for instance, would you remove it?"

"Oh, I don't know. In fact, here, I've got it on my key ring now." He threw his keys on the table.

"Yes, very interesting," Crosby said, holding up the coin. "It looks quite old."

"It is, if that matters."

"Do we understand correctly that you purchased this coin at about the same time you bought the car?"

"Yes, I think so."

"And you've had it ever since?"

"Yes, of course."

"And you kept it in the Jaguar?"

"Well, like I said, sometimes I did and sometimes I didn't."

"Do you recall when you removed it from the Jaguar and put it on your key ring? When was that?"

"It could have been weeks ago or months ago. I don't remember."

"I see. So, this coin is special to you?"

"It has very personal associations. Is there something wrong with that?"

"No. But this raises another issue, which I'm afraid is not a 'little' thing. You see, Mr. Roberts thought he saw a coin hanging from the Jaguar's mirror on the day of your party, when the two of you drove to pick up a cake. He explained it was a 'talisman' of sorts, which played into some kind of running gag among you all about Greek philosophers."

"On Saturday?" Charlie said, feeling the pressure mount. "That can't be right. I'd have remembered."

"Exactly! And the thing is, we also have a photograph, taken by one of your guests. It was Ms. Howard; she was kind enough to provide us copies. Two of her shots, in particular, show Mr. Gilroy seated in the Jaguar the day of the party." He passed the photos to Charlie.

Charlie brushed sweat from his forehead. Crosby picked up the coin again and said, "I think you can see pretty clearly this same coin was hanging from the Jaguar mirror the day of the party. We surmise, then, that you removed your 'good luck charm' on Sunday before you left town. Possibly, the coin was something you wanted to preserve and you suspected something might happen to the car while you took an unscheduled trip out of town?"

Charlie collapsed. Joan reached for him, but he pushed her away. Miller rose and stood behind him. "Charles Piedmont," Crosby said, "I'm arresting you on suspicion of the murder of Theresa Piedmont."

Chapter 46

Ansel lay on his bunk in lockup. He wished he had something to read to take his mind off the throbbing in his head.

An officer came by his cell. "Looks like you'll be leaving us, Professor."

"What do you mean?" he said and jumped to his feet, grimacing in pain.

"Slow down, pal. We just got word the detectives will be by to spring you. Must have been a break in the case."

Soon he was led to an interrogation room, and moments later Detectives Crosby and Miller breezed in. "Dr. Tone," Crosby said. "We've got some good news. Charles Piedmont has confessed to rigging the Jaguar and killing his wife. You are free to go."

"I…" Ansel stuttered, "I don't know what to say."

"Well, maybe it's the two of us who should say something. For myself, I'm sorry we put you through this. It's the hard part of the job when you have to shake up bystanders to get to the facts." He reached out a hand and Ansel shook it, feeling the weight of the world lifting from his shoulders.

Miller added with genuine concern. "We're also sorry your jailer wasn't able to keep you safe."

Ansel shrugged this off, he was so full of elation and then curiosity. "How did he do it, do you know?"

"Very much in line with a technique *you* suggested. He cut the brake lines under the hood and taped them closed. He figured there would not be enough of the car left to detect the tampering. You, I should note, suggested a less detectable way to accomplish the same thing, by jamming debris into the brakes. That was what first led us to think the sabotage was *not* the work of someone with *your* knowledge of cars."

Ansel marveled at this. He had been so convinced his confession about knowing how to disable cars was a mistake.

"Now, you should understand," Crosby went on, "you will likely still face charges of speeding and reckless endangerment, although we will not, as agreed, pass along any information about illicit drugs. But with Nora French on your side and seeing as how this was a first offense and you were under some considerable stress—and spent some unpleasant jail time on a charge that was dismissed—I'm guessing you'll get off with community service."

"Right," Ansel acknowledged. He could only imagine facing his department head and his publisher. But one step at a time; he was sprung!

Miller slid the black and white photo of Ansel and Tess across the table. "We made several copies of this to identify the printer. I thought you might like one."

Ansel stared at the photograph. She *was* a beauty. The image thrust him back to a time of innocence. "Thank you, Detective," he said sincerely.

"Oh, and one more thing," Miller said, "if you don't mind?" She handed him a copy of *Redux: Stick it to the Man.* "I don't imagine you'd consider signing my copy?"

"My adoring public," he laughed, and wrote on the half-title page: "Thanks for getting the story straight. Ansel (James Bond) Tone."

A patrolman drove Ansel back to the city. He entered his empty apartment feeling like he'd been gone for months. After a shower and a bagel from the freezer, he picked up his phone. "True, guess what? They found the guy who did it! I'm free!"

"Yippee!" True shouted. "I knew you'd get out!"

"I'm so proud of you, how you stood by me."

"Does this mean we can go to the beach now?"

Ansel laughed so hard he cried, and his nose ached. Regaining control, he asked to speak with Florence and filled her in. "I still have to face the police chase and some things about Dublin, but I have to thank you for believing in me and for raising that amazing kid."

His next call was to the university. "Ansel," Ed Flagel said, "good to hear from you. Very unfortunate you had to get mixed up, uhum, with the police and all. The Trustees will be relieved this was resolved."

"Yes, sir, but other things will come out. We should meet and I'll walk you through it, so no one is surprised." There was no hiding the incidents at Trinity. Ansel was certain they would derail his tenure and doubted the university would even keep him on as a lecturer, but it was worth a try.

Next on the list was Leah.

"You're out!" she said in her usual deafening tone. "Congrats. I couldn't believe you would kill someone, but then social media decided that's why you ran. It was the biggest car chase since O.J. Simpson!"

"Thanks, although it wasn't much fun from my seat. And my question for you is whether Wiley will still publish the fake news book."

"Hard to say. The morals clause gives them an out. But they are businessmen; if the book will sell, they'll publish. Harvey may wait to see which way the wind blows but, in the end, I should be able to convince him. The publicity about your false arrest, with all the fast cars and the beautiful Theresa Piedmont, will send advance sales through the roof. And, with Donald Trump now the Republican candidate, the concept of fake news couldn't be more current."

"That's terrific, Leah. Please do what you can and thanks, for this and for all the other times I didn't say it."

"O…kay," she said. "Did you hit your head during that chase, Ansel?"

"Not during the chase, but you might say I had some sense knocked into me along the way."

"Well, anyway, if he goes along, Harvey will insist on early completion of the manuscript, with strict milestones. He'll want to market the book while the incident is fresh in the public's mind."

"No problem there. I'm not likely to have any more obligations at the university. My lawyer thinks I'll be collecting trash by the side of the Thruway on the driving charges, so I'll have plenty of time to think about the book. Just agree to whatever schedule Harvey wants. I'll start working right away."

He stepped out on the balcony. A large sailboat headed up the Hudson under power. He took a deep, careful breath of freedom. His world was shaken. The backstop of the teaching job would disappear, which meant losing the university apartment. He was going to need a new place, something simple but with two bedrooms so True would have a room. With nothing holding him to the Columbia neighborhood, he figured he should look around Chelsea, to be nearer his son. In any event, he'd cut back on drinking to social occasions and lay off the drugs, not even look for a connection to replace Henry.

He would have to see what Trinity College decided. Maybe there was something he could do about Digory, too, if it was not too late. Did the old guy have any family? If not, he could make a donation to the school, maybe something to spruce up those crumbling philosophers on the Campanile?

Acting on his new resolve not to put off unpleasant tasks, he called Jordan. "Father, it's Ansel. I've been released. The husband confessed to killing his wife."

"I'm very relieved, Ansel."

"And I want to thank you, sir, for sending Nora to help. She's a consummate lawyer and was an enormous comfort to me."

"It's good to hear. In the end, Ansel, we *are* all the family we've got."

"Ah, about that…."

"Yes, Ansel. What?"

"Well, this may come as something of a shock, but there's someone you have to meet."

"You're *not* getting married again?"

"No, but this *does* involve my marriage with Florence."

He waited for Jordan to insult Ansel's poor judgement or impulsive behavior, but he only said, "Tell me, what is it?"

"Well, you have a grandson."

"A what? When? Who is he?"

"Florence had a baby after we divorced. I steered clear of them all these years, except to send money, but circumstances pushed us together."

"You and Florence?"

"No, I'm not back with Florence, although we have become friends again, and she is an exemplary person and a great mother. But there's the boy. His name is 'True.' I'm not sure you remember, but you met him…at the shop?"

Ansel waited. For the first time he could remember, his father was speechless.

"Dad, are you still there?"

"My…grandson?"

"Yeah, and you'll see: he's a terrific kid! Really smart and funny and full of energy. He's even got the car bug. But most of all, he loves his mother, and as to the father who deserted him when he was born…I don't know why, but he seems to love me, too."

"Ansel, I don't know what to say. May I see him? Will you and Florence let me spend time with him? What can I do for him and his mother? I treated her so badly; she must hate me."

"No, Dad, Florence doesn't hate anyone. You'll see just what kind of person she is. We'll work it out."

After another moment, Ansel went on. "I know I haven't always been the son you wanted, and I have a lot to make up to you. I just want you to know I'll try."

"Listen, Ansel. Things have never been right with us since your mother died. We both have ground to make up."

Ansel explained about the remaining charges and what might

happen in Dublin. "We'll keep Nora on the case," Jordan said. "She's got contacts overseas, so we'll have her do what she can to resolve the legal issues. We—you and I together—we've got this in hand."

A few days later Leah called to say Harvey would not terminate the publishing contract if Ansel produced a finished manuscript by the end of September. Later, Nora reported the authorities in Dublin would not file charges in connection with Digory's death. Trinity College, on the other hand, had verified the plagiarism. Ansel's academic record would be revised to reflect an incomplete on his year-long tutorial. Ansel was pretty sure he still had enough credits to keep his bachelor's degree but decided it might be best not to press that subject with Columbia.

Saturday morning Ansel walked to the local Avis garage and rented a Ford Fiesta. Henry was no longer on call, and MacTone Motors had retrieved the Zagato from the Sanctuary Inn to display in its showroom, where it was drawing crowds. That was just as well. Ansel's wrist would have made operating the manual transmission uncomfortable.

It felt freeing to drive an ordinary car, like he had become one of the people. He brought Florence a bouquet of blue delphinium and Hattie a bottle of sherry. The boogie board for True he left in the trunk as a surprise.

The moment he entered the door, the ten-year-old launched at him from across the room, bringing pain to his wrist but a salve to his heart.

"Oh, Ansel!" Florence said. "Your face!"

"Life on the chain gang," he said with a smile. Actually, True's excitement had washed away the trauma of his time behind bars— although the injuries would take time to heal, and he was not sure his face would ever look quite the same.

The Fiesta had a backseat but Ansel buckled True in beside him.

"This is not as cool as the red car," True said. "Why did you change?"

"Came back to earth. I guess I'm just a dad like all the others, driving his son to the beach."

As they approached the exit for the Meadowbrook Parkway, True perked up. "The sign said Jones Beach! We didn't turn!"

"Oh, don't worry, son. We're taking another route to the very center, where there's a boardwalk and a pool."

True was visibly relieved when they saw another Jones Beach sign and turned south. After they crossed an inlet and the air smelled of salt, they approached a tall, copper-roofed brick tower on the grass median in the center of the parkway.

"What's that?" True asked.

"It's a water tower that supplies the whole park. Pretty awesome, huh?"

"Wow. Can we go up in it?"

"Afraid not. But I wanted to see it again. Your great-grandfather once told me they built it to look like a tower in Venice, something they call a 'campanile.'"

True scrunched up his nose at the Italian word. "Is that why you wanted to see it?"

"Well, actually it reminds me of another campanile in Dublin. I'll show you someday."

THE END

Acknowledgements

Several books were helpful in my research: *Trinity College Dublin: A Beautiful Place*, edited by Lynn Mitchell and Elizabeth Mayes; *Trinity Student Pranks: A History of Mischief & Mayhem*, by John Engle; *Advice to the University of Dublin*, by multiple contributors; *Ireland: The Propaganda War*, by Liz Curtis; and *Propaganda: The Formation of Men's Attitudes*, by Jacques Ellul. On the art of the novel, I also owe a debt to several classic texts: *Aspects of the Novel,* by E.M. Forster; *The Art of the Novel*, by Milan Kundera; *Lectures on Literature*, by Vladimir Nabokov; and *How Fiction Works*, by James Wood.

Several friends and colleagues were even more helpful. Clair Battle walked me, virtually, around the Trinity College campus. My cousin John Barber—and his expert consultants—advised on the care and disabling of luxury sports cars. Former Assistant District Attorney Benjamin Schneider counseled me on criminal prosecution in New York. And a number of readers helped with the manuscript as a whole: Drew Dawson, Mary Behan, Julie Cummins, Ann Marshall, Robert Arenella, and a contingent of relations: my daughter Katie Ried, niece Jennie Samoska, and brother Greg Ried. I owe thanks as well to my proofreader, Alyce Townsend Kay, and to Mikhail Starikov d/b/a michaelstar* for his cover design and patience. And behind it all was my editor, Christine Keleny of CKBooks Publishing, who schooled me on point of view, story arcs, and nearly every other facet of keeping eight major characters distinct and on point. Finally, once again and always I must thank my wife, Megan, who helped me formulate the story while we hiked in Andalusia, read my first draft back home in Manhattan and the final draft while we kept company in COVID-19 isolation and has sustained and encouraged me throughout the process.

About the Author

William Michael Ried was born on Long Island, graduated from the University of Michigan and Georgetown University Law Center and practices law in New York City. His first novel, *Five Ferries*, was a finalist in the 2019 American Fiction Awards for Best New Fiction. He lives with his wife in Manhattan.